Praise for the novels of
OLGA BICOS

"Bicos has definitely found her niche…
a sizzling summer read!"
—*Romantic Times* on *Perfect Timing*

"A terrific writer who knows how
to keep the reader turning the pages."
—Jayne Ann Krentz

…ng plot
…unning."
…iew

sprinkled with just enough magic to be believable."
—*Library Journal* on *More Than Magic*

"The emotion is intense, the sensuality powerful…
creates both thrills and chills."
—Long Beach *Press-Telegram* on *Wrapped in Wishes*

"Romantic suspense fans can rejoice
as superb author Olga Bicos adds her voice to this
spellbinding genre. *Risky Games* reaches out
and ensnares readers from the first page!"
—*Romantic Times*

"Olga Bicos is a genius!"
—*Affaire de Coeur*

"Amusing and highly emotional… True romance."
—*Los Angeles Daily News* on *More Than Magic*

OLGA BICOS

DEAD EASY

MIRA®

ISBN 0-7783-2076-6

DEAD EASY

Copyright © 2004 by Olga Gonzalez-Bicos.

All rights reserved. Except for use in any review, the reproduction or utilization of this work in whole or in part in any form by any electronic, mechanical or other means, now known or hereafter invented, including xerography, photocopying and recording, or in any information storage or retrieval system, is forbidden without the written permission of the publisher, MIRA Books, 225 Duncan Mill Road, Don Mills, Ontario, Canada M3B 3K9.

All characters in this book have no existence outside the imagination of the author and have no relation whatsoever to anyone bearing the same name or names. They are not even distantly inspired by any individual known or unknown to the author, and all incidents are pure invention.

MIRA and the Star Colophon are trademarks used under license and registered in Australia, New Zealand, Philippines, United States Patent and Trademark Office and in other countries.

www.MIRABooks.com

Printed in U.S.A.

To Everette and Vicki Jordan,
for their love and friendship all these years.

To the ladies who taught me the myth,
my mother and grandmother,
Olga and Consuelo Carreras.

And to Andy, Lexi and Jake, my grand adventure.
Never has a woman been so blessed.

A special thanks to my very own Brains Trust,
James Ball, Mike Vanier, Ken McCue
and my sister, Leila Gonzalez, for sharing
their knowledge and time.

Los Angeles—Police answering a 911 call arrived at the scene of a burglary to discover the only thing taken was a human brain. In what police are calling a college hazing incident, two youths have been charged with the theft. The brain was part of a research project on human memory conducted by a local pharmaceutical company specializing in herbal remedies. The brain remains missing.

Reuters News Service

Prologue

The woman sitting in front of the computer worked with frenetic energy, legs pumping, shoulders hunched. Nails bitten to the quick flew over the keyboard as waves of color reflected off her face from the twenty-one inch monitor. Completely focused on the flat-panel display LCD screen, she typed as if she were taking dictation, giving values to the simulation program she'd named Neuro-Sys as a joke.

She began writing Neuro-Sys two years ago, but the program needed constant updating. She'd become a late-night fixture in the lab, easily recognizable for her spiked near-white hair and funky contacts that turned her eyes to anything from two tiny eight balls to hypnotic swirls. The system at the university ran Linux, the hacker's choice, and it was fast. Still, she thought she had time to get a cup of coffee before Neuro-Sys coughed up results.

The offices spanned just two rooms connected by glass doors. Six flat screens and recessed lighting showed the yellow brick path of foot traffic pounded into the carpet as she made her way to the Mr. Coffee machine. After she poured herself coffee bitter from overheating, she glanced at the clock. She was behind schedule, but no biggee. There wouldn't be any traffic at this hour.

With the air-conditioning out, the computers heated the room to just shy of hell. But she needed to stay awake, so she loaded the coffee with sugar and the powdered creamer some students called "White Cancer." She wasn't worried about cancer.

In the next room, she heard the software she'd installed on the computer sound off, a sudden burst of "Hallelujah!" from a choir singing Handel's *Messiah*, alerting her. Time to check her results.

Back at the computer, the screen showed a three dimensional image of a brain. Horizontal lines designated cross-sectional slices. Neuro-Sys allowed her to rotate the brain in any direction. Once she clicked on a line, the cross section would float out toward the front of the screen as the image of the brain receded to the upper right-hand corner. Like the PET scan used in hospitals to measure brain activity, Neuro-Sys displayed activity levels of the brain cells themselves. These results looked promising. A lot of red.

She printed the data from several slices, glancing at the clock—she'd really have to floor it on the 405. She jotted notes in the margin before slipping the sheets into an interoffice envelope, then plugged a one-gigabyte memory stick into the USB small port to back up. She moved the cursor to log off, then hesitated.

She told herself it was nothing, the file. Just some bullshit someone was using to mess with her head. Her company was onto something big—anybody, even someone on the inside, could be trying to sabotage the project.

But that wasn't what she really believed. That wasn't why she'd come here at the last minute or why she had a plane ticket tucked away in her backpack.

Before she could change her mind, she added the file, "LYNN STRATFORD." The past couple of weeks, she'd been messing with the operating system. She'd disabled the logging to keep anyone from finding out which files she'd copied.

Rushing out of the laboratory, she passed a small plaque: Phoenix Pharmaceuticals. She rounded the corner and stopped at the honeycomb maze of mailboxes where she pushed an envelope into the slot marked "Gunnar Maza."

"Freakin' asshole," she said under her breath. The Gunman thought he knew what was best for her, always calling the shots, telling her what to do. But tonight she was one step ahead of her brother.

It wasn't until she turned for the double doors leading out that she saw something jammed inside her own mailbox.

She stopped, frozen in place, her heart pumping like some junkie's getting a hit of something too strong. She'd emptied her mailbox just before going into the lab tonight. There'd been the typical stuff: a flyer for another kegger Friday sponsored by the Greeks, a candlelight vigil to protest Yankee Imperialism, a bunch of junk mail.

Only now there was something else. A folded envelope.

Stepping back, her first instinct was to run. *Don't*

look! Don't even touch it! But she needed to make sure. She couldn't just walk away—she had to see if it was real and not some sort of mirage.

She pulled out the envelope and opened it, breathing hard. A plain sheet of paper slipped onto her hand. The writer had clipped letters from a magazine to spell out his message, so that the whole thing looked cockeyed, the letters forming a roller coaster of highs and lows in rainbow colors.

The threats came almost every day now. She never tried to find out who sent them. She hadn't reported anything to the cops. She didn't want to have anything to do with these letters. She just wanted to push the delete key and run away.

She wadded up the paper and jammed the ball inside her jacket pocket. *All gone. Disappear.* She shoved past the doors and raced down the steps, skipping several. She caught her foot and stumbled into the middle of the small quad, almost falling to the ground.

She turned, scanning the darkness of the college campus. *Disappear.*

She realized she was trying to catch her breath, scared and shaking like a baby…only, she didn't see anyone. No strange car, no loitering man.

But he could be there, waiting. Watching.

"Ana. I have to find Ana," she said under her breath. "We have to get out of here."

Plunging into the dark, Rachel Maza hurried to her Jeep, hoping that tonight she could outrun her ghosts.

From a distance, the soft click of a camera followed her every move.

Watching her drive away, a man stepped out of the shadows, camera in hand. He'd set the film speed and exposure to register in the moonlight. The photographs he'd develop later would show her image as a ghostly blur.

He whispered the words he'd put in his letter, almost as if reminding himself.

"I can see you. I know who you are. There's no escape."

1

For Ana Kimble, to stare at a blank page was an exercise in terror. The lines and spaces on the paper almost shouted, "I dare you to be good enough!" Which was why, sitting at the counter of the near-empty diner at Los Angeles International Airport, Ana could think of absolutely nothing to write.

Luckily, time was on her side. Ana was on vacation. A vacation delivered courtesy of a select group of men and women who had recommended to the regents at the college where Ana taught (Slaved? Sold her soul? Gambled away her best years?), to reject her bid for tenure. Ana Kimble was out of a job.

Oops! Sorry it didn't work out for you, Ana. See ya.

The Dean of Faculty himself, Jim Bannor, had delivered the news. *Thanks, Jimbo!* He'd looked Ana square in the eye and told her—the author of several critically received publications, voted outstanding professor two years running, not to mention Bannor's personal lackey—that she was fired. And for that special touch, Norman Fish, her ex-husband, had headed the committee of the slice-and-dice, kicking her out of the collegiate nest with the ease of the library's timer-bound lights.

Ding! Her time was up.

I know I let you down, Ana. Fish was always at his best delivering bad news. *But enrollment is down and heads are rolling. There's even talk of Darth Bannor wiping out entire departments to get around tenure. Two X chromosomes and a smattering of Cuban blood ain't gonna save you, though don't think I didn't shake that branch until my wrist hurt.*

"And the jungle devoured her," she said into the silence at the diner, paraphrasing Rivera, a beloved author whose writings she had made her life's work…work the committee in their esteemed wisdom had judged irrelevant.

"Downward spiral alert." Elbows on the counter, Ana massaged her temples. "Hit…abort…stat."

She told herself she wouldn't weep into her Colombian roast tonight. Better to regroup. To slug back the lukewarm caffeine and convince herself that Jim and Norman had actually done her a favor, by golly, because Ana was moving on. She would not, as feared by friends and family, go quietly into the nightmare of updating her curriculum vitae. No siree, she had chosen The Dream: to write the Great American Novel.

"Oprah, here I come," she told the blank page.

She gestured to the waitress behind the counter for another cup. The only other person in the diner was a man bellied up to the bar wearing jeans, a Tommy Bahamas shirt, and oddly enough, sunglasses. She was just wondering if the overhead fluorescents might be too much for him—perhaps some rare genetic condition—tapping her pen against the counter, when she turned to watch the concourse beyond the plate glass for Rachel, her protégé and instigator of vacation plans.

Better late than never—Rachel Maza's life creed.

Not that Ana couldn't excuse a little tardiness. It had taken the force that was Rachel to scrape Ana like lichen off the hull of her responsibilities, arriving as she had in the wake of Ana's pink-slip tsunami.

"They freaking fired you, Ana! You owe these people nothing, so don't give me this 'I can't take off in the middle of the term' crap. Look, I have this friend. He has a place in the Caribbean," Rachel had coaxed. "Think suntan lotion, piña coladas and young men with hard bodies. There's inspiration for you. Come *on*, Ana. This is your chance. Finally, you can take the time to write your book."

Oh, she'd made it sound tempting. The island magic of distant shores, rain forests a mere hop, skip and a puddle-jumper away. And crazy. How the staunch little worker bee in Ana had resisted escape, plowing ahead with classes, grading papers, braving staff meetings.

But even Ana had limits. When they moved her out of her office and into the copy room, she'd hit a wall inside herself. *Sorry, Ana, but the faculty library needs expanding and your office is perfect. Why wait until summer to start construction when we don't plan to replace your position?* Jimbo, in top form.

In the weeks that followed, the constant *whoosh thwack* of those copy machines was enough to goad even the most loyal into a midterm mutiny. She could still remember the indignity of shutting her door against the invasion of the Copy Snatchers when she'd been forced to conference students in that hot stuffy room. *Whoosh thwack!* The looks of pity from colleagues, expressions that, like the photocopies, appeared hot and identical: relief to have dodged her bullet, concern that unemployment might be catching like the flu.

And the last straw—Rachel coming to Ana in tears last week, announcing that she was leaving, with or without Ana. Because Rachel's brother and guardian of the family purse strings was pulling the plug on his sister's doctoral program at Harbour College. Gunnar Maza wanted his sister to give up her beatnik dreams of writing poetry and join the family business full-time. Unlike Ana, Rachel was not above running away.

Lost in thought, Ana looked down to find that she had a little rhythm going with the pen tapping on the writing pad and the spoon against her coffee cup. She glanced at the diner's clock, then checked her watch, thinking she'd give Rachel another five minutes before allowing panic to set in. Only the sight of her wrist bare of jewelry except for her sensible Timex served to remind her that she'd left her lucky bracelet at home.

She told herself she wasn't superstitious. "Lucky bracelet" was merely a turn of phrase. Still, she could almost hear her grandmother whispering: *Jet. To ward off the evil eye.*

The fact was, she'd searched her condo for her bracelet before scurrying off empty-handed when she realized she'd be cutting it close if there were traffic on the 405 Freeway. Grabbing her bags, she'd told herself small beads of jet and gold couldn't protect her.

Only, she'd just remembered where she'd left the bracelet. Downstairs, on the kitchen counter. And there'd been no traffic, it being the middle of the night. She'd checked her bags, bought Mentos mints and a power bar along with several magazines. She'd reconnoitered her gate and was even now watching the waitress pour another cup of coffee.

Too much Kimble and not enough Montes. The ob-

servation came with affection from her mother, the
Latin artist who had fallen in love with Ana's steadfast
Yankee accountant father. *La americanita,* the Montes
side of the family had dubbed Ana—a comment on her
accented Spanish and a body that, at five feet ten inches,
was better suited for the runway than the rumba. She
couldn't even cook rice.

And she carried the burden of her father's timeliness,
while Rachel would arrive just seconds before the plane
closed its doors to pull away from the gate.

Once again, Ana had come too early—she'd been too
prepared. Too much Kimble and not enough Montes. A
pattern she'd come here to break—even as she synchro-
nized with the diner's clock, sending up a little Catho-
lic prayer that Rachel would do her the courtesy of not
missing their flight.

The man smoothed his hands over the surgical greens
before setting to work. The clothes made him feel comfortable, more like his old self. The laboratory was of
his own invention. Makeshift and dreary, easy to trans-
port. Everything in the room he'd found discarded or
bought over the Internet.

She was running. He'd expected that.

Humming softly, he huddled over a dissected portion
of a human brain, carefully setting aside the hippocampus and dropping it into a beaker filled with saline.
Glossy black-and-white photographs covered a cork-
board hanging on the wall. He'd taken most of them
using a telephoto lens.

He stopped his work with the scalpel to press his fingers to one photo, a rare moment when the lens had captured her laughing. She didn't laugh so much these days.

The past few months, he knew she could almost sense him there, watching her. His fingers stroked the photograph. He'd scared her with his little notes. But he wanted her frightened. If she was scared, she'd make mistakes. Like now.

He couldn't afford mistakes. Mistakes would take him back to the clinic with its cracked and barred windows and leather cuffs strapping him to the bed, the smell of Lysol and urine overpowering everything. Mistakes would bring the doctors with their incessant whispers: *Frédéric? What do you see now?*

The man turned back to the section of the brain. A pinkish gray and shaped like a sea horse, the hippocampus was thought to be involved in the process of memory formation. Lesions in this part of the brain had been known to cause amnesia. He'd stored it in saline, to keep it alive. A fixing solution like formaldehyde would kill the cells.

Every so often, he would glance at the photographs of the woman and whisper to himself, making promises. On the table where he worked lay a sheet of paper, a printout of the passenger manifest for American Airlines flight number 509. He'd circled one name in red. *Rachel Maza.*

When he was ready, he dragged out a blender. Placing it on top of the desk, he reached for the plug. It was a little worse for wear, the blender. He'd bought it at a garage sale. But it served his purposes.

Taking the beaker containing the hippocampus, he dumped it and the saline solution into the blender and hit frappé.

2

After an hour and a half of watching the dwindling foot traffic at LAX—no sign of Rachel, of course—Mr. Sunglasses was beginning to look interesting.

Other than the Ray•Bans, he appeared fairly ordinary. Clearly this was no movie star or reality-show celebrity preparing to take flight incognito. There was nothing particularly noteworthy or striking about him. And still, Ana found herself staring.

For a moment, she considered the possibility that it was his very conventionality that drew her. That and the fact that she was so mind-numbingly bored that the patterns on the Formica were beginning to suck her in. *Oh, look. Right there by the napkin holder! Squint a little, and the grainy pattern looks like a rabbit.* He sat directly in her line of vision, turned to watch the concourse as if he too might be waiting for someone, allowing her to observe him unnoticed.

He was attractive in a dark, swarthy sort of way. Hardly her type. Ana preferred more elegant looking men like Norman (I know, Dad. Big mistake). She glanced down at the paper where she'd been doodling: Mucho Macho Man. Lips pursed, she turned to a clean sheet.

Like George Clooney, or that Irish actor, Colin Farrell, he appeared a man's man. A total guy. The clothes, the posture, the need for a shave. The more she thought about it, the more she realized he represented an archetype. Everyman.

And here was this handy sheet of paper, all blank and inviting.

Quickly she jotted down: *A face that remembered...* Going with the flow, she added: *the echo of a soul lost long ago.*

Maybe it was the coffee, her third cup, or simply boredom. Or perhaps she was inspired by her bubbling fears that any minute now the esteemed Gunnar Maza might march into the airport diner, police in tow, to accuse Ana of abducting his baby sister—should Rachel bother to show, that was. Whatever the reason, Ana's thoughts turned to her mother, recalling the day Isela learned about her daughter's fate at the college where they had both taught.

Ana had been home sitting cross-legged on her couch eating Oreos and drinking Chardonnay, her fingers curled around another yellow pad. She had dozens of such pads, booty from the college's requisition center, an Aladdin's treasure trove of paper clips and pencils that Ana visited with something akin to a kleptomaniac's worship.

She'd been thinking how much she would miss those perfect pens—they came in three hues—the multicolored folders and pads of paper, the tools that had for the past five years brought order to her life, when she'd glanced down at the page where she'd written across the top: Losing my job—pros and cons.

The doorbell had rung. Twice. Followed by the

pounding of a fist. Her mother had never been a patient person.

"*Animal! Bestia!*" her mother announced in Spanish as she stepped into Ana's condo. A lithe woman, she barely managed five feet unless she wore teetering heels. Which she did. Often. It didn't slow her down a lick as she maneuvered around an enormous ottoman Ana used as a coffee table.

Isela paused before the couch. The act of sitting came in three parts: descent to sofa, the recline back, a toss of shoulder-length curls. Isela dyed her hair a deep red, a color that somehow worked on a sixty-two-year-old woman when it should not.

"That he could do this to you," her mother continued in Spanish. "Just to hurt me."

"Who mother?" Ana asked, answering in English. Because that's how they operated, she and her mother. Ana, the American, responding in English, facing off the Cuban exile ever clinging to her roots.

"Bosque." The word came out a clipped staccato. Her mother lifted her chin, the gesture of a woman well acquainted with the lecture podium. "Come, Anita. All he needed was to put the wrong word in the right ear. I have watched him these years, how spiteful he can be. To let such a little thing as my superiority to his dog's talent bring him to this petty revenge."

Professor Armando Bosque had sat on Ana's tenure committee. Now her mother perceived a connection between her daughter's demise and the man's discontent with Isela. Like many of her countrymen, Ana's mother found conspiracy in every wrong done.

"The man has venom in his veins," her mother continued. "He never forgave that I was given the Nobel instead. As if everything he's written hasn't been done better by Marquez and Fuentes."

Isela Montes had received the Nobel some fifteen years ago. A poet, she'd been credited with the creation of the Neo-Romantic movement. Some of Ana's first memories were of her mother at book signings, the pride she'd felt as her offspring. Ana, who next week would be scanning the want ads for a job.

"He is the worst a writer can be, Anita. He is derivative! But he has half the trustees at the college thinking he's God. He came to me last week asking for consideration for a novella he'd presented to *Editorial Sudamericana*. Pure pornography, I assure you, but then hasn't that made a name or two? I turned him down, of course. And now this is his revenge."

Her mother had been fully engaged in her role as the lioness protecting her cub, reveling in the cauldron of her Latin temper. But in the silence that followed, her face had softened, reflecting that rare transformation from famed poet to concerned parent.

"Anita? How shall I fix this?"

As if she could. As if it were possible.

Ana stared down at the pad of paper on the diner's counter. The words she'd written in pen began to blur. She shut her eyes, knowing that whatever she'd written in those discreet ruled lines couldn't redefine half a lifetime. She was thirty-two, long divorced and without children. She had nothing to show for the insanity of draining her lifeblood into the succubus of her career.

And she wanted more. She *needed* more. For the first time, she dared to search inside herself for a touch of her mother's magic. As she opened her eyes, she almost willed the extraordinary, determined to see the world a different place.

Until quite suddenly, she did.

The walls surrounding Ana disappeared. The waitress, the concourse, her worries, all seemed to vanish as if in a puff of smoke. A low buzzing filled her ears as a mist clouded her vision like some movie special-effects trick.

For the first time in staid, practical Ana's life, imagination took over. Just as her mother, the famed Cuban poet and Nobel laureate, had warned would happen, Ana Too-much-Kimble-and-not-enough-Montes entered the world of a writer.

Across the counter, the jungle she'd nurtured through years of research in dusty tomes began incredibly to take shape. Vines crept and tangled across the Formica. The air hissed sauna hot with the jungle's very breath. The rush of torrential rain drummed past the tree canopy as it filled her ears to drown out the cadence of frogs and insects.

She stared at the man seated at the counter. His sunglasses and clothes had vanished so that he wore nothing but cutoffs. Muscles glistening with sweat tapered under a pelt of dark chest hair to disappear into the waistband of his jeans. The top button remained undone, as if he'd been in a hurry and couldn't be bothered with that last vestige of propriety. A machete rested across his knees, held there by his powerful hand.

As he turned to look at her, she realized his eyes were dark green, like the deep waters of the Amazon.

A name came to her, whispered from somewhere deep inside. *Raul.*

"Do you want a warm-up?"

Ana sent her pen spinning across a now very ordinary counter, vines and trumpet flowers mysteriously absent. She looked up to find the waitress hovering, coffee carafe in hand.

She glanced back at the man seated at the counter, sunglasses and clothes firmly in place as he stared out the plate-glass window, none the wiser of her scrutiny.

The waitress gestured to the coffee cup, ready to pour.

"No. No, thank you," Ana told her.

She stared at the coffee cup, wondering about the visionary properties of caffeine. She knew from Rachel's experience with rain forest pharmaceuticals about the hallucinogenic effects of some compounds, but she didn't believe caffeine fell into that category, no matter how much she'd tanked up on the stuff.

Still, the alternative seemed equally unlikely. That sensible Ana Kimble had just spent the better part of ten minutes daydreaming.

She snatched back her pen, a gift from her parents, and pushed it and her writing pad into her carry-on. After wrestling out the appropriate amount in change, careful to leave a generous tip, she headed for the nearest exit. She kept her head down, studiously avoiding the man seated at the counter.

As if he might notice her quick departure. As if he'd even bothered to look at her.

Outside the coffee shop, she focused on her Timberland hiking boots, shocked and a bit scattered. Ana never daydreamed. Daydreaming required a release of control that was part and parcel of who she was. She couldn't even be hypnotized, for goodness' sake.

But back there, in the diner, she could swear she'd lost time.

Behind her, a familiar voice called out her name. She turned to see Rachel race past, holding up a pack of cigarettes as she pointed with the Marlboros to the atrium where the smokers did time before their flights. She wore drawstring khakis and a man's undershirt that exposed her stomach where two tattooed kittens curled around her belly button as if playing with a ball of yarn. As she watched, Ana felt suddenly weighed down by her sensible trousers and twin sweater set that minutes ago appeared perfect travel gear.

Ana gave a wave and dug back into her carry-on. At least now she knew Rachel would not be vaulting into the cabin of the aircraft as Ana half feared just as the flight attendant reached to lock the doors. She fumbled through the carry-on's maze of pockets, locating the one packed with gum, her arsenal against decompression on takeoffs and landings. Now that she'd found Rachel, she told herself she could relax. Whatever had happened back there at the diner—fear, monotony, caffeine overdose—she had more than enough time to explore its implications while working on her tan.

She smiled, envisioning herself sipping some exotic concoction housed in a coconut and overflowing with colorful fruit. Poolside, she would counsel Rachel on how best to deal with her overbearing brother in particular and life in general. After all, not everything that idiot Maza espoused was tripe. As he'd pointed out to Ana when she'd confronted him about Rachel's unhappiness, Phoenix Pharmaceuticals was Rachel's legacy.

My sister is capable of great genius. Rachel, with her gifts, can change the world.

Only, Ana wasn't so sure. Rachel was nineteen, a woman grown. Shouldn't it be her decision whether to lock step and follow in the familial path? And didn't Gunnar as her brother and guardian have the responsibility to let her decide her own future? It seemed wrong on so many levels that Gunnar, with Norman at his side as Rachel's watchdog, could trap her in their mad scientist lab, whether she wanted to work for Phoenix Pharmaceuticals or not.

Ana's arguments, of course, hadn't made a dent in Gunnar's arrogance. The thirty-nine-year-old mogul believed himself Zeus on high, seldom venturing from his mountain kingdom of the Phoenix Corporation to converse with mere mortals like Ana. No, she couldn't blame Rachel for running away, hoping to outlast her brother until her twenty-first birthday when Gunnar would be forced to hand over control of Rachel's trust fund.

In the meantime, Rachel faced the monumental decisions of her youth. She plotted her future. She'd asked her brother for a little space and got threats of a ball and chain in response.

Which was precisely why Ana had agreed to tag along, leaving midterm to follow Rachel into paradise. The way Ana saw it, her only obligation was to keep Rachel safe. Because even at nineteen, Rachel—who had never known anything other than the life of a sheltered prodigy—was much too naive to go it alone.

Not that the trip couldn't serve as a working furlough for Ana. She planned, as advertised in the glossy brochures tucked away in her carry-on, to visit every rain forest within a puddle-jumper radius of their island destination, Guadeloupe, seeking inspiration for her novel. And while a small part of her wanted to leave the English department in a lurch (Throw me out, will you!), she'd handed the reins of her classes to her Nobel laureate mother, an unexpected treat for students and faculty alike.

Ana patted the canvas bag. Should disaster strike and her luggage be a no-show, she was prepared to wait out the arrival of her bags at the villa where they'd be staying, having packed her vitamins, a toothbrush and spare underwear in her carry-on. She wasn't quite sure why Rachel had insisted on a duffel-style suitcase, but in the end, it had been a wonderful choice. She could have packed her entire closet in one of these babies—

"Ahh!" A force like a linebacker plowed into her from behind, sending Ana and her bag careening to the floor. Suntan lotion, Dramamine, writing pad and pens sprayed across a good three-foot-perimeter, along with her toothbrush and panties.

Before she could get her bearings, the culprit zigzagged through the crowd ahead, not giving so much as a backward glance at her prone figure on the floor.

"Neanderthal!" she yelled at him.

But she was wasting her breath. People like him didn't care if you insulted them. They expected it.

To add insult to injury, she'd recognized the Neanderthal. Mr. Sunglasses himself. Her Raul.

"Of course," she said, dumping the underwear into her bag and reaching for the Mentos. "A complete lack of judgment when it comes to men."

Even the fictional kind.

CLASSIFIEDS
Health Services:

Augment your income and improve your memory. The Seacliff Memory Clinic needs volunteers for research in determining memory functions and supplements that improve human memory. Qualified volunteers will receive a free physical as well as compensation for their time.

3

Norman Fish walked up to the podium, climbing the steps to the stage as the chaos of the lecture hall settled into a semblance of order. He calculated he was a good fifteen minutes late. He liked to make an entrance.

As usual, the hall was filled to capacity. Norman considered himself the Pied Piper of an exciting new field, and today's topic was a favorite. Technology's search for the wonder drugs of the future was a subject guaranteed to keep even the cheap seats filled.

Norman shielded his eyes with his hand and squinted against the overhead lights. He shook his head in dismay, the gesture conveying the room's endless proportions, the teaming throng in attendance. There came a murmur of laughter from his audience, followed by a rustle of pages turning. Pens raised, they waited at attention, a collective bated breath. Waited on Norman to weave his tale of bio magic.

Despite his orchestrated shock, Norman was not surprised by his popularity. With a superpneumonia raging through the planet and the proliferation of pathogens resistant to today's antibiotics, who wasn't interested in a new source for drugs—not to mention the cure for AIDS and cancer? Rain forests and coral reefs had become the brave new world for bioprospecting, the soil itself holding the promise of new cures.

But such knowledge did not come without a price, and more and more, pharmaceutical companies were loath to pay. The golden days of the "rape and run" operations for drug companies had come to an unhappy end with talk of intellectual property rights for indigenous peoples. More than ever, corporations had been scared off by the high costs of developing rain forest pharmaceuticals.

That's where Rachel and her brain child Neuro-Sys came in, turning the world upside down with her revolutionary computer model. If Rachel succeeded—and Norman had little doubt that she would—her simulation program would unlock the secrets of any compound found in nature, allowing Phoenix Pharmaceuticals to develop drugs at a speed and cost that would put the company at the forefront of a billion-dollar industry. Neuro-Sys could give Phoenix the inside track into the most lucrative drugs for the baby boomer generation. And though the current project had hit a bit of a snag, her progress on Neuro-Sys held the promise of an imminent breakthrough.

"Good morning, boys and girls," he began. Holding up lecture notes, he called out, "Manna from heaven! Or at least, small insights that might serve to keep you awake at this *ungodly* hour. I see someone in scheduling didn't get a Christmas card."

Laughter waved across the hall. Norman smiled, just warming up. He caught the delectable Miss Wilson watching from the first row. Judging from her last test score, the petite blonde wasn't here to improve her mind. His gaze dropped to her breasts, pressing against her cotton sweater like two apples outstretched to Adam. Not for the first time, he wondered if she wouldn't benefit from some one-on-one tutoring after class.

"I hope all of you dusted off your copy of Mr. Plotkin's book, *Medicine Quest: In Search of Nature's Healing Secrets,* and are prepared to discuss both the moral and spiritual issues at hand as we face the greed and stupidity of Corporate America—not."

More laughter filled the room as Norman straightened his papers on the podium. Not that he needed the prop. He'd memorized every word. The pages provided only details for those who would later approach to ask the deeper questions. He liked to think of this lecture hall as his own little kingdom. Here, to these men and women, Norman was God.

"But let us not jest at the expense of the great Mr. Plotkin. I merely present a different paradigm than that of the warm and fuzzy ethnobiologist. Today, I ask the question, What if computers and not men could discern the importance of compounds found in nature?"

He flipped out his reading glasses with a flourish and peered over the lenses. He assumed some knowledge on the part of his audience, which allowed him to avoid any lengthy discussion on the limitations of today's computer technology to achieve what he proposed.

"The shotgun approach to bioprospecting—travel to some coral reef or rain forest, collect sundry flora and fauna, grind them up in the laboratory and screen the resulting products—has proved less than effective. The alternative, befriend the local shaman, invest in what insights his special knowledge can provide, then share not the expense of such research, but only the profits it *might* grant, was simply too risky a venture. What I propose is entirely different—and, possibly, commercially viable, thereby making all of Mr. Plotkin's supposed conservation efforts worth pursuing because, frankly, we need more bang for our buck. The American Way, as it were."

He stepped from behind the podium, hating to keep anything between him and his audience. "Ladies and gentlemen, here are the facts—the cost of developing a new drug is astronomical. Somewhere in the hundreds of millions. And of those organisms found in nature, on average only one in ten thousand results in a commercial compound. Not to mention that it can take a company ten to fifteen years to bring a new drug on the market. Thank you very much, FDA."

Norman hiked down from the stage, approaching the front row of students. What he didn't mention was the profits to be gained from a drug with sales exceeding one billion dollars. Still, what he proposed removed any risk of governments from developing countries horning in on the lucrative money through profit-sharing schemes.

"But what if we could design a computer program that analyzed the effects of these compounds right there on site? Create a program so sophisticated that it could simulate brain functions, mimic how the brain responds to certain chemicals?"

"Whoa, dude, are you talking about getting the computer high?" someone called from the back row.

"No," Norman responded through the laughter. "But with a brain-simulation program we might just discover which pathways are activated, and perhaps determine what long-term effects, if any, exist for marijuana use, something for which our gentleman there in the back row might be a poster child. What do you think, dude?"

This time, the laughter was peppered with applause. Leaning back against the apron of the stage, Norman waited with arms crossed, his expression contemplative. "So the question remains—can computers become the shamans of the future? And can we go even further? Can we, with a sophisticated computer program capable of simulating brain functions, make animal trials—even human trials—obsolete? And more important, will any of this boring crap be on my quiz tomorrow?" he asked, so that the room burst into laughter.

After the lecture, Norman stayed behind to answer questions from the more tenacious, did the proper amount of hand-holding for the dense muttons who struggled along in their attempts to overachieve their pathetic potential. He made certain to take an extra minute or two with the yummy Miss Wilson. Bright eyed, the silly thing informed him that she was premed—as if she had a chance of getting into medical school. *Not even Guadalajara, sweetie, so stop wasting your parents' money.*

By the time he reached his office, he was feeling high. He was, above all, a performer. He loved his job.

Once inside his office, that all changed.

The message on his desk said to call for the company limo. He'd been summoned. And Gunnar Maza didn't like to be kept waiting.

The staff referred to this section of the Phoenix complex as the Black Tower. The room Norman entered had no corners, its masterpiece an enormous fish tank filled with batfish, moray eels and monstrous boxer crabs.

The tank spanned the room, blending seamlessly into the bank of windows as if the batfish that crept eerily along on pectoral fins might somehow take flight into the blue skies beyond.

"Rachel left town," Gunnar announced. "With your wife, apparently."

Seated behind the black lacquer desk, Gunnar Maza sounded as manicured as his appearance. The Milan suit fit him to perfection, its steel-blue complimenting Gunnar's pewter hair. Norman had to admit he was a touch envious as he tugged at his reasonably priced sports jacket, the uniform of academia. Still, there was something about the eyes that didn't fit the image of a successful business and family man. A flat, malignant brown, they brought to mind the batfish crawling along the aquarium floor.

Norman dropped into the leather seat before the throne of Gunnar's desk. "You mean my ex-wife? I hadn't heard a thing. Where are the girls off to now?"

Gunnar flipped a sheet of paper across the desk so that it glided to just within reach. The note was short. Norman recognized Rachel's handwriting.

"Ah," Norman said. "A vacation at the family condominium in the mountains?" He tossed the note back onto the desk. "Ana always did like it there. I suppose Isela will cover her classes? Though it's a bit unlike Ana to leave before the semester is over, but I suppose the tenure committee's decision stretched even her bountiful loyalty—"

"And do I give a shit?" Gunnar asked. "The note says she's planning to stay a few weeks. I want Rachel home by Monday."

Norman reached to stroke his goatee, but caught

himself in the nervous gesture and stopped. He remembered Gunnar had once referred to Norman's goatee as an alarming attempt to blend with the student body, a remark that still smarted. He found it disconcerting that a man several years his junior could so unnerve him.

Once upon a time, Phoenix Pharmaceuticals had been a small mom-and-pop operation specializing in natural remedies. When baby boomers caught on to the benefits of echinacea and gingko biloba, Gunnar's father, Javier Maza, had been able to capitalize on a phenomenon that would make more than one man rich beyond his wildest fantasies. What quickly became a million-dollar company specializing in rain forest pharmaceuticals evolved to even greater heights under Gunnar's tutelage. It was Gunnar who'd had the foresight to move the company to the heart of what Gunnar referred to as "Silicon Beach" in Newport, California, before the real-estate boom. He liked the weather here.

He also liked Harbour College, which turned out to be a bonus for Norman. Phoenix Pharmaceuticals had become a major contributor, making the laboratory where Norman ruled the crown jewel on campus.

The Japanese had been doing it for years, creating a cushy nest for themselves in the bosom of America's technical colleges. The formula of choice was to donate sufficient funds to erect a building, granting a foothold for the Japanese researchers to keep close. By interacting with the American students and professors, the Japanese made use of that coveted American know-how. It was also cost effective. The students worked essentially free and the company had joint ownership of all patents.

For Phoenix, Harbour College provided high-quality research at a reduced cost. It was a partnership that greatly benefited Norman. The addition of Gunnar's brainy sibling six years ago played a vital role in how lucrative that partnership had become.

"You're pushing too hard, Gunnar," he said. "She's showing the strain."

"Rachel needs discipline. Work gives her that."

"She's young—"

"She's not allowed to be young." Gunnar flashed his perfect white smile to soften the message. Almost gently, he said, "For once in her life, Rachel has direction. You have given her that, Norman. Don't weaken on me now."

Norman sighed. "Sometimes I wonder if Ana isn't right about you. Don't kill your golden goose, Gunnar."

"I know what's best for my sister."

"And who am I to say otherwise," Norman added.

Gunnar took his duties as elder brother and guardian strictly serious. A child prodigy, Rachel had moved in with Gunnar and his family, Magda his wife and Juliet their daughter, when Rachel had enrolled at Harbour College at the age of thirteen. Now, six years later, she was finishing a doctorate in poetry while working alongside Norman at the company laboratory on campus—until Gunnar had pulled the plug on her studies, informing his sister that it was time to toe the line.

Rachel's answer: disappear. And, of course, Ana would complicate Norman's life by facilitating the girl's escape. Gunnar liked nothing better than to keep close tabs on little sis.

The relationship between half brother and sister had always intrigued. Even though Javier Maza had abandoned Gunnar's mother for Beatrice, his mistress and Rachel's mother, Gunnar had never been bitter. Quite the opposite. With the age difference, he'd practically raised his half sibling as his own. And he spoke of Beatrice with nothing short of reverence.

Unfortunately, despite her beauty and genius, Beatrice had been delicate mentally. She'd committed suicide when Rachel was only five. Gunnar had been the one to find the poor woman's body.

"Bring Rachel home," Gunnar repeated. "The sooner the better."

Norman gave a tired smile, feeling suddenly sick of his role as watchdog. But he didn't have the luxury of refusing Gunnar. "Monday it is," he said congenially, as if he didn't feel old and decrepit and under the man's thumb.

He was halfway to the door when he heard Gunnar say, "One more thing. The clinic called. They found Frédéric." Still speaking to Norman's back, he said, "It's not good news."

Norman stared at the lacquered door, his hand stretched out and reaching for the knob. *Not good news, not good news, never good news…* He felt hot, then suddenly cold, unable to turn to face Gunnar.

"He's dead, Norman. A fire in some dilapidated hovel where he'd been hiding the last months. Without medication…well, there wasn't much of chance for him now, was there. Dr. Rozieres thinks it was suicide."

Norman closed his eyes. Six months he'd been waiting to hear these exact words. And still, the news shocked.

"We'll start over, of course," Gunnar said. "We've made progress. We have that much at least."

Norman nodded, then forced his feet forward, refusing to turn around. *Open the door—get out of sight.*

He made it as far as the bank of elevators before he sat down, thankful to find himself alone. He took his time, catching his breath.

He thought of all the ramifications of the man's death, the possibility that now more than ever they were running out of time. The optimism that had begun the morning slowly leached from his body, making room for unwanted fears and doubts.

Frédèric is dead.

All that promise gone, leaving just another body to hide.

4

Ana squinted against the glare of the airplane's overhead light. She adjusted the angle of the computer screen, powered down the screen's light using a button she'd discovered on the side of the laptop. She flexed her fingers and typed:

> PREFACE: THE JUNGLE MYTH
> "And the jungle devoured him." José Eustasio Rivera's prophetic words bring closure to his novel *The Vortex,* and aptly describe the essential character of one of the most enduring personages in Latin American literature, The Amazonian jungle. The *novelas telúricas,* novels of Super Regionalism, combine natural geography and Indian mythology to create a hereto unknown world.

Sensing Rachel hovering beside her, Ana glanced up from the screen. Rachel was reading over her shoulder, a peculiar expression on her face.

"Kinda high on the snooze factor, don't you think?" Rachel asked.

Ana stared at the paragraph. She'd been working on

how to start her book for a good hour, trying to discern just the right approach. She hadn't asked for Rachel's opinion, but suddenly the manicured words appeared in a totally different light.

The novela telúricas, novels of Super Regionalism, combined natural geography...

Zzzzz...

Ana stabbed at the delete button, watching the cursor gobble up the words like a Pac-Man video game. In composing a preface, she'd thought to educate the reader before plunging them into the fantasy of her story, so that they might better appreciate theme and sequence.

"I suppose I should have started with something catchy," she told Rachel. "Something like, '"Don't shoot!" the woman screamed, facing the business end of the Glock.'" And when Rachel looked pensive, as if that might not be a bad idea. "Oh, puleeze!"

Yes, it made her angry. She was trying her hand at fiction, but must she cater to the lowest common denominator?

"What would you ladies like to drink?" the flight attendant asked from the aisle.

"I'll have a rum and Coke," Rachel chirped.

Ana almost informed the flight attendant that Rachel would have a soft drink, petty revenge. But she said instead, "I'll have the same," and tugged her purse out from beneath the seat in front of her.

Once served, Rachel sucked on the rum and Coke with an enthusiasm that implied the next step might be an intravenous infusion. She brought the perspiring can to her forehead, her spine melting into the seat.

"This is great." She practically moaned the words.

Ana smiled, taking a sip of her own drink. For the first time in weeks, Rachel appeared her old self. Relaxed, even happy. It was a nice change from the nervy teenager haunting the halls of the English department the past few months or chain-smoking in the courtyard at Ana's condo.

"We needed this, Ana," Rachel said. "Just to get away."

An emotion Ana could only term as "warm and fuzzy" rushed through her. Here was a woman who had grown up without a mother's guidance, bearing the weight of her genius and talents alone. Ana could more than understand the warring forces inside Rachel, a blessed poet and computer whiz. She'd spent too many years herself wondering on the proper course of her life as she warred with the Hispanic Übermom. Isela never did accept her daughter's decision to analyze great literature rather than create it.

Gunnar, of course, couldn't care less about that conflict in his sister's life. He wanted complete control of Rachel, never allowing so much as a misstep. And while at nineteen, she was certainly an adult by legal standards, Gunnar had money and malice enough to keep his stranglehold, and woe to anyone who got in his way.

Unfortunately, the push-me, pull-you of Rachel's creative and technical abilities tugged at her in ways that her brother's demands could only exacerbate. Growing up, Rachel's lot never included anything as mundane as a date for the prom or grad night at Disneyland. Instead, she'd entered college at thirteen—a doctoral program shortly thereafter. Always too young, never quite emotionally prepared. And perhaps most telling of all, at thirty-two, Ana counted as her best friend.

My sister is capable of genius. Gunnar's words. Well, certainly Rachel was an extraordinary woman. But Ana suspected that despite her punked-out hair, tattoos, and eye-popping wardrobe, the young woman sitting beside her wished only to be disgustingly normal.

Ana reached across the seat to give Rachel's hand a squeeze. Rachel flashed a smile, raising her plastic cup in a mock toast.

Watching her, Ana made a silent vow: She would give Rachel this one chance at normal...even if it meant making herself a fugitive from Gunnar's martial law.

Tapping her glass to Rachel's, she sealed the promise. "Here's to escape," she said.

"Amen, sister."

Drink in hand, Ana returned to the blinking cursor and tried to clear her mind of the distracting buzz of lost tenures and possible jail sentences. She focused instead on the computer screen, striving for objectivity, reminding herself that she'd edited enough articles and short stories in her capacity as reader for several prestigious publications to know that an author wasn't always the best judge of his or her work.

Perhaps her analysis of the jungle had crossed the line from educational to soporific. Rachel could be right. Ana had forgotten her audience.

The voice of the pilot crackled over the intercom to announce they were flying over Montserrat at a time of volcanic activity. Ana peered through the window, squinting down at the tiny island.

Rachel leaned closer to gape out the window like a child. "Boy, will you look at that."

Below, smoke plumed from the island's interior through a cover of clouds. The image reminded Ana of a match snuffed out between pinched fingers.

"There's inspiration for you, Ana."

"You may be right," Ana whispered.

A million images flooded her. Nature as mother goddess, nurturing new life from the funeral pyre below, the forces of nature as the vengeful god punishing man, eradicating any sign of his existence.

The jungle devoured him.

In her mind, the likeness of Raul—sexy and Herculean—appeared like a transparency projected from an overhead. Machete in hand, he looked like a god sitting at the counter where she'd first imagined him…the picture of a man who could both battle and romance the heated jungle below.

The idea came then, brilliant with inspiration. By coming to this island paradise, living her adventure rather than experiencing it through books, Ana might breathe life into writing that before now lay static on the page. Perhaps here, in the midst of banana leaves and jungle rot, she would write words that climbed upon the mundane counter of a diner, transform beige facts into Technicolor fantasy.

And it could all begin with the character Raul.

Struggling to get out of her seat, she almost doused herself with her rum and Coke. She put away the laptop, allowing Rachel to crawl into the vacated window seat. Searching through the overhead compartment, Ana struggled to dig out her writing pad.

It was something instinctive, this need to give Raul life, a force she dare not question as she returned to the aisle seat. Caught by inspiration, her pen and yellow pad on the tray table before her, Professor Ana Kimble remembered the wisdom of her mother.

You lack only the experience of life, Anita—let its color show you the words.

Lynn Stratford had been a student at Gold Coast College for two years. She loved history, her specialty being Renaissance and Reformation. She was thinking she'd get her master's degree. By then, Bobby Melton, her boyfriend (almost her fiancé, really), would graduate. Bobby was going to take five years at UCLA. He was having a hard time as an engineering student, but those were tough classes.

Lynn wasn't having any trouble in school. She pulled straight A's every semester. Maybe it was because she liked school so much that she was interested in the flyer from the Seacliff Memory Clinic. Lynn heard ads like these all the time on the radio, so she knew it was legit. A bunch of them from the dorm had gone down to check it out, but only Lynn made it through the interview process. She was kind of proud about that.

And they were paying good money. Six hundred dollars a month. Lynn was putting herself through college with student loans and work study, so she could really use the cash. Bobby had been all for it. He was just sorry he hadn't passed the interview.

The clinic offices were really nice and not far from school. It looked like a hospital because everything was white and clean. The doctors were nice, too. She even liked the questionnaire because it asked things that really mattered, things such as: Have you ever had a past-life experience? That was really cool.

The only thing she didn't like was the pills. But they

said they would improve her memory, which was great when she thought about all the tests she had to take. A good memory would really help out. Some of the kids took herbs and stuff that they bought at the health food store, like DHEA and gingko. Lynn figured this was better because the stuff she was taking was monitored by doctors. You never really knew what was in those herbs. It's not like the government regulated the stuff. Not like real drugs.

Her sister, Kathy, had been worried about the clinic. That's because she'd seen a show on television where people had volunteered to get shot up with malaria and stuff for medical trials. She said the doctors were more worried about getting results than the safety of the volunteers.

But the memory clinic wasn't like that. And the research could really help some bad conditions, like Alzheimer's and Parkinson's. President Reagan had Alzheimer's. It was really sad.

Lynn had been going to the clinic for the past six months and everything was going great. Today was her first time in hypnotherapy. She felt proud that she'd made it this far. Not everybody did. That's what Hal, the tech she worked with, had told her.

Lynn showed her badge at the entrance to the clinic. Hal, the tech, was waiting for her and she waved. She skipped ahead, excited about the next step.

She was getting paid to help people. In her book, that was a pretty sweet deal, any way you looked at it.

A Novel, by Ana Kimble

Raul was born under a lucky star, blessed with a keen intelligence and a life experience that bred a potent charisma. His father was the Brazilian consul in Los Angeles where he spent his formative years, a place he returned to for graduate work.

We were students together when I made the unfortunate mistake of sleeping with him. A lot. And, oh, yes—I asked him to marry me. To which, Raul, the son of diplomats said, "Let me think about it," as he searched my condo for the most sublime spot to park his Barca-Lounger.

How naive, how utterly devoid of common sense and self-preservation love can make a woman. I remember the night he disappeared. We were sitting in the coffee shop at LAX, watching the foot traffic through the plate-glass window, waiting for Raul's flight. He was leaving for the Amazon on a research project for Mystics Inc., a pharmaceutical company with a philosophy friendly to indigenous cultures where we both worked after finishing our studies. I was crying and looked a mess—he looked like a god, his eyes appearing so green they startled.

But it was his mouth I tried to memorize as I sat beside him at the counter. He could seduce a woman with that mouth.

5

"It's a boat," Ana said.

Rachel toed off her sneaker and hopped aboard the Fiberglas deck. The custom-built, fifty-five-foot cata-maran moored at the floating dock sported a state-of-the-art GPS navigational system. Its double-hull design allowed both speed and stability, not to mention the four airy guest cabins and spacious main salon, all with warm wood accents… These statistics rattled off by Rachel as if read off the jacket of a brochure.

Isn't it just killer, Ana? Downwind, I bet this baby books. Bruce really outdid himself with this trippy color scheme.

In three-foot-tall letters, the name *The Green Flash* undulated wavelike across the bow.

Rachel skipped down into the shaded cockpit of the afterdeck where she informed Ana they could dine al-fresco. She tossed her duffel bag on the bench-seat cushions reflecting a vibrant Caribbean blue.

"Isn't it hot!"

Rachel was not referring to the weather, which at late-morning local time was just a notch below sweltering.

Ana stared at the catamaran. A mere hour ago, they had landed at Pointe-à-Pitre's newly refurbished airport, a complex whose modern concrete-and-glass architecture had hinted at resort riches just beyond. Alas, a mere fifteen-minute cab ride later, they had landed here, at a singularly unimpressive marina.

She realized it was a comment on her character that she was, in fact, horrified.

When Rachel, heiress to the Phoenix bazillions, had mentioned that they were staying at a "friend's place," Ana had imagined, well, a villa. The palatial estate had risen in her mind's eye from the slick pages of *Condé Nast,* a resort worthy of the jet set. Nestled on a crescent of white-sugar sand, palm trees tipping the horizon, native charms and moneyed comforts awaited Ana. It would be a refuge where she could sunbathe with her notepad or zoom around in bath-tepid waters on one of those nifty personal watercrafts.

Now she stood on the dilapidated dock of a run-down colonial harbor, staring at a boat without a crew. Gone were her dreams of cabana boys and Sea-doos. She glanced at her duffel bag, realizing why Rachel had insisted on the luggage. Easy to carry, simple to store.

"It's...a boat," Ana repeated stupidly.

"And it takes only two to crew. Think about it, Ana. We can go *anywhere.*" Rachel bounced down the gangplank and picked up Ana's duffel. "I was thinking we'd head for The Saints tomorrow. Bruce says it's way cool there. They have these six-foot-long iguanas. Wouldn't it be wild if we saw one?" She leaped back onto the deck, doing a little dance move before springing toward the entrance of the main salon. "Come on, Ana. It's even better inside!"

Ana stepped gingerly onto the gangplank, balancing

like a tightrope walker as the boat moved beneath her. "I can only hope."

Inside, Rachel directed Ana past the galley to the cabin where Ana would sleep. Ducking her head, Ana stepped down into the miniature kitchen that doubled as a hallway between the aft and forward cabins. Why, if she stepped sideways and crab-walked past Rachel, she might even call it roomy down here.

Once inside her cabin, Ana's sense of claustrophobia shot into high gear. The closet, bath and queen-size bed Rachel had rhapsodized over were sandwiched into a space smaller than Ana's walk-in closet.

"Wow." Rachel slipped past Ana to swing open the door to the bathroom. "Look at the head. You even have your own shower—though Bruce says we'll probably want to take most of our showers on deck. It's a real treat after a swim."

A voice—her voice—whispered inside Ana's head: *Help me, Jesus.*

"Hey, look at this." Rachel high-jumped onto the bed just above a bench seat that served as a storage compartment. She pointed to the hatch scant inches from her nose. Lying with hands folded across her stomach, all she lacked was a sepulchral lily to complete the pose. "I bet you can see the stars at night from here."

Ana backed out of the cabin. She needed air.

Scrambling through the double doors of the main salon, she hoisted herself topside. On deck, she counted ten deep breaths. She could feel the boat's motion hinting at a queasiness she feared even her ample stores of Dramamine might not conquer. Only the sky, an almost painful blue, seemed to give back the sense of space the small cabin had sucked from her.

"It was supposed to be a villa," she said to herself. "Servants would bring exotic drinks in coconut shells. A cabana boy would massage lotion on my sunburned shoulders."

"You're okay with this, aren't you, Ana?"

Ana turned to find Rachel waiting halfway up the steps from the cockpit, her boy-cut hair a peroxide-white in the sun. In board shorts and a midriff tee, she could be an advertisement for the newest teenage movie rage. *Scream XII—Axed on my Catamaran!*

But standing there, Rachel also looked incredibly young and eager to please, her desperate need for approval shining bright and transparent for Ana to see.

And there you have it, Ana thought. Her purpose for coming here. Not to sunbathe and frolic, but to help Rachel just as she'd vowed to do on the airplane. Despite all the sensible starch in her spine, Ana couldn't sit back and allow Gunnar Maza to rob his sister of everything— even if it meant spending three weeks sailing in a coffin.

Making her way gingerly over to Rachel, Ana said, "Yes, this will be fine."

She tried not to sound resigned. The truth was, she was here. She would make the best of it. There really was no turning back.

"Now, explain to me the part about you and I sailing this thing."

"So you see, it's really no biggee." Rachel pored over the charts she'd laid out on the salon's table where she'd projected a course on a laminated map showing Guadeloupe and its surroundings. To the untrained eye, she did indeed appear to know what she was doing.

"We won't even use the sails," she told Ana. "We'll just motor over. It takes about two and a half hours, tops." She pointed to the island chain on the map that appeared enticingly close to the shores of the main island. "Tomorrow, you can take a couple of practice runs with the anchor."

Ana had been assigned the task of dropping anchor, making sure it had a solid grip on the ocean floor. Rachel had mentioned that it would be "very bad" if the anchor failed to hold during the night, bringing forth images of waking to find *The Green Flash* in the path of a three-thousand-ton cruise ship.

"By the time we get there, you'll be a pro. What do you think?"

Ana cradled her cup of decaf between her hands, wondering if now wasn't the time to suggest one of those cute hotels they'd driven past in town. During the day, she'd become acquainted with *The Green Flash,* walking from stem to stern, telling herself it really wasn't so small. By golly, with the right medication, she could sleep right through the night in her floating casket of a bed.

"You're disappointed."

"No, honey," Ana said, her expression deadpan. "It's an embarrassment of riches here."

"Okay, okay. So maybe it's not what you expected…and maybe I sort of knew that and forgot to mention Bruce's place was a catamaran."

Ana frowned. *Lured here by imaginary villas…*

"But you came, Ana. When I needed you the most." Rachel scooted over, bringing her knees to her chest, looking vulnerable. She had removed her colored contacts so that brown replaced the eerie false green irises of the morning. "Please don't be sorry."

"I came because you asked me. Even if it had been a rowboat, I would have come. Don't lie to me, Rachel. Ever. Even through omission." But Ana knew it never did any good to lecture, so she added, "When do I start my training?"

Rachel smiled, knowing she'd been both absolved of misdeed and given her prize. "In the morning. I'll wake you bright and early with the best cup of coffee you've ever had."

"Aye, aye, Captain," she said, giving a mock salute. Rachel was so genuinely enthusiastic, infectious in her excitement. "Just what I needed. Manual labor."

"Girl, what you need is a tan," Rachel said.

"You mean a good sunscreen," she said, referring to her pale skin. "And a short walk before bed." She patted her khaki shorts over her stomach. "By the way, how did you manage that amazing dinner in Minnie Mouse's kitchen?"

"Are you kidding? Bruce has this thing supplied to the gills. You'll see, Ana," she said with a wink. "Be prepared to be pampered."

Ana thought wistfully of her villa. "I can't wait."

Back on deck, Ana could hear music coming from the town, a tinny merengue. She stared at the stars and black sky above, the echo of them in the lights from the bars and restaurants reflecting off the water of the marina. It was two weeks before Mardi Gras, and the town had already begun to blossom with celebration.

Turning, she glanced at the steps leading back to her cubical. Ana shuddered. Just the idea of the room incited claustrophobia.

"Hey, Rachel," she yelled down. "I'm going into town for a bit." To herself, she added, "To buy myself a very large drink."

Her writing pad and pen safely tucked in her bag, Ana walked down the gangplank, her body swaying to the sound of distant drums. She took in the island's ambience, feeling primed to create. Everyone here spoke French, and with its Caribbean architecture, the quaint streets and shops reminded Ana of New Orleans. There weren't many tourists, she realized, the congestion common to most holiday spots blissfully absent.

Passing a dance troupe parading down the street, the source of the drums, she stopped to watch the men and women wearing colorful African tunics and elaborate headdresses. One man came to her with a wooden dish, into which she dropped two euros. He lifted his tunic to reward her with the sight of dainty women's panties worn over his drawstring trousers, then flirted with the crowd, gathering applause and money.

Ana felt herself buoyed by the exotic as she continued down the street. The marina presented a vista of West Indies charm valiantly fighting off the encroaching industrial concrete. Only the occasional neon sign washed out the glow of old-fashioned frosted globes lining the sidewalk. Strolling couples—some white, most black, or a beautiful combination so often seen on the islands—passed Ana as she headed toward what appeared to be the quarter's main restaurant.

The outdoor eatery sported an enormous plastic bull dressed in a tux and holding a walking stick, touting the restaurant "Home" of the "Rhum Steak," à la Creole. Hazarding a walkway of rough planks dropped on crabgrass, she found a table and took a seat, enjoying the Caribbean Top Ten piped through loudspeakers from the central quad.

A few tropical moments later, French from the neighboring tables drifted on the breeze, exotic and fragrant. Ana hummed along with a samba and plucked her notepad from her tote. Across the top of the page, she'd scribbled "Ana's Novel." She'd come up with a title later, after she knew more about the characters and plot.

Flipping past her notes, she skimmed the scene she'd been writing on the plane, jotting a few ideas in the margins as she read. She'd already decided to use the jungle as her starting point, taking her characters through an *African Queen* adventure à la Bogart and Hepburn. Along the way, she planned to introduce the imagery that had so captivated her in her studies of the jungle myth, attempting to bridge the gap between educational and entertaining.

Ana read to herself, following the narrative she'd chosen to write in the first person: *How naive, how utterly devoid of common sense and self-preservation love can make a woman.*

"You said it, sister," Ana said, correcting a dangling modifier. She was totally engrossed in writing, tapping her foot to the beat of another merengue, when her drink arrived.

Apparently, the drink piña colada was far from universal.

The waiter set before her a glass filled with a milky liquid that smelled of licorice. There was no umbrella, no pineapple, not even a cherry stabbed through the heart with a toothpick.

She pointed to the drink and asked, "Piña colada?"

The waiter frowned, saying a word that sounded like "toothpaste?" His tone implied the slight heat of umbrage, as if she'd made a contract and was now trying to renege.

"Right." She stared at the drink, a few slivers of ice lazily melting at the top. "And doesn't it look yummy?"

The waiter smiled, his expression saying it all: another satisfied customer. Watching him walk away, she told herself she wouldn't allow such a simple thing to ruin her mood, even as she felt it slip a notch.

She picked up the glass. "Note to self. Look up how to say piña colada in French, pronto—"

"It's not a piña colada," she heard someone say behind her. "Not even a bad one. Is this seat taken?"

She turned, about to discourage any interloper who might quell the free flow of ideas, when she saw him.

The man at the airport. From the diner. Her Raul.

He stood before her in three-dimensional splendor as if he'd just now stepped off the page where she'd taken the liberty to describe him. Same nose, angular but strong. The now-familiar dark hair, short so that it didn't quite look disheveled despite the constant run of his fingers. And the sunglasses, on board despite the late hour.

He didn't wait for her to answer, but rather sat down. "It's your basic anisette drink. A staple of France. Most of the places here cater to French tourists. Pastis," he said, nodding at the glass, repeating the word she'd mistakenly heard as *toothpaste*.

He took the glass from her hand and set it aside. "I'd skip it."

No kidding, she thought, still speechless from his sudden appearance.

"The name's Nick. You're American, right?" To the bartender now hovering, he said, "Carib, *s'il vous plaît*."

Nick gave her a questioning nod, prompting her to add her own request. "Red wine, please." After the piña colada, she thought it best to stick with the basics.

"Vin ordinaire," he translated, watching her from behind the dark lenses.

To depict the man as an assault on the senses seemed overdramatic, and yet that described him precisely. It was as if his sudden appearance were some trick. She'd been writing about Raul, creating a background and story, and *voilà!* Imagination comes to life.

As she watched, he took off his glasses and rubbed his eyes. She saw that they were green and squelched the urge to flip through the pages of her notebook to make certain she'd described that very color.

Coincidence, Ana-the-practical explained. *Lucky guess.*

But a more tempting rationale came to mind, flowing from the realm of literature. The idea that sometimes fantasy preceded reality. A basic tenet of the great writer, Gabriel García Márquez, and his form of magical realism was that words could give life, influence as well as be influenced. Imagine Raul first and reality will follow, granting truth to the illusion. In the world of magical realism, Raul became inevitable. Kismet.

She reminded herself that "Raul" had more or less tackled her to the floor at the airport, never so much as glancing back to assess the damage. A man she'd insulted as a Neanderthal.

And yet…

She stared down at her notepad on the table, the corners slightly curled from turning the pages. On the plane, she'd written: *But it was his mouth I tried to memorize as I sat beside him. He could seduce a woman with that mouth.*

Ana glanced up, now staring at Nick's mouth.

Ah, yes. And yet…

"You speak French?" she asked.

"Hey, I'm not fluent or anything," he answered when the bartender delivered her red wine and his beer with a glass. He passed the untouched cocktail back to the waiter along with enough euros to soothe the insult. "Just taught myself a couple of key phrases. In a few languages, actually. So, am I right? You're American?"

She smiled, sensing her advantage. He hadn't recognized her as yesterday's roadkill, which presented an interesting opportunity.

When she'd put pen to paper on the plane, Raul had evolved into an intriguing mystery, so much so that she'd determined to write the ideas inspired by those moments at the diner to see where they might lead. She planned, oh so slowly, to reveal his character and motivation, none of which she'd particularly nailed down.

And here was a chance to guide that vision. To meet her character up close and personal, as it were. Magical Realism being all well and good, the fact remained that sometimes imagination needed a jump start. Tinder for the fire.

Rachel's "snooze factor" pounding its jungle beat in her head, Ana took a drink of her wine. On the plane, she'd determined to create a larger-than-life hero. A man who could melt hearts with a wink and rescue damsels with a sweep of his arm as he swung Tarzan-like from the jungle canopy…by golly, her Raul would save the rain forest and make it into trade paper.

And judging from how he filled out the Hawaiian shirt and the faded blue jeans beneath, Nick would do nicely hanging from that vine. Best of all, she sensed an intensity about him, an aura that virtually oozed testosterone, a solid plus for a character in a book.

"So," she said, putting down her wine. "Why the sunglasses? A disguise?" she added, half-joking but at the same intrigued at the possibilities.

"The Jack Nicholson routine? They're prescription," he said with a wink. "Contacts were killing me."

Even the color of his eyes struck her as unnaturally vivid. The restaurant's Chinese lanterns gave them an almost iridescent quality, a color that mirrored the jungle's heart and blood.

Perfect!

Ana picked up her pen, casually trying to pretend she was doodling on the corner of her pad as she scribbled. *As dark and mysterious as the depths of the mother river.*

At that moment, she thought of Rivera, a writer many claimed had memorized every word in his novel as he explored the jungle, never forgetting so much as a comma until he reached civilization and wrote it all down. Well, Ana needed a few field notes.

"How did you know I was American?" She returned his smile, forcing eye contact so he wouldn't notice her scribbling, hoping that she could later make out her chicken-scratch scrawls. She felt slightly giddy at her subterfuge. Ana Kimble, writer-sleuth, at your service.

He never so much as blinked, his smile for her only. "You were either French or American," he said, referring to the fact that she didn't exactly blend with the natives. He took a drink from the bottle, ignoring the glass. She quickly made a note of the gesture.

"Then again, could be I'm homesick," he said, as she shorthanded: *flashing that I-could-be-a-movie-star smile.* "Wishful thinking?"

"Tell me about yourself, Nick." A little too direct?

"What brings you here to paradise?" A good recovery, she thought. Almost slick. So un-Ana like.

"Actually, I'm here on business."

"Really? Oh, I'm interested to hear all about it." But her enthusiasm sounded forced. She cleared her throat, trying to bring down the volume. She'd been on exactly two dates since her divorce and one of those courtesy of her mother. *Rusty* wasn't the word for her small-talk skills.

"What kind of business?" She raised her wineglass.

"I'm in the import business. Produce, actually. I'm looking into some new outlets. Hey, are you all right?"

She held up her hand, nodding that she was fine as she struggled to catch her breath, choking on her wine. "An entrepreneur," she said when she could manage. "How…fascinating."

Not to mention utterly dull. She thought about the words she'd chosen to describe the man sitting beside her: *He looked like a god…lean of muscle, bronzed of body…* The image didn't quite jibe with importer of coconuts.

"How about you, Ana? What brings you to paradise?"

She glanced up, startled to find his eyes on her. Because she knew what her face would show. Surprise…even shock.

Because he'd called her by her name. Ana.

She had spent the past five years navigating the highly charged waters of university politics. Oh, she may not have succeeded in breaching the shores of that Avalon—tenure—but she'd withstood enough sobbing students with hard luck stories and college committees seeking volunteers to be careful with her words…none of which had included her name the past ten minutes.

The silence between them lingered, raw and telling. Ana set aside her wineglass. "I don't recall telling you my name."

"When I sat down." He flashed a grin as forced as her flirting. "How else would I know it?"

"Of course." But she was already standing, losing her nerve as she tucked her writing pad and pen back into her tote.

"You're leaving?"

"Well, it's getting late. I need to head back. My party wants to make an early start of it."

He grabbed her hand, the smile gone. "I came on too strong?"

"Not at all." But she wiggled her fingers free, the sensible Ana taking the reins. Sitting alone at a bar with a man she didn't know, far from home or help, no longer seemed so inspiring. "It was nice meeting you, Nick. Honest. Who knows? Maybe we'll…slam into each other again."

He shook his head. "I was afraid you recognized me from the airport. Not my finest hour."

"And there you have it."

Walking away, she never bothered to glance back, giving Nick the same courtesy he'd shown her at the airport.

But it didn't take Ana long to reevaluate. Making her way back to the quay, she wondered if she'd been premature, her sense of fear exaggerated. This just in: Professor loses her job, only to have a crazed maniac follow her to paradise. She was writing a book, not living it.

And she'd been so wrapped up in taking notes while simultaneously flirting. *You've never been able to multitask, Ana.* She could have very well told him her name.

It was the only thing that made sense. *Res ipsa loquitur.* The facts speak for themselves.

And wasn't it just like her to figure that out now, on the edit.

Back on board the catamaran, Ana stared at the blur of the Milky Way above, trying to convince herself she'd done the right thing, to exit, stage left. *Best to be cautious.* At the same time, with the boat weaving beneath her, the regrets came—*too much Kimble, not enough Montes.*

How was she to write adventure if she couldn't allow herself to live it? Where would she find the palette to color her words if she fled from the extraordinary? A real writer—her mother—wouldn't have run away. The incident would have intrigued her. Isela would have stayed and asked her questions, pressed for more.

The latter comparison in particular weighed heavily on Ana as she headed down the stairs to her cabin. Kicking off the rubber-soled clogs she'd bought for the trip, she felt suddenly as stolid as the shoes advertised for their comfort. She stepped inside the bathroom, thinking of her mother in her ever-present three-inch heels, her flamboyant red hair, her compulsion for eyeliner.

In the mirror, Ana saw only a feminine reflection of her father: bee-stung lips, hazel eyes, chestnut hair she wore in a flip à la Mrs. Peel. There was a catlike quality to the features that could be played up to look striking and exotic, but which merely showed Ana-the-sensible in their natural state.

Once again, her mother's words echoed in the empty cabin. *You lack only the experience of life, Anita—let its color show you the words.* Making her wonder.

What if she'd stayed? What if she'd asked?

* * *

At the table, Nick Travis finished his beer. "Brilliant."

He turned back to the waiter and asked for another drink. The man smiled, having witnessed what he thought was Nick's crash and burn.

As clumsy as hell, calling her by her name, he thought. But he was out of practice, stumbling over the story about the import business. The minute he'd said it, he'd seen it on her face, the doubt.

Her disbelief left him uneasy. It seemed to come out of nowhere—suspicious of his lies as if she could see right through him. In the silence that followed, she'd looked too much like a woman mulling over the truth and finding him lacking.

Not to mention she'd recognized him from the airport.

He'd been tailing the Maza kid the past couple of weeks, always careful to keep out of sight. But now, it was the professor who concerned him.

He hadn't thought she'd be a problem. He'd seen his opening and he'd taken it.

"Brilliant," he repeated.

When the waiter came back with the bottle of Carib, Nick Travis tossed a generous tip on the man's tray. Speaking in French, he asked, "Do you know where I can rent a boat?"

6

Numbers floated inside her head, constellations dropping from a void into the blueprint of her own making, coming into focus. Rachel opened her eyes.

"There," she said.

For the next two hours, she typed feverishly on her laptop. Even short pauses to ease the cramping in her fingers frustrated. She needed to get it down. Needed to make things right again. *No more screwups.*

Earlier, she'd plugged into the Internet using the satellite phone, looking for information. You could find anything on the Net these days if you had the patience to sludge through the mountain of cyber-crud. She managed a few sites that were useful, some electronic magazines, even a couple of college papers. But she hit gold with the article on recovered memories.

It was just a footnote, really. Imagine, all these weeks of work and she finds her answer in a stupid footnote. Now she would have to hurry. It wasn't going to take the guys back home too long to figure out their billion-dollar baby had flown the coop. Then Gunnar would come after her.

Typing on the laptop, she thought of the past few weeks, working to find her "out," a plan that could give her options when for the past few months she'd seen only No Exit. Finding that file on Lynn Stratford had made everything so horribly real. She knew she had to do something, even if it felt like freaking suicide taking on the Gunman like this. But she told herself she still had control. She wouldn't pull the trigger unless she had to. Neuro-Sys helped, because no one knew the computer program like Rachel. She was betting they wouldn't figure out what she'd done. Not until it was too late.

Eventually, she sat back in her booth where she was working in the salon of the catamaran, the small of her back a fiery agony. She pushed a diskette into the drive to back up. Tomorrow, she'd run the program through some tests, maybe fine-tune.

Flipping the diskette out of the A drive, she stared at the label: YBN. The initials stood for the Youthful Brain Project, Gunnar's brainchild and something she'd worked on for two years using Neuro-Sys. She bit her lip, then carefully peeled off the label and wadded it into a ball. She tossed it into the trash. From her backpack, she pulled out a new label and wrote Ana's Poem across the top.

"Okay," she said. Just in case.

She was skimming through the last article she'd downloaded on neurotransmitters in the brain, her fingers nervously tapping the diskette, when she noticed the bottom of her screen. An exclamation point appeared next to the icon of an envelope. She had mail.

She knew who it would be. Fish, checking up on her, doing his baby-sitting thing for Gunnar. She could almost recite what he'd say. *Hi, Angel.* That's how he always started when he wanted something from her. Then he'd write something cute like, *How's tricks?* That was Fish, always wanting to fit in. Just one of the gang… when he was really Gunnar's watchdog.

Not that she was any better. Bringing Ana here. Using her. Ana, the only person who really cared about Rachel. Sure, Magda was okay. But she was Gunnar's trophy wife. Basically, the Gunman was god-on-high for everyone back home. That's why Rachel needed Ana. Even if it meant lying to her a little.

Rachel had got the idea last month when she'd shown up at Ana's with her eyes all red and her mascara raccooned from crying. She'd just had it out with Gunnar. He'd been talking about how she was wasting her time with her doctoral program. What he really meant was, she was wasting *his* time. He needed her to work on his dreams full-time and the hell with whatever Rachel wanted. At the same time, she was getting these freaky letters full of threats, talking about all this really scary stuff that was supposedly going on at the lab.

Ana had immediately gone into mother-hen mode, tucking Rachel into the sofa bed. Making her hot chocolate. Rachel smiled, remembering how she'd felt so safe, curled up on Ana's couch sipping chocolate and watching old romantic movies as if her world weren't falling apart. But Ana could do that, make the bad go away. She'd done it for years. Fighting Gunnar, badgering Fish into giving Rachel some space.

From the first day she'd met Ana Kimble, Rachel had found her fairy godmother. Ana had still been married to Fish back then. He'd brought her to a party for Phoenix Pharmaceuticals, some launch for a new clinic. Seacliff something or other. Ana had stepped outside where Rachel was smoking a cigarette, furiously writing all this dark junk about Gunnar and her father making her start college because she was some brainiac. How awful it was to walk around campus. *Look at the thirteen-year-old freak!*

Rachel remembered Ana had sat down beside her on the bench just outside the French doors and grabbed the cigarette right out of her mouth, then tossed it into a planter. "I'm sorry, but I simply cannot watch children smoke." That's what she'd said.

And then she'd taken Rachel's book and asked, "May I?"

Asked. Not demanded. So that Rachel totally forgot about the cigarette burning away in the planter.

Rachel had been five years old when her mother killed herself. After that, her father basically wanted nothing to do with Rachel. Gunnar said because she reminded him of Beatrice and it made Javier too sad to be around her. He was always traveling on business anyway, letting Gunnar run the show at Phoenix Pharmaceuticals. Why not let him run Rachel's life, too? Even though Gunnar talked about Beatrice a lot, Rachel couldn't remember her mother.

But just then, with Ana acting all nurturing, Rachel had this fluttery, fuzzy memory. Something had just sort of sizzled and popped in her gut when Ana looked at her. After that, Rachel made sure Ana was part of her life. Majoring in English, taking all of Ana's classes, staying on for her doctorate. All she wanted was to be with Ana.

Sitting in the salon with her laptop on the table before her, Rachel played with the cigarette in her hand like a prop. Belowdecks was a designated No Smoking zone. Ana never did get her to quit smoking, but the writing. Yeah. She'd taken all those words full of teenage anguish and guided them into something Rachel could be proud of, even as she struggled with that artist inside.

"The struggle is what makes you special," Ana had told her once. "Don't fight who you are."

Unlike Gunnar or Magda, Ana really understood that struggle. She lived it every day. Because she tried to be this stuck-up English professor, but Rachel knew there was this passionate artist waiting to bust out.

Ana was an amazing person, really. Nothing fazed her. Even the Isela-the-great thing, she took in stride. She was proud of her mother. And now, she was showing a lot of guts, writing her own book when Isela was this icon.

And Fish. Everybody knew he'd screwed around on Ana when they were married. Fish, who thought he was so important because he'd managed to land Isela's daughter. As if that was all Ana was worth.

The thing was, Ana didn't even hate him for it, though she'd been smart enough to dump the douche bag. In the end, they were even friends. Like she'd forgiven the whole thing.

Maybe she'd even forgive Rachel. That would be just like Ana.

Not that she would do anything to really hurt Ana. No way. This was going to work out for both of them. If Rachel played it right. She wasn't really manipulating her or anything.

Only, this little voice in her head kept saying *You know what you're doing.* And she did. Down to her crocodile tears when she'd gone knocking on Ana's door last week, plane tickets in hand.

"I'm leaving, Ana."

"Oh, Rachel. Not like this."

"Exactly like this. I'm not giving the Gunman the satisfaction of finding me, either. He doesn't know anything about my friend's place in Guadeloupe. But I don't want to go alone..."

Rachel stared down at the diskette she'd labeled Ana's Poem. She guessed that when it came to Ana, Rachel wasn't any different than Fish or the Gunman.

Taking a breath, she pushed past her guilt. It was like Gunnar said—if she was going to do it anyway, why be all martyr about it? Just do it. Accept the consequences. That she was going to lose Ana's friendship.

It's pretty much what she deserved anyway, she told herself as she clicked on the mail icon, knowing she would only make things worse if she ignored Fish's e-mail. Waiting for the message to load, she tried to think how she might make it up to Ana, what she was doing. If everything worked out, if she got her chance.

Rachel frowned when the single message appeared on the screen. She didn't recognize the address. It wasn't much of an addy, really. Just a bunch of numbers. The subject line was blank.

Junk mail, probably. Still, with all the stuff that was going on, it made her kind of nervous. She had software that was supposed to screen out the spam. She picked up the diskette and thought about logging off without opening the message. But then something changed her mind, instinct taking over. *Just get it over with!*

She double-clicked on the e-mail.

The message read: *You can run, but you can't hide.*

Rachel's hands jerked off the keys, as if the computer

had turned burning hot. She didn't move, just sat there frozen, reading the words over and over. Each time, she heard the warning getting louder in her head—*you can run*—making her stand and back away, bumping into the Nav Station behind her.

The stalker guy. He'd found her.

She told herself to get a grip. E-mail wasn't any different than those dumb notes he'd left at her apartment and the mailbox at the lab. Sure, he could find her e-mail address. It wasn't a secret.

Only, this was the first time he'd contacted her through the computer. Almost as if he knew she wasn't around anymore.

She circled closer to the laptop. Behind her, the compressor on the opposite side of the Nav Station hummed along, a strange insectlike buzz she hadn't noticed before. She stepped around the table of the main salon, finally sliding into the bench seat. She was breathing hard, trying to catch her breath.

She asked herself what was she afraid of? As if it could get any worse. As if he might reach out from that screen and grab her neck and squeeze.

She pressed her lips together, angry now. How long was she going to keep running from this guy? How much longer did she have to endure that sickening rush of adrenaline that turned her stomach and made her weak at the knees? Like she was some lab rat and he was running the maze, testing her.

She pulled the laptop toward her, staring at the words on the screen. Before she could change her mind, she punched in her own return message.

EAT SHIT AND DIE, YOU PRICK!

All in caps. Like she was screaming at him.

It felt good to fight back. Not to be so scared all the time and play the mouse. Even at LAX, she thought someone might be following her. The creepy feeling wouldn't leave, and she'd been on edge the whole trip. It wasn't until they'd locked the doors to the plane, Ana sitting there beside her, that she'd felt safe.

On the screen, an exclamation point suddenly reappeared by the mail icon.

Rachel kept her eyes there, staring at the icon. It was like somebody else guided the mouse, bringing up the mail. Some other woman stared at the addy that she now recognized, the single line of numbers.

He'd answered her mail. He'd been online, waiting.

This time, the message was a single word.

Gotcha.

Rachel disconnected the computer from the satellite phone. She slammed the laptop shut. *Snap, click.* Grabbing the diskette, she ran to her cabin, careering down the hall, feeling the movement beneath her like a funhouse ride where the floor shifts under your feet as you try to reach the next door. She thought about what she'd just done, contacting him here from on board, using the satellite phone.

Could he trace it somehow? Triangulate her location?

Inside her cabin, she jumped on the bed and grabbed her pillow, clutching it to her chest. She felt weak from fear. And worse. She felt violated.

"It wasn't supposed to be like this."

He wasn't supposed to find her here.

In the dark, she curled up on the bed, holding the diskette in her hands.

"I'm safe here. It's just some dumb asshole getting his rocks off, screwing with my head." Her tormentor wouldn't have the equipment or resources to track her.

"I'm safe," she said, repeating the words over and over to herself in the dark.

Nick punched off the cell phone.

He'd known it wouldn't be easy to get the information he needed. Still he was a little surprised the guy had hung up on him.

Don't call here again.

"Right," Nick said, dropping the phone on the nightstand. "No problem."

That seemed to be happening a lot lately. People hanging up, doors slamming shut in his face, women leaving him high and dry at restaurants. Which only made him smile.

"I must be getting close," he said to himself.

Nick imagined the guy on the phone back in his little bar fiefdom in San Francisco where Nick had first met him, flying there on a hunch. The place pretended to plop you down in the middle of some South Pacific isle, palm fronds and ukuleles everywhere, the help wearing Hawaiian shirts, a style Nick himself was partial to. He knew the bartender had a doctorate from Harvard. So how had he ended up Top Kahuna behind the rail pouring drinks for a living? Inquiring minds wanted to know, Nick had told the guy.

The man's answer had been simple enough—*It's a God-given talent.*

But Nick had another idea, that hunch of his kicking in. The overeducated bartender was hiding from something. Running away. Just like the Maza kid.

Nick sank down on one of two twin beds pushed together in the middle of the aging colonial room he'd rented. He tried to keep in the path of the breeze slipping through the window, figuring he'd worry about mosquitoes later. He plumped up a couple of pillows and leaned back against the headboard. Apparently, this part of the world did not believe in box springs.

He picked up the beer he'd brought up to the room and drank straight from the bottle. It might take a few, but he thought he wouldn't be too worried about the heat or mosquitoes by the time he was done.

Halfway through the second bottle, he was still thinking about the phone call. The bartender had been his first connection to Phoenix Pharmaceuticals. The guy had been fired from his job at another company with ties to Phoenix. Flying out to San Francisco, Nick had hoped to find a man angry enough to spill some secrets. God knows Nick could use a break. Now, it looked like he'd reached another dead end.

But the call hadn't been a total waste. At least the guy had given Nick an idea. He picked up the cocktail book he'd bought at the airport and studied the index page.

"'Slow Screw on the Beach,'" he read out loud, then flipped to the page describing the rum drink. "As good a place as any to start."

Half an hour later, the small print began to blur. He put the book on the nightstand next to the cell phone. Directly beneath, a black spiral notebook waited, the kind kids used for schoolwork. You could buy them in any grocery store.

There was a number scribbled in pen at the top. Twenty-six. As if maybe there might be a number twenty-five somewhere, which Nick figured there would be. Only he hadn't found it.

He grabbed the beer, feeling the sweat slip down his chest as he threw his head back and drank. He knew it wouldn't help. A lot of people were depending on him. Stupid to let his guard down and get buzzed. He was here to get a job done, and he was beginning to see some disturbing patterns. Like the bartender in San Francisco hanging up on him when he'd mentioned Paul. Nick could smell the man's fear over the phone.

He knew what he needed. What they all needed. For Nick to be that guy again, the one who had worked his ass off all those years for nothing. Absolutely nothing. Because in the end, he'd just worked and worked, and all he had to show for it was the knowledge that he could work himself to the point that he didn't care anymore.

The work was the goal. Another notch on the belt. Nick the asshole, alive and well. And alone.

The thing was, Nick the asshole always got the job done.

Raul eventually become the poster boy for Mystics. For a while, we were the "hot new" pharmaceutical. Our philosophy, to learn from native healers and translate their knowledge into modern medicine. At each public relations event, it was Raul's face that graced the television cameras, his charm that sold newspapers and company stock. *Discover* magazine named him one of their up-and-coming scientists for the new millennium. There was even a profile in *People* magazine. He had the rugged good looks of an Indiana Jones—a man as familiar with the classroom as the jungle. Alas, he looked even better with his clothes off.

7

In the clearness of morning, the sky and the water became reflections of each other, creating the illusion of endless blue. Flying fish landed before the eye could capture a glimpse so that only the sound of splashing and the foamy white ripple that followed evidenced they were there at all.

On this bright beauty of a day, Ana knew she was dying.

No, dying would be too easy. The great god of the sea had passed judgment, keeping the deck rocking beneath her in a nauseating rhythm that just might do her in. But not before she suffered, long and hard.

"The Dramamine isn't working?"

This sage observation came from Rachel, standing at the cockpit, steering the catamaran's wheel with her foot so that she could navigate toward the horizon. She was wearing cutoffs and a lime-green bikini halter that appeared to glow against her tanned skin. She wore a toe ring.

For her part, Ana remained a human sacrifice on one of the mats set for sunbathing. She didn't move, didn't speak. The constant motion was something she couldn't stop, couldn't control. Like life. Skewered again.

"Bruce has some stuff in the first-aid kit." This from Rachel—perky, fully functioning Rachel—who'd magically shed her Gothic mood of the morning once Ana agreed to motor off into the sunrise. "You just rub it on the inside of your wrists and pow, you're good to go. It's inside, just under the—"

"No!"

Because that's how all this misery had started. Ana going belowdecks, stepping inside the mouth of the beast, or so it had seemed once she reached her cabin. Blazing hot, stuffy and airless, the walls immediately closed in. The room careened with the motion of the waves, a carnival ride belowdecks.

"If you take the wheel for a sec, I could go down and get it."

But Ana shook her head. If she moved off the mat, all would be lost.

"Maybe if you sat in the bow seat?" Rachel suggested. "Kept your eyes on the horizon?"

Rachel nodded toward the two seats that stretched out across the water, one built into each of the catamaran's hulls, giving the appearance that the ship itself reached out with both arms toward distant shores. Following the motion of the waves, each seat rose and fell as much as ten feet, the ocean spray drenching the occupant on splashdown. It was Disneyland with a kick.

To reach one of the seats, Ana would have to maneuver across a deck made slippery by salt water, her only purchase the slim wire that served as a handrail and an occasional metal handhold built into the Fiberglas deck. As a sports climb, she'd give it a ten for difficulty.

Even if she could reach the seat, there was still the trick of getting into it without being tossed into the black and blue water. When the deck fell out from under your feet, you were Major Tom. Weightless, floating toward who knew what fate. Ground control to Major Ana. Can you hear us, Ana?

She peered up at Rachel. They'd shoved off from the floating dock twenty minutes ago. It would take hours to reach The Saints, their island destination. Now, athletic, seaworthy Rachel wanted Ana to shimmy into the bow seat. No sweat.

She realized now that despite her best intentions of the morning, she was going to let Rachel down.

Ana said, "Turn the boat around."

Nick found Ana scrambling up the quay at the marina, her hands clawing at the railing to hoist herself onto the fractured sidewalk. The way she stared at the concrete, he thought she might do the Pope thing, drop down on her knees and kiss mother earth.

At his whistle, Ana froze. He could see from the look on her face when she turned that she'd known all along who would be standing there, and she didn't like it. He was pretty good at reading lips, but it came out, "The Neanderthal," which he figured was all wrong.

Ignoring him, she sat on the concrete bench stained with fish entrails and bait. She managed to project a woman of pride despite her head firmly lodged between her knees. A neat trick, he thought. Even at her height, which he clocked in at a solid Julia Roberts, she looked rather insubstantial when his shadow fell across her, blocking out the sun.

She peered up at him. That expression, green around the gills? The way she looked now, Ana could be a poster child.

Nick dropped down beside her and tipped back his sunglasses, making eye contact. He'd rehearsed this part enough that he knew he had his smile just right when he asked, "You ever have a really lousy day, Ana?"

"I think I'm having one now. This very second, in fact. I'd move aside just a smidgen if I were you. In case it suddenly gets worse."

His smile turned genuine, which surprised him. "You probably guessed I was on your flight over." He shook his head. "She broke my heart, the lady who put me on that plane here all by my lonesome. I guess when I plowed into you at the airport, I must have been angry at the whole of womankind—though it's no excuse. You might not believe me, but I'm not normally such a thug. In fact, when I saw you sitting a few rows up on the plane, I thought of eking out an apology right then and there."

"Why do I hear a 'but' coming?"

"Spelled with a double *T* at the end. Look, I was rude and I knew it. To make things worse, while I was contemplating how I might make it up to you—maybe send over another one of those rum and Cokes for you and your friend—I sort of listened in on your conversation. That's how I knew your name."

"I see."

"At the restaurant." He threw in a shrug. "That's when I thought I'd buy you a drink, after all."

"Instead of just apologizing?"

"Ass backward, I know, but there you have it."

He saw a whole lot of emotion slip past her face, suspicion being the prime one before settling into the sick look of someone who shouldn't sail for recreation.

Taking pity, he said, "You know, there's a cure for what you have."

"There is no cure from this death."

He wouldn't have pegged her for the dramatic sort, not with all that professorial starch evaporating off her in the moist heat of the afternoon.

He stood and held out his hand, and when she didn't take it, he added, "It's my secret formula." He winked. "I call it life after death. Think you might be interested?"

8

Ana wasn't much of a drinker. Even during her undergraduate years, when most students adapted to dormitory life like Greeks basking in the freedom of their newfound city-states, she'd been a picture of moderation. She'd drunk her first glass of champagne at her cousin's *quinceañera,* a coming-of-age party where a Cuban girl would dance with her beau and fourteen other couples in a stunning formation that was a cross between a wedding and a Fred Astaire musical. At fourteen, Ana had been the runt of the pack, assigned to a partner nicknamed "Elbows." As it turned out, the name was a reference to his unique rumba style.

Her duty done by Elbows, she sought solace in a fountain effervescent with champagne. The plastic punch bowl included dramatic lighting where the champagne spouted with the flair of a Vegas floor show. It was the first and last time she'd drunk too much. Before now.

She called it "self-medicating." And why not use a little alcohol to dull the edges? She was thirty-two, in a transitional period. She no longer had to influence students or impress faculty. She'd wanted to let her hair down, pop out of her professorial cocoon and transform into a butterfly of writing talent. And those umbrella drinks seemed long overdue.

Enter Nick, not just a supplier of coconuts as things turned out, but very handy behind the bar.

He'd taken her to a place with sawdust on the floor and colorful bottles lining the shelves. A haze of blue smoke from French cigarettes clung to the rafters while a travel poster with dolphins and palm trees offered "A Day of Dreams" for those who called ahead for reservations. She held up the cordial glass, admiring the drink into which Nick had poured a thin line of Chambord over the back of a spoon so that the liquor floated on the surface, a distinct red tier separated from the creamy Irish liqueur below.

"What do you call this one?" she asked.

"A Cherry Kiss." He smiled as he spoke, standing behind the scarred counter of the bar. Only now that smile didn't seem practiced or false. In fact, she liked it quite a bit.

And she liked how she felt, floating like the Chambord, buoyed in a current of self-satisfaction as she worked her way through this, her third drink. They were all as sweet as nectar, the alcohol a mere afterthought, just a tap on the shoulder that said, *Here I am.*

She discovered she was drunk only when she moved. Her vision became stop-action then, a sequence of images that took a few seconds to catch up.

But she no longer felt seasick as three paper umbrellas lay side by side like trophies on the bar.

The room was deep and long, the sort of establishment that gave birth to the notion "hole in the wall." Toward the back, two men sat beneath a cloud of unfiltered cigarette smoke, the bartender moving his hands in a windmill of expression as he and his companion hovered over their coffees.

She toasted the men, neither of whom paid the least bit of attention. "How much did you have to pay to have the run of the place?"

"Does it matter?" Nick raised his own glass of dark cherry liquid and tapped it against hers.

"Ah. The mysterious Mr. Nick strikes again." A reference to the fact that in the past hour he'd heard too much from her and she'd yet to learn enough about him.

"Look, Professor. It doesn't take a rocket scientist to figure out that a lady like you isn't going to be impressed by my line of work, which limits the conversation a bit, if you know what I mean."

Apparently, the coconut importer was on to her. "So you think I'm a snob?"

"Hell, yes," he said, toasting her. "Of the worst kind. An intellectual."

"Well," she said, wondering if he hadn't served up a little insight with his drinks, "you may have a point."

She had never thought of alcohol as particularly inspiring, but she could see how writers might be seduced to seek its vision on occasion. Sitting at the bar, she could swear she'd garnered some sixth sense, a writer's sensibility that made her not only doubt her prior judgment of the Neanderthal, but question the direction of her book.

After her initial burst of inspiration on the plane, she was afraid to admit the character Raul lacked dimension. Having introduced the lethal combination of Rachel's brains into Nick's brawn, she wondered if she hadn't crossed some line into the fantastical, making

Raul more caricature than character. Perhaps what her hero needed was a spiritual crisis. Like the protagonist Arturo Cova in Rivera's *Vortex,* she could infuse him with a dreamy instability. Or chart a course to show defiant courage, like Marcos Vargas in Gallegos's *Canaima,* shouting down a tempest so fierce that even the trees of the jungle trembled in fear. Her inspiration could be the very *novela telúricas* she'd studied so diligently, stories in which men were capable of both weighty sacrifice and supreme cruelty.

Which brought her back to Nick, a charmer who inspired. The Raul who had appeared with his machete balanced on his knee seated at the diner's counter, his eyes daring anything as the jungle sprouted around him, stood before her. Heck, he even had attitude.

Under the glow of pineapple juice and rum, she thought it rather handy that she'd found Nick. So much so that over the past hour she'd been uncharacteristically chatty, recounting tawdry tales of lost tenures like a missed segment of a soap opera, hoping to inspire Mr. Mystery to do the same. Tit for tat, as it were.

And to think that she'd almost thrown this opportunity away with her hasty retreat last night. But here was a second chance to learn from Nick—who really had a talent behind the bar—a man with no cerebral accomplishments to mar the picture and a truckload of flaws no doubt.

Which meant he would have a story. One that he might share. If she dug a little. If she pried.

"Earth to Professor," he said, waving his hand before her eyes.

"Sorry." She turned the cordial glass, watching the buoyed line of red, thinking about a different sort of research. One that didn't require the pile of tour books she'd purchased in town.

She held the drink up to the muted light. "A Cherry Kiss? You're not making that up?"

He leaned forward, shaking his head. "A Cherry Kiss. Just that."

She sipped from the glass, expecting the tropical sweetness of the previous fare. She pursed her lips. "I liked the Painkiller better."

"One more of those and I'll be carrying you home. Slow down, Professor," he told her, when she closed her eyes and half drained the glass. "The cure doesn't work if you overdo it."

But she didn't want to slow down. The alcohol was doing its work, speeding things up, granting elusive connections. She couldn't stop, not when she thought of those lovely pages waiting to be written with the inspiration of this man.

"How can I slow down when you offer me such ambrosia?" she asked, attempting a flirtatious smile.

"What can I say?" He leaned in closer. "It's a gift."

Looking at his mouth, she felt her heart beat faster. "Were you always in the import business? Did you go to school?" And here, her imagination igniting. "And what about the woman who broke your heart? The one who put you on the plane to paradise? Why don't we talk about her?"

"Why do I suddenly feel like there's a microphone shoved in front of my face?"

She pushed her glass away, coming clean. "I'm writing a book. And I've come to an impasse." Quite early on, but he didn't need to know the details. "I thought you might be able to help."

He let out a whistle. "Really? A book? So what do you need, Professor?"

"I thought I would write one of those ordinary man thrown into extraordinary circumstances stories. My specialty is the jungle. The Jungle Myth in particular. You might give me some perspective on the main character. In many of the *novelas terlúricas* the jungle is the personification of a god so powerful that he can lead a man to his downfall or redemption—"

"Whoa. Back up. You lost me, Professor. Novels Delurica?"

He placed his drink on the counter and reached for her hand. As she watched, struck dumb and staring, he lined up his palm with hers as if this were some logical next step. She could feel his pulse beating against hers.

Suddenly here was another treat served up from behind the bar, charging the air around them with a strange energy. She closed her eyes, seeing the sparks behind her lids as her fingers curled around his.

She felt like Marcos, shouting into the storm.

"*Novela telúricas,*" she said, opening her eyes, taking a breath. She warned herself not to misinterpret. His hand in hers was no more intimate than a handshake. "A regionalist novel, a book of the earth. Also known as novels of Super Regionalism." The words tumbled out, faster, neater, as if she might simply talk her way back to where she'd started, thinking about character and plot. "They emphasize the special characteristics of nature found only in the Americas."

He opened his fingers like petals, releasing her hand so that he could pick up her glass. He held it out to her, but she didn't take the next step, reaching for the cordial and decorum. Instead, she let her hand rest empty on the scarred wood. Waiting. Wanting.

"I have an interest in the myth of the jungle," she told him weakly. "It's personification as demon or savior."

"You have me hot and bothered just hearing you talk about it."

He set her glass aside. This time, he took her hand in earnest, grasping it between his two. He did this thing with his thumbs, caressing her knuckles, sending teasing charges up her arms.

She hadn't dated much after Fish. In point of fact, she hadn't dated at all after her divorce. She realized she could very well fall for an insanely handsome stranger with an easy pickup line. If she weren't careful. If she weren't wise.

She cleared her throat, something she might do with a student. It was like a little nudge. Listen up!

But Nick took the sound as the green light, bringing her hand to his mouth to kiss those very same knuckles still burning from his touch.

"You look all excited, Professor." He drew her closer. "Tell me more."

"In the jungle." She told herself to relax. *You still have your intellect as a weapon!* If she just concentrated, spoke her facts, she might well find normal Ana again, lost somewhere among exotic potions with silly names like Painkillers and Zombies. "You can travel through time."

"No kidding?"

"Carpentier in his book, *The Lost Steps,* wrote that the deeper into the jungle you venture, the farther back in time you wander, until you reach the jungle's heart, the primordial soup of creation."

His eyes dropped to her mouth. "I like the way you say that."

"Creation?"

"No. Soup."

With surprise and shock, she acknowledged the possibility of wrapping him up and taking him home like a present. Her only problem—home was currently docked in the marina, moving up and down with the motion of the waves slapping against the hull. And of course there was Rachel to think about, no doubt waiting for Ana in her cabin adjacent.

"Are you really in the import business?" she whispered, her eyes on his mouth.

"Why do you ask?"

"I thought maybe something else," she said, not sure about the conversation, that inability to multitask again at fault.

She wanted to kiss him so very much.

"Yeah?" he asked, inching closer still. "Like what?"

"I don't know. Anything really. Maybe you're a private investigator."

His smile froze—she'd taken him by surprise. But she realized she meant it.

With the alcohol warming her, it was an easy step from lust to logic. After all, he kept showing up unexpectedly. At the airport and the restaurant. "But that wouldn't make sense," she said. "Why would you be following me?"

"You got me," he answered, sweeping in for that kiss.

At the touch of his mouth, she felt burning up, lust rushing past to shove out logic. *Don't think! Ana vanished with the Zombie—the Painkiller kept her low. Don't be her!*

"I can't believe I'm kissing you," she said. With only the counter between them, she was tall enough that she could reach over and dig her fingers into his hair. He wore a dark green T-shirt that sported the phrase Why Not? in bold print, making her think the obvious. *Why not, indeed!*

"I don't know anything about you," she whispered, kissing him even as she came up with reasons not to.

He coaxed her on deliciously. "I promise. I'm an okay guy. Normally, I don't even do this sort of thing, but Professor, all that stuff you keep talking about, the jungle and those delirious novels. You make it sound sexy as hell."

"Really? That's a bit unusual." She could imagine what they looked like. Her fueled by three drinks, half-climbing out of her bar stool, kissing him. "Studies show that with every degree a woman earns, she diminishes the pool of candidates for her mate. Because the man needs to have equal or better education."

"No kidding?"

"And the older she gets, the chances of marriage fall dramatically. Exponentially."

"Exponentially?" His tongue reached hers, just a taste, then more. "Right now, I am exponentially hot for you." He placed his mouth next to her ear and whispered, "Let's go to my place. Before we do it right here on the bar."

She thought about her life. The choices she'd made. Methodical, careful Ana, never acting in the heat of the moment.

"I can't stay overnight," she heard herself say.

He really had such a wonderful smile. "So I figured."

* * *

She couldn't stop talking.

"This is what I've been doing wrong all along." They kissed as she helped him unbutton her shirt, at the same time grabbing for his, as if she couldn't make up her mind what should come off first. "Going for men who are my intellectual equal. I should have been dating truck drivers, construction workers, bartenders." She leaned into him, looking into those dreamy eyes. "Importers of coconuts."

She wasn't sure if it was the alcohol, but somehow he'd pushed the "on" button inside her, and she couldn't seem to find the switch to turn off the insanity of the moment. She'd come to his room and barely passed the threshold before she threw herself at him, kissing him wildly.

"Tell me more about these novels delusional," he said, keeping her going. "When you talk about that stuff, your eyes get huge and full of light, like you're all worked up. It makes me want to think of where we could take all that energy radiating off you."

She tried to remind herself that sex just wasn't like this. Normal Ana would ease into the physical, getting to know a man long before sex even became an issue. She didn't just meet a stranger in a bar and jump into bed, the consequences be damned.

"I can't touch you enough," he said, kissing her neck, his hand on her breast. "I can't kiss you enough—can't get near enough."

Take a breath, Ana. Get oxygen! "This is so much more fun than being seasick."

"Didn't I promise you a cure, Professor? Ah, man. Your breasts are perfect. They fit right in my hands."

Perfect. That's what this was, she told herself. A grand adventure beyond anything she'd imagined. She was letting go, really living, taking chances, seeking inspiration.

Having hot sex.

She reached for his jeans, but in that moment, he pulled away, surprising her. He leaned his forehead against hers, breathing hard. In the awkward silence that followed, she tried to find some semblance of the old Ana. Kneeling half-naked on his rumpled bed, she told herself things were happening too fast.

"Look, Professor." He brushed back her hair. "Maybe you should take a second to think about this. You've had a lot to drink and I don't want to take advantage—"

"I want to have sex with you," she said, the words coming out all breathy. "That's all right, isn't it? If we have sex. I really want to, so don't stop. Okay?"

He seemed for the first time to wake up, really see her. She thought for a moment he might gather up the clothes strewn on the floor and escort her back to the boat.

Instead, he said, "It's your call."

He couldn't get his pants off fast enough.

He was talking about what he thought was her best feature, what he called her long showgirl legs, when she saw the notebook.

The room was small, just saggy twin beds pushed together and a vanity where the veneer was peeling off and the mirror showed only a cloudy shadow of a reflection. They'd pushed most of his stuff off one of the beds when they'd come in. A notebook, its pages flipped open, had landed on the floor.

Staring up at Ana from the lined pages were the words Rachel Maza, written over and over in neat precise print.

Ana felt her heart stop. She didn't reach for the book. She just sat up, taking the thin cotton sheet with her.

She didn't look at Nick, just stared at the book as she said, "You're not in the import business."

She dressed quickly. On the bed, Nick didn't move, didn't say a word, which somehow made everything so much worse even as she silently begged that he say nothing. She managed to put on her shorts and shirt and stuffed her bra into her purse. When she had her hand on the knob, she looked back at him for the first time.

"Tell Gunnar," she said, "that she's safe with me. And she'll come back when she's damn good and ready."

After she closed the door, she ran down the steps. She'd wanted adventure, something to fill the pages of a book.

Reaching the street, she hailed one of the dilapidated cabs, only too ready to make sure that anything she wrote in the future came from nothing more interesting than good old make-believe.

Rachel was scared.

She wanted to tell Ana everything—tell her about Gunnar's stupid project and the stalker guy—but she couldn't. She'd only make things worse if she did, making Ana a bigger target then she already had by bringing her here.

It had been the hardest thing in the world to turn back when Ana got seasick. She kept thinking about the satellite phone, the call she'd made to get on the Internet.

What if that weirdo found her? That was totally possible. Crazy people might have all sorts of creepy equipment to find their victims.

She pulled up her legs under her on the bench seat, holding her arms tight around her stomach. But she couldn't make herself feel better. She'd wanted to reach The Saints today. Just disappear. Out there, she and Ana could get lost in the island chain where nobody would ever find them.

She needed to sneak a cigarette. Only she'd promised Ana just that morning she'd try to quit, making this whole ceremony out of throwing away her carton, at the same time keeping a hidden stash. But she didn't want to go up on deck. He could be out there right now watching.

She needed to think of something to tell Ana. Not the truth, but some other reason why they needed to set sail. Right now. This very second.

Only, before she could think of anything, she heard Ana scrambling back on board. Rachel jumped to her feet as Ana burst through the door into the salon, looking completely messed up, like she'd been dressing on the run. And her hair was sticking out at odd angles. She was really upset, too, looking sicker than ever. Rachel felt her heart drop, knowing they weren't going anywhere.

"We have to leave," Ana said.

Ana's voice sounded totally different. Really strong. Just like when she gave seminars in the big lecture hall and her words could fill the room.

"When can we get started?" she asked, again taking Rachel by surprise. She sounded so sure of herself.

Rachel caught her breath. She was thinking it was all

twisted that she was doing this to Ana. But she knew she had no choice.

"Right now," she said, trying to sound all casual, at the same time choking on the words because her throat was tight from crying. "There's still enough light to get there before sunset."

Ana stared out at the open sea and nodded. "Yes. Now would be best."

Rachel felt as if she were floating. Her feet were two inches off the ground. It was like this miracle had happened. Everything that had been bringing her down just seconds ago vanished. Even her guilt.

They were taking off, getting away.

Stepping over to set their heading, she knew they were safe now. In two hours, they'd be gone. They'd be history.

9

Gunnar preferred the restaurant, Crustacean. He liked the fish tanks.

One serpentined its way through the room, built right into the floor like a river topped with Plexiglas. Foot-long koi swam beneath Gunnar's Oxford Berlutis. The decor resembled Beverly Hills chic meets the Orient, the food, exquisitely the same. But tonight, he'd come here for neither. He and Norman sat at the bar, Norman doing the heavy drinking for both of them.

"You're sure he's dead?" Norman repeated over his merlot, following up with a bovine shake of his head. "There's no mistake?"

"You need proof? Dental records? Perhaps a DNA test?" As if that were possible. "Grow up, Norman. He's been dead for months now. They merely found the body."

The fact was Frédèric had escaped long ago. They recently discovered his remains, a corpse burned beyond recognition. The decay showed he'd been dead almost from the day he'd managed to break out of the clinic, which wasn't surprising given his condition at the time. The man was beyond mad. They'd only been able to recognize him by some belongings found in the hutch where he'd been hiding out.

"And that's supposed to be good enough?" Norman frowned, deepening the grooves around his mouth. "We found the body, end of story?"

"That's right. Dead and buried."

"How did he escape in the first place?"

Gunnar shrugged. "A plastic spoon. He'd fashioned it into some sort of knife and hid it under the sheets. He caught them by surprise. The doctors thought they'd seen some improvement."

"They weren't keeping a close enough watch."

"Apparently."

It was something he didn't care to talk about, losing Frédèric. So he thought of Magda, his wife. She wanted him at some silly fund-raiser tonight, no excuses. She said Juliet needed help in school. If he couldn't make the time, they should hire a tutor. Gunnar thought of the fine rice chips they kept behind the bar at the restaurant, well seasoned and light.

"Your father gave his life for this project," Norman prodded. "Now, we could lose everything."

"Then we'd better be careful that we don't have any more disasters like Frédèric."

"So it's my fault?"

"I think there's plenty of blame to go around. What about the data Rachel left behind? Any progress there?"

"I'm not sure," he said, avoiding Gunnar's eyes.

Nothing then, Gunnar thought, disgusted. Gunnar didn't suffer fools like his father, whose noblesse had begun to smother. These days, the dreams Gunnar had inherited were beginning to look too difficult to keep.

He watched Norman drain his glass. "Haven't you had enough?"

"Not hardly." Norman nodded to the bartender for

another. "I'm sorry. I can't manufacture your sophisticated dispassion. Jesus. I had such hopes."

Magda wanted skylights in the kitchen. Juliet asked if he could take her fishing at the pier. "Which is why we need Rachel back. I don't have time for teenage rebellion."

Again Norman shook his head. "I think it could be a good thing, Ana taking her away. If there's trouble."

"For God's sake, Norman. The man is dead. What trouble can he possibly be?"

But Gunnar was remembering Beatrice, Rachel's mother. How sometimes the dead could haunt you. And his daughter, Juliet, who now needed a tutor. The irony of that lack when compared to Rachel's genius.

Disgusted, he asked for the bill, the evening now a total loss. Even the attractive restaurant wouldn't ease the worries of the day. "Tomorrow," he said, getting the business over, "my driver will be by at seven in the morning. We'll take the helicopter over to Seacliff."

Norman choked on his wine. "When the whole thing has gone to shit? Can't they handle the cleanup?"

"It's not a cleanup," Gunnar said, dropping money on the bar. When Norman looked up, he added, "Don't look so concerned. It's good news. We have another prospect."

"They were cowards," the woman's voice rang out, mechanical and grating from the tape recorder, "burning their stick figures in effigy, defiling El Libertador. I couldn't allow the insult. They called me shameless the next day, but I was unafraid. My years with the general taught me how to fight."

There was a pause followed by the interviewer's voice, "Tell me about Bolivar."

"The first time I saw him, I stood upon the balcony and watched him astride his great white horse, our own Napoleon. We danced that night, and by morning, I was his forever. We made love for the next fortnight. He called me his lovable fool, because I would do anything, endure anything, for him."

The recorder clicked off, having reached the end of the tape.

"Wow," Lynn whispered to Dr. Clavel. She stared at the machine. "That was me?"

She couldn't believe it. But the voice was hers—only it wasn't.

The woman on the tape believed she was Manuela Sáenz, concubine and confidante to the greatest revolutionary of all time, General Simón Bolívar, the liberator of South America. She talked about things Lynn had never heard or read about, events she couldn't possibly know anything about.

Only, it was Lynn speaking on the tape telling the story.

After months of filling out questionnaires, endless interviews, being poked and prodded, she had finally made it into the final stages of the program at the memory clinic. Hypnosis.

At first, it was just some psychiatrist checking out to see if she was whacked in the head or something. Pretty boring stuff. Lynn had seen a counselor once with her mom, because her mom thought she was maybe getting an eating disorder. It was just some stupid diet with grapefruit and cantaloupe that messed up her stomach so bad she threw up for a month. That had been embarrassing, talking about stuff like that in front of her mom.

But this wasn't like that at all. This was cool.

"I was her?" She barely whispered the words. "I was Manuela Sáenz?"

"We're not sure," Dr. Clavel said. "We think these are memories you've inherited. From someone in your family, passed along to you through your mother. But we need more evidence. In the meantime, we're learning incredible things about the brain and memory. These sessions, with people like you, Lynn—the ones that make the final leap—" he reached across the table and squeezed her hand "—they are invaluable."

Dr. Clavel said she was a great subject. That's because she could go really deep. It kind of scared her when they wanted her on the IV. Up until now, she'd only taken the pills. But Hal the technician who worked with her explained she needed to go even deeper. He told her it would be okay, the drugs. That she was one of the special ones and she could help them a lot if she hung in there. Lynn trusted Hal and Dr. Clavel, that they wouldn't let her do anything dangerous.

Now she was glad she'd gone through with it, because when she woke up with Dr. Clavel, they weren't alone anymore. Lots of people were gathered around. She could tell from the excitement on their faces that something big had happened. It was really exciting. Now she was sitting in one of the interview rooms, listening to the tape of her session with Dr. Clavel and Hal.

"I can't believe it," she said again, feeling stoked. "How come I wasn't speaking Spanish?"

"It doesn't happen like that," Dr. Clavel told her. "It's you, relating memories. Sometimes people speak in a foreign language, sometimes not. It just depends."

"But it was really me?"

"Yes." Dr. Clavel said, enjoying it, too. "It was you. I swear it."

"Way cool."

Dr. Clavel wouldn't admit it—they were keeping things under wraps at the clinic—but Lynn knew. What she'd experienced, it was bigger than that hokey past life stuff because this was real. Manuela Sáenz, she'd existed. And now, she was coming back to life through Lynn. Through her memories.

Smiling to herself, she asked, "When can we do it again?"

When I bid my love goodbye in that airport diner, my heart breaking at his loss, Raul had left me a surprise. His confession waited back at our condo, long after he'd safely boarded his jet for warmer climes. In his practically illegible script, he admitted he'd doctored all the files at Mystics to take credit for my research. And though he would surely regret his deception someday, at the moment he was in a bit of a bind and didn't see many options other than to skewer the woman he loved.

He wrote, "I just hope that someday, when you look back at this moment, you'll realize I'm doing this for your own good. You know how much you hate fieldwork."

The lowlife. The amoebae. The pond scum.

10

Ana carefully stepped onto the deck, medicinal coffee in hand. They'd arrived at The Saints the night before, just as dark closed upon the hills of the island, turning everything a deep purple black. She hadn't been able to enjoy the beauty of the sights then. She took it in now.

The island rose from the water like green humps, some with cliffs of bubbling black basalt that appeared sculpted of molten lava. Organ tubes, Rachel called the formations, and certainly the towering shapes seemed to be just that. Thick and round and clumped together, they waited to start their fugue for the audience of houses clinging to the hillside. But only a persistent rooster and bleating goats broke through a hush so heavy it blanketed the morning.

Ana turned toward the breeze, letting it stroke her face and hair. She had stepped into a postcard.

She reached behind her for the bench seat in the cockpit of *The Green Flash,* groping for the cushion like a blind person before sitting down, sloshing coffee over the rim of her cup. She couldn't know exactly how many different kinds of alcohol she drank last night. The drinks came multilayered, each tier glowing with a different color of rum. She thought she remembered most of what happened, though her memory gave certain moments a film-noir effect that appeared more like scenes from a movie than her life.

She of the paper umbrellas now considered the possibility that the man she'd dubbed the Neanderthal had poisoned her. Of course, it had all been calculated, yesterday's bacchanalia. His plan had been incredibly simple: get her drunk, induce her to tell all. And heck, why not throw in a little sex as a bonus?

The lowlife. The amoebae. The pond scum.

The crossing had been monstrous, but she knew the trauma had saved her from alcohol poisoning. Gripping the rail, she'd cleared her system of just about everything but her embarrassment.

As it turned out, the bow seat had been a godsend. With the water spraying up at her bare feet, her face turned into the wind, she pretended to be a living figurehead, clinging to the hull. When she'd closed her eyes, she could almost believe the ten-foot drop and swell was a carnival ride, and she was just lucky she didn't have to return to stand in line for her next thrill.

She'd worn earphones, listening to loud CDs she'd borrowed from Rachel. She'd sung lyrics about "carrying on," and "another day," until her voice grew hoarse.

Now, with the catamaran securely anchored in the calm waters of the bay, caffeine hot-wired into her system, she could finally enjoy the view. Another day under her belt.

If Pointe-à-Pitre was rural, The Saints were pastoral. The green of the hills made an electric contrast to the cobalt-blue waters surrounding the island chain. It was early, just dawn. The boats anchored in the harbor bobbed gently with the movement of the water. Once again, a rooster crowed in the distance.

She sipped the coffee, taking in the beauty of it all. Just as Carpentier had foretold in *The Lost Steps*, Ana had taken her steps back in time. She smiled, peering at a world so completely different from the concrete jungle she inhabited. In this place that still managed a foothold in the old mother earth and father sky, she might just find the inspiration to throw off the weight of last night.

That's when she saw him—with freedom in her sites—looking straight across the water at their boat.

"No." She rose, spilling more coffee, burning her hand as she set the cup down. "I don't believe it."

He stood on the deck of a sailboat anchored some 200 feet from *The Green Flash*. He was perfectly naked as he dived into the water headfirst.

"Wow. Now there's something to wake up to." Rachel had come up behind her, catching part of the show as she appeared on deck with her coffee in hand. "What a hottie."

Ana made no comment. Like a child peeking through her fingers at the screen of a scary movie, she was trying to remember the night before, trying to bring back tiny wisps of memory.

An image of tangled limbs flashed through her mind, making her wince.

She drank her coffee, trying for more sober thoughts. Like body hair—the fact that he had quite a bit, a sure sign of an overload of testosterone.

"You've got to love those French guys," Rachel said, her eyes glued to the sight of Nick cutting through the sheet of blue water, stroking out to sea.

"He's not French." Ana watched Nick double back, his muscles rippling like the water as he glided past. At his boat, he pulled himself effortlessly onto the swimming steps. Grabbing a towel, he gave the women a quick peek at what Ana remembered was a lovely posterior before he wrapped the towel securely around his hips.

"Look, Ana. He's waving." Rachel waved back, smiling. "Hey, I think he's checking you out, girl."

Ana grabbed Rachel's hand. "He's a private investigator. Hired by your brother. He followed us here."

Rachel froze. "How do you know that?"

"I confronted him yesterday," she answered, leaving out the colorful details. "He as much as confessed." Then, seeing by Rachel's expression that she needed further convincing, she added, "I saw him at the airport, at LAX. Later, he came up to me at a restaurant at Pointe-à-Pitre. Yesterday, he was waiting at the quay."

Rachel visibly paled. Suddenly she put down her cup of coffee and ran toward the bow of the ship. She looked back at Ana, an afterthought, then stopped, coming back around to the engine side. "Raise the anchor, Ana. Now!"

"Hold on." Ana had barely managed the crossing from Guadeloupe. It wasn't going to be so easy to get back in the saddle. Even if they could lose him—which seemed unlikely—the naked Neanderthal might be a better option to another run across with the catamaran.

But Rachel was shaking her head, her eyes glazed and wide open.

"Rachel?"

Without another word, Rachel fell into Ana's arms. Ana held her, wondering if this could be a bout of nerves brought on by her family's omnipresence. Or something else. Something more sinister.

"Hey. It's okay," she told Rachel. "We'll call Gunnar. We'll set him straight. I should never have let you run away. That kind of escape never solves anything."

"No." Rachel pulled away, looking more composed. "I'm okay. He just surprised me, that's all." She took another deep breath. "I told Gunnar I was taking a few days off with you at your family's condo in Big Bear." She shrugged at the lie. "Now he knows I was screwing with him. Kind of makes me wonder how long he's had someone watching me, that's all. It's creepy, you know?"

For a moment, Ana tried to imagine what it had to be like for Rachel, her every move monitored by Big Brother. Gunnar couldn't give her the respect of allowing even the smallest freedom.

But she offered the pabulum. "He's just concerned about you."

"I'm okay," Rachel repeated, picking up her coffee and heading back inside. "Don't call Gunnar, okay? Don't give him the satisfaction."

But she wasn't all right.

Rachel waited inside the main salon, scrunched in the corner on the seat, her legs tucked under her as if she could somehow make her body smaller, something so insignificant she might disappear.

He'd gotten here fast. Or maybe, he'd been here all along.

She couldn't tell Ana. It reeked, what she was doing, but Rachel was too afraid to come clean. Anyway, now it was too late.

"It wasn't supposed to be like this."

She'd set it up so that Ana wouldn't get hurt. Rachel was going to Marie-Galante alone, leaving Ana here while she checked things out on the neighboring island. Ana wasn't supposed to be in any danger.

But Rachel hadn't counted on the creep actually finding them.

It was almost too crazy to believe, like maybe Ana was right and the guy was just some P.I. jerk sent by the Gunman. In fact, the more she thought about it, the more it made sense. If the stalker guy really believed all those things he'd accused her of, wouldn't this be the last place she'd come to hide?

"It's not him. It *can't* be him."

She could hear Ana pacing up on the deck. She figured Ana was pretty upset. She'd be thinking about Rachel, how much should she push? Ana always wanted to make things easy for everyone but herself.

Rachel didn't know how long she waited, listening to Ana walking around. She imagined Ana lifting her hand to knock on the salon door, then talking herself out of it. *Give her some time.*

Rachel sighed, then slipped down into the captain's chair. Over the past month, she'd gotten to know the prick who was following her pretty well. If he really was out there, this close, he wouldn't be able to keep it to himself, not Mr. I'm-Watching-You, I-Know-What-You-Did. He would let her know somehow, just to watch her squirm.

She picked up her laptop, then stared at the case for a long time. But she figured not knowing was worse. Because it was eating her up inside.

She opened the case and logged on using the satellite phone, almost afraid of what she might find. Afraid of the truth. That someone wanted to hurt her. That he might be close.

She felt really stupid when she brought up her e-mail. What a dweeb, she'd been, thinking it could be this easy to get away.

Staring at the screen, she could see that there was a long row of messages from the stalker guy. That's when she knew nothing would ever be easy again.

She took a breath. "Okay," she told herself.

She clicked on the first message. Then the next. She kept going down the row, on automatic.

It was almost funny how every message was the same. His idea of a joke, she figured. Just three words typed over and over:

The Green Flash.

Ana watched him. Nick, in turn, watched Ana.

They both sat, silent and unmoving, continuing their strange game of chicken. It was getting dark now. Crimson and fire from the setting sun reflected off the water. He really should do something about that five o'clock shadow, Ana thought. He was probably one of those men who should shave twice a day but thought it was too much trouble.

"I've lost my mind," she said.

Because she still found him incredibly attractive despite the fact that he was the enemy, Gunnar's henchman. A man following her as if she had a price on her head.

A wanted woman. Wanted for all the wrong things.

Last night, he'd whispered urgently in her ear, *I want to make love so bad I think I'm going to explode.* And she'd laughed, thrilled by the thought.

Her problem, of course, was simple. She was afraid that her lack of life experience would turn her into a dried-up prune of a woman, wishing for the mysteries of sex that had somehow passed her by. The first man she'd ever slept with had been a Swedish exchange student in college, a tennis player and a great fan of Bjorn Borg. He'd been tall and heavy, and she remembered thinking he felt very much like a door pressing down on her on the bed.

Fish had been a bit better, though not by much. Her mother had introduced them at a university function, something she claimed she now confessed regularly to Father Kerry at church. And Fish, scenting fresh meat, had given chase. Of course, once she'd made the colossal mistake of marriage, she'd stuck by her choice. Until it became painfully obvious it was time to admit failure and move on.

An old expression of her mother's came to mind: The best way to remove a nail is with another nail. After three years, she'd thought Nick might be that other nail. Only, she wasn't sure what she was using him to dig out from inside her. Loneliness, perhaps.

She'd wanted him feverishly, as if she, little Ana Kimble of the Ph.D. and tailored suits, could don some bright island plumage and become the kind of woman who could walk into a bar, down a few and take home the bartender. Only, as it turned out, he'd been much more than that.

"I liked you better when you were just some jerk buying coconuts," she said, matching him glare for glare.

She hadn't called Gunnar, and she wouldn't, abiding by Rachel's wishes. The girl had spent the day holed up in her cabin, coming out only for a listless meal where she did some lovely Impressionist work with the food on her plate. Certainly, Ana knew how complicated family could get. Her mother and father had a tiny bit too much say in her life at the overripe age of thirty-two.

But Ana had come to terms with her family, knowing it was part and parcel of her cultural heritage. She'd discovered as much her first year at college, living in the dormitory. She'd been the only student to call her parents every night, the only one to disappear each weekend, returning to the familial roost. Everyone frowned on her dependence, so immature, almost un-American.

But the following year, she'd moved into a dormitory for international students. She'd been accepted into the Spanish hall, one inhabited mainly by native speakers. In an era before there'd been a cell phone attached to every fist, she'd waited in line to use the hall phone each night. On weekends, the unlucky few who didn't make it home awaited visits from their parents.

That's when she'd learned that, despite her very Kimble exterior, there was still plenty of Montes inside. Things she couldn't explain because they were just part of who she was, like the color of her eyes and the length of her nose.

Ana was reminded of her mother's lecture about her colleague, Bosque. Perhaps Isela was right, after all. Why not take the Latin approach and see conspiracies everywhere? Best to be proactive.

Ana stood. "All right," she said softly.

Feeling very Montes, she signaled Nick.

It was time they meet.

11

Norman didn't have a good feeling about today's business. A heaviness burdened the air around him like a physical presence. *Something wicked this way cometh...*

Settling into the leather seat, he closed his eyes and ordered himself to relax, putting on the headphones to drown out the noise from the helicopter. He tried not to let the interview at Seacliff get to him, tried not to be distracted by the image of Gunnar, in a rare display of emotion, mesmerized by that poor girl on the other side of the one-way glass. Norman thought his CD player might help. He could lose himself in the glories of Bach. Music did that, wiped away the bad.

But those devilish doubts stayed with him, even through the lovely piano concerto. Little voices whispering, *Think of Frédèric. In the end, they all die.*

He adjusted the headrest, frowning. He didn't consider himself a cruel man, one of those sterile scientists who could justify anything. But the fact was their research with the Youthful Brain Project could change the world. And the girl's regression was only a first step. They'd learned a lot through Frédèric. These days, they were taking greater precautions.

And the way she'd accessed the memories. It had

been clean and quick, no confusion. Certainly that spelled progress.

"It's because she's so young," Gunnar had pointed out during the session, his hand on the one-way glass as if he might reach out and touch her. "That counts in our favor."

Only Norman wasn't so sure. What if their efforts were merely hit-and-miss? He was deeply committed to the project, but recently, too many things weren't adding up. *Too many people dying...*

But isn't that exactly the point, a little voice whispered? Theirs was a great purpose, and therefore worthy of a great price.

Norman clipped off the earphones, putting them away. He cleared his throat. "Did you make arrangements for...the disposal of the body?"

"No, Norman," Gunnar responded. "I kept it around the morgue, hoping the local authorities might catch on to what we're doing. Jesus."

"I just thought—"

"You didn't. Think, that is."

Harsh, but possibly true. At least, of late.

Because he kept losing when Norman was used to winning. And now, well it mattered more than ever that he win. He'd already lost too much. Ana, who seemed to be slipping through his fingers. Even Rachel.

Or was it just his nerve he was losing?

He still believed in what they were doing, didn't he? God only knows he planned to take credit, at least academically, which was what mattered most to Norman. Money wouldn't be a problem. Gunnar had always been generous to those who were loyal. And there'd be plenty to go around. Barrels of it, if Gunnar's projections stayed true. He should take heart in this new subject and the progress she measured.

He tried to silence his concerns. He managed, he thought, for a good long while before asking, "What have you been telling Rachel? Lately, I mean?"

For his sister, Gunnar managed to crack open his eyes. "Why?"

He cleared his throat again, wondering if he was getting a cold—or, God forbid, a nervous habit, like a twitch. "The data we've been giving her lately. She's not stupid. She's bound to have questions."

"Has she had any questions?"

Meaning that he, Norman, was her watchdog, after all. If Rachel had any problem with the data, it wouldn't be Gunnar she'd ask, not by a long shot.

Norman glanced away, wondering if he had in fact missed something. A while back—possibly months ago—Rachel had talked to him about their progress, suggesting that the data coming from the clinic seemed almost too good to be true. Surreal, that's how she'd described it. At the time, he thought she was hinting about some sort of malfeasance on the part of the lab, possibly the doctoring of data.

He'd been nothing but reassuring, of course, letting her know that it was her brilliant work with the computer program Neuro-Sys that allowed such incredible progress. Now, in retrospect, he wondered if she had meant something more sinister—if she'd begun to suspect the true subjects of those clinical trials.

But it wouldn't do him any good to admit such a thing to Gunnar. Not now, with Rachel missing. The girl was his responsibility, after all. He'd made enough mistakes already.

"I took the opportunity of speaking to Dr. Clavel at the clinic today," Norman said in a quick change of subject. "He thinks there might be a problem with some of Rachel's more recent findings. How did he phrase it? The well might be drying up?" A bit of an exaggeration, but surely the situation at hand allowed for embellishment. These days, it might take the equivalent of a nuclear explosion to get Gunnar to reevaluate their course, pushing Rachel as he had.

He waited for Gunnar to process the information, weighing the words. Watching him, Norman realized he didn't much like the man. Not like he'd liked his father, Javier…not like Rachel, for whom he held quite a bit of affection, even love.

"This trip of hers with Ana. Have you ever stopped to think it might be a good opportunity for Rachel?" he continued. "There's no use keeping her locked up at the lab, Gunnar. Let her stay with Ana at the condo for now and refocus," he argued gently.

Gunnar seemed to think about it. "You think it will help?"

"How can it hurt?"

"I disagree. Your wife has an unhealthy influence on Rachel."

"She's my ex-wife, and she's far from a bad influence, give her that much." When Gunnar didn't respond, he pressed, "I'll call the girls at the condo tomorrow. See what I can do to persuade them to come home. But these dictates of yours, Gunnar. It can get very old to always have Big Brother telling you how to live your life. In two years, even you can't stop Rachel from getting her hands on her trust money, and God knows what she'll do with that kind of freedom if she's never had a taste."

Gunnar appeared almost surprised that he might find himself agreeing with Norman's sentiments. But in the end, his only answer was to settle back into his seat, leaving Norman to interpret the silence.

Yes, Norman thought, *it does get rather old.*

But he kept his dissatisfaction to himself. He had bigger problems than Gunnar's enormous ego, the man's incessant need to have his way. Because Norman had been calling the condominium at Big Bear urgently since Gunnar had told him to bring Rachel home. No one answered. Nor had either Ana or Rachel bothered to return any of the messages he'd left on their cell phones.

Norman put his headphones back on. He'd been trying to buy himself some time, suggesting that Rachel stay put with Ana in Big Bear. But the truth was, he had a bad feeling about the girl's disappearance. And after talking with Dr. Clavel about the newest data Rachel had sent—how disappointing her work appeared—that feeling in his gut was starting to feel like an ulcer.

Well, he still had a trick or two up his sleeve, he assured himself to the strains of the piano concerto. Ana had given him a map to the family roost last year when she'd let him use the condo for a ski trip with his students. Well, student, anyway, not that he'd told Ana as much. This time of year, the ride up the mountain took only a few hours. He might even do a little fishing, once he found Rachel and set her on the proper course.

They rode Nick's Zodiac to shore, Ana agreeing on the basis that if anything went wrong, it was only a good swim back to the safety of *The Green Flash* anchored in the harbor.

The quay resembled an unfinished freeway, a concrete ramp that just dropped off into the big wide blue. There was a single set of steps, and plenty of traffic waiting to use them considering the size of the ferry herding visitors to shore. Apparently the island chain was a popular destination for locals and tourists alike.

At the town's entrance, a tiny hand-painted sign welcomed you to Terre-de-Haut. Pink and gray squares paved the central plaza like a checkerboard while a bust of Marianne, the date of the French Revolution stamped on her towering Corinthian column, stood front and center, facing the bay, adding to the lively fishing village air. Striped awnings and red tin roofs sprang from buildings glowing with whitewash. Flaming red hibiscus and bougainvillea crept along the cracks in the concrete.

They settled on an outdoor eatery whose name, Nick told her, translated to The Creole Gardens. It was crowded, which Ana took as a good sign. It was nearly dark, the plaza just coming to life. Children played beneath Marianne's very republican stare, making it seem relatively safe to sit with Gunnar's spy and have a cuppa.

"It's a traditional cake made here, " he said, pointing to the round coconut tarts he'd bought, then pushing the plate toward her. "Love's Torment, they're called." He winked. *"Tourment d'Amour."*

"You certainly know a lot for someone who isn't fluent in the language," she said, stirring a cube of brown sugar into her coffee.

"I get by."

She could see the boats near the shore bobbing on the water by the light of the dying sun, anchored on the surf close to the beach. Above them, the white facade of the fanciful "Houseboat" reached out into the bay like a great frigate ready to set sail. Nick said a doctor lived in the ship-shaped home that resembled the prow of a ship sprouting from the hillside. Above it, one of Napolean's famed fortresses lay in ruins, home to Rachel's six-foot-long iguanas and a diverse variety of cacti and succulents according to the tour book Ana had bought.

"The fishermen from The Saints are considered the best in the Caribbean," he said, biting into one of the coconut tarts. He nodded to a boy with a string catching minnows beneath the quay. "The ones caught close to shore, you don't eat. They have this bacteria that sets up house inside you. For years, you get violently ill any time you eat fish. Only the locals are immune."

"Delightful." She wondered if he had his own little tour book, he was such a font of information.

She'd already formed a plan, though not necessarily a good one. The Neanderthal was the enemy, but an enemy that could be had. She just needed to figure out what it would take to get him to board a plane and run along home. Or more likely, how much. The fear she'd seen in Rachel's eyes wasn't the kind she could ignore.

What surprised Ana was her own lack of fear. But then, maybe she couldn't be afraid of a man she'd clung to like a barnacle while she'd begged for more. But she told herself to stay on guard. She was no Mata Hari.

"So, why was I following you?" Wearing his sunglasses, he used his dimples to full effect. She realized that his lips were full and square, that his ears might be considered too big. And yes, he needed a shave. Today's T-shirt de rigueur warned Crazy Doesn't Begin To Cover It.

"You guessed right," he told her. "Her brother. Or her family, at any rate. They hired me to keep an eye on her." He looked away, as if hesitating. "She hasn't been acting like herself."

It was a simple ploy, the kind that asked for information but gave little in return. She'd served on too many advisory boards for academic journals and cornered too many students with excuses not to recognize the tactic. She did her best to reposte.

"Maybe she has her reasons," she said, taking a sip of the espresso. She'd be up all night, but the coffee tasted heavenly.

He popped the rest of the tart into his mouth and talked around the mouthful. "And those would be?"

She gave him a bland look of misunderstanding.

"Come on, Ana. Maybe I can help...." He reached across the table, giving her fingers a squeeze. He had large hands with long fingers, reminding her of an artist or a musician. She remembered noticing his hands while he'd poured liqueur over a spoon, using the alcohol like paints.

"If we work together," he continued, all earnest compassion, "wouldn't that be for the best?"

She could feel the charisma beaming from him, the warmth of his hand beating against hers. He took off the sunglasses, that Everyman face broadcasting his message loud and clear from across the tiny table: *Trust me. For Rachel's sake.*

"Oh, you're good," she said, reclaiming her hand. "Were you going to sleep with me to accomplish the job, Mr. Johnny-on-the-spot? Or was that just some R and R back there in your room?"

"Maybe I couldn't stop myself."

"As in, 'I'm too good to resist'? You must think I'm an utter simpleton."

"Shit, no. But you could ease up on the thesaurus, Professor." He leaned over the table, getting close. The demitasse cups rattled in their saucers, portents of what was to come.

"Did you ever think maybe that kid was involved in something?" He said it softly, like a threat. "That maybe I was here to keep an eye on her for her own good? Stop her before the trouble got started?"

"What are you talking about?" The sudden shift in his mood made her feel unbalanced, which, of course, would be his intent.

"What do you really know about Rachel?"

"I know her favorite color is periwinkle-blue," she said without hesitation. "Though I'm not sure if it's the name more than the color she likes. I know there's this song she listens to over and over, so that she actually ruined the CD. I know what time she gets up in the morning, and when she goes to bed. That she thinks men her age are stupid, which they are, of course, only she's too young to know they don't get any better. I know which star she wishes on at night, though she'll never say for what."

"Maybe that's what she's counting on. That you trust her. What are you doing here, Ana? What did she tell you to bring you along?"

He was all soft consideration now, the intensity only in his eyes as they narrowed on Ana, reading the crystal ball of her. She could feel the doubts sprouting, seeds planted with the memory of Rachel's behavior the past month.

She jerked back, realizing she'd been oh-so-slowly

inching toward him. She felt suddenly out of her depth. Clearly she'd underestimated the enemy.

She stood, shaking her head. She saw what he was after; he wanted her to side with him against Rachel. The fact that he could make her doubt Rachel, even for an instant, let her know something was very wrong.

"Coffee and coconut," she said, staring at the pastries on the table. "It might be a poor combination," she warned, thinking of another blend altogether.

She ran for the quay, signaling for a water taxi, a little sorry she would forgo the drama of jumping, fully clothed, into the water to put distance between her and her misgivings. But stepping into the boat, she hazarded a glance back, seeing that Nick was still watching her, the sunglasses firmly in place again and a smile on his face that said he had nothing to worry about.

Rachel was typing furiously, her fingers flowing over the keys as if she were playing a concerto. She smiled.

She was in that place in her head where answers fell from the sky and there was a solution to every problem. It was like shopping at the mall, you just reached right out and grabbed whatever you wanted. *Release of the messenger chemical peptide would occur only during simulation of fear associated with primary urges. The extraordinary situation must be sufficient to trigger an evolutionary survival instinct.*

Here, in her head, she wasn't pathetic, some loser living a nightmare, waiting to turn into worm fodder. Here, *she* had the power, not some moron stalker.

She was sweating, her fingers cramping, totally oblivious to whatever was going on around her. She didn't hear the knocking, didn't realize anyone was on board. She needed to finish.

"Rachel?"

She looked down from the bunk bed where she'd been typing on the laptop. Ana stood at the door.

"I knocked. When you didn't answer, I was worried something might be wrong."

She felt instantly guilty. And on guard. She glanced down at the diskette on the bed beside her where she'd scribbled Ana's Poem across the top. She reached for it now, trying not to call attention to what she was doing as she covered it with her hand.

"I'm just doing a little work."

Ana looked as if she wanted to say something more, but Rachel needed her to leave. Before she lost the flow.

"I'm really tired, Ana. Today was a big day, you know? So, I guess I just want to go to bed early. I don't want dinner or anything, okay?"

Ana frowned. "Are you sure? You didn't eat very much for lunch."

"You sound like Magda," she said, thinking about Gunnar's wife, who she pretty much liked because she'd do stuff with Rachel, like rent a movie or go shopping. But she was also a pain sometimes, overdoing the mother thing. "Like you're reaching over to cut up my steak or something." Magda had actually done that once, right after she'd cut Jules's into bite-sized pieces. Rachel and Juliet had cracked up, laughing their heads off.

"Point taken," Ana said. Even though she sounded hurt, she smiled. "Call if you need anything."

"Sure. Yeah."

Ana closed the door behind her. Even though she felt

guilty, Rachel was relieved. She wanted to get back to her computer.

She didn't like people messing with her mind, and this guy pretty much got his jollies making her feel like the village idiot. But here, in that place in her head where even he couldn't reach her, she knew she could beat the bastard. She could beat them all.

She started typing, faster still. She'd been at it all day, barely stopping to eat. When he made his move, she'd be ready. She'd make sure of it. Because once she finished, he wouldn't be able to hurt her—he wouldn't be able to hurt anyone.

All she had to do was be faster and better. Preferably before she got to the scream-all-you-can scenario and it was too late.

12

He was seated at the table covered with lab books, the jungle's pulse just outside the window keeping rhythm with his heart. Racks of test tubes, Erlenmeyer flasks, Epindorf tubes and beakers waited like good soldiers. He was reaching for a glass pipette when the attack came.

He focused, pushing back the anger, trying to fight. The pipette in his hand snapped in two. Blood dripped down his hand as he struggled to keep a piece of himself.

He was strapped down in a hospital gurney. They were feeding him the pills. He spit them back, tearing out the IV.

"Not real," he shouted in the empty room. "Not…real!"

But he couldn't fight anymore. He'd waited too long between injections, caught up in his search for a miracle. He was regressing, going back to a time in which he didn't exist.

"No!" he screamed.

Because he didn't want to become that dead man, didn't want Frédèric back, taking over, didn't want to see the world through those cold eyes…and he didn't have a choice.

* * *

Nineteen-forty. The German army occupied France. They had come. Expected but unwanted guests.

Frédèric stood on the terrace, keeping watch as the uniformed visitors scavenged his office, overturning furniture, emptying drawers. Jackals pawing through remains. This was not the first such occasion, nor, he was confident, would it be the last. The possibility of such visits had precipitated the need for certain actions on his part, sending Irène and the children away while he remained here, the watchdog.

Lighting one of his beloved Gitane cigarettes, he quietly gave the men his salute, a solidly raised middle finger they were too dull witted to see. The hatred he felt now was young, this smugness, newly fashioned, allowing him to smoke on the terrace and casually watch these dogs hunt.

Today they would find nothing, certainly not the discoveries he and Irène had deposited in a simple envelope at the *Académie des Sciences,* awaiting better times. As he and his beloved had to wait, his gentle Irène, a woman who had taken his name, and whose name, in turn, Frédèric Joliot-Curie had taken, making them equals in the sight of God and man alike.

Frédèric looked away from the soldiers, his memories making him ache. Stubbing out his cigarette, he crossed the terrace for the sight of Paris below, Irène's beloved city, seeking that connection.

Only, it wasn't Paris he saw. Instead, Frédèric perceived a dingy room, small and rank, a hovel reeking of jungle rot. The furniture lay overturned, and he lay curled up on the floor staring at his bleeding hand, unable to move.

Frédèric Joliot-Curie began to scream.

* * *

As suddenly as it came, the attack ended.

He woke up on the floor surrounded by broken glass, his head pounding. When he was able to, he dragged himself to the overturned desk and stood. He righted the desk, then leaned against it, catching his breath.

Not so bad this time. The new formula helped.

He stepped over a bench and pulled out a drawer from the bureau. Finding the vials, he prepared a syringe, then shot himself directly in the vein.

Euphoria surged through him with the drug. So lovely to feel the pain gone, the fear of those memories disappear. He smiled, falling into a chair. There, on the floor at his feet, lay one of her photographs. It had fallen from the desk. He picked it up and pressed his finger to her face, humming softly.

Very soon he wouldn't have to settle for photographs. He would have her flesh and blood right here in his hands. He found himself looking forward to their meeting—the day he could put his nightmares to rest.

Hers were just beginning.

Coffee and coconut...it might be a poor combination.

"Right," Nick muttered, watching Ana board a water taxi.

He pushed away from the tiny ice-cream-parlor table that barely left room for his knees, almost rising to follow her. Changing his mind, he dug his fork into the *Tourment d'Amour* and finished the pastry in two bites. Damned if he'd let the professor ruin his appetite.

Only, he could already feel his stomach rumble, as if she'd put a curse on the pastry. He dropped his fork to the plate, wondering if they practiced voodoo in

Cuba. Not that the professor looked Cuban. From what he'd seen, she was one-hundred percent uptight American bitch.

He'd tried to play nice, but those skills were damn rusty. And now, she'd taken off again, making it clear she thought he was in league with the enemy, Big Brother himself.

"Fine by me," he said, heading for the Zodiac he'd left at the quay. He wasn't here to rescue the professor.

He'd been trying to do her a favor back there, letting her know the kid might not be all that she seemed, which was pretty much the conclusion Nick came to after he got the call from San Francisco.

Turns out the brainy bartender and Nick had some friends in common.

After the guy had hung up on him a couple of nights back, he'd made a few inquiries. Once he got the thumbs-up on Nick, the guy did him the courtesy of calling back. The news wasn't good. Not for the girl, Rachel. Not for the professor, either.

So he'd tried to warn her. Tried to get her to cooperate, using all those skills he'd learned back in his army days. Only, the professor thought she knew better—or maybe she couldn't help herself, protecting the kid.

Nick tied the rubber dingy to the schooner and jumped on board. He told himself it did no good to worry about Ana Kimble. He'd done his best, given her a heads-up. The professor was a big girl, let her figure it out.

Only, a few hours later, he was still thinking about Ana. How she rubbed him the wrong way—actually, how much she rubbed him just right.

The other day, he'd almost made love to her.

And now, he couldn't get the idea out of his head. How she smelled, that sexy little noise she made deep in her throat when he kissed her. How much she'd wanted him so that he could tell it had been a long time for both of them.

He took a drink from the bottle of beer he'd brought out on deck and stared up at the night sky. He couldn't help thinking it was all the Maza kid's doing, Ana being here. That's the kind of thing he'd learned in tradecraft. How people used each other. The kid and the professor fit the profile. The two were tight. The kid was in trouble. Why not lean a little on the professor?

Not your problem, Niko, he told himself, draining the Carib. He had enough on his plate finding Paul. He needed to keep with the big picture. That's one of the things they drilled into you in training. You had to take a step back, keep objective. Emotion was the enemy.

Paul had been really good at pushing away the emotion, staying on task. Nick...not so good.

He wondered sometimes how Paul might have done things differently if it had been Nick who'd disappeared. Like the meeting with the cops in D.C. The scrappy-looking homicide detective in his cubicle at the station, pushing Nick's buttons.

He remembered watching the guy rummage around his desk until he managed to pile half the crap into a stack, then moved it to the other side. Problem solved. Nick thought that was a pretty neat trick for killing time, getting them nowhere fast.

Detective Isaacs had asked Nick if he wanted a cup of coffee. Nick had answered he wanted the cops to get off their ass and find Paul. He figured Paul would have shown a bit more finesse.

The detective explained how, according to the law, there wasn't really any problem here. So the man's sister lost touch? It seemed Paul took some mystery job that required a lot of travel. She kept things going on the home front, watering the plants, feeding the cat. Then, boom, no more letters home. No more calls to ask if Tiger'd choked on a hairball. So the guy takes off? Where's the crime?

Down in the galley, Nick bypassed the beer, going straight for the Scotch. The thing was, Detective Isaacs didn't know Paul. He hadn't spent twenty years of his life with the guy as Nick had. No way Paul would just up and disappear.

And now, Nick was halfway around the world chasing ghosts, his gut killing him from those coconut tarts and some Cuban curse. Lusting after a woman he couldn't have. Not if he knew what was good for him, because anybody could see the professor played for keeps.

Trouble, Nick thought, easing into his bunk with the Scotch. Nothing but.

The jungle crept into Ana's dreams.

Liana slid out from the trees, winding across the ground to wrap her up tight, a smothering cocoon from which she couldn't wake up or escape. A dark fretwork of leaves above, the jungle's canopy beckoned. Climb higher! Seek the sun!

As knowledge often comes in dream, the truth struck. She had lost her way.

The Amazon was a witch, the foliage so thick it echoed back voices, appearing to whisper like a mistress, seducing her deeper into her heart until Ana feared her destiny was madness. The sun was the key. And so in her dream she climbed higher, to pierce through the blanket of canopy to search out the dawn's first light.

Suddenly she heard voices below her weeping. She was their only salvation! She could not lose heart, the voices urged her. Climb higher! Seek the sun! She forced herself up, knowing they spoke the truth. She had to climb above the canopy's thick leaves. If she weakened, all was lost.

But another danger lurked above in the lacy branches, a black storm of death. *Tambochas!* Fire ants, capable of sweeping through the jungle, killing everything in their path.

The sweat beaded beneath her breasts. Her arms trembled from exhaustion and fear. She screamed, *"Tambochas!"*

She had to climb down. She had to warn the others.

Only, when she began her descent, it wasn't some hapless band that she found waiting on the jungle floor. It was Rachel.

She held a gun pointed at Ana, screaming that she had to go back. Climb higher! Just a few more feet and she would reach the top. And when Ana felt the first bite of the swarm crawling over her flesh, loosening her hold so that she slipped even farther, she saw Rachel raise her gun.

She fired.

Ana opened her eyes. She lay in bed, the stars appearing clearly through the hatch above her.

She sat up, her heart racing. She knew to the page the scene she'd just lived in her dream as well as the fate of the characters. *The Vortex,* by Rivera. Two brothers escaped from the brutality of the rubber plantation only to have their guide become lost in the jungle.

What the men had endured was possibly the most disturbing passages she'd read in the jungle novels she'd studied. Leeches, hunger, the aching fatigue of forcing yet one more step, even army ants driving them into a swamp as the swarm devoured everything in its path.

In the end, one brother had ordered the other up a tree to seek the direction of the sun. When his brother screamed that *Tambochas* were still high up on the branches, he'd been shot by his own flesh and blood as he tried to descend, a rage overtaking the murderous brother because his kin had not revealed the way out of the jungle before descending in fear.

She remembered reading a review of the novel that claimed the author's depiction of the jungle had been too unforgiving, too bitter and dark. The Demon Amazon, the destroyer.

Tonight had been the first time she'd ever dreamed about the jungle. All those years of careful study and not once had the Amazon crept into her sleep.

Picking up her yellow pad, Ana straightened the crumpled pages where her shoulder had crushed the paper. She had fallen asleep writing. She was wondering if the passage could have inspired her nightmare when she heard a strange noise just outside.

She listened, hearing the sound again, louder this time. A splash?

She frowned. At first, she thought she'd heard only the lapping of waves against the hull. But now the sound seemed suddenly more substantial. She'd assumed it was the brutality of her dream that had woken her—that image of Rachel raising the gun and firing. But could her fears be closer to home?

The noise grew to a thumping. Someone directly outside her door, searching the cabinets?

She glanced at her watch and hit the Timex Indigo light to see that it was almost one in the morning. Carefully she crawled down from her bunk, telling herself she wasn't really searching her room for a weapon. In the end, she settled for one of her Pradas with chunky heels, the pair she'd packed for that after-dinner dancing that wasn't going to happen at the club that didn't exist.

She probably looked ridiculous with that Prada shoe held overhead. Rachel was standing just outside Ana's door, raiding the icebox in the galley.

She raised her hands in surrender. "Don't shoot. I'm on a mission of mercy." Rachel nodded at the carton of milk on the counter. "I'm starving."

Ana tossed the shoe back into the Barbie-sized closet. She realized she'd been holding her breath. "Pour me one, too?" She grabbed the plate of cookies covered with plastic wrap.

They sat in the main salon eating Rachel's chocolate-chip cookies and sipping milk. It would have been nice, that companionable silence—if Ana had felt companionable at the time.

"You know how difficult it is to get this stuff out here?" Rachel asked holding up the glass of milk and smiling. "Bruce says you have to be ready to buy whatever you find in the stores." She wiped away her milk mustache with the back of her hand. "He says it's made him a better cook."

"I can imagine."

A mercurial change had come over Rachel. Even though it was the middle of the night, she was wearing makeup, something she hadn't done the past few weeks when she roamed the hall outside Ana's copy-room office at the college like the walking wounded, biting her nails and mumbling excuses about lack of sleep. She'd gelled her boy-cut hair in a style that made her eyes look even larger, and she'd put in her contacts, which were merely cosmetic. She had perfect vision.

Tonight, her eyes appeared gray-blue. She'd used hair mascara to give herself red streaks in her spiked blond hair. Ana clocked grooming time at a minimum of twenty minutes.

It was crazy how Ana thought about her dream at that moment, with Rachel sitting across the table, all kohled eyes and milk mustache. Stranger still to realize how parallel their relationship was to that of the brothers in the book. Because she loved Rachel like family.

What are you doing here, Ana? What did she tell you to get you to come? Nick's voice inside her head, whispering suspicions.

"Did you finish what you were working on earlier?" Ana asked.

Rachel slapped her hands clean of crumbs, all lit up with her accomplishments. "Yup."

"What was it?"

Rachel appeared for a moment to have trouble understanding the question. She reached for her glass of milk. Too casually, she said, "Something for you actually. A poem."

"A poem?"

She remembered how Rachel appeared when Ana had first come aboard that afternoon, feverishly hunched over the laptop, perspiring from effort and the muggy heat. It wasn't Rachel's creative mode. Like Ana, Rachel preferred a pad and pen for her writing. When she worked on the computer, it was usually for her brother.

The fact was, she couldn't remember the last time she'd seen Rachel write her poetry, something that used to be a daily activity. She'd complained of writer's block. Lately, she seemed to have time only for her computer and her work for Phoenix.

What did she tell you to get you to come?

"When you suggested this trip," Ana said, answering the question in her head out loud as if it were Rachel who had asked, "you made it sound like a whim. Something you came up with because I'd lost my chance for tenure. But later, you said you wanted to leave, whether I came along or not." She played with her glass on the table, turning it in her hands. "And then there was the surprise of Bruce's place." She gestured to the interior of the catamaran.

"Hey, I apologized for that."

"I have to tell you," Ana said, smiling to take away the sting of her words. "I'm feeling a bit manipulated."

"Don't look at me like that." Rachel gave a weak laugh. "I'm not lying or anything. Jeez, it's just a poem. I thought you'd be happy that I was writing again."

Rachel stood and walked over to the captain's console where her laptop waited. Quickly she logged off. She unplugged the laptop from the satellite phone and tucked the computer under her arm.

Rachel wasn't looking at Ana, very busy with some button or latch on the computer. "Look, the Gunman just got to me, okay?" She shrugged. "He's been putting a lot of pressure on me lately. Apparently, there was this attempted takeover thing, and he thinks this new project he has me working on can save the company. I guess things weren't happening fast enough."

Ana felt her heart pounding in her chest. "Really?"

She turned then, looking at Ana. "You know, Ana, just because you don't want to run away doesn't mean everybody is like that. Stay and be all brave. That's you, Ana. Not me." She rolled her eyes. "Come on. My brother's a prick and you know it."

"Who did you just e-mail?"

She wasn't sure why she asked. Some instinct had taken over as she'd watched Rachel scurry over to her laptop and log off. And now the look in her eyes confirmed Ana's fears. *She's hiding something....*

It felt like one of those moments in the Westerns. A standoff on some dusty street, tumbleweeds rolling across their path as each waited for the other to blink.

After a minute, Rachel shrugged. "Gunnar." She raised her chin, defiant. "I e-mailed my brother. I wanted him to know I was in on his little stunt with the P.I."

"You're lying," Ana said, never more certain. No way Rachel would contact Gunnar. Not now.

Rachel rocked back on her feet, shocked by the accusation. But even the gesture seemed forced, an act, making Ana wonder how many times she'd been lied to, if even this new takeover story was some tale concocted to stop her questions. She wondered why she hadn't wanted to recognize the ploy before.

"I want to help you, Rachel. I can't do that if you lie to me."

Rachel peered at Ana in the semidark. Something in her face changed. A coldness that Ana had never seen before masked her expression.

"Hey, I'm not lying," Rachel said, watching her. "But if that's what you think, maybe it's time you go home, Ana."

Rachel turned, heading for her cabin. Ana let her leave without a word of protest, making no attempt to negotiate a truce as she would have in the past.

Rachel was still lying, and no amount of cajoling was going to get her to tell the truth. She was too scared.

After Ana crawled back into the cubicle that served as her bed, she wondered what to do next. How to make sense of it all. After a while, she gave up on sleep, turning on the overhead light. She flipped through her pad to where the writing was no longer neat or precise but rather hastily scratched words that came too quickly for her hand. She'd been writing notes about the story taking place in her head. Raul's grand adventure.

"It's not what you think," she whispered, dropping the pad. "The Neanderthal has put these ideas in your head."

Making her doubt Rachel.

She'd come here to help Rachel, not to challenge her. All right, she was lying. The question was why? Ana shouldn't imagine herself the doomed brother in the tree, the eternal victim of fratricide. She wanted to protect Rachel from any threat, real or imagined.

But Ana couldn't help if she didn't know what they were up against. She needed to be more persistent, she told herself, easing out of her bed, bare feet hitting the floor.

Maybe it was time to press a little, became more involved. Perhaps it's what they both needed.

Down the steps to Rachel's side of the boat, Ana thought she heard another sound. A loud thump and a scrape. In two steps, she was in front of the cabin.

"Rachel?" she called, pounding on the door.

She heard a muffled cry.

Ana grabbed the knob and pushed, but the door stayed shut. She shoved harder, panic setting in.

"Rachel! What's wrong?"

"I'm fine," Rachel called out, but there was a strained quality to her voice.

"Rachel—" she pounded again on the door "—let me in!"

"Leave me the fuck alone, Ana! You're not my mother, so stop checking up on me. Okay, I lied. I fucking lied to you. Just leave me the fuck alone!"

Ana stepped back from the door, all the adrenaline of seconds before charging in a different direction. She had never heard such foul language from Rachel, had never experienced the girl's anger. It startled her enough that, for an instant, she didn't know what to do.

As it turned out, Rachel made the first move. The door still closed between them, she said, "Look, I'm sorry, okay? I'm just tired. I need some sleep. We'll talk in the morning."

"Of course," Ana said, feeling ridiculously upset. "In the morning, then."

She turned back from the door, not quite sure what had just happened, but feeling black-and-blue from the encounter. Climbing back topside, she looked up at the stars that were incredibly dense, almost cinematic, as if someone had painted the sky like a backdrop. The emptiness of it felt suddenly bigger, as if it might swallow her whole.

She'd known Rachel six years. She'd watched her grow up, making the delicate change from student to friend, child to young woman. There had always been a little bit of the maternal between them, because of the age difference.

Maybe she'd crossed some line, gotten too close—taken too much for granted. She came from a family that didn't believe in limits. If you loved someone, you were allowed a certain tolerance to pry and to influence.

Don't be like me, Ana, her mother had once warned her. *Don't care so much.* And hadn't Ana learned to rein in those feelings? To be sensible, like her father? She'd tried to live her life using reason, to not be ruled by the emotions that troubled her artist mother.

And now she was thirty-two, stuck on a flimsy boat in the middle of the Caribbean, waiting for a nineteen-year-old to give clues on the course of her fate.

"Oh, Rachel," she said.

Because, no matter what Rachel had done, Ana knew she would forgive her. With Rachel, it was just too late to hold back.

Mystics hadn't received specimens from Raul for months. Rumor reached us through a colleague that Raul had "gone native." That's when his final missive arrived asking for me to come. I was to bring a spectroscope and I was to come alone. As if it weren't too much to ask that I become his errand girl, when all I could remember was the sting of his betrayal.

The need for haste came from statistics. Everything in the Amazon Basin appeared on the verge of extinction. The indigenous population itself had dwindled from two hundred distinct ethnic groups to a third of that number. The company had gambled on a few key projects, leaving Mystics vulnerable to a nasty takeover. If the company were to make money, it would have to be soon. And I thought Raul was hiding something, the weasel.

So mine was essentially a salvage operation. And in the end, I would return home and seek a teaching position. I would forget Raul. I would.

Or so I thought. The jungle had other plans.

13

Ana had never experienced a panic attack. She didn't know she was hyperventilating when her lungs seized up and she felt like one of those fish flopping on the concrete pier as the fisherman removed the hook. She only knew she couldn't breathe. There just wasn't enough oxygen in the room.

It was morning, just past seven. And Rachel was gone.

Gone was perhaps the wrong word. You weren't "gone" in the middle of the night, not from a boat anchored off the shore of a tiny, isolated island chain in the French Caribbean. Under the circumstances, you made a decision to leave. You packed your duffel and told the woman you brought along "to go to hell," so that you could sail off in a rubber dingy exercising your right to full-blown teenage angst.

She'd left a note. *I'm sorry things didn't work out.* Just that.

Which only made everything worse. The lack of oxygen, the shaking hands, the sense that if she couldn't find Rachel *right this instant*—know that she was safe— Ana would surely collapse like one of those balloons that slipped from your fingers before you could tie a knot.

Rachel was nineteen, looking too daring with her boy-cut hair, colored contacts and tattoos. And she'd just disappeared into the big bad world.

Ana stepped out onto the deck still wearing her pajamas. She'd bought the cotton boxers and T-shirt top that buttoned down the front from a catalog, intrigued by the description, "vacation-fresh stripes in blue." She stared out over the white expanse of Fiberglas that suddenly stretched for miles rather than fifty-five feet and scissored her legs over the wire rail. Just ahead, Nick's sailboat remained exactly where she'd seen it anchored the previous night.

She'd always thought of herself as a woman of the world. She'd traveled from Mexico to Morocco with her mother; she'd lived abroad as an exchange student in Spain. She could quote full passages from literary masterpieces, tear them apart and put them back together to show the author's intent. She counseled students on their future, helped them set goals and strive for gains.

But right now, the only thing that mattered was that Ana Kimble was a damn fine swimmer.

She jumped, surprised that here, close to the equator, the water could still feel so cold.

Nick dreamed of Ana. The vision of her slipped in and out of his grasp, a mirage, making him fight to keep her right there, him holding on to sleep.

Concentrate. Think only of soft thighs and a bow mouth.

He figured the Scotch helped. He'd been fantasizing about Ana before he'd even closed his eyes, reaching for the good parts, where she was all tangled up with him in a way that made it difficult to know where she ended and he began.

But ice-cold water dripping on his chest didn't fit the mood he had going. Neither did the grating voice that followed.

"How absolutely fitting," he heard Ana say.

He opened his eyes. She was standing over him, soaking wet so that her hair and clothes oozed water and her eyes disapproval. She was holding the half-empty bottle of Scotch, her knuckles popping white around the neck.

"You're drunk."

"Technically—" he propped himself up on his elbows "—I'm hungover."

He thought she was wearing pajamas. Like maybe she'd gotten wind that he was having this erotic dream and through some psychic connection zapped right on over, beaming her disdain. *Put my clothes back on, you pervert!* White with tiny blue stripes, the wet cotton hinted at the best of her.

"I had this pitiful hope that you might have actually done your job." She sprayed water and Scotch as she waved her hands at him, high dungeon in every gesture. "That you were keeping an eye on her and knew where she'd gone."

The fact that she was yelling threw him more than her sudden appearance in his cabin. It seemed too overblown for the professor. He was just thinking the whole thing surreal, that just maybe, he was still sleeping or drunk, when she followed through with a hard slap to his face.

She hit him again, like maybe she hadn't done a good enough job of it the first time.

He didn't move from the bed, didn't give her the satisfaction—though it did occur to him to grab the bottle out of her hand and put it down.

But it wasn't until she collapsed to the floor weeping that he really knew what was wrong. That look of utter misery on her face—he knew how that felt, how it burned so hot that nothing could cool the pain of it. He considered himself a specialist in that sort of loss.

In his family, the women wept like Academy Award nominees—they practically pulled their hair and beat their chests. But Ana, she cried without making a sound. Her voice wasn't even choked up when she said, "Gunnar paid you. It was your job."

"When did she leave?" he asked, getting the picture. The kid had taken off.

"She was still there at one this morning." She knuckled off the tears before they reached her mouth. "I fell asleep after that. But I heard something earlier. She might have been provisioning. I found her in the galley, in any event. And later, when I tried to come inside her room, she wouldn't let me. I think she might have been packing."

"You don't think she just went into town? That maybe she's on her way back right now?"

"She left a note."

He nodded, swinging his legs over the edge of the bed. "Then we better get started."

The kid had taken her time about leaving, that was for sure. No drawers hanging open, no clothes on the floor. Everything was as neat as a pin.

"What are you looking for?"

Ana watched from the door, as nervous as a cat, like

maybe she expected him to steal the towels or something. She'd changed into khaki shorts and what looked like a man's undershirt, but somehow managed to look sexy and wholesome at the same time. She kept tapping her finger against her arms, in a hurry for something though she hadn't budged an inch.

"Do you see anything?" she prompted. And when he gave her a look, she added, "It just seems like you're taking awfully long."

"Yeah," he said, backing out of the room. "Like about five seconds. Nah, I don't see anything."

Still he opened a drawer here and there as he crowded her into the hall, wondering about the fact that there wasn't so much as a pencil or a bobby pin inside. Ditto the bathroom.

"Do you have any training for this sort of thing?" she asked. "I mean, did you go to school or something?"

"The Dick Tracy Institute for Investigative Engineering. I got this neat gold badge and a laminated degree that says I was a star. Calm down, Professor. Give a man some space to think."

She was holding her arms tight around her stomach when he turned to face her, her fingers still keeping time like a metronome. She'd slicked her hair back into a ponytail, which made him notice her face even more.

He'd always thought she was just your basic white chick, so it surprised him a little that she looked suddenly exotic, as if it might not be such a stretch to find her here in The Saints where women could be anything from Asian to African. She'd gotten a little color since the airport. And with her hair out of the way, there was something about her cheekbones—high and delicate— and her eyes. The color, maybe. He could swear they would change depending on her mood and what she wore.

"What is it?" she asked, touching her face, as if she might brush off some dirt.

He turned away. "Nothing."

After what turned into the longest silence of the morning, she told his back, "I'm sorry I hit you."

"No big deal. Didn't even hurt."

"Yes, it did. You still have my handprint on your face."

He smiled. "No kidding?" The damn thing hurt like hell. "Bet your hand feels worse."

She rubbed it. "Maybe. A little."

He kept looking around, though he didn't know who he was pretending for, the professor or himself. So he leaned up against the bed and crossed his arms to look at her straight on. "You ever hit anyone before, Professor?"

She took a moment, then answered, "Yes."

"So I'm not your first asshole?"

She lifted her chin. "My ex-husband. The second time I caught him cheating on me."

Now that shocked the shit out of him. Who would be stupid enough to think the professor wasn't enough? "And did you apologize afterward?"

"Not on your life."

He grinned. "Atta girl."

He could tell she was barely keeping it together. The fact that the kid had taken off brought up some interesting possibilities. It also made him wonder what the hell he was going to do about it. He didn't have anything invested here, he kept reminding himself, not with Ana, anyway.

"I should call her family," she said.

He shook his head, way ahead of her. "I don't think that would be such a great idea. I mean, what's scaring this kid so much?" When she didn't fill in the blanks, he elaborated. "She took off before, right? So what's she running from? Her family? Okay, so maybe I work for the guy, but I wouldn't want to be part of anything like this," he said, keeping it vague. "I'm one of those guys who likes to wear the white hat." He gave her what he hoped sounded like sincere. "That kid is hiding something, Ana. Maybe we should find out what before we call in the troops."

He could see she was considering her answer carefully. She said, "It's probably my fault that she's gone. I may have goaded her into leaving. I accused her of lying."

He was still leaning against the bunk. It took everything he had to look concerned rather than satisfied. "So you believe me now about the kid lying to you?" When she played the statue, he added, "Come on, Professor. You just got yourself a private dick, and I use the term loosely. Tell me what you're thinking in that supremely overeducated head of yours?"

"What I think is that I don't trust you."

"Oh, honey." He liked that he could smile saying it. "Right now I'm all you got."

"And why doesn't that make me feel any better?"

"Maybe you just need some coffee." He winked, then scratched his chest, making a show of it until Miss Priss looked away. Like she hadn't seen it all before, up close and personal. He threw in a nice big yawn. "I could sure use some myself. Maybe clear up the cobwebs. What do you say?"

She gave him an exasperated look. She either didn't need coffee as much as he did, or she wasn't used to being the one making it. But she walked out just the same, so he called after her, "And some aspirin. Yeah," he added to himself, still looking around. "A big fat bottle of it."

Like he'd said, the room was as neat as a pin. Except when he looked in the closet. That's where he found her computer.

It was jammed way in the back, hidden behind some loose boards. Easy to miss if you weren't careful. Someone had smashed it to shit, which made him nervous.

He was holding it, telling himself the kid could have kicked it or thrown it across the room in a huff. She could have hidden the evidence, not so sure it had been a good idea to take out her aggression on such an expensive piece of hardware.

Staring at it, he was trying to convince himself it wasn't the obvious. It didn't have to mean that someone else had destroyed the laptop and the information on it. Someone who might want to hurt the kid.

The diskette was a little different. He found it tucked under the mattress. Sitting there, he had to ask himself the hard questions, the ones the professor wouldn't like.

If the diskette was so special to be hidden, why hadn't Rachel taken it with her?

He turned the diskette over in his hand. Someone had written Ana's Poem, across the top in this funny, fancy script.

He hated himself that he put the computer back where he'd found it, so that the professor wouldn't see it. He wondered how in hell he was going to get it off the ship without her knowing.

But Nick the asshole was on the job, and his instincts told him to play it close to the chest until he found out more about the situation. *Don't forget why you're here,* he told himself. He'd traveled clear across the world, and he'd be damned if he'd make anybody else his priority. God knew he owed Paul and his family that much.

If he could help the kid, sure. Why not? But his agenda came first, he told himself, heading down the hall to find the professor.

The fact was he couldn't afford to trust Ana. Hell, he couldn't afford to trust anyone.

She didn't trust him.

"Come on, Fish. Pick up. Pick up!"

She was on the satellite phone. Her cell phone wouldn't work on the islands, and the cell phones she'd assumed would be readily available for purchase at the airport hadn't existed, after all. She was calling her ex-husband, hoping to get a hold of him before the stranger she'd invited on board a catamaran she didn't own and couldn't sail discovered what she was up to.

Ana could hear the coffeemaker coughing and spitting in the galley through its brewing cycle. She wanted to ask Norman a very important question. Because down in Rachel's cabin, all smiles and full of concern, Nick's sudden change of heart seemed about as real as her mother's acrylic nails.

But it was Norman's answering machine that picked up. Biting her thumb, she waited for the classical music to end and Norman's unctuous voice to shut up.

"Norman? It's Ana," she whispered urgently into the mouthpiece. "I need to talk to you, but it's complicated.

Whatever you do, please, please, please, don't tell Gunnar I called. Really, it's nothing to worry about." And because she knew where Norman's loyalties lay. "Oh, for goodness' sake, Norman. Show just a tiny bit of shame. For once in your life, do this for me. Give me at least a few days before you tell Gunnar, all right? You can do that, at least." She heard footsteps. "It's important to me and in Rachel's best interest. I'll call you later tonight. Be there!"

She hung up and turned just as her private dick, as he called himself, walked up the steps into the main salon. She hoped she looked casual as she led him into the galley.

"Did you find anything?" she asked over her shoulder, taking the carafe from the drip coffeemaker and pouring two cups.

"Would you believe me if I said no?"

He had one of those faces that could look tough. With his arms crossed, it made his biceps bulge from beneath the sleeves of his T-shirt. An enormous smiley face stretched across his chest with the caption Cute But Psycho. Despite the silly shirt, you might think him belligerent. If he frowned at you like that. If he kept quiet and studied you as he was doing now.

"Do I have a choice but to believe you?" she asked, handing him the coffee. "As you so bluntly put it, you're the only game in town."

He gave her a smirk and held out his hand. "I found this," he said, holding out a diskette with Ana's Poem written in Rachel's script.

She felt her stomach drop, remembering her argument with Rachel the previous night. "She said she wrote me a poem," she said softly, taking the diskette.

"Here's what we're going to do, Professor. We're going to have a look at what's on this diskette, see if she left any bread crumbs for us to follow. Then, first chance, we're going to shore to contact the local gendarmes. You comfortable with that?"

The police sounded good. "Yes. All right."

He took the diskette back. "You have a computer?" And when she nodded, he stretched out his hand, the gesture indicating that she should lead the way. "So let's get cracking."

She hadn't switched on the Toshiba since the plane ride over Montserrat, having ditched the computer for her more familiar yellow pads. She actually had to dig out the laptop from her luggage in the closet and try to remember how to switch on the darn thing. When she fidgeted with the screen, searching for the knob to hike up the brightness, the Neanderthal took over, mumbling something under his breath she was sure she didn't want to hear.

She watched him pop in the diskette. She took a step back, thinking about Rachel. That she was gone.

Just a few hours ago, Rachel had been safe here, even happy. And those smiles beneath Rachel's milk mustache, why so cozy if she'd been planning to leave, to write vapid notes that said nothing at all?

From the computer, Nick said, "Here we go."

Ana peered down at the screen. Numerical gibberish marched across like hieroglyphics so that, even before she asked, she was afraid she already knew what it might mean.

"It's encrypted," Nick said.

His fingers flew over the keys, showing that, at least

in this he had some skills. She supposed that in his profession computers might come in handy, cyberspace being the best place to snoop.

She stood behind him as he picked at the keys using only four fingers, a self-taught typist making up his own rules while still managing impressive speed. When he finally leaned back to show her the screen, he gave her a wide smile of satisfaction—while Ana felt suddenly ill.

The screen was covered with equations. The kind of work Rachel did for Gunnar.

"She wasn't writing a poem." But she'd known. She'd been certain it had been something else.

"Nah," he said. "She was writing code."

Now there wouldn't be any bread crumbs. Certainly not for Ana and Nick. Not on these pages with all those symbols.

As if confirming her fears, Nick popped out the diskette. "Mind if I keep this?"

"Well, I can't make sense out of it." But then, thinking better of the carte blanche. "I'll want it back, of course."

Nick didn't appear the least insulted. He wasn't even paying attention. He had folded up the computer and was whistling under his breath. "You got a picture?" he asked. And when she stared at him blankly. "Of the kid? You got a photograph of Rachel?"

"No. No, I don't," she said, realizing it just then.

"No kidding?" Again, that smile. "I guess it's a good thing that I do."

Fish sat back listening to the aria of music surrounding him in the salon of his apartment overlooking Newport Harbor. He was thinking of Ana. How much he missed her.

He was sitting in his coveted Warren McArthur chair—one of the pieces that had survived the war effort when much of aluminum furniture had been melted down—drinking his Beringer zinfandel, 1992. An excellent year.

Just that morning, he'd returned from his visit to Ana's parents' condo in Big Bear where he'd gone to find the girls. The place had been perfectly empty. The caretaker said no one had been up in months.

Which meant the worst-case scenario. Rachel had vanished. Of course, she'd dragged Ana along for the ride.

He took another sip of the zinfandel. He'd driven directly from Big Bear to Lido Island where Gunnar lived. But rather than race to the entrance of the Mazas' palatial home with the information that all was lost, he'd sat in his BMW, the engine running, contemplating his next step. In the end, he'd determined to postpone any revelations he might make to Gunnar.

There was Ana's message on his machine, of course—the rub of it, letting him know exactly how trustworthy she considered him. But there was also the vague inclination to wait for her call tomorrow. For Ana, he found suddenly that he wanted to be a better man.

And so he'd driven back to his apartment, was even now drinking the delicious zinfandel to douse his fears. Ana had always brought out the best in him, even if it hadn't done her a lick of good.

When the aria ended, he finished the glass of Beringer and poured another so that by the time he strolled into the room he used as a home office he was feeling a bit light-headed from the wine. He sat in his leather chair and shoved his hands through his hair, the chant running through his head, *What to do? What to do?*

Rachel's e-mail to him changed all that.

He read it and laughed. "Ah, Rachel," he said, touching the screen. "How you do intrigue."

When the jungle burns, the first thing you notice is the smell. Thick, tasting like cadavers, it is essentially death, or so I would come to think. My purpose here was altogether different than most. No weekend adventurer, no Chico Mendes crusader, I had traveled to this, the last destination on earth, for a man I'd hoped never to lay eyes on again. Of course, I would have to find him first. Knowing Raul, he wouldn't make it easy.

Daily I creep forward with his spectroscope, entering the jungle's heart with respect and fear. Tomorrow, I will leave the security of João, my English-speaking guide, for an Indian and a dugout. Raul lives with the Urutu-Pau-Pau tribe, rumored to be pygmies who perform strange rites of passage that may or may not include cannibalism.

For the first time, I feel utterly lost, wondering at the madness of love.

14

As it turned out, the locals weren't up for much.

Apparently, the constable was off-island on business. In the meantime, the Gendarmerie National at the Terre-de-Haut anchorage gave the term laissez-faire new meaning. Rachel was nineteen. They were confident she would return. She'd been missing less than twenty-four hours. Come back tomorrow. Better yet, come by next week. Presently, they had their hands full with festivities for the local Mardi Gras.

After Ana had done her stint walking up and down the square, throwing her hands in the air and shaking her head in despair, Nick pointed out that, on an island the size of Macy's parking lot, Rachel didn't have far to run. The worst she faced before they found her was bad shellfish or a rabid iguana. Honestly, they didn't even allow cars here. If the kid was agile enough to avoid an oncoming moped, they were home free.

They nixed the idea of returning to the consulate on Guadeloupe, fearing that officials there would contact the Maza family. The diskette Nick had found made an even stronger case that Rachel was running from Gunnar, having possibly disappointed him in some regard.

Leaving the island without Rachel was completely

out of the question—not without first conducting a thorough search.

To that effect, Nick and Ana decided to split up, flashing photographs of Rachel to anyone who would stand still long enough to take a gander. Which led to the past two hours, a complete and utter waste of Ana's time. She wasn't getting very far with pantomime and a French dictionary.

"*Perdu,*" she said, tapping the photograph of Rachel. "*Jeune fille. Perdu.*"

"*Ah. Mais, non. Je ne l'ai pas vue.*"

Whatever that singsong phrase meant, the facial expression that accompanied the remark did not encourage.

She felt utterly lost. Back home, it was Ana who could step in at the local grocery store for a quick translation for those caught in a communications bind. Now suddenly she was the foreigner so that, the past half hour, she'd stared at the pay phone longingly, feeling its irresistible pull.

Call Fish. Call him now. Don't trust the Neanderthal.

Was it merely a desire to speak English? Or was she being too cavalier not contacting Rachel's family? Dare she sabotage some secret plan of Rachel's? Rachel was nineteen, after all, a woman grown, capable of making her own decisions.

Not that calling Fish necessarily jeopardized Rachel's wishes. What Ana needed was information. Under the circumstances, Fish might be her best bet— a frightening concept, but there you had it.

She'd told him to expect her call later tonight, which would be early morning stateside. But it was late evening in Los Angeles now. Surely he would be home.

Ana ran to the phone and dug out her American Express card. She punched in code numbers, access numbers, international prefixes, until she heard Fish's line ringing, her eyes scanning the square for signs of the Neanderthal.

Fish picked up on the second ring.

"Where are you?" he demanded, recognizing her voice.

"Did you talk to Gunnar?"

"Of course I didn't talk to him. And thank you very much for that vote of confidence. Put Rachel on the phone. I need to speak to her."

Ana closed her eyes, wondering if she was doing the right thing. *Who to trust?* But then she caught sight of a familiar silhouette coming down the narrow street, heading right toward her.

"She can't come to the phone right now," she improvised. She squinted, a little nearsighted, thinking that, yes indeed, she recognized those broad shoulders, that rolling gait.

"I need you to find out something for me, Norman." She spoke in a hushed, hurried voice. "Try to be subtle, but I need to know if, possibly, Gunnar might have hired a private detective. To follow Rachel."

"I don't need to ask because I know he did no such thing. Otherwise, he wouldn't be hounding me for the number to your parents' condominium in Big Bear, which, by the way, is where he thinks Rachel is at the moment. This morning, I finally ran out of excuses and gave him the damn number, knowing full well that you weren't there because I just got back myself from trying to chase you down. Had a lovely afternoon by the fire wondering where the hell you were. Now, Ana," he said, switching to his best this-is-for-your-own-good voice, "what's this about a private investigator? Are you in some sort of trouble?"

Ana ducked farther inside the booth, which wasn't a booth at all, but rather a clear plastic shell. She could feel herself breathing too deep, not exhaling, her head growing lighter with each rush of air. "I'll call when I can."

She hung up, Norman's warning doing a nice little samba inside her head. *Are you in some kind of trouble?*

He wasn't a private investigator.

Maybe she'd known from the beginning. Call it woman's intuition. Without looking, she slipped out from the booth and sat at one of the benches facing the ocean. When she thought she had her heart rate below cardiac arrest level, she glanced up. The Neanderthal was walking toward her, looking congenial—not the face of a man who might suspect he couldn't be trusted.

He wasn't a private investigator. At least, not one hired by Rachel's brother.

So why the notebook with Rachel's name written over and over, dozens of times, almost obsessively? Why follow them all the way from Los Angeles?

"Ana?"

He had come up behind her, so that she practically jumped out of her skin even though she'd seen him approach. But then, as things turned, Nick wasn't near through with the surprises.

Sitting beside her, he said, "I think I have a lead on the kid."

Fish hadn't told Gunnar shit.

Still holding the phone, making an ass of himself because he'd spent a good two minutes berating Ana before he realized she'd hung up, he felt instantly on guard.

She'd wanted to know if Gunnar had hired a private investigator. Which meant—wherever the hell they were—Ana and Rachel were being followed.

Of course, it wasn't Ana they were following. She wasn't the least important in the scheme of things. Good Lord, there wasn't a bone of intrigue in Ana's body. But her nurturing instincts were certainly overdeveloped, making her vulnerable to Rachel's machinations.

He should have given her children when she'd asked. She never would have left him if he had, despite a few peccadilloes.

Back in his office, he reread Rachel's e-mail, trying to decide what exactly he should do.

She'd written, *Made a breakthrough. Neuro-Sys is up and running and you won't believe how slick this thing is. Will contact you soon. Don't tell my brother. He'll be greedy.*

She'd attached a series of instructions he was to follow when she delivered the newest version of the program.

A breakthrough. What they needed most, what he prayed for day and night. For Rachel's genius to give them their get-out-of-jail-free card.

Neuro-Sys is up and running.

The possibility seemed too incredible to believe. A functioning brain-simulation program was practically science fiction.

But then so was mapping the human genome and cloning.

Made a breakthrough...will contact you soon.

"Not soon enough," he said softly.

Last night, he'd actually begun to believe they'd succeeded. No one else needed to die. With a functioning brain-simulation program, human experiments were no longer necessary. They could use Neuro-Sys to fine-tune their formula at the clinic risk-free.

Maybe this was what Rachel had needed all along, time away from her tyrant of a brother. Perhaps that's why her work had suffered the past months, as Dr. Clavel suggested at their last meeting. The overbearing Gunnar, a man too controlling by half, had pushed Rachel into some sort of mental block.

But Gunnar was also a powerful man, and he had resources Norman could only dream of. If Ana had called him rather than Norman, Gunnar wouldn't be sitting with his head in his hands, bemoaning his fate.

Now Ana was asking about a private investigator, and Norman was experiencing a crisis in conscience. Because he didn't want Ana or Rachel hurt.

Feeling extremely weary, he picked up the phone. He punched in Gunnar's number.

"Hello, Magda dear," he said into the mouthpiece. "Could you put Gunnar on the phone. It's about Rachel."

15

"I don't understand," she yelled over the roar of the moped pumping up the hill like a winded horse, the *clackity-clack* of the kickstand dragging on the asphalt adding a sort of dirt-bike thrill to the turns. "Are we going to find Rachel now or not?"

"Hold on, we're almost there." Nick gunned the scooter to a full fifteen mph, wondering if the damn thing was going to make it up the road to the fort.

The idea of bringing the professor to Fort Napoleon had come in a burst of inspiration brought on by the sight of her with the phone plastered to her ear staring at him as if he were Manson out on bail. Which, most likely, he was from her point of view.

After he'd managed to ditch her, Nick had put in a little phone time himself. Because of what he could decipher from the diskette, he wasn't feeling good about the kid's little vanishing act.

He hadn't been able to run the program on his laptop, as it was massive, requiring more capacity. So he'd looked into the guts of the code by using a translator to get readable text. Most programmers included comment fields in their programs, pieces of information that the computer ignored but explained the function of each section of code for the programmer's sake—or anyone else who might want to know how the thing worked. Reading the comment fields, he realized the code was some sort of computer brain-simulation program, designed to analyze the effects of pharmaceuticals on the brain.

Suddenly alarm bells were going off in his head. Only, he couldn't get anyone at any of the alphabet agencies to talk. And now he had this bad feeling that whatever Paul had been doing, he'd either screwed up or gone rogue.

Then there was the bartender in San Francisco. According to him, Paul traveled to hospitals and clinics all over the world, a different time zone every week. He made the job sound just a cut above the drug reps carrying freebies for the docs. That didn't exactly gel with what Paul's sister thought her biochemist brother did for a living.

But it was a perfect cover, which Nick figured the bartender already knew given the friends they had in common.

Nick turned sharply up the winding road so that the blue sky came screaming at them, mirroring a postcard view of the bay below. He gave a little wiggle with the front wheel, like maybe he was losing his balance—the damn scooter was a slug chugging up the hill. The professor grabbed on, holding on to his waist. A cheap thrill, but there you had it.

He hadn't had a lot of time when he'd come up with the story about getting a lead on the kid. He was trying to give himself some options before the cavalry arrived in the form of Gunnar Maza. Because, sure as shit, the professor had sounded the alarm on that pay phone.

That's when he'd thought of the fort. It was situated 120 meters above sea level and delivered a 360-degree view. The old relic had been commissioned by Napoleon himself, hence the name. The place drew tourists by the droves and bragged eighteenth-century cannons and, for the eagle-eyed, six-foot-long iguanas hiding in the foliage surrounding the fort.

But the real beauty of the place was its location. No way in hell the professor was getting away from him until he had his say.

At the entrance, he bought two tickets and signaled to the woman at the gate that Ana was with him. Hurrying up the crumbling ramparts past Pope's Head cactus and Flamboyant trees, he came to a stop at the edge of the world.

About five minutes later, Ana hiked up alongside him, staring out at the ocean haze beyond. When he turned to smile at her, he imagined the eyes behind her sunglasses narrowed, distrust perfuming the air as heavily as the wild orchids growing in the gardens below.

"All right," she said. "Where is she?"

"Come on. You can see La Soufrière on the other side."

She grabbed his arm. "I don't want to see La Soufrière—"

"Sure, it's not erupting, but it's still worth a look."

"Is this a joke? Do you even know where Rachel is?" Then, with an impatient hiss, she dug her fingers into his arm. "You tell me about this lead of yours, and tell me this second."

"So have a look at La Soufrière."

Amazingly enough, she came up alongside him, making these little huffing noises that he figured the professor thought expressed how really pissed off she was. When they were finally alone above the yellow stone barracks by the third magazine, he said, "Someone spotted the Zodiac. She hugged the coast, going to the neighboring island." He nodded toward the island of Terre-de-Bas just visible through the haze. "I figure she's probably there—unless she's rented a boat. But she didn't take the ferry. I slipped a few of the ferry guys some euros and flashed her picture around."

"So why aren't we there?" she asked, waving ahead. "On this other island? Shouldn't you be…tracking or trailing or something?"

"I want to talk to the guys who saw her, get as much information as possible before we set out like a couple chickens with our heads cut off. But first, we have to get things straight between us. I sense a certain lack of trust."

He saw it then. All systems shutting down.

She adjusted her glasses, cleared her throat. "Lack of trust?" She spoke as if it were some foreign phrase she was trying out for the first time.

"I can't work like this, Kimble. Always watching my back, you making calls…."

"If you must know." She crossed her arms and stuck out a foot, so that her hips hitched up on one side, the body language saying it all. She was going to lie. "I called my parents."

"I was thinking family was involved, but not yours." He stepped closer. "You really think they have her best interest at heart? Because, listening to you, I think it's interesting that I'm the only one worried about her brother coming down for a look-see."

She stared at him for the longest time, assessing behind the tinted glasses. He gave the blurry reflection his best Boy Scout grin.

"It's a little difficult to believe, Mr. Travis, this sudden change of heart on your part. Presumably, her brother hired you to spy on us."

"No kidding? But here's the thing—you don't have to know my motives, or even approve of them. But imagine what I look like if my client gets a call about his missing sister being in trouble and I don't have a clue where she is? So now maybe you understand that we want the same thing. Keep the family in the dark until further notice."

"And we find Rachel?"

"And talk to her, see what's the beef. Then, if everything looks kosher, I call Gunnar Maza and collect my fee. You take the kid on home."

"And what exactly do you want from me?"

"From here on out, we work together. No more calls." He pretended to brush something off her shoulder, using the contact to keep her attention. "See, you're making everything messy, clouding up the relationship so we don't know where we stand with each other."

"I believe you and I know exactly where we stand." But after a while, she stepped back and held out her hand. "All right," she said, waiting for him to shake on it.

You had to love the professor, her lovely view of the world. One handshake later, and it's all official. Hell, they'd practically taken a blood oath.

He liked her grip though, nothing clammy or limp about it. Just a nice firm shake as she said, "And the call was personal."

He winked. "Gotcha. Now, here's what we're going to do."

On the walk back down, she listened as he told her about checking out the rental places, hostels and restaurants on Terre-de-Bas, see if they could pick up the kid's trail. Nick figured she still didn't trust him, which was okay. He just wanted to keep her off the damn phone. If she wasn't lying about calling Maza, they still had time.

"Does Rachel speak French?" he asked as he handed her the motorcycle helmet.

She shook her head. "Not to my knowledge."

"Good. She'll stick out." He straddled the bike, waiting for her to do the same. "Hold on tight, Kimble. And watch the hands." He felt her stiffen as he punched the bike, forcing her to grab hold of him. Over the cannon fire of the belching scooter, he yelled, "I'm only human, you know?"

Lynn didn't feel so good today.

By now, she was used to the headaches, but this was different, like nuclear winter stuck inside her head. She'd even called Sandy, her best friend. She had to have sounded pretty bad because Sandy didn't even ask what she wanted, just said she'd be right over.

Lynn wished she'd hurry. She didn't want to be alone if anything happened.

She'd been reading up on that Manuela woman. She was supposed to be some famous courtesan. The lover of Bolívar, the guy they'd named the country for, the liberator of South America. Lynn thought it was really cool how in the sessions, she could remember all that stuff. But she didn't want it to happen all the time, like some crazy person.

Today, she was a little worried that's exactly what

had happened. In class, she thought maybe she'd become that Manuela chick, only she hadn't been hypnotized or anything. All she remembered was Professor Rodriguez talking about some crisis in the Church in Rome during the fifteenth century. She thought she might have dozed off, but when she woke up, everyone was staring at her so that she knew something was wrong. She'd picked up her books and ran out.

Okay, maybe that was a little far-fetched, to think she'd become Manuela during class. It's not like she'd stopped to ask anybody what happened. But it felt so much like after her sessions with Dr. Clavel, that eerie feeling that she'd been "gone." And the headaches were getting worse. Right now, she felt so bad that she almost fell trying to reach the bed to sit down.

She scrounged through her nightstand drawer. Hal, the tech at Seacliff, had given her new medication just yesterday. Something special he said she might need if her headaches got suddenly worse. But he'd warned her to hold off on the strong stuff, but now she thought she'd waited too long.

And, boy, had she ever. When these pills kicked in, she was even sorry she'd called Sandy, she felt so much better. The clinic didn't want her to talk to anyone about the stuff she was involved in. It was all confidential. She'd signed this paper—a nondisclosure agreement or something. She'd get in a lot of trouble if she told.

She could feel herself drifting off. She tried to focus on what she'd tell Sandy. A migraine, maybe.

Tomorrow, she'd go back to the clinic, she told herself, curling up into a ball on the bed. At the clinic, they'd know what was wrong with her. Really, she didn't need to worry. She shouldn't have called Sandy.

Drifting off to sleep, she told herself everything was going to be okay. She didn't need to freak out or be scared. Dr. Clavel knew what he was doing. If she started whining about stuff, they might even cut her out of the program at Seacliff and that would be a real bust.

She should just keep to the plan and follow instructions. She was part of something special. In a few weeks, it would all be over anyway. And then she could go back to focusing on school, just like before. Pretty soon, everything would be back to normal. She just had to be patient.

Relax, she told herself, drifting off. Everything was going to be just fine.

"Are you coming to bed, Gunnar?"

Magda stood at the door to his study. She was dressed in an elegant peignoir that complimented her green eyes. She wore her blond hair in a simple knot at her nape, so that with the pull of a few hairpins it would flow past her shoulders.

"Gunnar?" she prompted, that hint of irritation in her voice that she sometimes allowed.

"Not now, my love. In a while, maybe."

He always called Magda by pet names, but that's all they were. He didn't love her and they both knew it. Gunnar had loved only one woman.

Perhaps that made him defective somehow, unable to move beyond the loss of true love. But he preferred to believe that he was discriminating. He treasured the experience and wouldn't cheapen it by pretending that something so special could be repeated.

No, he didn't love Magda. What they had was commitment, and in that he considered himself a superior husband and father. He provided for Magda and their child—he never questioned a single expense. He gave them social standing. He'd never broken his marriage vows, hadn't even been tempted. Not once.

He did care for Magda. A great deal. He didn't want her hurt. And that's exactly what would happen if she didn't leave him the hell alone right now.

"Gunnar, I know you're worried."

About Rachel, she meant. The fact that she'd vanished and he had absolutely no idea where to find her. He didn't know if she was hurt. If she needed him.

"Rachel's a big girl. She'll call and let us know where she is when she's ready. Gunnar, what can you possibly accomplish tonight?"

"Go to bed, Magda."

"Don't you think I'm worried, too?"

"Magda, dear, I don't fucking care. So do us both a favor. Shut the hell up and go to bed."

He didn't look up, because he knew what he would see, a look of pained rejection on her face. She was such a regal woman—it's what had drawn him to her from the first. She didn't make these overtures often. He couldn't stand to see her demean herself for him.

"Thank you for that," he heard her whisper. "For reminding me just how much I matter in the grand scheme of things. You can be such a bastard, Gunnar."

He smiled, liking her wrath better than her sympathy. He sipped the cognac he'd poured minutes earlier, ignoring her as she slammed out the door.

"That's right," he said. "Leave the bastard alone."

They should all be happy that he was such a bastard. It's what made everything possible. This house, the vacation homes, their daughter's dance lessons and voice lessons and horse obsession, all of which cost a fortune just so Magda could pretend the girl had some talent when they both knew Juliet would never accomplish anything other than what Daddy's money could buy her. The girl hadn't even managed her mother's good looks.

Gunnar finished the cognac and placed the glass in the sink at the bar. He stood in front of the fireplace watching the embers glow.

He should have expected Rachel's rebellion. He was off his game, too focused on Seacliff. He should have anticipated this move on her part, kept one step ahead. She'd spent her entire life fighting him, after all.

And now she was gone and he was having trouble catching his breath.

What surprised him most was the stabbing sense of betrayal he felt. The fact that he could just about wring that bitch Ana's neck for taking Rachel away, filling her head with stories when all along he thought he'd neutralized the woman's threat.

He'd hoped Rachel would come to understand, as he did, the greater ramifications of her genius, what she wasted, daydreaming over poetry. She had a great gift, one that he had nurtured, tutoring her himself until she surpassed what he could accomplish, then finding Norman for her, although he suspected these past few years Norman was only helping himself.

She had an obligation to fulfill her potential. She had no idea the great things she could achieve—what she had achieved.

And didn't he know firsthand what could happen if she let that brilliant mind lay fallow? It wasn't just what the world would lose, but Rachel herself who might be lost. Juliet suffered no such threat prating about with her mindless friends. What else did she have to do with her days? What more could she accomplish? The girl was beyond average.

But there was danger in letting Rachel's genius waste away. He didn't want to walk in and find her dead on the floor, a bottle of pills empty beside her like Beatrice.

It was a delicate time for Rachel. She needed him there to guide her through the choices ahead. Of course, he'd pushed. He'd witnessed firsthand how she could lose herself in the numbers and theories in her head.

He couldn't let her fail—throw away what Beatrice had given.

He turned off the fireplace, getting ready to go to bed. Magda, as always, was perfectly right. There was nothing he could do tonight. And he needed to be fresh for tomorrow.

He imagined his wife would be sleeping in the downstairs bedroom. She did that more and more these days. He'd been distracted. And now with this new situation…

Switching off the light, he told himself Magda would just have to understand. Rachel needed him. He'd never hidden anything from his wife. She'd known from the beginning he had a prior obligation, that Rachel came first. He'd promised his father, Javier.

Tomorrow he'd find her. And then, he would be able to catch his breath and the pain in his chest would ease. He would be able to think clearly about their future.

And he'd make damn sure she never left him again.

16

Nick stood on the schooner's deck, ignoring the bottle of beer he'd been nursing the past hour. Out over the black water, the lights from the village reflected off the glassy surface to create a perfect mirror image. Music from a club granted a nice accompaniment.

The Green Flash lay anchored just a stone's throw away. He could just make out Ana's silhouette as she sat scribbling on a notepad topside. Writing her "book," no doubt.

He remembered that first night she'd talked about writing her book, asking for input on the character she was creating. He wondered if she still considered him hero material.

He'd been watching her most of the night, having a hard time getting his head into the game.

He stared down at the untouched sandwich he'd made himself earlier, the nearly full bottle of beer he'd been carrying around as if he had any intention of finishing it.

And now, he'd lost his appetite.

"It must be love," he said, picking up the plate and heading for the galley.

The interesting part of the puzzle and what he'd been

mulling over the past twenty minutes was his reluctance to follow the more secure path. Duty called, right? No way he should be giving Ana alone time, basically trusting her to keep her side of that handshake back at the fort. What he needed was to be on that catamaran right there alongside her, keeping a close watch instead of sitting here like some teenager mooning over her from afar.

"What the hell are you afraid of?" he asked himself.

But he knew. The professor was a hell of a distraction.

He tossed the sandwich and poured the beer down the sink. What he needed was some sleep, not that he was getting any. The professor again. The woman had taken over his dreams.

He figured that's what three years of celibacy did to a man. One taste of Ana a couple of days back and sex was all he could think about. He could still smell her on his skin.

He glanced at his watch. Midnight. He closed his eyes and breathed a long sigh.

Sitting down in the salon, he took his wallet from the back pocket of his jeans and slipped out Valerie's photograph. He never went anywhere without her picture. He wondered if Paul did the same thing. He knew Paul had loved her every bit as much as Nick had.

Or maybe more. Nick stared at his wife's photograph. He'd always wondered about that. How things might have been different if he'd done the right thing. Walked away and given Paul his happy ending.

He dropped the photograph on the table, Valerie staring up at him. Happy. Loving him still.

That saying, how it was better to have loved and lost instead of missing out on love altogether?

"Bullshit," he said under his breath.

He dug back into his wallet. Like a magic trick, he flipped out his business card so that it, too, landed faceup next to Valerie. The act had the familiarity of ritual. He looked at the two, reading them like tarot cards. The warring forces in his life.

He tossed the wallet onto the table, shaking his head. "God, I need sleep." As if regret could change anything.

Maybe that's what this was about, his surly mood. The professor bringing it all back. In a weird way, she paralleled the past. Paul was his job—no, his duty. But then Ana came along, clouding things up, making him wonder about the kid. What kind of trouble she might be in. If Paul could be part of the trouble.

He told himself it didn't matter. Whatever the truth, Rachel Maza was the key to finding his friend. That notebook told him as much. So had the bartender in San Francisco. And the diskette the kid left behind. Rachel Maza and Phoenix Pharmaceuticals.

But then there was Ana, who probably didn't deserve what was coming down the pike. The woman had collateral damage written all over her.

He'd learned a lot about different personalities when he'd been training for Intel. Ana was one of those nurturing fools who drew people to her, usually the wrong sort. Like that dick, Norman Fish, marrying the Nobel Prize winner's daughter. He could imagine how the idiot had introduced her at cocktail parties, wearing her on his arm like a badge, how uncomfortable the unassuming Ana would be with the protocol.

And Rachel. After reading what was on the diskette, he figured he knew why Paul was involved. A program that could simulate the workings of the human brain? No way that kind of research was going on without some sort of government interest—and maybe more than just the government. So she'd dragged Ana here, afraid to go it alone.

And now he was the latest of the needy to cross Ana's path. He had to admit it, what happened in that hotel room with Ana hadn't been right. A lapse he couldn't forget. His wanting her so badly. Still wanting her. Hell, it was almost too easy, falling back into that rhythm with Ana. Scary easy.

He smiled despite himself just remembering. She made an adorable drunk.

"Novels delusional," he said, laughing a little. Ana, taking it all so seriously. Especially when she'd looked deep in his eyes and said she wanted to make love to him. That wasn't the kind of thing you messed around with, a woman who looked at you like that.

"Delusional." That just about covered it.

He reached across the table in the salon to where he'd put his latest discoveries from the catamaran, a wadded-up label and a package of cigarettes. Hell, if he wasn't going to sleep, he could at least get some work done.

He imagined the label he'd found in the trash was probably the original on the diskette now entitled Ana's Poem. Like maybe the kid was starting to get paranoid, something new making her take the added precaution.

He had no idea what the initials YBP stood for.

His second discovery was just as troubling. A package of cigarettes Rachel had hidden in the galley. He knew the kid smoked—had seen her plenty of times— but he'd asked Ana just the same. *Rachel smokes, right?*

You had to hand it to the professor. Not a bone of subterfuge in her. She'd told him Rachel had quit recently. Had made this whole ceremony of tossing out her supply.

She'd been hiding the cigarettes from Ana. Which meant, whatever reasons Rachel had for leaving, she hadn't taken her secret stash of cigarettes along.

It might not mean anything. But under the circumstances, he thought it might mean a whole hell of a lot.

He glanced at his watch again, getting up to retrieve Rachel's computer. It hadn't been hard to get the laptop off the catamaran, after all. Ana, the trusting type, hadn't exactly hovered over him while he'd been on board.

He hooked up the computer to his laptop, using it like an external hard drive. He'd have to break through some major firewalls. After reading what was on the diskette, he didn't figure the kid was going to make it easy.

Ana's mother once described writing as a "delightful torment." Sitting alone in the salon with her writing pad before her, Ana was trying to figure out when the delightful part entered the picture.

It wasn't so much that she was having trouble writing. The words flowed effortlessly—long, detailed, *tortuous* passages about Nick. She rhapsodized about his hair and the color of his eyes; she celebrated the texture and tone of his voice and how it could zing right up her spine to land inside her head. The sound of him would plant itself in her heart, never giving her a moment's rest as she consumed countless *exhausting* hours trying to think what exactly it was about that voice that could turn a woman inside out.

None of which had anything to do with Raul or the Amazon or writing her book.

She flipped back to the beginning of the pad, telling herself she had completely lost her mind. No, it was more than that. It was something much worse. She'd become obsessed.

Ana sat up straighter with the realization. Yes, she thought, looking down at the pages inspired by a single afternoon with Nick. She'd become obsessed with the man.

But sometimes obsession was just a form of distraction.

She dropped the pad and made her way to the bathroom sink. She scrubbed her face, trying to wash away the worry. *Rachel.*

She stared into the tiny bathroom mirror, her face red from scrubbing. She wondered where Rachel was right now. If she was hungry. Scared. If she was safe.

"Arghh! Don't think! Don't think! Don't think!" she said breathlessly.

She buried her face in the towel, trying to stop all those crazy ideas running through her head from coming together into coherent thought. Think of beautiful green eyes instead. Of dark hair and a crooked smile. Muscles.

"Obsession is okay. Obsession is good."

It kept her from going completely insane worrying about Rachel.

She stared into the mirror, the bewildered look on her face reflected there. The past twenty-four hours, she didn't know if she was coming or going. So she'd pulled out her familiar yellow pads, looking for escape from just this kind of panic. Somewhere along the way, Raul of the jungle melded into his flesh-and-blood counterpart, Mr. Private Dick himself.

"Well," she said, hanging the towel with a sniff, "enough of that."

Fifteen minutes later, she'd made herself a cup of chamomile tea. She was sitting at the table in the salon, focusing on the pages of her book, analyzing the flaws in her writing to avoid dealing with the flaws in her life—only to discover an overlap.

She'd been wondering about her decision to write from the point of view of a scorned woman, as if she might be working through her own disastrous romance life. "Well, why not?"

She smiled, scratching out the name of the story's villain. With a flourish, she wrote another name to replace it. *Nieman Trout.*

She underlined it. Twice.

"Now, that's inspiring," she said, putting pen to paper, once again searching for the delightful part of her torment.

17

Rachel woke up in the Zodiac, wanting to heave, her head on fire. He'd tied her hands behind her back with duct tape and dumped her on the floor of the raft so that, when she opened her eyes, all she saw was the side of the inflatable.

But she knew the guy was there. She could hear him humming to himself as he steered the boat.

She tried to get up, maybe even throw herself overboard. He grabbed her and put the handkerchief over her nose again. She had a faint impression of intense eyes and dark blond hair before another blanket of darkness fell over her.

The next time she woke up, she was lying in a bed, her hands tied to the bedposts. There was a slightly sour smell to the sheets. Light shot through the cracks in the wooden shutters covering the window so she knew it was day.

She tried to sit up but with her wrists anchored to the bedposts she felt pinned like some stupid bug. The place wasn't much more than a shack. She rolled over, trying to get a better look around when out of nowhere again, a handkerchief covered her mouth.

She hadn't seen him, didn't even know he was

there. She tried not to breathe, to fight. Again darkness descended.

Now she woke up moaning, almost waiting for that handkerchief and its acrid smell. And when it didn't come, she rolled slowly to her side, still tied in that sour-smelling bed but by loose cords of rope.

She tried to imagine the freak hovering over her while she was out cold. What he might have done to her when she was passed out.

She saw him then, in the corner hunched over a table, eating. He was shoveling food into his mouth as if it were this totally normal thing to have her tied to his bed.

She didn't say anything. She didn't dare move. She was too scared. She knew this was the guy who had left all those messages, and now he'd done exactly what he'd said he'd do. He'd found her. He'd neutralized her threat.

"Don't pretend you're not awake. I heard you," he said.

He kept eating, not turning, acting as if he had eyes in the back of his head. She felt the air freeze up inside her chest as she watched him swab the bread around the bowl. He picked up the bowl and took it outside, giving her a glimpse of some kind of jungle growth. The shack was small and hot, the humidity here, suffocating. She didn't know if it was the drug he'd given her, but she couldn't move. She didn't even try to struggle— or maybe she was just tired of running.

She kept staring at the door, waiting for something to happen.

Maybe he'd use a gun. That would be fast. Dying like that wouldn't be so bad. She just didn't want to be tortured or anything. She'd seen movies where things like that happened to women. It made her sick just to think about it.

He'd been waiting for her in her cabin. She'd been so stupid, so blind to his threat. Instead, she'd been all upset because Ana had ruined things by accusing her of lying—which she had been, of course. But Rachel was so close to making it all okay again. So she'd been angry that Ana suddenly gets a clue. Kind of ironic, really. Because Rachel wasn't going to make anything okay now.

Inside her cabin, he'd grabbed her and taped her mouth and wrists using duct tape. He even taped her ankles together. After he'd turned on the lights, he'd gone around the room picking up her stuff and jamming it into her duffel bag. The cabin was a pretty small space, so she waited until he was walking past her and kicked him. He had to have hit her because she'd blacked out.

The next thing she knew, she opened her eyes and her head hurt something awful. He was still there, pounding her laptop against the bed. He'd looked up and, seeing her, he'd smiled, giving the laptop one more good blow, staring at her the whole time, like maybe he wished it was her head he was caving in.

He'd written that she was evil, that she deserved to die. She knew he hated her. But she'd never had anyone look at her with such emotion. Here was this stranger—but he hated her guts. Wanted her dead, even.

When he tried to stuff the broken laptop into her duffel, the bag wouldn't shut. And then Ana had come pounding on the door, so he'd shoved the computer inside the closet behind some loose boards. He'd made a leap for the door, just as Ana tried to come inside.

He had this wiry frame. When he tensed, pushing the

door closed, she could see cords of muscles at his throat and on his arms. He moved fast, like a hunted animal, grabbing a knife from some holster at the small of his back.

He held the knife at her throat, then put his finger to his lips, making it perfectly clear what she should do as he peeled back the tape on her mouth.

She'd been crying when she'd screamed those awful things at Ana, and she'd meant every word. She'd wanted to say more. *Get out of here! Leave! Run before he gets you, too.*

She wanted to tell her that she was sorry. She shouldn't have brought Ana here. She'd known it was wrong and she'd done it anyway because she's been too scared to come alone.

After Ana left, he'd sat on the floor to write something on a piece of paper. She thought maybe it was a ransom note. Or worse yet, a letter making it sound like she was just taking off so Ana wouldn't even come looking for her, wouldn't ever know what really happened.

He could probably do that—copy her handwriting or something. She knew he'd been planning this for a long time.

He'd used the chloroform after that, so that the next time she awakened, she'd been in the Zodiac, staring up at the stars as they zipped over the dark water.

When she'd e-mailed Norman, she'd been so stoked. *I won!* she'd thought. She'd beaten them all. At least, that's what she'd been telling herself when she'd punched the command to send her message.

When she'd hidden the diskette under the mattress, she'd thought she'd celebrate with milk and cookies. Why not? She'd felt as if she were on top of the world.

Now she was trying to convince herself that she wasn't going to die some horrible death as she watched Creepy Guy open the door and step back inside the shack. He'd changed, wearing khaki shorts and a T-shirt. His hair was wet, like maybe he'd taken a minute to wash up outside or something, but he hadn't brushed it.

The sour smell of the bed wasn't coming from him, she figured that much. He smelled faintly of sweat and sun and soap.

He looked so totally normal. She might have passed him on the street a dozen times. Even smiled at him on campus.

"So now what, you prick?" she asked.

She could have bitten her tongue. She always did that, pushed people when it was better to shut up. Right now, she couldn't afford to mess up, act like she had some chip on her shoulder. She could still bargain for her freedom maybe. If she could get him to listen. If he didn't kill her first.

Ignoring her, he went over to the table and pulled out a black leather kit from a bag on the floor. He opened it, unfolding the leather to show a series of ampoules and syringes. He filled a syringe from one of the ampoules and her heart just stopped.

She didn't want to be shot up with anything. She'd never done any drugs, not in her whole life. She barely even drank.

He had the most intense eyes. The pupils were really round so that they appeared almost black with only a thin rim of color. Holding the syringe up to the light, he pushed the plunger just a little. A squirt of liquid popped out from the top. Then he sat on the chair, leaning forward, elbows resting on his knees. The hand held the syringe loosely, almost casually. Like it was nothing that he was holding this needle while he stared at her with his hot eyes.

She didn't know how long they stayed with locked stares like that. But he finally turned back to the kit and retrieved some rubber tubing. He tied the tubing around the top of his arm, just above the elbow, and held it tight using his teeth. He shot the needle into his vein.

When he finished, he threw his head back and moaned with what sounded like a rush of pleasure. It was both sickening and fascinating to watch, how he just sort of transformed. All those tight muscles around his neck melted, and he smiled as he ran his fingers through his hair, sitting there, humming to himself.

It took him a while to remember her. He put away the medical kit and stood to walk over, his smile spreading with each step so that she could see he had slightly crooked front teeth. She didn't think anybody evil should be good-looking.

He dropped down in front of her, kneeling there on the floor before the bed. She'd thought he was in his forties, but he looked years younger now.

"Hello, Rachel," he said gently. "I told you I was coming."

"You're full of shit! I don't believe any of that stuff you wrote." She wanted to scream at him. Only, the words came out all hushed. Just this small sound, like a child arguing. "You're some crazy guy who found out my family has money and now you're going to try and cash in."

He nodded, as if he agreed. "That's why you came here? To the islands? Because you don't believe me?"

She didn't answer. It would have been stupid to say anything just then.

"My family's loaded," she told him instead. "They've got barrels of cash. They would give you anything to have me back. Call Gunnar. You'll see. Millions."

"What about your father?" He tilted his head like a bird, the smile suddenly gone. Like he might actually be concerned. "Why don't I call him?"

The question took her by surprise. She hadn't thought about her father in a long time.

"What do you know about my father?" Because it was such a weird thing to say. No one ever asked her about Javier. They always talked about Gunnar. He ran the business and her life.

He stared at her with this funny look. Like he felt sorry for her or something. "Your father. He hasn't been around lately?"

"He's…he's in Argentina."

But she wasn't sure. She was never sure about Javier. She used to ask Gunnar why he didn't live with them when she was little. But Gunnar finally explained that Javier couldn't be around her because she reminded him of Beatrice. That she should understand how much that loss hurt Javier. And she had Gunnar and Magda. They were family, right? They were enough.

"Argentina?" He watched her with his strange eyes. He ran his fingers through her short hair, still acting all gentle. "How strange. A father who never visits or calls. How long has it been? Maybe a year?"

She knew she was breathing too fast. She told herself to get a grip, that the nightmare was just starting and she needed to keep strong. *Suck it up!* But she couldn't figure out how he would know that kind of stuff about her life—not when she wanted to believe that everything he said was lies.

"Did I ever tell you I met your father?"

"That's bullshit," she said, jerking her head out of his reach so he would stop touching her. "Like everything else you've told me."

He laughed, long and hard. Like it was a joke or something, the stuff about knowing her father.

"Well," he said, standing, "I suppose after all that, I will have to kill you. Maybe tonight. If I feel up to it. I'll think about it."

And then he walked out, humming softly to himself.

The headaches came back, this time in the middle of the night. By morning, Lynn couldn't stand it anymore, the pain was that intense.

Even the pills the clinic gave her didn't help. Sandy, who'd spent the night, was worried she was taking too much. She'd gotten all freaky, wanting to call Lynn's parents, which she sort of wanted to do, too.

Only maybe they were all wigging out about nothing. It was just a really bad headache, right? She should call the clinic, see if they could help her before she punched 911 and got her parents involved.

She pretended everything was okay, to get Sandy to leave. Then she called Dr. Clavel. He'd always been so calm, and he'd always helped her.

"You've taken too many pills already," he told her. "You have to stop. Or at least, slow down."

"Then give me something else," she begged.

"It's not like that, Lynn." Dr. Clavel was silent for a long time. "It wasn't supposed to be like this. Not with you, Lynn. You were special."

She wanted to be special. That's how Dr. Clavel and everybody at the clinic had made her feel. That's why she'd never really worried too much about the drugs or the IV. Because they'd always treated her like she was the special one.

"You have to trust me." Dr. Clavel was whispering now, like maybe someone was listening and he didn't want anybody to hear. "You need to be strong, Lynn. It will hurt at first, but you need to stop taking the pills. They have…a side effect. They cause the headaches, do you understand? You take the pills because that's the only way we know to control Manuela. Look, I can't explain right now, but I'll try to meet you tonight. I'll bring something then. Only…"

She almost couldn't hear him now, his voice was so soft.

"Lynn, don't contact me here at the clinic, okay? I'll give you the number to my cell."

And then it happened. Manuela came back.

Lynn knew Manuela had taken over because she lost time. When she came to, she wasn't in her room anymore. She was in the middle of the quad, students passing her with these strange looks as they hurried to their classes. She realized she was wearing just a T-shirt that barely brushed the tops of her thighs and she was barefoot.

She almost took another pill when she got back to her dorm room, but then she remembered what Dr. Clavel had told her. She was supposed to trust him. He was going to help her.

But when he didn't answer his cell, she fell down on her bed, crying even though crying hurt her head even more. She was still holding the bottle of pills, the really strong ones, the ones Hal said she had to be careful taking.

For a second, she thought of taking every single one. Just one pill after another until everything went away.

She screamed, throwing the pills and the bottle across the room. She didn't want to die, did she? She wouldn't really kill herself, would she?

"Oh my God. I need help."

When she called the clinic, the receptionist patched her through immediately. Only, it wasn't Dr. Clavel who answered.

It surprised her at first, even scared her. After everything Dr. Clavel had said, it seemed bad that they'd put her through to someone else. But the new doctor explained that he could help her. That she needed to come back to the clinic. She was having a bad reaction to the medication, and they needed to give her an antidote.

She thought an antidote sounded right, like she was having an allergic reaction or something. And they were going to call her parents.

"You wrote their number on the application, didn't you, Lynn?" he asked.

She kept thinking about what Dr. Clavel had told her. *Don't contact me at the clinic.*

"Are you there, Lynn? Are you all right? Should I send someone over? I can, you know. I can send someone right over with medicine to help you."

Don't contact anyone at the clinic.

"Yes, okay," she said, crying now. "Send Dr. Clavel, please. Send him right now."

Perhaps it was the jaguar meat at dinner that brought on the dream. I saw myself sitting in my office back at Mystics Inc., a copy of Scientific American opened before me. There was a Post-It note from the company's vice president of Research and Development, Nieman Trout, at the top of the article. It read, You've been robbed!

The title and short abstract alluded to mysterious ceremonies in the Amazon Basin involving accessing tribal memory—research I had spent the past two years nurturing into relevance. Raul's name appeared as the sole author, though he did cite my dissertation several times.

Now I lay feverish in the jungle, dreaming of betrayals yet to come, wondering who might rescue me if this should end badly. But then, who can save a woman from her own regrets?

18

Isela had once told Ana that, in order to be a good writer, you had to write what you know. Ana had taken her mother to mean that she should focus on topics familiar to Ana. She'd chosen the jungle, a subject over which she'd acquired considerable expertise through the years.

Lying in bed, her feet crossed at the ankle, her toes brushing a ceiling set too low for comfort unless you were a sardine, she was thinking about the jungle in Rivera's book, *The Vortex*. How Mapiripana, high priestess of springs and lakes, would ride on a turtle shell drawn by dolphins, singing by the light of the full moon. She would lure animals away from hunters who dared make noise on her riverbank—she could squeeze clouds of rain to create streams, supplying the Amazon and Orinoco rivers from her tributaries.

But the legend as retold in *The Vortex* centered on a corrupt priest, a man known for his drunkenness and lechery. As it was his mission to destroy all superstition, the priest lay in wait on the river's shore, determined to burn Mapiripana as a witch.

But Mapiripana tricked him by appearing as a beautiful young girl and luring him into a jungle cave. There, she punished him for his lewdness by sucking the blood from his lips and giving birth to two offspring, a vampire and an owl. The priest's progeny followed him for the rest of his life, tormenting him: the vampire, by sucking his blood, and the owl by casting the incessant glow of his eyes upon the priest.

In the end, the priest returned to the cave to beg Mapiripana for protection. Her response was simple, and one that Ana had never forgotten.

"Who can save a man from his own regrets?" Ana said out loud, reciting the passage.

She sat up, slipping her legs over the side of the bed, letting her feet dangle over the bench seat below. She'd had a lot of time to think since Rachel's disappearance, the days filled with empty moments during which she'd been forced to analyze past acts, seek truths. *Opportunities for discovery...*

If she were honest, coming here, following Rachel—had it all been a labor of love, overseeing Rachel's quest for freedom from her brother? Or had Ana been like the priest, filled with regret and begging for a second chance?

She wasn't a woman ruled by impulse, but she'd allowed just that in her decision to follow Rachel here. She'd accused Rachel of running away, but perhaps Ana, too, had fled, a refugee from the university and all it represented, afraid because she'd never once stepped off that straight and narrow path to adulthood—education, job security.

The truth was, having reached the end of her chosen path as a teacher, she'd found the road blocked, a dead end, leaving her confused and suddenly without context. And so she'd come here, to the islands, hoping she wouldn't wake up one day and realize she'd never given breath to the artist inside.

It was supposed to be an adventure.

She picked up her latest yellow pad, then set it aside, wondering if this was what happened to impulsive women. The humility gods were always ready to strike—*So you wanted adventure?*

Only, now the events in her life seemed as vivid and punishing as Mapiripana's ruthless sentence of the priest. Rachel was missing, and Nick, a man she didn't trust, offered her only hope to finding her.

True to his word, he had a lead on Rachel.

Yesterday, past blind curves lined with quaint white-washed homes, braving hillsides that tested both the scooter and Ana's nerve, they had eventually come across a bare-chested native in swim trunks carrying a plastic laundry basket brimming with fish. Behind him, another island resident—his brother as it turned out—pushed a wheelbarrow full of what Nick later told her was tuna. According to Nick, these two were the source of information on Rachel's whereabouts.

Nick's rudimentary French gave way to a smattering of German, which the fishermen managed just fine. Amazing, what a clever private investigator could pick up these days.

The bare-chested Henri hired out his boat for recreational fishing to tourists. He and his brother had spotted a Zodiac heading for Terre-de-Bas, a neighboring island, a rare enough sight that the two natives took notice. Tourists seldom used the rubber dingy for anything other than water-skiing and going ashore once they'd anchored their yachts in the deep waters of the bay.

After that, Nick had somehow convinced her that

they needed to "pool" their resources. His words, not hers. It had taken most of the day to make arrangements so that he'd left his rental at a local marina with instructions on the boat's return before he ensconced himself into the front cabin of the catamaran that afternoon.

She hadn't argued the matter. The fact was, she needed to find Rachel. She didn't know how to sail. Nick did. The arrangement suited her purposes. Or at least, that's what she'd told herself during the crossing today as she'd trained her eyes on the horizon during their short cruise to Terre-de-Bas. It was a practical consideration.

Practical, practical, I'm just being practical.

Once she'd sunk the anchor and watched it keep its hold against the pull of the motor as Nick tested the anvil's grip, she'd stared at the rocky shore ahead. She buried her misgivings, rationalizing that Norman might not be as well informed of Gunnar's intentions as he claimed. Nick certainly acted like a detective on the job. She shouldn't exaggerate what was already a dramatic situation. Come morning, they'd be on solid ground again. They'd resume their search. Right now, that's all that mattered.

"Hey, Professor. Get up here."

"Speak of the devil," she said, jumping down from the bunk bed and heading for the door.

Up on deck, she found Nick with his binoculars up and ready. He stood with his back to her, wearing cutoffs and no shirt, looking disturbingly like she'd imagined him that day at the diner at LAX. Switch the binoculars for a machete and he was Raul, her hero, come to life.

"Hurry up, Kimble. Conditions are perfect."

Only, Raul didn't have eyes on the back of his head as Nick appeared to. He'd done it before, sensed her presence, making her wonder if she made too much noise entering a room, alerting him somehow with her awkwardness.

Still not turning, he said, "You're going to miss it."

Nor had she imagined Raul with that cocky edge to his voice.

"Miss what?" she asked, coming up alongside him.

He was staring at the sinking sun through binoculars. She was just about to mention the possibility of burned retinas when he said, "The green flash."

Those words, of course, were painted onto the side of the hull, but she'd never bothered to ask what they might mean. With Nick thrumming with excitement, binoculars trained, she wondered what disaster lay ahead. Not a lot of good things had happened over the past few days. The unknown became immediately suspect.

"It's an atmospheric phenomenon," he explained. "Here."

He stepped aside, putting the binoculars in her hand, directing her to look at the horizon. He then reached up to squeeze her shoulder as if to steady her, keeping it there even after she gave his hand a blistering stare.

Moving behind her, he pointed ahead to the setting sun. "Don't blink or you'll miss it."

"What am I looking for exactly?" she asked, focusing the glasses.

He stood uncomfortably close. She wondered if he did it on purpose just to get her goat, and then thought, *of course*. Nick the Neanderthal, always looking for a cheap thrill.

An Important Message from the Editors

Dear Reader,

Because you've chosen to read one of our fine books, we'd like to say "thank you"! And, as a special way to thank you, we're offering you a choice of two more of the books you love so well, and a surprise gift to send you — absolutely FREE!

Please enjoy them with our compliments...

Pam Powers

Peel off Seal and
Place Inside...

THE EDITOR'S "THANK YOU" FREE GIFTS INCLUDE:

▶ 2 Romance OR 2 Suspense books

▶ An exciting surprise gift

YES! I have placed my Editor's "thank you" Free Gifts seal in the space provided above. Please send me the 2 FREE books which I have selected, and my FREE Mystery Gift. I understand that I am under no obligation to purchase anything further, as explained on the back and opposite page.

PLACE
FREE GIFTS
SEAL
HERE

▶ DETACH AND MAIL CARD TODAY! ▶

Check one:

ROMANCE
193 MDL DVFJ   393 MDL DVFL

SUSPENSE
192 MDL DVFH   392 MDL DVFK

FIRST NAME

LAST NAME

ADDRESS

APT.#

CITY

STATE/PROV.

ZIP/POSTAL CODE

(BB1-04) © 1998 MIRA BOOKS

The Reader Service — Here's How It Works:

Accepting your 2 free books and gift places you under no obligation to buy anything. You may keep the books and gift and return the shipping statement marked "cancel." If you do not cancel, about a month later we'll send you 3 additional books and bill you just $4.74 each in the U.S., or $5.24 each in Canada, plus 25¢ shipping & handling per book and applicable taxes if any.* That's the complete price and — compared to cover prices starting from $5.99 each in the U.S. and $6.99 each in Canada — it's quite a bargain! You may cancel at any time, but if you choose to continue, every month we'll send you 3 more books, which you may either purchase at the discount price or return to us and cancel your subscription.

*Terms and prices subject to change without notice. Sales tax applicable in N.Y. Canadian residents will be charged applicable provincial taxes and GST.

If offer card is missing write to: The Reader Service, 3010 Walden Ave., P.O. Box 1867, Buffalo, NY 14240-1867

BUSINESS REPLY MAIL

FIRST-CLASS MAIL   PERMIT NO. 717-003   BUFFALO, NY

POSTAGE WILL BE PAID BY ADDRESSEE

THE READER SERVICE
3010 WALDEN AVE
PO BOX 1341
BUFFALO NY 14240-8571

NO POSTAGE
NECESSARY
IF MAILED
IN THE
UNITED STATES

Which meant, she would rather roast in hell than let him know he was bothering her.

Unfortunately, there were just so many things that did bother her about Nick. The fact that he appeared to have a two-day shadow by dinnertime even though she'd seen him shave right on deck just that morning. The T-shirts he wore with careless grace—today's sporting the logo from The Stones, a rainbow-colored mouth with the tongue sticking out—so that he never appeared hot or sweaty, while she was dying cocooned in her natural fibers. The sunglasses that added a certain panache, when the last thing she needed was to be attracted to the man.

And jealous of him. Because Nick Travis was an advertisement for the good life. Your carefree Everyman indulging his wanderlust. Watching him these past days strut his stuff about town, chatting up the locals, she realized here was a man who had lived life to the fullest.

Just being around him made her feel burdened by her education, the alphabet of letters at the end of her name. Her training required that she make something of herself. She hadn't had the same freedoms as someone like Nick, able to choose recreation over achievement.

"Focus, Kimble," he said, getting her attention. "Any second now."

She stared through the binoculars, watching as the sun melted into the flat of the horizon. The shrinking sphere submerged into a suggestion of light threatening to disappear altogether until, just as she was about to ask what the fuss was about, a flash of light swept across the horizon, emerald and distinct.

She lowered the binoculars. She'd seen the Northern Lights once, in Scotland with her mother. The experience felt much the same, as if she'd been given a glimpse of God's hand at work.

Pink glowed auralike above the waterline. It had been almost instantaneous, that flash of green, and yet, she could have sworn it radiated like a wave for seconds.

"Do you know how rare that is?" he said, standing behind her.

Rare.

In that instant, she wanted to run down to her cabin and write it all down, everything she'd just seen. She didn't want to lose a word. At the same time, she wanted to quiz him. How rare? What perfect conditions? Will we see it again? Can you videotape it? Or was it something so unique that it made you special because you alone had seen the magic of it.

"I wish my mother were here," she said, her eyes on the sunset, replaying the image inside her head to fix the experience into her memory. The green flash was just the kind of thing Isela could breathe life into. "She could make you experience it all over again with her words."

"Is that what you want?" he asked. "To be like your mother?"

The way he said it, the body language that accompanied the question. A judgment—one that had come her way one too many times.

"Would that be bad?" she asked, feeling suddenly defensive, a little of the Latin coming through.

He shrugged, but the look he gave her…

"My mother is a Nobel laureate," she said, because he didn't know what he was talking about, ignorant of her life, of her culture.

"And does that make you chopped liver?"

"I should be threatened by my mother's success? Is that what you're implying?"

"You wouldn't be the first."

"Well, you couldn't be more wrong."

She turned back to the horizon, sorry she'd spoken, not wanting to appear vulnerable before him. They'd shared something special and, with its glow, she'd let down her guard, allowing him to see too much.

"The green flash." She kept her eyes on the horizon. "How did you learn about it?"

He waited a long time before he spoke, as if he needed to get the rhythm right in his head—or line up the story he was planning. "I know a lot of things, Professor. Like the fact that a formal education doesn't mean shit."

She sniffed, because she'd been thinking just the same moments before. "Maybe it's common knowledge among the fishy set."

He laughed. "Nah. I'm into astrology."

"You mean astronomy?"

He snapped his fingers. "Yeah. That's right. Astronomy. The study of the stars."

For a moment, she felt it was all an act, his ignorance. How could a man who knew about this mysterious green flash, who spoke what sounded like a smattering of several languages, mix up astrology with astronomy?

"Or maybe it's something they teach you at detective school." He winked. "Yeah, that's where I learned it. Right along with how to set my Dick Tracy watch into decoder mode."

He was making fun of her, Professor Kimble, the progeny of the sheltered world of intellectuals. As if she'd taken some misstep—what, she couldn't guess—

and he was secretly chortling when she was unclear about the subtext.

"I didn't mean to make fun of your lack of education," she said, looking for clarification.

He stared at her for the longest time, then shook his head. "You know, Professor. You're too easy." He leaned down, whispering, "Don't make it so fun or I won't stop." Walking away, he added more casually, "Dinner will be ready in twenty minutes. The bar is over there. Make yourself your own drink, Kimble. I don't want to be accused of trying to get you drunk again, though God knows you could use some loosening up."

She watched him step into the main salon and descend into the galley, which, since he'd come on board, he'd made his own. She felt the witty retort that hadn't quite come to her die on her lips. A bit breathless, she wondered why it was that everything she learned about the mysterious Nick Travis simply posed more questions.

Well, perhaps their quest would be like Rivera's character, Cova, after all. Strangers relying on each other out of need.

She just hoped for a better ending.

A long time ago, so long Nick couldn't even remember how old he'd been, his father had taught Nick how to cook black-eyed peas. He'd been cutting up tomatoes, green onions already frying in a little olive oil, telling Nick, "You eat these the first day of the year, Niko. It will bring you luck the whole year long."

That's the sort of thing his old man believed in. Luck. Nick wasn't so sure. But hell, he could use a little help right now.

He stared at the boiling pot. He'd set the beans to cook after they'd dropped anchor off Terre-de-Bas, the only other inhabited island of the chain. Now he drained the black water and filled the pot again, just covering the beans. For a minute, watching that water drain, he wondered why a man couldn't do the same. Soak away the bad and dump it down the sink.

"There you go, Niko," he said to himself, taking the chopped onions and sautéing the pieces. "Philosophy of Life 101."

He opened a can of tomato sauce—his father would kill him if he knew Nick used canned tomato sauce—then emptied it into the pot. He stared at the beans like some bubbling cauldron, the can still in his hand.

He shouldn't have asked about her mother, Mrs. Nobel Prize Winner. The professor's self-esteem meant squat to him.

You know better, Nik.

He didn't want to care about the professor. Didn't want to get involved. He and Ana weren't a possibility.

Then, seeing the onions going up in flames, "Shit!"

He grabbed a potholder and snatched the skillet. In the sink, he dosed the onions with water and caught his breath, waving off the smoke.

"Come on, buddy," he told himself. "Focus."

It took a while to get up and running again, way past the twenty minutes he'd promised. He could hear her pacing on deck, getting impatient. But she wasn't coming down. Hell no. Too much starch in her Cuban spine for that.

He left the beans simmering and stepped into his cabin, which basically opened onto the galley, just like Ana's, so that there was only two doors and a kitchen between them. If he'd been a gentleman, he would have taken the other cabin. If she hadn't been such a major prude, she might have suggested he do just that with a little more gusto than *Don't you think you'd be more comfortable somewhere else,* and a sidelong glance at the cabin across the main salon.

Nah. He liked it right here just fine, he'd told her. Because, these days, Nick was dotting his I's and crossing his T's. Best to keep a close eye on the professor, he thought, sitting down and pushing aside the maps and guidebooks to reach into his duffel bag.

It took about ten out of his twenty minutes to set up Rachel's computer. He futzed with it a bit, bringing up the files he hadn't gotten to yet, still listening to Ana pacing on deck.

When he'd come across the two brothers and their fish, he'd switched to German. He knew the professor was fluent in Spanish and French had a Latin base, a romance language just like Spanish. The past few days, he could see she'd started picking up a word here and there, and he'd wanted all the details before he passed along any information to Ana. Panic wouldn't help them a lick, and if she'd heard the brothers' version, the professor would have had kittens right then and there.

Turns out, three nights ago a couple of guys were out night fishing. They saw someone transfer a woman onto a launch around *Pain de Sucre.* The woman had looked sick or unconscious, so the men had come in for a closer look, which was when the guy took off.

They'd chased him as far as Terre-de-Bas, thinking the guy was up to no good before he'd gone to ground. That's when they'd lost him, carrying the woman into the trees ahead. The next day, the news got around.

Everyone checked to make sure that no one's kid or wife or sister had gone missing.

But Nick had a feeling he knew who was in that launch. The descriptions matched perfectly.

His last night on the Newport schooner, he'd worked into the wee hours getting Rachel's hard drive up and running, doing a fair bit of tinkering. He'd been looking over the files she'd kept, hoping to find something to help him.

Only now, looking at the list of folders, he found himself clicking open the one she'd named "Jerkface." He'd read the file several times. He followed the long list of threatening e-mail that Rachel had backed up on her drive like evidence.

He was starting to get the picture. Why Rachel had come here to the sunny Caribbean.

The kid was running for her life.

I woke in a groggy state in my hammock, my stomach aching I hoped from the jaguar meat and not from something more lethal. I took my time sitting up, feeling worse than ever as I reached for something to drink in the muggy darkness.

It had to have been the curse under my breath that alerted him. He struck a match, so that a bleak light filled the hut. When a candle flared to life, I realized it wasn't indigestion that had brought Raul into my dreams that night.

I'd anticipated changes in his appearances. Leathery skin beaten by the sun's unrelenting radiation. Cheeks sunken from an exotic diet of ants and grubs. Perhaps a missing tooth from a recent bout of scurvy?

Unfortunately, he looked adorably the same.

"Hello, Beth," he said. "What took you so long, babe?"

19

Ana ate black-eyed peas for dinner. Nick said it would bring her luck.

They were seated across the table from each other like two combatants at a chessboard. She wanted to ask about the dish he'd cooked with such ease, envious that in this, too, he'd bested her. Ana's meal choices tended toward things that went *ding!* in the microwave.

She'd never eaten black-eyed peas. She'd eaten black beans and rice and her grandmother's *congri. Fabada* and *caldo gallego,* both made with white beans. *Potaje* with chickpeas and *chícharos* with split peas. She'd eaten a world of beans courtesy of her grandmother and mother, none of which she'd managed to master.

The dish prepared by Nick tasted Southern, certainly something ethnic. Not that she'd asked for details. She had, in fact, done her best to ignore Nick, Mr. Trivia, who'd spent the evening playing tour director.

"Did you know they call Guadeloupe *Le Grand Papilion,* on account of the island's shape, like this enormous butterfly?"

The information flowed off his tongue. Honestly, the man could be a game-show host. He'd certainly cranked up the charm the past hour.

Ana tore off a piece of bread, keeping mum.

"The region here is known for its banana plantations." He raised his bottle of beer, taking a long pull. "There's even a botanical garden with petroglyphs, the work of the island's original inhabitants, the Arawaks. I think those were the guys in Cuba, too, but the Spaniards came and knocked them all off, which you probably already knew. And there's this Hindu colony at Capesterre. Could you figure that?"

As if he'd purchased and memorized every guidebook in print.

Ana, who had purchased her own share of books, had been limited to picturesque photos with sparse captions in four languages. Any book with substantive print had been published in French. Which raised the question where Nick, the ever-resourceful detective, had unearthed his information. He'd told her himself he wasn't fluent in French.

Ana took a tentative sip of wine, wondering why it should bother her that, while she'd been wholly unable to find even a thin tome to research their destination, Nick had turned into a walking encyclopedia of knowledge about the islands? But she told herself it could very well be part of his job description as a private investigator, a sort of literary reconnaissance before arrival, standard procedure, as it were.

"The Cousteau Reserve is here, too. As in Jacques and the gang. Ever watch that show as a kid?" He stuck a piece of bread on the end of his fork and swabbed the bowl before popping it into his mouth. "When Soufrière erupted, Basse Terre had to be evacuated. It's the administrative capital of Guadeloupe. The eruptions pretty much made Pointe-à-Pitre the economic hub."

"Fascinating." Her first word of the meal, not that he seemed to notice.

"Right up the side of the damn volcano you can see those bad-ass banana leaves, waving in the breeze. The place is full of waterfalls. Wouldn't mind seeing one of those."

She bit the inside of her lip. She wouldn't say another word. Not one.

He dropped his fork into his now-empty bowl. *Clank.* He nodded at the beans she'd barely touched. "It's not poisoned, you know."

She folded her hands on her lap, meeting his gaze across the lamp-lit table, thinking to herself that she knew no such thing.

He nodded. "I know. It's the sexual tension—you can cut it with a knife. Makes dinner conversation a bitch. What do you say we go down below deck, have wild sex, and just get it over with?"

She closed her eyes. Counted to ten. When she opened them, he was smiling.

"Kidding," he said. "So you think I lack education?"

She hated that he could do that, turn the tables on her. "I never said any such thing."

He thought about it a minute, as if he were going over the exact phrasing. "Nope, that's actually what you said. You apologized for making fun of my lack of education. Therefore, ergo, that means I *lack* education."

Suddenly the evening's parade of facts came under a brand new light, making her feel slightly ashamed. "Not everyone needs a doctorate." It certainly hadn't helped her, she almost added out loud. "You have endless practical knowledge. Under the circumstances, I might add, that's nothing to sneeze at."

He was leaning back, arms crossed over his chest, that grin beaming across the table. "I love it when you go into teacher mode. Man, it's sexy. But don't start with that delirious novel stuff or I can't be held responsible." He winked. "Come on."

He took her hand, as usual, interpreting any reluctance on her part as encouragement. He dragged her over to the steps of the boat leading to the water and gestured ahead at the black horizon, the sky covered in stars.

"The Southern Cross should be rising just after midnight," he said, guiding her toward the water lapping against the boat. "Might be worth staying up to see that. In the meantime…"

He sat down and pulled her alongside him. Easing his feet into the water, he kicked gently.

Immediately, a million pinpoints of light burst around his legs, igniting the black water.

"The plankton here is phosphorescent," he said. "Try it."

Ana lowered her feet into the water, warmer now compared to the ambient temperature. She stared, mesmerized as sparks of light swirled around her ankles.

He took off his T-shirt, wadded it up into a ball and tossed it back on deck. Wearing only his shorts, he dropped into the water.

Everywhere he moved, tiny specks of light danced around him. "Come on in, Professor."

"I don't have my bathing suit."

"Oh, well," he said, pulling her in.

She went completely under, caught by surprise. She dog-paddled back to the steps, spitting and treading water for all she was worth. It was one thing to know those little creatures were in the water when you couldn't see them, but now, the water was literally coming to life with each move of her hands, every kick of her feet.

She grabbed hold of the steps and watched Nick swim effortlessly away. As he cut through the water, he left a trail of lights. The wake glowed behind him like a beacon pointing the way.

She dipped her hand in the water and tried to catch the fleeting spots of light as they poured through her fingers back into the ocean. She could still see the faint glow of him out in the distance.

"Wait!" she yelled, swimming after him.

He had to have heard her. He stopped, treading water, watching and waiting. When she reached him, she came to a stop just a few feet away. It was so dark here away from the boat, that she could barely register his features in the faint glow from the water and moon.

But he was smiling. "Well, well. A woman who doesn't like to be left behind."

She felt weighed down by her shorts and shirt, at the same time exhilarated. "I've never done anything like this," she said.

"I bet you haven't done a lot of things," he said, back-stroking toward the boat.

She frowned, not liking the subtext of his observation. But she followed just the same, watching lights shoot out from her fingers as she cut through the water, for the first time, not thinking about the words that might capture such a moment.

They stopped alongside the catamaran. She grabbed the stairs and watched her legs through the water, making tiny bursts glow to the surface with each kick.

"I think you have a misconception of me," she told him, not really sure why she'd even brought it up, as if she needed to explain herself to him?

"Really? Then set me straight, Professor."

"Exactly. The way you keep calling me *Professor.*" She made a face. "That's not who I am. I mean—indeed, I was a professor."

"Indeed," he repeated gravely, so that she could see he was still making fun of her.

But she didn't care. She wanted to make her point. "That was only my job. And now it isn't," she said, working it out in her head as she spoke. "I am not this stale intellectual who lives her life through books. You have no idea the things I've seen and done."

"None at all," he said with a flat expression.

"I've traveled abroad—all over the world, as a matter of fact," she answered, searching for highlights, events that might stand even his life-on-the-extreme scrutiny. "I've drunk sangria with Gypsies in the caves of Albaicin in Granada and watched them dance flamenco. I've toured the pyramids of Mexico, including Palenque, where I entered the Temple of Inscriptions and descended into the burial chamber. I've climbed the Alps."

"Wow. The Alps? I'm impressed."

But for some reason, the story sounded forced even to her ears. She was making a list, giving another tutorial.

And she could see he thought the same, the way he was watching her, as if fighting himself not to smile.

"I'm lecturing again," she said.

He looked out across the water. "It's not a bad thing."

"Then why does it feel like a bad thing?"

That she couldn't shed her orderliness even here, in the midst of chaos and crisis.

Her mother had always told Ana she was strong. She'd been raised to believe that her ability to analyze—step back, take in the whole picture—was a strength. *Don't be like me, Anita.* Volatile, incendiary. Plotting her revenge against Bosque and anyone else who might seek to harm her or the people she loved.

While Ana waited and watched. Lectured.

Beside her, she heard Nick ask, "Did you dance the flamenco in those caves with the Gypsies? And when no one was looking, did you dip your fingers into the inscriptions on the tomb—or did you just read the boxed translations set out for the tourists?"

She stared at him, caught off guard that he could see so clearly inside her.

"My mother did," she whispered, giving herself away.

Isela had kicked off her shoes and thrown her hair back, mimicking the steps of the Gypsies, urging her daughter, who'd been sixteen at the time, to join her. But Ana had shaken her head, content to sit with her father, a fellow observer, and clap in time with the music.

At the Temple of Inscriptions, she'd seen her mother touch the tomb and its hieroglyphs as if reading the stonelike Braille with her fingertip, while Ana watched their guide, afraid that her mother would get thrown out for her daring. Instead, Ana had focused on the plaque explaining how archaeologists interpreted the symbols.

But she'd had regrets, wishing as their group was ushered out that she'd been more daring.

"The Alps," he said. "Tell me about climbing in Switzerland."

She shook her head, because she'd been misleading him and she didn't like her subterfuge. She'd been trying to make herself sound like someone else, someone a man like Nick might find interesting and exciting, on a par with his own life experience.

"It was more like a hike," she confessed. "They'd hammered out these steps into the rock. And there were chains for handrails."

She remembered feeling as if she were seated at the top of the world, holding on to those handrails for all she was worth, far from the ledge. There had been goats and flower patches on the other side on the hike down.

She turned back to Nick. "But didn't I sound wonderfully daring for once? I climbed the Alps."

Because she was still living her life in her head, taking the facts and adding color. Extrapolating a more interesting existence.

He watched her now, as if trying to think of something to say. As if he might understand what she was feeling inside when he couldn't even come close.

"You were probably just young," he told her, giving the excuse.

Because he didn't want her to feel bad.

She pushed away from the stairs of the catamaran, easing out into the water. She turned to look at Nick. He was watching her as if he expected her to say something more. That was her strength, after all, to educate through words, not actions. But she realized she didn't want to talk, didn't want to explain away her choices.

Taking a breath, she dived underwater.

She opened her eyes, watching the plankton light up as she reached into the darkness and kicked her legs, swimming down, down. She could feel her lungs getting tight, but she kept swimming, pulling at the water, watching it light up around her, her hand reaching into the darkness toward the sea floor.

Run away!

An arm slipped around her waist, Nick guiding her around. Taking her hand, he pulled her to the surface so that they broke through the water at the same time. ·

"Hey!" Nick was treading water in front of her, not touching her anymore. They were right in front of the catamaran so that the boat loomed over them. She almost didn't recognize him, the expression on his face completely foreign.

He looked frightened. Afraid for her?

She swam toward him. He drifted back, anchoring himself to the steps as she reached him. Floating in front of him, she grabbed the rail at the side of the stairs with one hand to steady herself and smoothed that furrow between his brows with the other hand, wondering what on earth she'd done to frighten him so.

"Vida y muerte han faltado en mi vida," she said in Spanish. "Jorge Luis Borges, a very famous writer said that," she told him.

Life and death have been lacking in my life.

But he shook his head. "What do you know about death?"

"That's not the part I'm worried about missing," she whispered, coming closer.

Everywhere they touched, the water lit up. She'd kissed him before, that first night in his room.

But now she wondered what it would be like to kiss him here, with the water glowing around them. To wipe away the look of concern that made him appear too vulnerable. He was Raul, after all. Her hero. A man who should never know fear.

She reached up and slowly pressed her lips to his, kissing him on the mouth, not boldly, but with tenderness and care, allowing objection. He kept his hands at his sides, not so much a participant, taking the subordinate role.

She closed her eyes and kissed him in earnest, this time, opening her mouth, elated when he did the same, no longer passive. He pressed into her, then turned them both so that she was up against the boat. He pinned her hands to the steps, deepening the kiss, taking her breath away.

He pulled away, watching her in the moonlight. The fear was gone, replaced by an enigmatic expression she couldn't read.

"Like I said," he whispered. "I'm impressed."

And then he did the strangest thing. He turned and climbed up the stairs, leaving her in the water.

Alone.

Nick dropped down on the bench seat in his cabin, soaking wet.

He should have kept it simple. Sex was simple. Tender was complicated.

Falling for the professor—well, that just wasn't happening. The two of them weren't even a possibility. Ana was a line he wouldn't cross.

But hadn't he been saying the same thing since he laid eyes on her? And still he found himself searching her out, wanting to keep close—and not for the right reasons, the ones he kept trotting out as if he had everything under control.

She was this beautiful person. Inside and out. Of course, he was drawn to her. He just had to keep those emotions in check.

"What the hell are you doing, Nick?"

He found his wallet and took out Valerie's photograph, then dried his hands on the sheets, careful not to ruin the photo. He didn't like what was happening. Circles bothered him. Paul and Valerie and Ana. Full circle.

Up on deck, he could hear Ana coming back on board. He should go out there and explain. Tell her about Valerie and why he could never love another woman.

Funny thing, all night he couldn't keep his mouth shut. But now he couldn't think of a single word to say.

Ana wasn't at such a loss.

The door to his cabin swung open. She was standing in front of him just as wet as he, waiting for some explanation. He wanted to smooth that furrow from between her brows. Wanted to kiss her and make it all better.

"What just happened out there?" she asked him, unable after all to wait him out.

He wondered about all the things he should say, the words coming up his throat and sticking there. In the water, she'd trusted him, maybe for the first time. He could use that to his advantage, keep the professor one-hundred percent on his side.

Only, he wasn't going to do that, all his expensive government training going out the window. Instead, he was thinking about Ana, what it might do to her if she discovered she should never have put her faith in him. That he was no better than the last man she'd fallen for—that asshole, Fish.

He heard himself ask softly, "Do you trust me, Ana?"

He could read the answer so clearly on her face.

"I want to," she whispered.

He smiled. "Now, see. That's because you're not thinking straight, letting all that physical stuff between us cloud your judgment. So let me give you the heads-up here. What do you really know about me?"

"You asked me the same thing about Rachel once," she told him.

"As I recall, you had a nice long answer about her favorite color and what star she wishes on at night. But the next day, she turns up missing and you know squat."

The professor was smart. It wouldn't take her very long to get where he was heading. Whatever she'd come to say to him—some stupid declaration of emotions he couldn't allow—he could see the idea die in her eyes.

He told her, "Why don't you start using that head you're so proud of?"

He watched her walk out, the door closing behind her. He picked up the photograph.

"There you go, Val," he said. "There you go."

20

Ana lay on her back, staring at the black sky through the hatch above her bunk.

Right up the side of the damn volcano you can see those bad-ass banana leaves, waving in the breeze. She closed her eyes, trying to shut out Nick's voice. *The place is full of waterfalls. Wouldn't mind seeing one of those.*

It had taken every ounce of courage she had—and a healthy dose of anger—to walk down to his cabin and confront him. Lit up like the water, she'd been caught up in a fairy tale, one she hadn't wanted to end. Only it had. Abruptly. Snuffed out by his simple logic.

What do you really know about me?

The implication being that she'd lulled herself into believing Nick safe. Raul, the Everyman, a benign character in a book she was writing. *Eat the beans, Ana. They'll bring you luck.*

Rachel he'd presented as a prime example of her lack of judgment—Exhibit A—as if to point out what do we really know about anyone?

And so Ana had spent the past hour evaluating just that, if the words she'd penned on her yellow pads had bred a familiarity that didn't exist. Plotting her story, had she created her own kind of make-believe, transforming Nick into a hero? By kissing him under the stars, had she merely sought a man who was flesh and blood rather than one born of her imagination?

When he'd pulled her to the surface of the water—the fear she'd seen in his eyes—she'd imagined herself like the heroine in *The Lost Steps,* Rosario cradling her lover to her bosom during the storm that threatened to capsize their canoe. With the same devotion, Ana had hoped to wipe away Nick's fears as they faced yet another trial together.

Foolish woman.

Earlier, she'd spent the evening lamenting a life as observer, quoting Borges and his famous regrets. But there were advantages to playing the detached intellectual. Sitting on the sidelines of life had polished certain skills. It's what made her so good at her job at the college.

She now accepted Nick's challenge, to step back and evaluate. She forced herself to think only of the facts, pushing away the emotion he claimed had clouded her judgment.

She'd never thought of the events of the past week as a story, something she could analyze. She'd been caught up in the day-to-day, letting Nick call the shots, allowing him to move the chess pieces. But maybe it was time to use those skills her mother loved to brag about so much. To forget his kiss and focus instead on the story behind the man.

What do you really know about me?

Clearly Nick had an agenda. The question was what? Why had he chased Rachel here, from half a continent away? Gunnar hadn't sent him, according to Norman.

Money, of course, was motive enough, the final slot

into which the ball might drop. Money was always motive enough. And certainly, the Maza family had plenty of it. A mountain's worth.

And there was the special project Rachel had mentioned, the one that might save Gunnar from the threat of a takeover. Ana had no idea what it was that Rachel did for her brother, other than writing the computer code that Nick had discovered.

Had discovered quite easily, in fact.

"Oh my God."

The image of Nick hunched over her computer, accessing information like a pro, came into sharp focus. At the time, she hadn't thought anything of his skill, believing the cyberworld a place investigators would frequent with ease.

But what if his skills at the keyboard derived from some other source—corporate espionage coming to mind as a good for-instance? Nick, who cooked beans and talked about the luck it might bring her, all the while plotting…

"Plotting what?" she asked herself.

The danger she sensed became a palpable heat inside the cabin. She remembered the fear in Rachel's eyes when Ana had first mentioned the possibility of being followed. Had Rachel known all along that someone was trying to find her? Had she run away not from her brother, as Ana had assumed, but from Nick himself?

What do you really know about me?

It was just after midnight, and fear transformed into a tinny taste in her mouth, taking her out of her stifling room, crowding her into the galley. She came to Nick's door, raised her hand.

But she didn't knock, quashing that desire for polite

confrontation. Instead, she listened, imagining him safely inside, asleep.

She crept back, quietly entering the main salon. Her heart racing, she switched on the satellite phone, trying to figure out who she trusted less, Fish, the womanizer, or Nick Travis, the supposed private eye who kissed so beautifully but could very well be a corporate spy. Hoping she had gambled right.

Fish picked up on the second ring.

"Norman? It's me, Ana."

"Dammit, Ana. Where are you? Where's Rachel? Is she all right?"

"I…I don't know. I think so. But we had a fight and she's run away."

"You did the right thing calling me. Ana, I can help."

"I hope so. Because I'm starting to think this is more than teenage rebellion."

"Yes, yes, of course. Your instincts are perfectly correct. Now tell me where you are. I can meet you. We'll look for her together."

The devil you know. "That would be best. You come here. But I don't want Gunnar to know." Already second-guessing herself. "Not yet, anyway. Can you do that for me, please, Norman?"

"Just tell me where, Ana. I just need to know where."

"But Gunnar—"

"Gunnar doesn't know a damn thing, and I plan to keep it that way as long as you let me know what the hell is going on—and that's not a threat, dammit. I'm just worried to death, Ana. Besides, I wholeheartedly agree that Gunnar will just complicate everything. All right? Do you feel better? Or do I need to cross my heart and hope to die? Now where and when?"

Suddenly she knew she was no longer alone. That if she turned around, she would find Nick standing quietly behind her, listening to every word. It hadn't mattered how stealthily she had crept here, checking his room first. Because Nick hadn't been in his room at all.

You can see the Southern Cross rising after midnight.

She lowered the phone. Norman's voice called out from the receiver as Nick reached over and cut him off.

"Dammit." Norman dropped the receiver in his hand, staring at it a full minute.

Gunnar paced across the Berber carpet, cell phone pumping up and down as he swung his fists with each stride. When the digital phone beeped, Gunnar flipped it open.

"Where," he said into the phone.

Norman had never seen Gunnar panic before today. The man was cold, like those damn fish in his office. But when Norman told him about Rachel, that she wasn't at the condo at Big Bear—that she'd never been there at all—Gunnar had gone ballistic. Even Magda couldn't calm him.

Norman, of course, hadn't mentioned that he'd already gone up to the mountains. He'd wanted to make it sound as if he'd contacted Gunnar at the first possible moment of revelation. *I left several messages with Isela before she got back to me.* That's when he'd found out the girls had never been. From Isela.

Of course, Isela would never confide in Norman, but Gunnar didn't know that. And watching him, Norman had wondered if the lie had been wasted. Did it even matter, the excuse he'd given. Gunnar had gone into automatic, completely focused on his search for his sister.

First off, he'd set someone to dial the number to the condo every five minutes, in case there were some mistake and Rachel might be there safe and sound. Of course, he'd hired a private investigator. In the meantime, he'd come here, to wait with Norman, anticipating Ana's call.

Norman didn't know what Gunnar had set up. Someone at the phone company? A private agency? He hadn't been informed of the details, only that he should try to keep Ana on the phone as long as possible. Now Norman waited, choking on every lie he'd told Ana, hoping it had been enough.

Gunnar powered off the cell phone. Norman couldn't tell from his expression if the news was bad or good.

It turned out to be both.

"She's in the Caribbean," Gunnar told him.

She's in the Caribbean. In the Caribbean. The Caribbean.

Norman broke the silence. "Ah," he said.

The simple sound unfroze the tableau of the two men. Gunnar flipped open the phone, making arrangements. They would leave tomorrow, taking the company's jet. There would be one small errand beforehand.

While Norman was thinking about the e-mail Rachel had sent. *Made a breakthrough—will let you know soon. Don't tell my brother. He'll be greedy.*

It was always Gunnar everyone wanted to keep in the dark. Yes, well, the man could be a son of a bitch.

"Pack a bag," Gunnar said, completing the arrangements. "We leave early tomorrow. We'll need to go to Seacliff first, so be prepared."

Norman turned, giving Gunnar his attention. "So soon?" *She's in the Caribbean. The Caribbean.* And when Gunnar didn't answer. he said, "It's the girl, isn't it? Something happened."

"Bright and early, Norman. Be ready," Gunnar said before he left.

She was using the satellite phone. She was on the phone, calling someone. On the freaking satellite phone.

Nick had been out on deck, stargazing, when he'd heard her, as quiet as a mouse, thinking she was so clever. He had to smile to hide his anger and surprise, kicking himself because he'd more or less pushed her to this point.

"Well, well," he said. "Not exactly what I meant when I said to start using your head."

She was seated in the captain's chair, her hands clenched on her lap. "And here I thought you were giving me your approval. You're not a private investigator. Or at least, not one hired by Gunnar."

"Is that right?" He was still smiling. "And what put that lovely little nugget into your head, Kimble? This Fishman you're calling?"

She didn't even look ruffled, instead staring cool as you please. "I have a right to know who I am dealing with."

"Sure you do." He walked behind her, then swiveled the captain's chair around. Very slowly he dropped down so they were face-to-face, his hands on her knees. She didn't move.

"Okay, Ana. Here it is, a quick refresher. You know about those, don't you, Professor? I'm here for my own reasons. What those might be, you don't need to know.

Only that I want to find Rachel and see her safe. We're on the same side, right?" Here, he cocked his head. "Or are we? Ana of the prestigious Harbour College."

She'd never told him where she worked. She hadn't mentioned quite a lot of things he knew about her.

"Ana of one-eight-zero-four-one Coral Circle." Like her address. "Prone to wearing sensible suits but who likes her heels, changing out of her Nikes right after she reaches her office at seven-thirty sharp. A man could set a clock to you, Kimble."

His hands stroked up and down her legs, feeling that cool, bare skin. "Ana, only child of acclaimed scholar Isela Montes, with the ever-prestigious Nobel Prize." He shook his head. "Tough shoes to fill, Ana. But you're doing okay, aren't you? Until they screwed you out of tenure. But the copy room had to be the last straw. Talk about office politics biting you in the ass. But hell, Ana—" he looked up "—who would ever trust a guy named Fish, much less marry him?"

He felt the goose bumps rising as he continued to stroke her legs, but Ana didn't say a word. No how-did-you-know, how-long-have-you-been-following-me? Not a peep from the professor. She was playing it cool. Only her quick breath gave anything away.

He shook his head, almost sorry he had to do it. He reached around her and pulled the plug on the satellite phone.

"Well. Now things are going to get interesting, aren't they, Professor?"

He pocketed the hookup and stood. This time, he didn't say a word as he went down to his cabin and shut the door.

21

Two days had passed and he hadn't killed her yet.

He kept her tied to the bed when he wasn't inside the shack humming like he was home-sweet-home. When he was around, he pretty much left Rachel alone. Always with her hands tied behind her back, so he had to help her with everything, even going to the bathroom, which was way creepy. She figured that's why Super Cretin did it.

He made a lot of dumb jokes, so lame she didn't even know he was kidding until he got that What? Not funny? look on his face.

He was too weird for words, and he scared her. A lot.

She figured he was just waiting for her to let her guard down. Then, *bam,* when she was used to the setup, all dependent on him and thinking, "Well, this isn't so bad, right? It's not like he's sharpening the ax?" That's when it would all go wrong. He was messing with her head, making it so much worse when the end finally came.

He took a lot of drugs, shooting up maybe three times a day.

She had to bite her tongue not to ask him things. He talked about this Frédèric guy a lot. She thought maybe he was scared of him. Like the guy was chasing him and he was running away, hiding somehow but always afraid he'd get caught.

Sometimes he would give her this look, like maybe he knew something he wasn't telling her. Something bad.

She had a lot of time to think the past couple of days, counting the beams in the ceiling. There were eight. The boards on the floor. Two hundred and forty-eight, more under this really ugly rug. She thought about the past few months, how scared she'd been. Stupid to come here, like she was some superhero and could solve anything.

She'd been thinking about her father. All the time, actually. Because Super Creep had brought him up. Asking her questions, making her think about things.

It's not like her father had ever been in the picture that much. Her mother died when she was five and after that, Javier couldn't even be around her. Gunnar said she looked like her mother, making it worse for Javier. But Gunnar wouldn't have those feelings. Beatrice hadn't even been his real mother or anything.

Growing up, her brother had always been there. She thought her dad would have been nicer about stuff like boys and school and teenage rebellion. The Gunman, he put the "dis" in discipline.

But her dad, he was, like, really old. Over sixty. And a little absentminded. When she'd visited him in Argentina a couple of times, he'd told her about the old days, how he'd gone to school at Berkeley, so he considered himself an American even though he had this really thick accent. Both his wives had been American, and she and Gunnar had grown up in California. Then, when

Gunnar married Magda, the Argentine-American princess, Rachel's dad had handed over the keys to the kingdom.

It's not that she hated her father or anything. You couldn't hate Javier. He was just too sweet. But his focus wasn't there. Not for her and Gunnar, anyway. His work, his company…yeah, that always came first. According to Gunnar, he traveled a lot.

But now, she wondered why she hadn't heard from him in so long. That's the kind of crap stalker guy put in her head with his weirdness.

She'd gotten a birthday card from Javier, sure, with a gift she could tell Magda had bought, a black velvet zippered jacket with faux fur collar. It hadn't bothered her. She accepted it, like when Gunnar told her she was going to live with him and Magda right after he got married.

But she wished maybe things could have been different. She wondered how it might have been if her mother hadn't died when she did, or the Gunman had a little more bend to his spine, or her dad hadn't been so…well, gone.

Because now, some guy she didn't know could say stuff about her dad and scare her. And she wouldn't even know if he was lying. She'd just sit in the dark and wonder when it would all end. The secrets…the lies.

She'd given up on the idea of rescue. Maybe she thought she didn't deserve it. Because she was starting to wonder about the things he'd told her, that maybe it wasn't all the product of a sick mind. Like the stuff about Neuro-Sys and what she'd been doing with the brain-simulation program, that it might be horribly true.

She hadn't asked the right questions about what they

were doing with her data. She hadn't asked *any* questions. She'd just acted without any thought about ethics or morals, focusing on her ideas, like some stupid scientist. She was no better than Norman. Maybe even worse.

She wondered sometimes if Ana had gone home. For sure, she would have called The Gunman. But she figured the crazy guy was smart enough to cover his tracks. Even Gunnar wouldn't find her here—wherever here was.

She thought Ana probably hated her. If what the crazy guy said was true, even a little, she couldn't just blame Gunnar and Fish for everything. Rachel had known enough that she could have put the pieces together, guessed what was going on. Instead, she'd been worried about only herself and getting away from Gunnar.

That had been a big part of it, actually, trying to get out from under the Gunman's thumb. She'd thought if she could accomplish this one thing—Neuro-Sys—she'd finally have control over her destiny. The program would give her freedom because it was so amazing. To be able to simulate the functioning of the human brain on a computer, she'd be like the key master at Phoenix. Finally she'd be the one calling the shots, telling Gunnar what to do. She wouldn't have to wait for her twenty-first birthday or some stupid trust fund to kick in. That was the plan, anyway, before she started getting the threats.

She'd come here to find out the truth. Now she was afraid she knew the truth.

She looked around the room. She felt really tired from the heat. She wanted to sleep, but every time she fell asleep, she'd have these nightmares.

Then she'd wake up and she'd realize that it wasn't a bad dream, after all.

"Welcome to my life," she whispered in the empty room.

* * *

Gunnar floored the BMW, watching the speedometer's needle tremble toward 120 mph. At one in the morning, the 405 became his speedway. Gunnar liked speed. Right now, he couldn't fly fast enough.

He'd found Rachel. He knew where she was. Safe, according to Norman.

In the Caribbean.

Where she'd gone to discover what he had been hiding from her all these years.

He could feel his rage pumping through him with the pounding rhythm of Guns 'n' Roses on the CD, making him punch the accelerator, then ease off. Gunnar didn't have a death wish. Quite the contrary. He'd make it through this disaster. He'd come out on top.

"Damn straight," he said, changing lanes, maneuvering past another vehicle.

Why hadn't she come to him? They could have talked about his intentions, how important it was for her to stay on task. She hadn't given him the opportunity to explain. Instead, she'd gone behind his back, digging for dirt. Finding it.

But he knew it was that bitch's doing, whispering in Rachel's ear. That constant thorn in his side, Ana Kimble, had never known what was good for her.

When Ana first called Norman, Gunnar had felt only relief. And a sense of triumph. As always, he'd been one step ahead. He'd been thinking exactly that—*I won! I beat you again, Ana!*—when he learned the call originated from the Caribbean.

He'd seen the panic on Norman's face, panic Gunnar refused to feel. Instead, he'd made his plans, forged ahead with his strategy. He'd find Ana, force her to tell him where Rachel was hiding.

And then he'd kill the bitch. Damned if he wouldn't.

He knew he could get away with it, too. Hadn't he gotten away with much more? He'd even considered the possibility before, mulled it over on quiet nights over a glass of port. But he'd settled for ruining her career. He'd thought once Ana left the college, he'd finally have Rachel back in the fold, where she belonged.

That's why he'd insisted Norman head the committee for Ana's tenure, egged him on to do just that. Dropping a word here and there, he'd carefully orchestrated her downfall. Everyone at the college knew the ex-husband and wife had an amicable relationship. Ana and Norman remained friends over the years, even hosted parties together. No one would suspect Norman of sabotaging his ex-wife.

But it hadn't been enough. Destroying her career had only made her dig in her claws.

No, Gunnar would have to kill her. Ana Kimble, the woman who'd stolen his family, needed to be taken down. Neutralized. But first he had to find her.

He wouldn't tell Norman, of course. There was only so much loyalty money could buy, and Norman didn't have the stomach for violence. The man was beyond weak. Even worse, Gunnar suspected Norman still loved his wife; he just hadn't been able to keep his pants zipped long enough to keep her happy. And so she'd left him to make her own sort of family, turning Rachel against the people she should value most. Gunnar, her real family.

He remembered exactly when Rachel had first started to follow Ana around like some lost puppy. How it sickened him to see her so vulnerable. Of course, she'd come to love Ana, a young vibrant woman who gave Rachel everything he couldn't. Time and focus.

At first, he hadn't even minded so much. He could see that Magda, with her own child to keep her busy, wouldn't be enough. Why not allow the friendship?

But Ana had encroached. She'd become a mentor to Rachel, casting a spell over her so that she'd begun to question Gunnar. She wanted to emulate Ana, a worthless schoolteacher, listened to her and not him on the course of her future.

And now, Ana had taken Rachel to the Caribbean. She would turn Rachel against him once and for all. And then Rachel would leave him. Just like Beatrice.

He knew how that felt. Like falling through the ice into a freezing lake so your heart stopped, just stopped.

To be abandoned. No, he couldn't live through that again. Losing Rachel felt the same. As if he'd been abandoned all over again.

And he wouldn't be able to stand it. He couldn't take another betrayal. Couldn't lose another person he loved.

So he would find her. He'd bring her back. And he'd make dead certain Ana could never hurt him again.

Raul was filled with stories of corporate espionage and harrowing escapes. He claimed to have lured me here out of harm's way, my research involved in some nefarious plot. I needn't be bothered with the tricky details, certainly not. That knowledge would only put me at greater risk. I should know only that he loved me and wanted me safe. We were on the same side.

Trudging along, the incessant drone of Raul behind me recounting the past months of his nomadic life, our Maçu guide brought us to a naturally occurring clearing. There, I fell to my knees in the white sand. As Raul shouted orders in the Maçu's language, I realized that my confusion was born of more than the jungle's maze. I was feverish, in pain, certainly suffering the effects of some disease, most likely malaria.

22

He knew where she lived—he knew about Fish.

Ana's fears circled the cabin, dark winged and fleet of foot. Before she could settle on one, another would take its place, never leaving time to prepare. She imagined Nick spying on her, walking down her cul-de-sac to her home, then slipping inside her apartment, stepping into her room, opening drawers, searching for…

"For what?"

She frowned, the words suddenly bringing her into abrupt focus, so that she sat up, hitting her head on the ceiling. "Ouch!"

What did she have to be afraid of? What did she have to hide? She had always been the very proper Ana Kimble. She had even once declared on her taxes a fifty-dollar gift certificate she'd been given by a local garden club for speaking at their monthly meeting on the myths of the Amazon.

And yet, he'd been following her. Little, insignificant Ana?

The past few hours, she'd listened as Nick banged around the kitchen, imagining him fumbling for a glass. She'd stared at the cabin door, straining to hear him pour, drink, then pour again, the pattern repeating itself until she'd scurried to lock the door, thinking that any minute now, he'd drink enough of whatever he was pouring to find the courage to break in.

Only there'd been no splintering of wood, not even a rattling doorknob. No drama whatsoever. Only fear. Until now.

She was cowering in her cabin because he'd pulled the satellite phone forcefully from its connection? Because he might be someone with evil motives, emphasis on *might?* And yet, thus far, he'd acted more like a used-car salesman with his grins and his lies.

For goodness' sake, she'd been half-naked in his bed when he'd asked for permission to make love to her. And when she'd walked out, he hadn't said so much as "boo-hoo."

And when she'd kissed him in the glow of the water, it wasn't Ana who'd been afraid. He'd held on to her, not the other way around, focused on keeping her right there in front of him, as if she might come to some harm otherwise.

Walking away, soaking wet and fleeing from that tenderness they'd shared, he'd merely made her the victim of his rejection. Nothing worse.

So what in the world was she doing here, frightened and waiting for his next move? Letting him call the shots when Rachel needed her to be strong?

When she found herself standing before his door, ready to knock for the second time that night, she thought better of the courtesy. Instead, she reached for the knob and pushed her way inside.

She found him half-dressed, half-asleep—half-in, half-out of his bed—snoring like a bear. That's when she decided why wake him?

She scanned the room for the satellite phone. Seeing his duffel bag in the corner, she dropped to her knees and crawled toward it. She'd be damned if he'd decide when and to whom she'd make her calls.

But quietly searching his bag, she found something much more interesting. Rachel's computer.

At least, she thought it was Rachel's computer. She recognized the Phoenix symbol on the top. Only, it couldn't be Rachel's. She wouldn't go anywhere without her computer.

When she pulled it out from the bag, she noticed it was attached. To another laptop. Sticking out of the A drive was the diskette Nick had borrowed, the one with Ana's Poem written on the label.

She didn't make a sound, little Ana Kimble, now a spy. She lowered the computer back into Nick's bag, then, when he moved suddenly, exhaling a deep sigh from the bed, she crept backward and dragged the lot out the door and up the stairs into the main salon.

At three in the morning, a light rain tapped against the deck. She eased into the bench seat of the salon table. She lifted both computers from the bag so that Rachel's laptop remained attached to Nick's.

She knew absolutely nothing about computers, but she had been married four years to a man whose life revolved around these machines. Surely she'd gleaned something from Fish besides distrust of men.

So she gave it the old college try and pushed the button marked On at the side of Nick's laptop. Remarkably, it worked.

The first thing she did was check the diskette, pushing it into the drive. She called up the file and it looked unaltered, just numbers, nothing she could understand.

She moved on to Nick's hard drive. Nothing much there, just more files with numbers, which he'd probably copied from Rachel's computer.

Around four in the morning, she made herself some coffee. Let him wake up and find her snooping. She'd take the risk for the caffeine hit. In the kitchen, she found a half-empty bottle of rum. "Hope he hurt himself," she said, picking up the bottle with two fingers, wondering if he'd even bothered with a glass.

Coming back to the table, convincing herself she was half-awake, she opened the drawer in the captain's desk, looking for pen and paper.

Tucked in the back of the drawer, she found the rental agreement for the catamaran. It was signed by Rachel. She'd paid in advance for a month.

Ana dropped into the captain's seat, catching her breath. Apparently Rachel had needed special documentation, for which she'd paid extra, making all her arrangements through the same rental company that had promised a Day of Dreams on the poster Ana had seen plastered on the wall of the bar where she and Nick had hoisted a few. The laws restricted anchorage to vessels flying French colors. Sailing here could be tricky. Rachel had certainly thought ahead.

Bruce has this thing supplied to the gills... Bruce says it's way cool in The Saints.

Bruce, with the accommodating boat, who obviously didn't exist.

The rental agreement was with Home Port Charters. The vessel was owned by Anthony and Samantha Burke. Ana was betting they didn't have a son named Bruce.

Of course, Rachel had lied. Of course.

The betrayal she felt wasn't painful. Too much coffee for that. But she did feel dizzy. Given the fact that she hadn't slept all night, she didn't think that was unusual.

She told herself what she felt was just like seasickness. If she distracted herself, if she concentrated on something else, that queasy feeling would go away and become bearable. That if she worked at it, she could breathe again.

It took her an hour to access Rachel's computer from Nick's. Apparently, she'd learned more than she thought from her ex-husband. Or perhaps necessity inspired. She found the file entitled "Jerkface," completing the evening of discovery.

The world she came from didn't include this kind of intrigue. The worst she'd ever dealt with was college politics, building power bases through committees and favors owed. But never this.

Nick wasn't a private investigator. He wasn't an importer. The man who had written these messages wasn't even in his right mind.

"What's your name?"

He was feeding Rachel oatmeal with a spoon, one mouthful at a time. Her hands were now tied behind her back, everything basically the same. But she figured why not push a little? She didn't plan to die in ignorance.

He didn't answer the question, just held the spoon up to her mouth until she turned her head away.

"What's the big deal telling me? I mean, if you're going to kill me anyway."

"Doesn't matter what my name is," he told her.

"Yeah, I know. I can just keep calling you Jerkface or Stalker Guy?" Just to be a smart mouth.

Instead of answering, he walked away, taking the bowl of oatmeal with him. He stopped at the desk, which she thought would have made great firewood but which he seemed to use like a mini science lab. He had a Bunsen burner, lots of test tubes and stuff. He even had one of those little refrigerators.

He spent a lot of time at his desk, reading thick tomes and writing in his lab book, doing the mad-scientist thing to the hilt. Now he put down the bowl and pulled out the top drawer. He grabbed something from inside.

It turned out to be an ID badge. He brought it over to her, holding the badge up like a prize. The name "Paul Hutchings" had been printed in boldface at the top.

"I didn't think it was a question that required visual aids," she said, staring at the photograph.

It was almost hard to recognize him. The photo was kind of blurry, sure, but the guy in the photograph wore glasses. He looked a lot younger. And he had this crooked carefree smile.

"I keep it to remind myself who I am," he said, turning the badge so he could stare at himself.

She pursed her lips, now getting to the uncomfortable part of the conversation. "Right. Because my brother did these weird experiments on you." She said it like she didn't believe a word.

She watched him put the badge away in the drawer, right front corner, carefully placing it faceup. Like a ritual. That was the sort of thing that made it real. The badge. That kind of detail made the other stuff he'd told her sound possible.

On the other hand, what did she know? Maybe that's the way crazy people did things. They made up the details because to them it was real.

"Does it happen to you a lot?" She didn't want to go there, right? So she should shut up and forget the questions. "You forget who you are?"

He came back and spooned up more oatmeal, holding it until she took a bite. She figured that was the best way to get him to talk. If she followed directions.

And then she got this idea. "Maybe you need someone around to remind you. I mean, to tell you who you are. When you forget."

"The badge works fine."

He had the palest eyes she'd ever seen. In this light, they appeared almost colorless.

Cold eyes. Mean eyes.

"Are you going to kill me?"

He didn't answer, just kept staring at her. He didn't blink for the longest time.

"Do you want any more of this?" he asked, holding up the bowl of oatmeal.

"Tell me about the clinic," she said.

He threw the oatmeal across the room. The dish smashed against the wall, oatmeal splattering everywhere. He jumped to his feet, tipping over the chair. He stood there, towering over her, looking really violent. And then he turned and ran out the door.

"Tell me," she yelled after him. "I mean, here's your chance, right? You wanted me to believe all that stuff you wrote was true. Convince me!" She wanted the nightmare to end.

Instead, he came back inside. He stomped over to the desk again, this time throwing anything that was in his way until he found the medical kit. He was shaking so hard, she thought he'd hurt himself when he started to inject himself.

She watched the familiar ecstasy fill his face, bringing light to his eyes. He was staring at her the whole time. Like he was daring her to judge him.

"Maybe I could help." She didn't realize she was crying. She didn't know when she started believing everything he said was true. She didn't need to go to Marie-Galante like she'd planned, after all, to prove this guy was lying. Because he wasn't lying at all.

"Don't you think," he said, his voice sounding too soft, "that you've done enough?"

"I…I didn't know." But even to her ears, it sounded lame. "Okay, I knew. But not like you think." She took a breath. The guy was crazy. He was going to kill her, and she was crying? Trying to make him understand? "I thought it was all theoretical. I didn't know they were testing the stuff on people."

"It wasn't theoretical to me." He held up the syringe. "This isn't theoretical."

He stood and walked over to her. "Do you want to know what it feels like?" He held up the syringe, like a threat. "The headaches? Sometimes, I want to kill myself just to stop the pain. I'd do anything. Even shoot this stuff in my veins. And the new formula. It works fast." Again, the syringe. "No, Rachel. This isn't theory."

"And that's it. You brought me here because you need revenge, right? Even if I could stop them, you don't care?"

He knelt down, now at eye level. "Killing you will stop everything."

And he was right. All he needed was to get rid of her. He didn't need to do anything else. Without Rachel, Phoenix Pharmaceuticals couldn't hurt anyone.

"Well, I'm sorry," she said, crying. "I didn't know. Oh, my God, I didn't know."

He was shaking his head, and she could see the truth in his eyes, his expression saying it. *Do not pass GO! Do not collect $200.*

Being sorry, well, it just wasn't good enough.

23

Nick woke up, rolling over onto his back before opening his eyes. That's when he saw his duffel bag. Or, more accurately, didn't see his duffel bag.

"Jesus!"

He scrambled out of bed. Acting out of instinct, he searched for Ana. In these tight quarters, she wasn't difficult to find.

Seeing him, she stood slowly, stepping away from the salon table, the two laptops opened before her. He tried not to notice her skimpy T-shirt and shorts. If he'd succeeded, he would have seen what was coming long before she pushed him aside and scurried past him for the galley.

He ran after her, cornering her there. Half-naked in that damn T-shirt and shorts, she reached behind her. Like a magic trick, she held an enormous butcher knife, clenching the thing in her hand like she meant business.

He took a couple of slow steps toward her, hands out to ward off an attack. It was a hell of a small kitchen.

"You're going to stab me now? Is that right, Kimble?"

"I will gut you like a mackerel if you don't tell me where she is," she said in a surprisingly level voice.

He managed a smile. "I almost believe you."

He grabbed the hand with the knife, swinging it away so that the tip only scraped across his arm. He pushed her back against the counter. Holding the weapon over the sink, he squeezed her wrist until she dropped the knife. He heard it clatter against the stainless steel.

With a twist of her arm, he brought her down to the floor and straddled her. He grabbed her other hand and clasped both over her head.

They were both panting, staring at each other in a standoff. But suddenly the professor smiled at him. And it was this incredible thing, her smile. He hadn't seen such an expression on her face before. She was always so serious, too intense. It was a hell of a turn-on.

She angled up, so that he knew what was coming. Helping her along, he met her halfway as she kissed him hard on the mouth.

The minute he let go, his hands reaching for her face, she rammed her knee into his groin.

The oldest trick in the book and he fell for it. Fell, quite literally. He didn't know how long he lay there, unable to move or breathe.

He made it topside just in time to see Ana take a beauty of a swan dive off the deck.

She had a good head start and was a surprisingly good swimmer. But he was better. She made for shore and scrambled up the sugar-white sand, diving into the vegetation with an abandon that bred awe—the woman was barefoot. He followed closely behind, letting the spikes and leafy thorns bite into the skin of his face and arms.

He could hear her better than he could see her, the panting of her breath, the occasional grunt of pain. He pressed forward, catching a glimpse of white shorts ahead.

"You took her! Where is she, damn you! Where are you hiding her?"

He didn't waste his breath to answer, just plunged on, following her through the jungle, tracking the sound of her voice.

It had been a long time since his training. He'd made it a sort of life's goal to forget everything he'd been taught since Valerie's death. But now he dug deep, becoming that man again. This kind of thing was second nature to the old Nick, coming back full force. *Focus on the goal.* He dived forward, downing her like a calf.

The fear in her eyes even as she fought him registered like an ache. But what had he expected? She should never have trusted him, and now she had proof that he was one of the bad guys.

When he finally managed to pin her down, he took a breath. Trying to sound calm, he said, "Okay. I'm going to let you go, and you're going to let me know exactly what this is about. Are we ready here?"

It took her a moment, but she nodded.

"So, I'll ask the obvious. What the hell is going on, Professor?"

"I found Rachel's computer," she said.

"Well," he said. "That much I figured out."

"You wrote those messages. To Rachel. You've been following her. Stalking her."

He didn't say a word, didn't even try. He stood, leaving her alone so that she could run away or do as she pleased. Of all the interpretations, this was one he hadn't prepared for or even considered.

But, of course, that's what she would think. What

else? He hadn't included her in his plans. Quite the opposite. He'd lied and manipulated her. All along, she'd been part of a strategy, trying to see how he could use her to get what he wanted.

And now, his job would be twice as hard. Because he couldn't tell her the truth. This one had to go by the book.

He shook his head. "I didn't take her, Ana. I was never stalking Rachel. But I think I know who was. Which means she's in trouble. A whole hell of a lot of it, I'm sorry to say. Because I don't think the man who wrote those e-mails you read is in his right mind."

They hadn't sent Dr. Clavel. They sent the men in the little white coats.

Lynn had been sedated and strapped into a restraining jacket, so she wouldn't hurt herself, they said. They brought her to the clinic in a private ambulance. Now she knew why Dr. Clavel had warned her not to contact the clinic, but it was too late.

They told her she had to sign some papers if she wanted medication. Commitment papers. They also told her they'd just forge her signature if she didn't do it because they had her signature on file.

At first, she refused to cooperate. Let the bastards do whatever they wanted. She wasn't signing anything. No way. But the headaches got so bad, and she knew the medicine would help. Soon it was her begging them. She told them she would do whatever they wanted if they brought back Dr. Clavel. In the end, she did whatever they wanted even before they brought him.

"Oh, God, Lynn," he said when they finally left them alone. "I didn't mean for this to happen—"

"No, it's okay," she said, because by then she'd figured it out. They had all the power. "I know. I know," she told him.

By the time her parents arrived, she was restrained in a bed, an IV. in place. She could hear them and see them, but everything was blurred, as if she were watching in a dream, detached and floating.

"In order to take part in our program here at the center, we do extensive medical testing," some doctor she didn't recognize was telling her parents. "Lynn's condition, however, is not so easily diagnosed. It wasn't until we started seeing problems that we asked for her permission to do the MRI. That's when we found the tumor."

The headaches were gone, and she had this great rush of euphoria from the medicine in the IV. But at the same time, she felt out of sorts. As if she didn't feel right in her own skin.

"What about the drugs you gave her?" She could hear the anger in her father's voice. "Did they speed up the…well, the growth? How many years did you cut off my baby's life?"

"Jim," her mother said. "Please, don't." She could see her mother wringing her hands, her head down as if she were afraid to look at her. "Not now."

"The experimental medication we gave your daughter in no way hampered her condition. In fact, we think it might have helped. She could have been…possibly worse." The doctor stepped closer to her father. "We are prepared to do anything to help Lynn. The company's policy is very clear on this point. However, in terms of legal responsibility, I think you'll find nothing was done without your daughter's full knowledge and approval."

"We'll want a second opinion," her father was saying.

They were talking about her as if she weren't in the room. As if she were gone already.

"Of course. We'll give you all the test results. But I'm afraid this is pretty straightforward. I'm sorry. Really I am."

Her parents looked like frozen people. Popsicle parents. They weren't talking, just listening, like they didn't know what to do. She could feel her mother squeeze her hand.

"As I said," the doctor was talking now. "You can choose to take Lynn wherever you want. But, as I showed you in the papers she signed, it was Lynn's wish to stay with our group when she committed herself."

"No," she said, shaking her head. "No! I don't want to stay here. I'm not crazy. Mommy, I'm not crazy."

That's when Manuela took over.

When she woke up, when she was Lynn again, they were all staring at her, except for the doctor, who was taking notes on his clipboard. He stepped over and injected something into the IV.

"You can visit her at the clinic," the doctor was telling her parents. "We'll do everything we can to help her."

"Oh, shit. Shit! That was horrible." Norman thrust a hand through his hair. "That girl. That poor girl. We did that to her!"

"Don't be stupid, Norman," Gunnar said. Clearly he didn't share Norman's concerns. "You knew the risks."

"Did I? Did I really?" Norman shook his head. "Your father—Frédèric—they were different. This girl was completely innocent. Duped by us. I'm sorry, Gunnar, but I am not like you. I feel for these people. What we're doing, it's not right! Why did you bring me here? Why did you show me?"

And there was the rub, the fact that ignorance was bliss. Like a child covering his eyes watching a scary movie, as long as he hadn't witnessed the mess first-hand, he had no worries. He'd gone on his merry way, coaxing Rachel to finesse her computer program, using the data he gathered from Seacliff.

He'd thought they were on the verge of something brilliant, something that could change the world. But they were only destroying lives.

Well, he had plenty to worry about now, didn't he? Because he would take the fall for anything that went wrong. Whatever happened next, he would be the one they blamed—Gunnar would make certain of it. He and Dr. Clavel were perfect scapegoats. Two mad scientists acting as rogue agents. He'd be ruined—possibly even put in prison—while Gunnar and the company would get a slap on the wrists for not keeping better tabs on their research personnel.

"This isn't good," he said, stopping his pacing, turning to face Gunnar. "This is *not* good."

"The only problem I see is that we failed," Gunnar corrected. "We're back to square one."

"Oh, I beg to differ." He shouldn't raise his voice to Gunnar. It actually surprised him that Gunnar hadn't shut him up. "Rachel is lost in the Caribbean. Frédèric is dead. And that poor girl is losing her mind courtesy of Phoenix Pharmaceuticals. Oh, no, Gunnar. We are not back to square one. We are fucked. Completely and totally fucked!"

"We find Rachel," Gunnar said. "We start over."

Norman closed his eyes, wondering how it could be

so easy for Gunnar. To dismiss that poor girl's pain just because they'd wanted to play God.

And yet, they were knee-deep into it. There wasn't anything he could do to fix what had already happened.

Or was there?

He thought about the e-mail Rachel had sent, the fact that she'd made progress with the computer simulation program. Using Neuro-Sys, might they not discover a way to help Lynn, a line thrown into turbulent waters?

He glanced at Gunnar. Well, maybe the man was right, after all. Finding Rachel was key.

Facing Gunnar, knowing what he had to do, he said, "Rachel. She thinks she's made a breakthrough. With Neuro-Sys. Let's pray to God that she's right."

A week passed as I lay cocooned in my hammock, rocked by fevered dreams. Malaria and food poisoning blurred everything, certainly my memory. But it was the yagé, the cold water infusion made from the crushed stems of a vine found by the Maçu, that I blamed most for my dazed state.

Raul fed me the infusion daily. In my foggy state, I began to suspect he was poisoning me.

24

Nick looked across the salon, meeting the professor stare for stare. They were back at the catamaran. They'd rinsed off, and he had a towel draped over his shoulders. He needed a drink but he'd make do with coffee.

"You want some coffee?" he asked.

"I want some answers." She didn't budge, just stood there, arms crossed.

Last night, he'd paced up and down the galley right outside her cabin, his hands balled into fists to try to keep from knocking on her door. He'd wanted to tell her how screwed up the whole business had become, how much he hated scaring her. This wasn't who he was, the kind of guy women ran from and locked their door against.

After a couple of shots of whiskey, he thought maybe he had his emotions under control, had loosened up a little. But instead of taking on the professor, he'd headed back to his cabin with the ever-practical thought that tomorrow was another day—only to fall asleep and dream about her all over again.

In his dream, they weren't arguing. She wasn't scared of him, either. They were making out, fast and furious so that when he'd woken up, groggy not so much from the whiskey as from the dream, he'd been thinking sex was the answer. Get it out of their system, erase the memory of that tender kiss.

That's why he'd fallen for that smile in the galley before she'd laid him low. He'd been halfway there in his head from the dream.

She didn't look like she wanted to kiss him anymore. She had this tense expression. He'd seen it before, her woman-on-a-mission look. No one did it better than the professor.

"You said you knew who might have taken her?" she asked.

"Yup. His name is Paul. Paul Hutchings. He's a friend of mine. His family contacted me to find him."

"And?"

He sighed. "Where to start."

"Now," she said, sitting down. She'd changed into shorts and a simple cotton shirt, her hair smoothed back behind her ears so she looked like one of those nature girls you see advertising face cream in the magazines. "You start now."

He nodded. He'd had plenty of time to come up with the right spin. "Paul and I grew up together, even went into the army together. He was like this real genius, and a prick. Good at the research but lacking in people skills, if you know what I mean. I hadn't heard from him for months, not since he'd started this new job. He was traveling a lot. But then his family called. To make a long story short, he disappeared and…"

Here he gave her a look, as if judging how much she could handle.

"Something pushed him over the edge," she said, finishing the thought for him.

"Maybe. The notebook with Rachel's name written over and over, that was Paul's. I found it in his apartment."

"But why Rachel? What's the connection?"

"That, I don't know, Professor. Look, there weren't a lot of clues about his disappearance. The police, they see a guy who takes off. They're thinking midlife crisis. No body, no crime. Only Paul's family thought differently. So here I am. I figured if I find Rachel, maybe I find Paul."

"Why do I feel as if you're leaving something out?"

"Beats me," he said, coming to sit next to her, running roughshod over her distrust. "Look, maybe she's just a name he came across and he's gone bonkers. The Jodie Foster thing. Maybe it's something else?" He took a moment, trotting out those acting skills. "Like that code we came across on the diskette. Do you know anything about what she was doing?"

"She worked for her family's company, some kind of research. They sell herbal medicines, the kind you buy in a drugstore. Maybe the code has something to do with that."

He nodded, going with it. Basically, she just confirmed what he'd figured all along. The professor didn't know squat.

"What about your ex. This Fishman. She works with him at the college, right?"

She crossed her arms, leaning back, her body language saying she didn't like where the conversation was heading.

And here he was about to step on the accelerator.

"Look, Ana. I'm just going to lay it out for you. The kid was running from something, right? She brought you along because she trusts you. We have a complicated code she's labeled Ana's Poem. Like she wanted to hide something, and you're the only one she trusted. So I'm thinking, maybe it's not such a bright idea bringing the Fishman in on this."

The professor had this face. You could read it like a book. Right now, the pieces were coming together, making a picture she didn't like—and she didn't know the half of it.

"You said you had a lead on Rachel," she said. "So where is she?"

"Those two fishermen on Terre-de-Haut? That boat sighting they were telling me about was a little more complicated than I let on."

"What a shock."

"Right. And I'm a jerk for holding out, but lucky for you, I happen to know what I'm doing here, so listen up. Someone saw a girl. She was being taken to Terre-de-Bas by a man." He let it sink in. "The description fit Paul and Rachel."

He had to give her credit. She processed the information quickly.

"We have to find them. Now."

She stood, as if she were going somewhere. But he grabbed her arm, knowing what she was feeling. She'd have this overwhelming desire to do something. Anything. She couldn't just sit around and twiddle her thumbs when the kid was in trouble.

"I'm working on it," he told her gently. "And I agree. We need to find her. The faster the better."

"This doesn't feel very fast," she said, shrugging off his hand.

"There are people I need to contact," he said, giving her that much. "The more we know about what we're getting into, the more effective we can be, trust me on that."

"But I don't," she said. "Trust you."

"Yeah, so I figured."

But he could see there was more on the professor's mind. It was right there on the tip of her tongue, the questions.

"Go ahead," he told her. "Ask me."

She nodded, taking it for granted that he'd read her so easily. But she had a couple of surprises of her own.

"Last night," she said, her voice dropping to a whisper. "When you dived after me in the water. Your face afterward...you looked frightened. I want to know why."

He lifted his brows, delighted and troubled by this unexpected question. But he knew what she wanted, a reason to trust him. He decided to give it to her. "I don't like it when people disappear."

"Like your friend Paul?"

"That's right."

"And someone else," she said, doing her own kind of assessment.

"My wife. Valerie. She was killed by a drunk driver." Saying it as fast as he could, with as few words as possible.

But that face of hers again, going all soft, making him look away. "I'm sorry."

"Don't worry about it," he said, turning for the door. "Just be ready."

Hoping that would be enough for the professor. Hoping it might buy him a little time.

The problem was, Ana didn't know who to trust.

Rachel had lied to her; Nick certainly had his own agenda.

Which left Fish, a man who held nothing sacred, including his marriage vows. And now, Nick claimed she'd made a mistake trusting him.

It was hard to swallow, Norman as the bad guy. He loved Rachel, Ana knew he did. He wouldn't hurt her, ever.

Or would he? The questions circled, round and round.

By noon, Nick had them docked at the marina at Terre-de-Bas. He said they were low on supplies, but of course, that was suspect. *There are some people I need to contact.* Their rapprochement did not include trusting each other enough to assume his quest would be a simple trek to the marketplace.

It wasn't until he'd left that she received the call.

She'd been sitting at the main salon staring at her yellow pad—why, she no longer could say. She was staring at the pages almost as if she thought she might find some answer there. As if these papers could somehow become her crystal ball.

When the satellite phone rang, she nearly jumped out of her skin.

By mutual agreement, Nick had reinstalled the phone, one of her conditions to their working together. She stared at the phone for what seemed beyond forever, then, considering it might be Rachel, she picked up.

"Ana?"

The voice on the other end was very male, very familiar.

"Ana? Is that you? It's Norman."

She took a moment to catch her breath. "How did you get this number?"

"Through a hell of a lot of trouble, no thanks to

you. Listen carefully. Take a taxi to Grande Anse. Meet me at a small outdoor café, À la Belle Étoile. Two hours. Bring Rachel. And tell her to bring the diskette."

The conversation had been quick and to the point, which was a little unlike Fish. He had to have been nervous. Like Ana.

Because whatever Rachel was involved in, it seemed fairly clear that Nick was right. Fish was part and parcel of it.

Not good, meeting him alone. She should probably wait for Nick.

But did she really have a choice?

"Don't be late," she spoke into the phone.

That's how the conversation had gone, after which she'd taken a taxi, ending up on a very picturesque drive of the island, reaching the location with time to spare. Her heart beat so hard in her chest, she felt sure Fish would see it pounding against her blouse.

She found Norman drinking coffee, looking his dapper best. Even in this crowd of manicured French, Academia's poster boy stood out.

"Ana." He stood and came toward her with open arms. "I'm glad you came."

She made sure to sit down before he could reach her. With Fish, it was best to be proactive.

"Where's Rachel? Is she with you?" he asked, sitting down, the tiny chair teetering beneath him.

She shook her head. The Mardi Gras parades were already in full swing. On the way here, she'd passed schoolchildren dressed in their carnival best. Even in this quiet corner, she could hear the music.

"She hasn't come back," she said. "Hasn't called—"

That's when she saw him. Gunnar was walking toward them, winding past the white tables.

Fish followed her gaze and cursed under his breath. "Damn the man. I said to wait." Turning to Ana, he said, "I can explain—"

She backed away, and when he reached for her, she turned and ran.

"I had to do it, Ana. It's for the best," she heard him call after her. "For Rachel's sake!"

She ran as if her life depended on it, thinking perhaps it just might. She found a cab and jumped inside, giving instructions and hoping she'd get enough of a head start to lose them. She didn't know if Nick was right or not, if Fish was the enemy Rachel had been fleeing all along, but there was something about Gunnar Maza that instilled fear. Fish's involvement with the man could be ascribed to naiveté or perfidy, it didn't matter. In either case, it did not bode well for her or Rachel that he'd brought Gunnar along.

She asked to be dropped off a few blocks from the marina. She looked around, paranoia a healthy side effect of her meeting with Fish. When she reached *The Green Flash*, Nick was waiting, feet propped up, looking too casual with his beer in hand and a baseball cap pulled low over his brow.

She was still trying to catch her breath, wondering how to break the news that they were no longer safe here, that by taking Fish's call, she'd brought the enemy to their door, when he asked, "What have you been up to, Kimble?"

Only, she wasn't sure who the enemy was. The bad guy could very well be the handsome stranger she'd invited on board, the very man who confused her with his half-truths and kisses. She tried to hide everything she was feeling. *Suppress!*

"I thought this relationship was strictly on a need-to-know basis," she said, trying to not sound as breathless as she felt.

He smiled, surprising her when he let it go. "Good enough." He took a drink from the bottle. "She's not on the island, but I know where she might be headed."

"I think we've played this game before," she said, still unable to catch her breath.

"Yeah." He stood. Tossing his bottle into the trash, he pulled a lazy-dog stretch. "So are you going to raise the anchor, or what?"

After three days, Rachel managed to get the tape loose enough to slip her hands free.

She waited, pretty much knowing the routine here at Creep Central. Paul would get up at the crack of dawn and hover over the boiling caldron of his test tubes, alternately shooting up and taking notes. Then it was time to feed the pet gerbil—that would be her.

She figured that's when she'd make her move, waiting until he left to go outside to wash the communal breakfast bowl.

She'd scoped out the place for weapons. Before he'd even closed the door, she was up and at the beaker holding what looked like—well, what *was*—a human brain preserved in some sort of liquid, saline she figured. When he came back inside, she was ready, hyperventilating behind the door, waiting for the right moment.

As soon as he stepped inside, she smashed the beaker on his head, brain to brain.

He turned, reaching for her. In that instant, she

freaked, thinking *It's not enough!* He was still coming for her, hands outstretched as she stepped back, and then, suddenly, he wasn't.

He dropped to his knees, grabbing his head. She backed away, almost slipping on the brain on the floor, watching it slide across the boards from under her feet.

He made this really horrible sound at the back of his throat, like he was choking for air or something. He was still holding his head, kneeling on the floor.

"No. No, dammit!" he screamed.

She should run. She could. He wasn't going to stop her. He was out of commission.

Only, what she saw—what she *knew* was coming— kept her there, staring. Waiting.

He raised his head, slow and calm, looking almost feral. His pupils completely dilated so that there was only a thin rim of gray. He didn't stand, but came at her just the same, prowling like a cat.

He was talking to her, but she couldn't understand what he was saying. And then, she did.

He was screaming at her. "Langevin in prison—Solomon executed!" She was the enemy and had to be destroyed. He wouldn't go back to that hellhole where they'd sentenced him.

"Jackals pawing through remains!" he screamed.

He leaped at her, tumbling her to the ground.

"You'll find nothing here, you Nazi dogs!" he continued, pinning her down, his hands reaching for her neck. "Nothing!"

"No, Paul!" When he rolled on top of her, she begged, "Please. It's me. Look at me. I'm Rachel, the girl you hate for a whole bunch of other reasons. Please, Paul."

He seemed to see her for the first time. He rolled

off her, huddling on the dusty floor, curled up in a fetal position. He started shaking uncontrollably, as if he were freezing in the muggy room or having some sort of seizure.

"Need...ampoule. Please."

She backed away, toward the door.

"Please..."

She reached behind her, her hand on the knob.

"No, Rachel. Don't leave me!"

She raced out, seeing the sky overhead for the first time. Stumbling forward, she made for the brush ahead, hoping to lose herself in the thick foliage. They were in the middle of some sort of jungle.

Not far from the hut, she tripped on a vine. She rolled to the ground, crying. "No, it's not true. He was making it up. All of it. Gunnar wouldn't do that. I didn't kill anyone."

She stood, and began running again, weaving past the vines and ferns and rocky terrain. The clouds were low here, like a fog, making the air thick. It smelled like sulfur and made her think of hell. Fire and brimstone. Hell, where she'd sent Paul and so many others.

The clinic. The horrible things he'd described. My fault.

She didn't want to die. If she went back there, he would kill her. He might not be able to help himself.

My fault. My research. My theories.

Do you want to know what it feels like? The headaches? Sometimes, I want to kill myself, just to stop the pain.

She was crying, unable to stop because she didn't want to go back. But she wasn't running anymore.

He'd told her people had died because of her. She hadn't wanted to believe him, but that didn't mean it wasn't true.

"Oh, God. Please, no."

If she'd been part of those horrible things…

"No, no." She dropped to her knees, shaking. "I didn't kill anybody. I couldn't do that."

But she wasn't sure anymore. The fact was, she hadn't been sure for a long time. That's why she couldn't write her poetry anymore. Why the words that had once brought her such comfort had dried up inside her.

And the last days watching Paul, how he'd dedicated himself to those test tubes and lab books—his obvious suffering—that last strand of faith in herself had begun to unravel.

He hadn't killed her. He didn't want to kill her. Because he wasn't a killer—he was a victim.

She lay on the jungle floor, staring up at the sky, wondering what to do, if there was anything she could do. She was nineteen years old and people were dead because of her?

She covered her face. It was too horrible to imagine it could be true. Experimenting on people. Giving her the data from those trials so that she could perfect Neuro-Sys, developing a simulation program that more closely mirrored the human brain. In turn, her findings using the sophisticated computer program helped guide more experiments.

That's why Paul had hunted her down, stalking her. To stop them.

And maybe he still could. With her help. If she had the guts to go back and face what she'd done. If she ran away now, it was so much worse. Because now she knew the truth. She'd seen it happen right before her eyes, Paul becoming someone he wasn't.

Someone who might hurt her, someone she'd helped to put inside him.

In the end, it wasn't much of a choice.

It took her a while to find the shack again. He was still on the floor, looking pretty much dead. She knelt, then held her cheek over his mouth, feeling for a breath.

"I wouldn't be so lucky," she said to herself when she saw he was very much alive.

She found the kit in the second drawer. After filling the syringe, she injected him, just as she'd seen him do so many times. It was hard to find a spot; he had a lot of tracks.

Afterward, she held him in her arms, humming, just like she'd always heard Paul do.

The yagé Raul fed me was a powerful hallucinogen, used during important ceremonies. Long ago, I witnessed just such a ritual, the shaman dipping the black calabash into the yagé to pass the drink to the men who would dance shoulder to shoulder, feathered headdresses crowning their hair and eagle's down covering their chests. In my delusion, I felt the rhythm of the seed anklets at their feet rattle to the beat of my heart.

But it was Raul's kiss that told me I was dying. His mouth on mine spoke his regrets. His tender touch extolled the story. In my fever, he was losing me, unable, after all, to persuade me back from the brink.

25

The catamaran bounced off the waves, Ana holding on for dear life. The sky burned white above the water, shining as if alive. She couldn't breathe her throat felt so hot with it.

While Nick stood at the cockpit, the wind in his face, hands on the wheel, doing the whole manly man thing to the hilt.

She couldn't read his expression, his eyes hidden behind the lenses of his sunglasses. Just looking at him made her tired.

Her fatigue went beyond the physical. Too much had happened these past weeks. Too much had been asked of her. *No more, please. Please!* Her failed career had become, in perspective, a minor inconvenience. But Rachel. Rachel, who had lied and plotted and could be—Lord knew where she could be.

But she was in trouble. A lot of it, apparently.

Concern for Rachel had drained Ana to the point that her limbs could float away and become part of that big white sky and she wouldn't even notice. Only a shell of her would stay on the deck to fret and worry and search out the young woman she'd come to call her friend. Rachel, who now weighed on Ana's shoulders with the persistence of Sisyphus's rock.

Now she knew Nick was right. Clearly Norman was in cahoots with Gunnar, the diskette Rachel had left behind a trophy they sought along with their girl genius. The fact that Rachel had fled here so far from home spoke of her desperation. With Fish and Gunnar hot on the trail, Nick's suggestion that they make haste to Marie-Galante seemed as good an idea as any, seasickness and distrust a distant concern.

According to "his sources," there was a medical facility on the island, something that had recently hit the radar of certain government agencies. Though he hadn't been able to connect the pieces to Phoenix Pharmaceuticals exactly, the pieces were there. Phoenix, as well as a company in Denver, was taking part in a joint research project financing a memory clinic in California. The Denver company in turn had ties to a doctor running a medical facility here.

Nick thought Rachel had brought Ana to The Saints planning all along to head for Marie-Galante. Why, he couldn't guess, but he thought it had something to do with the code he'd found on the diskette she'd left behind.

"So I figured we head for the clinic and get our next lead," he told her. Find Rachel and Paul. Piece of cake.

She tried to keep her eyes off the horizon, which was rising and falling in a rhythm guaranteed to reduce her to a puddle of motion sickness on the deck. *If you didn't look at the horizon, where did you look?*

"What do we know about this clinic—or do I want to know?"

"That would be a negative, Sparky." He leaned back against the rail and scratched his chest covered by a T-shirt pronouncing him God's Gift To Women. "I'm thinking pharmaceutical company, girl brainiac, clinic in the Caribbean far, far from the bothersome regulatory agencies."

"I see." She shook her head. Suddenly he had the colorful imagination? "Do you have any idea what was on that diskette we found? The one with my name on it?" The one Norman wanted along with Rachel.

"Bunch of numbers?" He pulled the baseball cap low against the sun. "Look, the kid's a genius, right? As in Einstein IQ? Couldn't she come up with something, I don't know, I may be reaching here…ingenious? As in, worth beaucoup bucks?" Nick took off his sunglasses. "You don't look so good, Professor."

"Did I mention that I really hate when you call me that?"

"Try deep breaths."

"Deep breaths, a glass of water, Dramamine, wrist bracelets. Lots and lots of alcohol. Nothing helps. Oh, Lord. I see your plan now. You have no idea where Rachel is. You brought me out here to do away with me."

"Right." He checked the autopilot, then stepped up beside her. He turned her to face him. "Come here, Kimble." He held her face in his hands, shocking her immobile. "Remember me? The man with all the cures?"

He kissed her, deep and tantalizing. All along it seemed as if she'd expected just this. Because she kissed him back, conveniently forgetting that everything in her life had turned so very confusing and wrong.

She wanted someone to believe in—or maybe she just wanted someone to hold.

She tried to remind herself she'd been fooled by love before. She knew better than to lean into a man's body, feel those hard muscles against hers and want more. She knew the price, and goodness knows the Neanderthal would have a high one. Possibly Rachel's safety.

And still she lingered, kissing him softly, then quick and hard, following his rhythm.

When he pulled away, he had this sleepy look to his eyes, making her wish he'd kept on the sunglasses. "How's that seasickness now, Professor?"

"With you, the cure is always worse than the disease."

"Ana," he whispered, lowering his mouth to kiss her neck, "I think I'm bewitched. I tell myself to stay away, but I can't keep my hands off you." He kissed her again, ignoring her lack of response. "Then I get to thinking, what's the matter with just having a good time?" Coaxing, he whispered in her ear, "Don't you think we deserve a bit of fun?"

"I couldn't tell you what you deserve."

"Every night, I dream about it. Just walking those two or three steps to your door and getting naked together."

"Getting naked? What a quaint turn of phrase." She forced him back a step, searching for breathing room. "Remember me? The woman you fed enough alcohol to that I actually considered going back to your shabby little room?"

"You did a hell of a lot more than consider."

"The point is, I've learned my lesson. With you, nothing is simple. _This_ isn't simple," she told him, "this thing, this energy zipping between us, driving me crazy."

"So why fight it?" he asked, stepping in for another round.

But Ana pushed him hard against the chest, keeping her distance. "Maybe I don't have a choice but to trust you to find Rachel—" she kept trying to turn the conversation into cool logic, splash water on the passion "—but I believe we'll be getting naked when, well, we're just not. Ever," she added, hoping the emphasis would make it all true.

She turned, ruining her exit by tripping so that only Nick's quick hands kept her from falling flat on her face. As soon as she gained her balance, she scrambled ahead, holding tight to the rail, going for the bowseat as the catamaran broncoed its way through the whitecaps.

He said it just loud enough for her to hear. "Admit it, Kimble. You're hot for me."

When she turned with a scowl, he dropped his sunglasses back into place with his knowing smile, his hands back on the wheel. "I'm there, baby. I am so there."

It had never been a question of whether or not he would kill her.

Rachel Maza was the danger. The evil.

He'd convinced himself of that long ago, to the point where he knew he could do anything, endure anything, just to eliminate that danger.

She was the job. His duty. Why he'd been sent—why he'd been altered. His calling before he died was to stop her.

He'd thought it would be a simple thing, that he was prepared. He believed the wildness she'd put inside him would take over, that killing her would be just a final step on the path he'd already taken.

A knife. He'd thought he'd use a knife.

But the demon he'd captured turned out to be young, hardly a woman at all.

After everything he'd suffered—what she'd put him through—he still hadn't killed her. And now he was beginning to accept that he never would.

She'd surprised him, coming back as she had. Despite his pleas, he'd never expected her to help him. But the young never thought about survival as much as they should. They believed themselves invincible. The girl had fallen prey to that belief, staying behind to take care of him, injecting him with the serum.

The episodes had been coming too close lately, more difficult to ward off. He needed larger and more frequent quantities of the serum. He'd developed a tolerance. He didn't even know how long he had before the serum stopped working altogether.

And there she sat, eating a peanut butter sandwich at his desk, leafing through one of his lab books. As if she were safe. As if it were nothing that he'd kidnapped her and brought her here, intending all along to kill her.

He came to stand behind her. She never so much as looked up from the lab book. She tapped her pencil where he'd written about scotophobin, a peptide in rat brains found to have transmitted the fear-of-the-dark memory from mother to offspring. He'd been looking at long-term memory storage in chemicals like peptides, believing that information similar to the rat's fear-of-the-dark memories could be transmitted chemically in utero in humans. His hypothesis: Chemically encoded memory could cross the blood-brain barrier, passing from mother to child.

"That's what I thought at first," she said. "Genetic memories." She shook her head. "Only..."

She glanced up nervously, then focused back on the lab book. "I don't think so anymore. It doesn't jibe with...some other stuff I came across. I wish you hadn't busted my laptop."

He could see she didn't want to tell him what she'd discovered. Something horrible, no doubt. Something that doomed him to this hell she'd put in his head.

"Leave," he told her.

She didn't even look up, jotting notes on the margin of one of the books. "I want to help you."

"You can't."

She never stopped eating the damn sandwich. "I started this. I can find a way to fix what I've done."

With one hand, he swept the dish and sandwich to the floor. He grabbed her, forcing her to her feet. "Listen to me. I'm offering you freedom. I can't promise you'll get another chance. I'm not who I used to be." The anger rose inside him, feeding off her innocent stare.

She should be afraid. She shouldn't be sitting and reading and eating her sandwich.

"I don't even know who I am anymore," he warned. "Don't make the mistake of thinking you're safe just because—"

"Because you haven't killed me yet?" she answered for him. Gently she pried his hands from her and sat down, dismissing him to return to the lab book. "Well, whoever you are, you sure know a lot about the research at Phoenix. Why were you running columns on the hippocampus extract?"

"It's the brain from someone who'd been altered. I thought I could isolate novel RNA, anything that wouldn't be present in a normal brain."

"Might work," she said, flipping to the next page.

He slammed his palm on the book, preventing her from turning the page. "I have these…episodes. I can't control them. I could become Frédèric. He wouldn't care how young you are or that you stayed and helped. I can't promise to stay Paul, a man who doesn't have the spine to kill you."

She didn't appear the least frightened when she stood to look at him. "Yeah, well. Someone already hurt me. He's my brother. And not because of what he did at the clinic. The Gunman was a hell of a lot more clever than that. He gave me just enough rope to hang myself."

She looked so small, tiny even, just standing there confronting him with her ridiculous bravery.

"You were right," she said. "I am a monster. And you or Frédèric or anyone else you might turn into can't hurt me anymore. I've done the job too well myself." She cocked her head, watching him. "You told me about the clinic, what happens there. You worked hard so I would believe you, and now I do. So don't worry about me. Okay? And don't waste your breath trying to get me to leave."

She sat back in the chair, shoving the lab book aside for another. "Just tell me what we need to do next," she said, opening the book.

26

It wasn't supposed to be like this. Abandoned halls, the smell of urine, broken windows and peeling paint. Cockroaches, and the constant babble of the insane.

Neglect was everywhere. The place wreaked of it.

"Norman? Are you coming?"

Norman turned. He hadn't realized he'd fallen behind. Dr. Rozieres and his assistant followed closely as Gunnar waited for him to catch up, while Norman stared at his broken-down dreams, wondering how the miracle of it had all gone so wrong.

He remembered the day he'd shown Rachel's father, Javier, her research, taking those first fatal steps into this quagmire. He'd been playing the proud parent. *Look, how brilliant. How talented! I did this! Yes, it's Rachel's work, but I inspired.*

Only later did he begin to see the true possibilities, that what Rachel had devised with Neuro-Sys was more than just a theory, something to publish—under his name of course, though he would have given her credit as a co-author. It could be a vehicle to greatness.

And so was born the Youthful Brain Project. His baby. Because it was Norman who had come across the obscure research on the Amazonian tribe and their ritual potions. Norman who had asked, "what if?" At the time, he'd shared his musings with only Ana, his faithful spouse.

But later, with the genesis of Neuro-Sys, he'd begun to wonder. With a computer program that simulated the workings of the human brain to guide them, couldn't Phoenix develop that simple tribal potion into something real, something viable? A window into the workings of human memory. How to put the brakes on the aging process in the brain.

And so he'd handed the reins to Rachel. "Here, darling girl, see what you can do with this." The symbiosis of Neuro-Sys and the Youthful Brain Project began, bringing about the trials at the clinic at Seacliff. It was going to be amazing. A dream come true.

But before this day, he had only visited that vision. Shiny, clean, state-of-the-art.

"In here, Norman."

He could hear the impatience in Gunnar's voice. But the grayness of the walls, the bored faces of the staff— it all wore at him, as did the memory of Mr. and Mrs. Stratford, whom he'd convinced to allow their child to be brought here. To recover.

At the entrance to the room, he saw the girl strapped to a bed. The IV bottle hanging on a pole beside her was held in place with white medical tape.

"They have begun the procedure, *monsieur.*"

Dr. Rozieres motioned him inside, holding the door open so that Norman could enter the dirty little hell where he'd sentenced Lynn Stratford. This room, at least, was relatively clean. Norman walked to the end of the bed. She was already deep in a trance, answering questions.

He took his place beside Gunnar, easing over, asking quietly, "I thought the Stratfords were supposed to visit here?"

Gunnar frowned, giving Norman a look that said *This isn't the time.*

"Look at this place," Norman said, insisting.

"When the time comes, I'm sure we'll find something more suitable." But Gunnar's attention was elsewhere, on the proceedings before him.

Which was where Norman should have focused, listening to the personality that his efforts had brought to life within the girl.

He found himself arguing instead. "But isn't that the point? Why isn't this elsewhere? I mean, look at this place. It's…it's a vegetable patch."

"Research costs money," Gunnar said, still not giving Norman his complete attention. "Seacliff is where the money goes, Norman, not here."

"Then she should have stayed at Seacliff—"

"She is exactly where she belongs. In the vegetable patch. She's gone, Norman. Just like the others."

Norman stepped away, backing himself into a corner as if he might disappear there, just shut his eyes and make the nightmare go away. There were only six people in the room, not including the patient, and yet the room felt crowded and hot.

This is where it all ended, then? This vegetable patch? This is where they'd brought Javier, a man Norman respected, even loved? Javier had lived out his days in this pestilence?

"This is where you sent your father to die?" he whispered, staring in disbelief.

Gunnar snapped to attention. Rising to his feet, he

came to stand over Norman. But Norman didn't care anymore. He had worse fears than Gunnar and his wrath to face at the moment. He'd sanctioned this place, had brought people like that poor girl here to die.

"Have you no shame, Gunnar?"

Suddenly Gunnar grabbed him by the arms and shoved him against the wall. He slammed him against the wall again and again, knocking the breath out of him.

"No, Norman," he said, smiling as Norman gasped for air. "I have absolutely no shame. Or regrets. *This* is where my father sentenced himself, a paradise of his own making. He forced my hand, or don't you remember whose idea it was to begin human trials in the first place? Javier couldn't be bothered with the FDA and its bureaucratic red tape, oh, no. He couldn't wait to follow proper procedure. Without my knowledge or counsel, he made himself that first test subject."

Norman knew the story only too well. How Javier had wanted to prove the efficacy of Neuro-Sys, that the computer program could circumvent costly testing, bringing about a viable pharmaceutical. But he wouldn't risk making anyone else his human Guinea pig, so he injected himself with the serum. He was the alpha group, the first man to experience the serum for the Youthful Brain Project, because Javier, a man who made his fortune selling home remedies, couldn't wait on tiresome government regulations.

Of course, his decision had forced Gunnar's hand. They couldn't very well stop research, allowing his father to merely disappear into the rogue personality he'd brought to life. They needed to move forward quickly, help Javier recover or achieve complete integration.

The cost had been Brobdingnagian, requiring that they leverage any asset, putting them all at risk.

"I didn't condemn my father to this hell, Norman. He brought himself here, dragging me along with him."

If either Norman or Gunnar had known what Javier was planning, there was no question they would have stopped him.

"He believed in his daughter's brilliance," Gunnar continued, his voice echoing the zeal of a convert. "Should I do any less? He wanted this, Norman. Now it's up to us to follow through, to make it right before it all goes to shit and we lose everything."

Which would be exactly what happened if they stopped now and admitted failure.

"So you see, *Norman,* I am here to fulfill my father's wishes. Nothing else. Nothing more."

"She's going to die," he said, hyperventilating. "They all die."

Gunnar lowered his head to Norman's. He whispered in his ear so no one else could hear. "So why not make her death mean something, hmm?"

What happened next came so quickly neither man had time to react. The girl on the bed sat ramrod straight, eyes open, no longer in a trance, but fully awake. When the doctor reached over to restrain her, the blow she delivered sent him crashing across the room.

She whipped her legs out from the bed. Grabbing the IV line, she yanked it from her vein so that blood spurted across the bed and onto the doctor's white coat. She seized the metal pole by her bedside where the IV bottle still swung precariously.

Grabbing it like a weapon, she jammed the end of the pole straight into the doctor.

Norman watched in horror as the prongs pierced into the man's abdomen like a pitchfork. Before the assistant could reach her, she smashed the opposite end up and under the man's chin with tremendous force. Norman heard the snap of the man's neck as his head fell back.

Suddenly she stood before Norman, holding the pole in her hands like a javelin. Eyes flashing, she smiled with the knowledge that for once, she had the power.

The sound of the explosion filled the room. The girl's eyes grew wide with panic as she fell forward, collapsing into Norman's arms. At the same time, the IV pole clattered to the floor.

Gunnar, a small-caliber pistol in his hand, knelt by the assistant, seeing that, indeed, the man was dead. The doctor had faired better. Taking the pillow off the bed, Gunnar pressed it to the man's stomach, motioning that he should hold it there. He stood and walked to the door, shouting for help.

Norman lowered the girl in his arms to the floor, trying to stanch the flow of blood pumping through the bullet wound in her chest. She was making these horrible choking sounds, the life bleeding from her.

Here lay everything that he had worked for. Only, it had never been real.

"You killed her," he said.

Gunnar looked back at the doctor. "I only wish I had done it sooner."

In that moment, Norman saw Gunnar as he had never seen the man before. He realized who exactly he was dealing with. Gunnar had taken a small company specializing in herbal medicine and created a kingdom, a kingdom that could very well topple because of risks taken by his father, choices made without Gunnar's knowledge or consent. And while Javier may have brought them here to this brink, Gunnar would be damned if he'd let everything he'd worked for fall into that abyss.

Holding the dying girl in his arms, Norman thought of Ana, fearing for her. Gunnar wouldn't hesitate to deal with her in just the same way as he had the girl he'd just shot without a shred of remorse, as he would surely deal with any threat to his plans, including Norman, leaving Norman very few options on the course ahead.

"Whatever you want," he told Gunnar. "You know I've always been your man."

They made Marie-Galante by sundown.

Ana and Nick didn't exchange a word. Not through the crossing, not during the long tense dinner. Only silence, which made being near him that much worse.

She could understand the attraction. There was probably even a name for what she was feeling. Something akin to celebrity worship syndrome. She'd created Raul in his likeness, and now the man had become this fantasy in her head.

Or maybe it wasn't that complicated at all. Maybe she just wanted him.

Of course, it bothered her, this lack of control on her part. How weak willed she'd become when Rachel needed her to be strong. Why couldn't she just vanquish those images of them in each other's arms? Certainly he was handsome and commanding. So what? Falling for a man she barely knew, risking everything on some gut feeling when she'd never before laid claim to such instincts? For goodness' sake, she couldn't even order lunch without thoroughly researching the possibilities.

And now she stood on deck waiting for him, knowing it was just a matter of time before he joined her. The sky was completely clear—not a cloud to be seen—and still, it began to rain.

Just before midnight, she sensed him standing behind her. He'd become this palpable thing, as if she'd developed a sixth sense called Nick Travis.

"See there," he said, knowing already she'd detected his presence. That was the sort of thing he could read off her body language. "In the southern sky, angled toward the west. About the size of your palm in front of your face. The Southern Cross. To the left."

"It's beautiful."

"The brightest star is at the base. Acrux."

She frowned, taking in that clear sky. "It's raining. But there's not a cloud in the sky."

"It's a fast-moving storm. They're up there. You just can't see them."

She turned to look at him. If there was ever a moment in life that a person knew she was about to do the wrong thing, Ana Kimble was living it. And still she didn't hesitate.

"Travis," she asked. "What kind of name is that?"

"My grandfather shortened it," he told her, coming closer. "When he first came to this country. A lot of people did that in those days."

She could feel the mist of the rain through her clothes. "What was it before?"

"You'll laugh."

"Try me."

"Travisomatis. It's Greek."

"It's a mouthful."

"Yeah." He smiled for the first time, bringing his hands up to frame her face.

"Do you want to hear my mouthful of a name?" she asked, using the question to get her breath back. "It's one of those Hispanic things where they all get strung together. Ana Magarita Kimble Montes Ruhland De La Cruz. They always make fun of those names on the sitcoms. How we do that."

"We?"

"Hispanics."

He was nuzzling her. She closed her eyes, leaning into his touch.

"You don't look Hispanic. Not one bit."

"Funny thing," she told him. "How we come in all sizes, shapes and colors. My father is American, some German, some Irish. He met my mother in college, this dramatic Latin woman who bewitched him, or so he claims. He hasn't looked back since. He said he wanted adventure."

"My mother is from Philadelphia, adopted and raised by a Greek couple. That's why she married my dad, another Greek American. They still do that sort of thing, the Greeks. They even tried to get me to go to Greek school."

"And did you?"

"Mou arasouna ta maliasou," he whispered.

"I have no idea what you just said, but I swear that's the sexiest thing a man has ever said to me."

"It means, I like your hair. Did I ever tell you that?" He was kissing her neck.

"I bet you tell all the girls the same thing."

"Kimble, there aren't any other girls," he said.

"—Haven't you figured that out? Now say something in Spanish."

"Dios ayudame," she whispered.

"God help me?" he translated. "Not exactly what I was hoping for."

She didn't know how to proceed, feeling awkward and out of practice. "How long ago did your wife die?"

"Three years. And I don't want to talk about Valerie." He kissed her full on the mouth, gripping her arms so tight it hurt. "I want to make love to you, Ana," he told her.

"It's what men usually want."

"But here's the thing. You're the kind of woman who plays for keeps. And that has me worried. I don't want to hurt you."

"Is that what you think?"

"It's written all over your face, Kimble."

And then, because she'd known all along it was inevitable, she took his hand and led him toward the open doors of the main salon. "Maybe I can prove you wrong."

It had been three years since he'd made love to a woman.

He sat in the cabin, watching Ana take off her clothes, standing so close she was practically between his knees in the small room. Her skin looked like alabaster in the moonlight, and he could smell a fragrance like sandalwood in her hair. That fever for her still burned inside him as he took in her amazing body, like an athlete or a model. Slim but with all the right curves.

"You're not undressing," she said.

Her hands on the buttons of her shirt stopped. She

looked startled, like a deer ready to take flight. Suddenly the mood in the room changed.

It wasn't that he didn't want to make love. It's all he'd been thinking about the past week, imagining all the things they would do together, dreaming about it. Tonight he'd simply given in to that hunger for her, thinking he'd get her out of his system and put to rest all those feverish thoughts.

But he couldn't move.

Ana knelt before him, her eyes never leaving his. She let her hair loose and it swept in a sheet of silk to her shoulders. He picked up a strand, thinking the sun had done its job, turning her hair the color of mink. She took his T-shirt and pulled it over his head. When he sat before her with his shirt off, she took his hands and put them on the buttons to her shirt, the next logical step.

"It's okay," she whispered.

He unbuttoned the first, then the next button, revealing her beautiful breasts. She wore a lacy red bra; the professor liked provocative underwear. Fire beneath the ice.

He felt such desire, yet at the same time, he was numb inside.

She leaned forward and rested her cheek against his chest. "You don't want to. You changed your mind."

"It's not that." He stroked her hair, liking the feel of it between his fingers. "It's just been a long time."

She looked up at him, those hazel eyes seeming almost catlike. Exotic. She was incredibly beautiful, the kind of woman they wrote poems about because her beauty was something from nature, grounded in mother earth. There was no artifice to Ana. The sooty-black lashes didn't need makeup; the silky hair had been highlighted only by the sun.

"Then maybe we should take it slow," she told him.

She took off her shirt, wearing only her bra and shorts, and pushed him back on the bed of the cabin. She crawled in next to him, spooning into him, her head resting on his chest. Those long showgirl legs entwined with his.

"Tell me about your family," she whispered. "Do you have any brothers or sisters?"

He almost laughed. Talk about slowing things down. "Sisters. Two of them. Both older and married with kids, a boy and a girl each."

"I'm not going to tell you anything about myself," she said, "because you probably know everything, including what I have for breakfast."

"Starbucks," he said. "Right before you go to work. Two Ventis carried in a tray to your car. You should lay off the caffeine."

"One was for Rachel. Sometimes she dropped by my office in the morning."

"So I figured."

He turned so that they faced each other. In the light coming from the hatch above she looked exquisite, someone he shouldn't touch or damage. "No, Ana, I don't know everything about you."

"The way you're looking at me now…that's how you looked after I dived under the water."

"I thought something had happened to you. You scared the crap out of me, Kimble."

She smiled. "You say the most romantic things."

"No," he said, meaning it. "Not really."

"Tell me about Valerie."

"I don't want to talk about my wife."

"Then tell me about your friend, Paul."

He frowned, because it was really the same story. He couldn't talk about Paul without talking about Valerie.

But then he thought maybe the professor was right. Valerie was in that room with them. There was no use pretending she wasn't. Even now, her picture waited in his wallet in the pocket of his trousers, like one of the icons at church. His mother always told him confession was good for him, and now Ana implied the same. He figured it might be easier somehow to start there, with Paul.

"Paul Hutchings was my best friend. We did everything together since sixth grade. Hiked Yosemite in the snow, worked at the library shelving books. Joined the army. We even fell in love exactly at the same time. With the same woman."

That face of hers again, giving away her shock. And it was shocking.

"You were both in love with Valerie?"

"He beat me to the punch, of course, because Paul always knew what he wanted. He never hesitated. Not like me. We met Valerie in the army. The three of us were friends, pretty much inseparable. Paul and Valerie got engaged," he said, giving the details. "Because Paul asked, and I was still trying to figure out if I was ready, all the long-term consequences, lining up my future."

"She said yes? She loved Paul?" Again, as if she couldn't quite see it, anyone picking another man over him. You had to love that about the professor. She showed that same damn loyalty for the kid.

"Oh, yeah. She loved him. Point of fact, we both did. And she wasn't so young, five years older than Paul and I, and that biological clock was ticking inside her and she didn't think I'd ever get around to asking. So there I was, odd man out."

"That must have been incredibly painful."

He nodded. "I didn't take it well, if that's what you mean. I tried. And that's when Valerie figured out that I loved her, too. She said…she said…"

He hadn't talked about Valerie to anyone for so long. It was hard somehow, to find the words, to tell the story just right.

He looked at Ana. "She said she loved me. That she wanted to marry me. And we were young and passionate. And we just about killed Paul when we eloped."

Looking back, it sounded like some damn soap opera. Just taking off like that because they didn't have the guts to face Paul, to let his pain convince them to hold off from what they really wanted.

"Paul disappeared after that. Transferred out and became this techno whiz kid. Never said a word to me again until Valerie died. He came back then. For the funeral."

She leaned up to look at him, her eyes luminous. "He wanted to help you through your grief."

He nodded, still marveling at the guy's forgiveness. "He showed up and just threw his arms around me. He never said anything about what happened in the past. Not a word. But that's Paul, a real mensch. Someone who always did the right thing."

Nick hardly remembered the funeral, only that in his sorrow he hadn't wanted to talk to Paul. Point of fact, he hadn't wanted to talk to anyone. Not his family, not the asshole who came up to him graveside, tears in his eyes, to tell Nick he was sorry about his loss—only, standing there, looking the way the guy did, he was confessing much more than that. Nick had known Valerie was having an affair, and now this stranger was letting

Nick know he was the one. As if Nick was supposed to do something about the guy's feelings when he had so much of his own to bear?

Nah, he hadn't wanted to talk. Certainly not to some asinine counselor like they asked him to do at work.

"I quit my job after that. I didn't leave the apartment for a week, didn't even step out for milk or food for the cat. Didn't answer the phone. That's when Paul showed up on my doorstep." He smiled at the memory. "He was like the freaking cavalry moving in. I think I even took a swing at him the first night. But he stayed. He brought me food and watched over me, like he thought I was going to lose it or something. Maybe hurt myself."

"He'd just lost Valerie. He didn't want to lose you both."

He stared at her in surprise. "You're good, Professor. That's exactly what he told me. He said that if anything happened to me, he really wouldn't forgive me this time. That a man only had so much forgiveness in him and coming back to help me, he'd used his all up— that's what he said. I remember exactly."

That's when Nick figured he needed to find the strength to live through Valerie's death. Because he couldn't let Paul down. Not again.

"At first, I didn't feel anything. I slept. A lot. But then, it hit me that she was gone. And I did a couple of wild things. I used to walk around the streets at night for hours. I'd walk out into traffic, weaving my way through the cars to cross to the other side, not really suicidal or anything—I mean, that's what I told myself. I was just crossing the street, you know? Almost daring the same thing to happen to me. Some stupid drunk driver."

"I've never had anyone close to me die. I can't imagine what you went through."

But the funny thing was, he thought she did understand. Those beautiful eyes of hers. She looked so sad. Yeah, he could see it there in her face.

"I still don't know how Paul did it. Got me thinking about life without Valerie. Like I said, he's not this particularly personable man. You have to get to know him. Quiet, in this nerdy way. But boy, did he ever get the message across. I had to come back to the living, for Valerie and for my family. For the people I cared about. For him. And after a while, I actually started to believe him, that Valerie wouldn't want me to die with her."

They lay in the bed, the moonlight crawling up their legs, her cheek against his heart. It felt incredibly intimate, how she fit just right against him, like some long-lost puzzle piece.

"Paul saved you," she whispered. "And now you're here to save him."

He looped a lock of hair behind her ear. "Yeah. Because I owe the guy. So that's my sad tale. Your turn, Professor. Tell me a story."

She didn't hesitate. "In *The Lost Steps,* the main character is a composer. He leaves the jungle and his true love to return to civilization to find paper and pen, so he can write his music." She was talking fast so he wouldn't interrupt. "But when he seeks passage back to the magical world where he left Rosario, his great love, the currents of the river have changed. The tide covers the tree trunk marking the entrance. Returning to the civilized world, he is like Sisyphus, his destiny always trying to achieve something only to lose it and start the quest again. The book ends with the character stating that Sisyphus's vacation had come to an end. There. That's my sad story."

"Good one. But that's not what I meant. Tell me about Fish."

"He didn't love me. He never did. I am like Sisyphus, always searching only to fail in my quest for love and start again."

He shook his head, wondering what she really believed. "What a load of crap, Kimble."

She kissed him and suddenly he was flooded by desire, feverish and hot. He practically tore her clothes, trying to get them off. He kissed her hard, everything rough—until he figured out what he was doing.

But Ana just stared up at him and whispered, "It's okay. I saw how you looked at me in the water. I'm not afraid."

They made love then, taking it slow. She found every scar; he kissed every inch of her. All the ghosts in the room vanished as he disappeared inside her, lost in the sounds she made, consumed by the texture of her skin—and her smell, that most of all. There was something crazy and intoxicating about her scent. And when they came together, he knew nothing would ever be the same.

They lay naked in the moonlight, their bodies linked so that there was no telling where one began and the other ended. He could feel the steady rise and fall of her breath against his arm, the pulse of her veins where he kissed her neck.

Looking at her, he saw everything he'd ever wanted.

He'd never been more scared in his life.

It was the first night since he'd kidnapped her that Rachel slept without her hands tied. That's why it startled her when she woke up, knowing it was still dark outside, sensing that something was terribly wrong.

Paul was sitting at the foot of the bed, watching her.

He'd left the door open; he had to have been outside. Moonlight filled the room so that she could see the knife in his hands.

She woke slowly, one thought at a time. *Oh, it's you, Paul. What are you doing up? A knife? Why a knife?*

He could have been anyone sitting there in the moonlight. She'd read the lab notes. How he'd become Frédèric Joliot-Curie, a man who along with his wife Irène—the daughter of Pierre and Marie Curie—had received the Nobel Prize in chemistry for developing new radioactive isotopes. Frédéric could be reliving the German occupation of France during the Second World War. He wouldn't even know who she was.

She sat up, moving slowly. "What is it? What's wrong?"

"You said you can stop them." He said it like a fact. "How?"

Paul, then, she thought. But still, Paul holding a knife.

How many months had he spent hunting her down? How carefully had he planned her death? Maybe the idea of killing her wasn't the sort of thing he could just give up.

And maybe he shouldn't. She'd been thinking about that the past few days. That this was all real, and that people had died. Maybe Paul, too, if she couldn't help him.

"I don't know," she said. "I think…yes. But I can't promise." Because she needed to be really honest now. She couldn't hide behind the arrogance that had brought her here, pretending anything was possible, not sweating the details.

"I should have known what they were doing," she whispered. "A million times I could have figured it out. But I didn't. Even when you started sending me all those letters, I made excuses. That you were just some crazy stalker guy, or someone trying to sabotage my brother."

She hadn't believed Gunnar capable of such things. But now it all seemed so clear. The data—it was just too good.

"I'm not afraid anymore, Paul," she said, choking on the words. "I want to help. Whatever it takes."

He held the knife as if fighting the urge to use it. He actually held it so tight that he cut his fingers on the blade, the blood seeping past his grip.

He dropped the knife. It clattered to the floor.

"I'm sorry." She was crying. Because at that moment, she'd known what he'd wanted to do. "I am so sorry."

He brought his hands to his face, staining it red.

She reached over and hugged him, crying in his arms.

"It's okay," he said. "It's okay. Just make it stop. Okay? Make it stop."

During the course of my illness, Raul never left my side. At times, he would whisper stories in my ear, his words slipping through the haze of my fever to take on the shape of a myth. A terrible monster had come to the mother jungle, he told me, entering in the guise of an enchanted maiden. Beguiling and sensuous, she promised riches beyond comprehension if a man would but lay with her. Of course, there was a price, as there was always meant to be in such stories.

27

Ana stared down at the neat black print. It was early morning, just after sunrise. She was sitting on deck, a yellow pad balanced on her lap. She had this surreal feeling that she was on the brink of some discovery, an elusive truth on the tip of the tongue.

She pressed her hand to the paper, wondering about that possible crystal-ball effect again, what it was she searched for in these passages she continued to write. Did she actually believe she could imagine herself to some happy ending, as if magical realism were more than just an art form? Here, on her Ouija board pad of paper, might she guide her pen to some personal breakthrough?

This morning, writing her story, she'd been thinking about the paradox of the two Anas.

She wasn't quite sure how she'd done it, but she'd managed to find this other person inside herself, giving birth to a brave new Ana, a reckless new Ana.

The new Ana appeared comfortable with risk, completely fearless. She claimed an almost mystical intuition. And she was falling in love with a complete stranger.

To the old Ana, the very idea seemed untenable. It

wasn't possible to feel such deep emotion for someone she'd known for a matter of weeks. Intellectually, she understood that crisis could bring a man and a woman together, fostering a false sense of intimacy. And still, the new Ana claimed nothing of the kind.

She trusted Nick. She thought he was "a good man." She based these assessments on not a single shred of evidence. She just "felt" he was safe, like some psychic occurrence, holding nothing back because that's what love meant.

Giving in. Taking that leap. Even if her feelings weren't returned. It didn't matter. They were *her* emotions. Not something to be controlled, only experienced.

"How very Latin," Ana said.

The old Ana, of course, was fighting "the good fight," holding on for all she was worth to some sense of sanity. She didn't focus her energies on herself—*go ahead, break my heart, I can take it*—but rather on her reasons for coming to the islands in the first place. Her first and only priority was Rachel. To find her. To keep her safe. And Nick had promised her just that.

She wasn't quite sure which of the two women kept writing on these yellow pads, seeking answers she didn't have. For some reason, she suspected it was both. As if only here, in Raul's story, could the two women come together. Or maybe she was merely trying to disappear here. Her mother once said that fantasy was the cure for all that ails a troubled soul.

But she hadn't found a cure. Instead, she returned to these pages day after day with increasing unease.

Something here—something important.

She flipped back a few pages. Her pen slipped from her fingers. "Oh, no."

She made a dive for the Mont Blanc, her favorite. On her hands and knees now, slapping at the white Fiberglas as the cherished memento rolled closer to the edge, always just out of her reach—until the pen skidded overboard and she watched it sink into the deep dark blue.

To Ana. Love Mom and Dad.

She kept her eyes on the pen, weighed down by a sense of loss that was anything but new.

Last night, they had dropped anchor at Marie-Galante. Come morning, she'd crawled out from beneath Nick's arm across her stomach, his heart beating next to her cheek, to escape here, on deck. She'd been greeted by the sight of a horseshoe bay of sand and palm trees trimming a dish of placid water—and the realization that last night had been a moment of lovemaking so tender she'd never experienced the like.

You're the kind of woman who plays for keeps.

She hadn't wanted Nick to be right. She couldn't be so silly, a woman who fell for a fantasy she'd created, then thought she could make him be forever. She wanted to be more sophisticated, savvy about the ways of men and women, able to look Nick in the eye the morning after and let him know that she'd already moved on. Welcome the reckless new Ana.

And the old Ana, following along, telling herself it was just sex, right?

Only, it hadn't been that at all. Instead, she'd found a connection, and something incredibly personal. Something she wanted to relive and trust. And she knew she couldn't. She just couldn't

She needed to get her footing back, to breathe. To remember who she was and why she'd come here, instead of watching her lucky pen slowly disappear to the ocean floor.

But even now that peculiar sensation crept upon her—knowledge just out of reach.

Until it wasn't.

Ana rose to her feet, the boat rocking beneath her, the beloved pen forgotten.

"Oh, God." She suddenly realized what it was she'd been writing about all along.

She stepped over to the pad of paper she'd dropped on the deck, kneeling to peer at the pages flapping with the breeze. What had she called these pages? Her Ouija board?

She thought she'd been writing a fantasy, filling her pages with make-believe.

She remembered an article she'd read about Gabriel García Márquez. His premise that fantasy preceded reality. As an illustration, the article discussed a scene written in Márquez's most famous book, *A Hundred Years of Solitude,* in which birds rained from the sky, an occurrence that wouldn't seem possible. But the article's author had come across a newspaper clipping discussing just such an event. Birds for some inexplicable reason flying into the sides of skyscrapers so that their bodies fell to earth like rain.

She picked up the yellow pad and stood.

Only, she no longer believed Raul's story was a case of fantasy preceding reality, that elusive knowledge coming to her at last. Writing Raul's story, Ana had not been creating but rather interpreting the world around her, her subconscious sending up a flare, warning her of what might lie ahead. *Beware!*

It seemed crazy and yet so right. All along she'd been trying to shed light on the path she'd taken, noting clues she would have otherwise ignored and writing them into her story to try to make sense of the crazy world she'd entered.

"Nick," she said, stepping away from the rail, continuing with those insights, seeing him suddenly in a blinding new light.

The fact that he spoke French fluently—he had to—that's why he knew so much about the islands here. Unlike Ana, he could read and understand those tomes she'd bypassed in the gift shops, settling for nothing better than picture books. Most likely, he spoke Spanish and Greek as well as German.

He knew about the green flash. He sailed and was a whiz with a computer.

And Rachel's diskette. All those numbers, the formulas, what had he called it?

"Code," she said.

She'd mistakenly thought he'd been referring to an encrypted message, something a private investigator might decipher. But he'd actually been more specific, saying just the single word: code. Just that.

Ana recognized the term. From Norman. It referred to the syntax, the words used to write a computer program. A term that was very sophisticated, well beyond the simple knowledge Nick claimed.

Ana raced for the steps behind her, climbing below-decks. She dropped the yellow pad on the salon table on her way to Nick's cabin. Once inside, she searched his drawers, the closet.

She didn't bother to hide what she was doing or stay quiet so that Nick, just waking, rumbled out of bed, then blinked in the light, smiling at her—until he realized what she was up to.

"You don't import bananas or coconuts," she said, grabbing his duffel bag, turning it upside down, dumping everything then searching through the debris. "You're not a truck driver or a bartender or a jack of all trades."

"What's going on, Kimble?"

"You're not a private investigator."

She picked up his pants and searched through the pockets. That's where she found it. His wallet.

She came across the first business card right away, before he was even out of bed.

Nicholas Travis, Ph.D. Technotrans Corporation. Specializing In Computer Systems Information Technology.

It took a little more digging to find the second business card buried in the back, as if he'd wanted to hide it, an old dog-eared card.

There was a logo with an eagle. In bold print appeared National Security Agency, followed by: Providing and Protecting Vital Information Through Cryptology. After Nick's name came the title *Information Technology Specialist.*

She stared at the card. Stared, as if maybe she'd forgotten the simple basics of reading.

Why should it hurt? Really? She'd known all along he was lying. Why should it *hurt?*

"When were you going to tell me?" she asked, still staring at the second card.

"Tell you what, Ana?" He grabbed her chin, forcing her to look at him. "What was I supposed to tell you?"

"This!" she said, shaking the business cards at him.

He grabbed both cards and ceremoniously ripped them in two, then four. "What was I supposed to say? That I'm not the dumb shit you think I am?"

"Yes. And, by the way, who are you? Who did I have sex with last night?"

He didn't answer. And she knew why. Because, if he spoke right then, he would reveal the lie of it all. From the beginning, every moment they'd shared together had been an illusion.

"That man," he said slowly, purposely, the way a person spoke when he or she was trying to get the words just right, not stumble over them and make a mistake, "that guy on those cards. You don't need to worry about him."

She stared at the little pieces on the floor, feeling somehow just as broken.

"Tell me," she said.

"Why? What does it matter that I have a doctorate in computer studies or that I run my own company? That I speak seven languages? What the hell does it change?"

But she was shaking her head. Because it changed everything.

He worked for the government. A spy. "You're hiding something. I can't trust you."

"But here's the thing. You can." He held her by both arms, the look in his eyes willing her to believe. "You can trust that I know what I'm doing. That I have training and special knowledge that can help you and Rachel."

She was stepping back, shaking her head. He was following her step for step. He grabbed her again, giving her a hard shake.

"The whole time, you were acting," she said, pushing him away. "Pretending you were—"

"Exactly the man you wanted me to be! Some stupid private detective straight out of the movies. That's what I do, Ana. What I was trained to do. Become the illusion. You saw exactly what you wanted, dammit, don't hate me for that!"

"You're some sort of spy. That's why you're following Rachel. This has to do with something Gunnar has done," she said, voicing the realization she'd made on deck.

That all along she'd been writing what she knew— what she'd been living through from that first day at the airport, taking clues from her everyday life. Mystics Incorporated. Nieman Trout. Rain-forest pharmaceuticals. Only, Raul wasn't a simple fantasy man fashioned into Nick's likeness as she'd always assumed. Raul wasn't Nick at all. Because it wasn't Nick who had fled from Mystics Incorporated and their rogue research. It was Rachel.

"Or maybe Rachel," she said. "Something involving Phoenix Pharmaceuticals and the government."

He stared at her in stony silence, a change coming over him. She could see it then, the government man assessing her.

"You should have told me," she said, defensive.

"And why would I do that?" Now, he was just as angry as she. "Why would I tell you a damn thing?"

"Because it might have helped Rachel."

"How could it help? What were you going to do? For God's sake, you're a schoolteacher, Kimble."

A schoolteacher. Only that. Not some super spy with special training like him. Not someone to trust and work alongside him.

"You're right," she said, stumbling back. "What a fool I've been."

She ran then, up the stairs and to the transom. She grabbed the line to the Zodiac, stepping on board. She was surprised how much she remembered from just watching Nick and Rachel because she had the dingy up and running by the time Nick came out on deck.

"Don't do this," he told her.

But she didn't answer. Because this time, it was Ana for whom the words backed up inside and wouldn't come out.

Paul had gone out. To rent a boat, he'd told Rachel. That's when the men came to take her away.

They broke down the door, racing inside and grabbing her before Rachel even knew they were there. For some reason, the image reminded her of Frédèric. The Nazis invading, coming to apprehend.

There were five of them, as if maybe they might need that many to restrain her. But then the Gunman always did like to travel with a posse.

At first she fought them, kicking and screaming. "No!"

She and Paul were so close to making a breakthrough. For the first time, with Paul to help her, she thought she could make a difference, make everything right again.

Now Paul would think she'd abandoned him. Scared of him after what had happened last night with the knife. He might even be happy that she'd finally given up and run away.

"How did you find me?" Rachel asked her brother, who was waiting at the door.

Gunnar came in from the outside, smiling as he took off his sunglasses. "Don't I always find you, Rachel?"

* * *

Monsters and phantoms crowded the street. Children lay in wait in dark alleys, eager to grab the unsuspecting with screams of delight, ready to chase those who were game. Music pumped up and down the narrow streets. *Les Jambes, les jambes, les jambes!*

Ana was crying enough that it was difficult to see. She pressed among the dancers, veering among the Mardi Gras revelers, wanting only to get away, to get somewhere…or just disappear among the mob until the whole crazy thing made sense.

This wasn't her, this woman running and trying to catch her breath, wearing nothing more than what she'd fallen asleep in the night before. Ana Kimble wrote stories about such things, she didn't live them. Ana Kimble led a nice safe life while she listened to her mother's colorful tales.

And she wrote the truth. On her silly yellow pads, she'd discovered what was happening to her and Rachel, making elusive connections within the fantasy in her head. Phoenix Pharmaceuticals—Mystics Incorporated. Raul—Rachel.

And while she wrote her fiction, those around her were doing the same. Telling her lies, using her.

Running through the streets, she felt like Alice in Wonderland. She'd grown too big, or shrunk so small. She couldn't find her way home again.

A man, his face chalk-white with makeup, grabbed her, spinning her into another's arms, as if she were one of them, just a dancer in the street. Turning, circling, from one to the next, until the sea of arms and faces parted, rushing her forward, pressing her into Norman's waiting arms.

"Ana." He grabbed her, holding tight. "I've been looking everywhere for you. Thank God I found you at last."

She shook her head, pushing him away. Crook! Thief! Liar! But the words stuck in her throat, her steps still part of the dance.

"No, no, no!" He reached for her as she backed away. "You have to listen to me, Ana. You're in trouble, my love. Please."

She kept backing away, but Norman kept pace. It would be a simple thing, to lose herself here among the costumed troupes. *Run Ana!* Like the jungle in the flat light of noon, everything looked the same and not the same. Her feet stumbled along in an awkward dance; she barely kept out of Norman's reach. The krewe just ahead, young men and women dressed in flaming colors, wearing masks and headdresses, resembled soldier ants marching with bored expressions.

Crack! The echo of the drums seemed to go on forever, sounding strange, not so musical, until she looked into Norman's eyes and saw his fear.

"Oh, shit" was all he said as another *crack* sounded. Not the beat of drums as much as a small *pop*, like in the movies, when the bad guy shoots the hero.

You're in trouble, my love.

"Don't run away from him, Ana. That will only make it worse." He was talking fast, trying to convince her, clawing at her while still seeming to dodge the danger, no longer a target beside her. "Please, Ana. Please."

She ran then, unsure if she'd imagined the gunfire. Unsure if the bad guys were real or just another figment of her imagination. She'd written this scene, hadn't she? Or imagined one just like it.

She turned a corner, then another, running through the crowded maze of streets, trying to outrun the danger, only to find it at the next turn.

A hand snatched her into the dark alley. The man standing there wound her tight into his embrace.

"Now you've done it, Kimble," he whispered in her ear. "They're trying to kill you."

Grabbing her hand again, Nick pushed her behind him as they ducked into the tangle of people ahead.

28

The clinic on Marie-Galante reminded Rachel more of an old farmhouse than a hospital. The buildings were low lying, crumbling apart, real museum material. The Gunman had brought her here in an ambulance, his men forcing her on board as he watched. She was a patient being escorted to a certain facility, a naughty girl being taught a lesson by Big Brother.

Now she found herself strapped to a chair in a room that looked straight out of some horror flick. They'd brought Fish along to baby-sit, a role he'd played to the hilt the past few years.

"All tied up and nowhere to go," Rachel said, watching Fish pacing across the room.

"Yes, well," Fish answered. "Your brother thought it might be best."

She'd never seen Fish look so miserable. Not that she cared. Because she could see that all his sympathy was for himself. He didn't want to be the bad guy, didn't want to face the plain truth about who he was and what he'd done.

"I think someone shot at her from the crowd." He was talking about Ana, acting as if he were all scared for her. "At least it sounded like gunfire," he said, biting his thumbnail, retracing his steps across the yellowed linoleum. "Could he really be trying to kill her? Would he go that far?"

"Don't play dumb, Fish," she told him in a dull voice.

She thought it was funny how easy it was for people to fool themselves, like Norman was doing now. She'd done it, too. All along, she could have put it together what they were doing, because the data was just too good. She should have known; she could have figured it out.

But she'd been focused on Neuro-Sys, getting the program to work. And she'd needed that data from Seacliff to fine-tune her code. So why question it? Instead, she'd given input to shape the course of the experiments, to get more data, one end feeding off the other.

Rachel watched Norman from where she sat, her bound hands tucked between her knees. There was a guard at the door as an added precaution.

"I know Gunnar can be ruthless with people. But Ana's out of the picture now. What could he possibly gain from hurting her?"

"The only other person in this world who might know what Gunnar and Phoenix Pharmaceuticals are doing here on the island?" she asked.

She saw the truth dawning on his face. That Ana wasn't safe. That maybe she never had been. She wanted to make him face what he was doing. He needed to choose to be the bad guy, not just get away with it and think he was still wearing the white hat. She needed to break that illusion he'd set up for himself.

"What you did," she said. "Taking my stuff and using it to hurt people? How could you ever think that was okay? This isn't like screwing around on your wife behind her back. People died. You destroyed lives."

He sighed, those blue eyes looking sad and burdened. "It's not so simple, sweetie."

"That's where you're wrong. It's dead easy to choose between right and wrong. Only people like you and Gunnar like to twist things around so you can make it all complicated. Feel good about screwing everybody."

"Rachel, I—"

"How did you do it, Norman? Would you like, put ads in magazines, maybe send out flyers to school campus or student hangouts? Do you want to improve your memory? Do better in school? And you'd get these volunteers. Only, they weren't volunteers, were they? Because, you're the ones who found them, who made sure they saw your flyers and gave you a call—you already knew what they had up their family tree."

"I know it's shocking, what you've learned." He was looking right at her, but she wondered if he saw her at all. "You need time to adjust."

"Once you had them at the clinic at Seacliff, that's when it would start, right? Your little program." She kept going, pushing harder, seeing from his reaction that she was right. "You do some fake interviews, run a few tests. Then, the pills and hypnosis…finally, the injections, until it gets so complicated with the headaches and the regression, they're pretty much hooked. They have no way out but to come back to you and your clinic for help."

He stood before her, trying a different tactic. "Neuro-Sys needed those experiments. And the Youthful Brain Project needed Neuro-Sys."

She shook her head, tired of the rhetoric. "I didn't hate you before, Norman. Not when you hurt Ana, or any of the stuff you did to me. I just thought you were weak, that's all. I made excuses. But I hate you now."

But Norman wasn't one to give up easily. He pulled up a chair and sat in front of her. "I can see you're appalled, and you should be. It is quite appalling. And still, still…"

He let the word hang between them, as if maybe she could fill in the blanks. Then he leaned forward, taking her bound hands and holding them in his.

"What if you're right? Rachel, what if it *can* be done? For all intents and purposes, we're cloning the human brain. Do you know what that could mean? What the Youthful Brain Project could lead to? The memories of Thomas Jefferson, Napoleon, Abraham Lincoln, weeded out through the centuries, brought back to life through one of their descendants…only integrated into the modern person, with their knowledge, their experience? Do you see what leaders we could bring to this lost world?"

She felt like spitting in his face, hitting him. She wanted to cry and scream at him. Cloning the human brain by accessing genetic memories? Not until she'd read Paul's lab books had she even known that's what they were trying to do. For her, it had all been about Neuro-Sys, finessing a better simulation program.

"It was just a dumb idea. I was just playing around, running models. You weren't supposed to hurt people. It was never going to work anyway."

"But it did—"

"No! You're so stupid, Norman. It wasn't working. It was never going to work. The science was bad. Neuro-Sys was wrong. These people weren't transformed into some past life. We weren't cloning the human brain. We were killing people. Just that."

His expression turned suddenly cold. It was a side

she'd seen before, when he was disappointed. *No, Rachel, that's not good enough. You can do better.* A side she could bet poor Ana had lived with much too long not to recognize.

"Some things can't be helped, Rachel."

She thought about Paul, what she'd done to him and others like him.

"I bet that went over really well during the Nuremberg trials," she said.

He stood, stepping away. She could almost hear what he was thinking. How to convince her? He needed her cooperation. He'd just ignore the part about it all being wrong.

She'd tried to do the same. Only, Paul had taught her about consequences. He was the consequence. And Fish couldn't see it. That Ana and Rachel were going to be his consequences.

"So save them," he said, "these poor people you fear for. You know how. Your last e-mail said as much. What is it, Rachel? What did you find?"

"Sure, I can help," she told him. "You get me out of here and we go to the police. We find Ana before Gunnar hurts her or maybe even kills her. You want that, don't you, Fish? To save Ana, the woman you married? The one you told me you still love?"

"More than life itself," he said, meaning it. "But this is bigger than that, Rachel. It goes beyond what I want."

"Wow," she said. "You really have lost it, haven't you?"

"Rachel, please."

Because he didn't want to hurt her. But he would. Just like the Gunman. If he had to.

"It's on the boat," she said. "Under the mattress in

my cabin. The diskette is marked Ana's Poem. It won't be hard to find."

He practically dropped to his knees, his relief was that huge. "You did the right thing," he told her, running for the door.

She watched him race out and sighed. "Yes. I know I did."

Nick had taken Ana into a small shop down the street, abandoned by all but the shop owner, who, after greeting them, stayed near the door watching the partygoers dancing in the street. The walls were lined with tie-dyed shorts and shirts in patterns and colors inspired by the sea. Nick took her into one of the dressing rooms, a small closet-sized space covered by a curtain with a stool in the corner.

She didn't beat around the bush, slapping his hands away. "What's on that diskette Norman wants? You know. You're some sort of expert. What are they after? Is that why you're following Rachel? Because of what's on that diskette?" she asked.

He was pressed up against her, wondering who in hell wanted her dead, only half listening to her questions. "She was running a model of the brain, seeing how it was affected by certain stimuli. Drugs, from what I could see. And no, I am not after her damn diskette. You gave it to me in the beginning, remember? I could have disappeared into the night with it if that's what I wanted. I didn't lie to you about Paul, Ana. I'm here to find my friend. Nothing else."

"But your friend. He's an agent investigating Rachel. That's why he was following her?"

He turned to look at her. He knew it wasn't safe to

stay here. They needed to move on. Maybe get back to the boat and get the hell off the island. He needed to get her to the airport and into some sort of protective custody.

"I wouldn't exactly call him an agent, but he had certain expertise. The kind of guy who would understand the information on that diskette. He was recruited for this job because he had some training way back when in intelligence, just like me, during our army days. From what I could find out, he's been working with a division of Interpol. Any time certain agencies get wind of the kind of technology Rachel was messing around with, it raises a red flag. My guess is Paul went undercover to find out what was going on. Only something went terribly wrong."

"I read those e-mails he sent. You said it yourself. He's not sane."

"Look, I don't know what happened to Paul, and this isn't exactly the time to play twenty questions. But I know how his mind works, his training. I don't think he'll hurt Rachel. But those guys out there mean business, Kimble. It's your ass I'm worried about right now, not Rachel's."

He'd said it straight out, still thinking about what would be safe. *Take her back to the boat?* He didn't think they knew about *The Green Flash*—that it was anchored out in the bay—but that could just be wishful thinking. He had to get back to Guadeloupe, put Ana on a plane. Once Ana was safe, he could focus on finding Paul and Rachel.

He was thinking ahead, not paying attention to what was happening there in the dressing room. It took him a while to notice she was quiet, to see the shock on her face.

He'd never seen anyone lose their color like that, but he recognized the expression, the realization striking that this was for real, people could get hurt, even killed. But he had to hand it to her, she rallied.

"We need that diskette," she said. "That's what Norman wants. The information on that diskette and Rachel. Maybe Paul wants the same thing. We can use it to bargain with Paul for Rachel's release if he has her."

As if she could understand. As if she could suddenly make sense of a situation he hadn't been able to decipher. Professor Ana Kimble, on the job, trying to do it all.

She was sitting in the corner of the dressing room. He knelt in front of her, not averse to a little begging. "Ana, you can't help Rachel anymore. You're a target now. Someone wants to kill you. They almost shot you out there."

But she was shaking her head, not listening. "I was writing this book. I thought I was making everything up, but I was just incorporating the things that were happening around me. Rachel, Phoenix Pharmaceuticals, even Norman. He's involved—of course, he's involved. Gunnar's lackey." She looked up. "Gunnar is the monster in the myth, but I'm going to beat him. We get the diskette for leverage, and then we go to that medical facility your sources told you about. Find out what Gunnar is hiding there that would drive Rachel to come all the way here with the diskette."

"That's insane," he said.

But she had this determined look. She stood. "The diskette. It's back on the boat. We have to get it."

He stood with her, shaking his head. "Absolutely not. They could be there already, waiting for you."

"It's our only hope."

She rocked back, stepping just out of reach. He made a grab for her. But she shoved the stool at his legs and ducked under his arms, slipping past the curtain.

He fell backward over the stool, taking her with him. They were both tangled in the curtain, the whole thing coming down over their heads. He grabbed a hold of her leg, but she kicked herself loose. Throwing off the curtain, he made another dive for her feet, but she was fast. Out the door and into the crowd.

He cursed, running after her. Looking through the faces in the crowd. Not seeing a damn thing.

But he knew where she was headed.

He took off down the alley. If he was lucky, he'd get there first, before all hell broke loose.

Ana had the Zodiac. Nick had come ashore in the damn kayak. Of course, she beat him back to *The Green Flash*. Closing in on the catamaran, he could see the Zodiac hitched alongside.

Once on board, he saw the place had been trashed. But he didn't see any sign of Ana, or anyone else for that matter, which didn't mean a thing.

It had been years since he'd used any of his trade-craft training. He hadn't been in intelligence long, just a few assignments before he'd settled into his job at the NSA. But it felt like instinct, coming on board without making a sound, crouching as he crept along the deck, waiting for the ambush, expecting it. But he didn't see any options. Not if he was going to find Ana.

His gun was in his cabin. He'd left it there, racing after Ana on the kayak. He hadn't been thinking clearly, watching her motor away on the Zodiac. Now he wished he'd been better prepared.

Whoever had been here had worked things over pretty good. Stuff was thrown everywhere, the cushions cut open, polyester fluff floating across the deck with the breeze like tumbleweeds. They'd be looking for something small. Something the size of a diskette.

The same story in his cabin. Everything littering the floor, the mattress cut open. He found his gun where he'd hidden it under a couple of boards, then made his way to Ana's cabin. Whatever they'd come for, he hoped they'd got it and had moved on before Ana got here.

No such luck.

He found her in her cabin, tied up on her bunk. Gunnar Maza stood beside her. He was holding a gun to her head.

A skinny geek of a guy was next to him. Nick figured he was the ex, Norman Fish. He was holding the diskette, having found where Nick had hidden it.

"Take his gun, Norman," Gunnar said.

Of course, whoever had dropped them off had motored away, hiding the launch so that Ana wouldn't suspect a thing. Just come aboard and fall into the trap.

He looked like a real winner, this Fish, taking the gun, holding it like the weapon scared the shit out of him. At the same time, letting Maza point one straight at Ana.

And Ana, well, for once, it was nice to see that goddess-glare leveled at another man.

"I'm sorry, Ana," Fish said. "I told you not to run, that it would only make things worse. I swear, I'll do what I can to help."

"Shut up, Norman," Gunnar said.

"Come on, Maza," Nick told him. "You have what you came for. So why not put the gun away and get out of here so Ana and I can get on with our vacation."

"Vacation?" Gunnar said, smiling as two other men appeared in the salon behind Nick. Backup.

Giving the sign, Gunnar watched the two spin Nick, delivering a jab to his gut, a blow to the head, taking him down. He could hear Ana screaming for them to stop as they kicked him.

"Well, I happen to know a lovely spot," Gunnar continued. "And really, I won't mind a bit taking you there."

29

It was Norman at his best.

"He's going to kill you," he said calmly, just a rational discussion on what she, Ana, should understand about her situation. *Listen to me, Ana, dear. I know what's best.* At the same time, a nervous twitch creased a corner of his mouth. "Unless I do something about it."

They were in a small hospital room straight out of the 1950s, linoleum tile floors and counters, stainless-steel sink, wallpaper a little worse for wear. There were bars over the windows. Ana didn't take that as a good sign.

Neither was the syringe and ampoule Norman set out on a steel tray beside him, making a tidy little row next to the rubber tubing and alcohol-soaked pad. She thought it was strange that he'd do that, worry about infection. And now, he was trying to reason with her in his typical Norman-conquest style.

He touched her hand at the wrist where it was bound to the chair. "I tried my hardest to save you."

"Norman, please. Let's cut the crap," Ana told him. "You aren't going to do anything to help me. The time for you to intervene on my behalf has long passed."

He stared at the stainless-steel tray. There was an attendant, a guard really, though he wore nurse whites. Ana remained strapped into her chair. And still Norman wanted her cooperation, her support, her absolution.

"Well, I suppose it would be difficult to understand," he said. "From your perspective."

"That's exactly what I was thinking. That this is just a matter of point of view."

"Ana, dear, you're abusing sarcasm. Believe me when I say this is difficult for me. Bringing you here. If there was any other way... But I do believe in what we're doing, though I can't say I agree with Gunnar's method. It's just too late to change course, that's all."

"You're a criminal, Norman. You're going to jail." Remembering one of her mother's favorite lectures, one Isela had learned from her own mother, Ana's grandmother, years ago, she continued, "To be a good man, you must fight. He who fights, triumphs. He who dedicates himself to the incorrect, he will always face misfortune, and, eventually, one day, just punishment."

"Lovely sentiments, I'm sure, but the fact remains that we have a problem. Gunnar wants you dead. I had to negotiate. I fought for your life, not that you'd understand." He lifted the syringe. "Unfortunately, this was the best I could do."

Despite herself, she could feel panic rising inside her as she watched him prepare the syringe. "What are you doing?"

He was sitting on a stool with wheels. He pushed himself closer, whispering, "Rachel was working on a computer model of the human brain. I was helping, giving her data so she could write and refine code. She was making incredible progress when she disappeared. I thought Gunnar was pushing her too hard, cutting off her schoolwork, making her focus on only Neuro-Sys. But when she came here, I began to suspect there was more to it."

The door behind her opened. Norman sat perched in his chair as Nick staggered inside, one of his eyes swollen shut, blood on his lip where it had split open. A guard ushering him in with a gun jabbed at his back, guiding him to the only other chair in the room.

Ana smiled at Nick, even though she didn't feel like smiling. But they'd been separated since they'd left the boat, and it was a relief to see him alive if a little worse for wear.

"This must be the private investigator you were asking about. The one you thought Gunnar had hired to follow Rachel."

But Ana didn't answer. She had no idea what Norman was up to, but she wasn't giving him one bit of information.

"It doesn't matter," he said. "He's already told us everything. He was playing you, Ana. He works for a competitor. He wanted the diskette just as much as we did, but stayed along for a little R and R with you. I'm afraid he used you, Ana," Norman said, his voice in the perfect pitch of sympathy.

They pushed Nick into a chair, then bound his hands around the back, anchoring his ankles as well to the legs of the chair. Ana was watching him, careful not to react to anything Norman said, thankful now that she'd found those business cards Nick destroyed. She couldn't imagine he'd be alive if Gunnar suspected he was a government agent.

"You must have been a damn good fuck, Ana, darling," Norman said crudely, his eyes on her. "He did an admirable job of begging Gunnar for your life. What he couldn't know—what I myself misjudged—is the depth of Gunnar's animosity for you."

"Tell him for my part, the feeling is completely mutual," she whispered back.

Norman returned to the steel tray and the syringe. That's when Nick lost control.

"What are you doing?" He lunged forward, stopped only by the two guards keeping him and the chair in place.

"It was the best I could negotiate for you both," Norman said, focused now, placing the syringe on the tray. "If it was up to Gunnar, you'd both be dead by now, feeding the sharks. But I couldn't let him do that. There's been enough death already."

"Think about what you're doing, man," Nick begged. "She was your wife!"

He wrapped the rubber tubing around her arm. "I don't want you to worry, Ana. You'll be part of the project we were working on with Neuro-Sys. The Youthful Brain. With all the talk of Alzheimer's and an aging baby boomer population, we've been studying medicines and procedures that could extend human memory. Along the way, we made an extraordinary discovery. That deep within each of us are memories passed along from mother to child, generation to generation."

Ana frowned, Norman triggering something. "Tribal memory?"

"That's right, Ana," Norman said. "I told you about it, remember? I believe it was a book on the tribes of the tropics. A Christmas gift from you, wasn't it? Imagine, Ana. In a few chosen people, those genetic memories can be accessed through a serum Rachel helped develop with Neuro-Sys. There's a clinic, Seacliff, where we did research."

"On people?" Ana asked, disbelieving.

"On volunteers," he corrected. "I can give you this one chance." He swabbed her arm with the alcohol-soaked pad. "I'm going to send you into the past now, Ana, to find someone inside you, someone with the knowledge and memories of another time and place."

He looked at her straight on, ignoring Nick's constant cries for Norman to stop, to think about what he was doing, which she, too, did her best to filter out. It hurt too much to hear Nick plead for her life. He didn't know Norman, how heartless he could be.

Norman appeared like a coach preparing his star athlete for a top performance. "That person can be you, Ana. An enhanced version of yourself."

It took both attendants now to hold Nick down in his chair. "You can't live two lives at the same time," he yelled out. "The science isn't there, man. Think about what happened to those people who volunteered at your clinic. Where are they now? Is that what you want to happen to Ana?"

"I don't have a choice. Not if I want to keep her alive," Norman said, concentrating on what he was doing. "I have seen an integration, Ana. And with the breakthrough Rachel promised—"

"You want to take that kind of chance with her life?" Nick was still struggling. "Look, you want a volunteer? I volunteer. I'll sign whatever you want, say whatever you want."

"No," she said, looking at Norman, forcing herself to sound perfectly calm. "No. It's me he wants."

She felt the sting of the needle in her arm, watching

Norman, trying to not listen to Nick shouting to take him instead. And when Norman finished, she said simply, "You were always such an asshole." She smiled, hiding her fear, feeling whatever he'd given her warming her blood, tingling inside her veins. "And Norman, I never told you—I didn't want your feelings hurt—but I think it's time you know the truth. You were never very good in bed."

It didn't take long before her vision blurred and Norman's voice became barely a hum, like music carrying her somewhere. She could still hear Nick at times, telling her things like *You're going to be okay,* and *I'll take care of you, Ana, I swear*—alternately railing at Norman, then begging him to stop, to save her.

She wanted to tell Nick not to plead with Norman, that it pained her to hear him begging a monster like him for anything. But she couldn't talk, not like before. The words were thoughts that floated away like notes, no longer important.

Norman was talking about her mother, about Isela, his words painting the image of her inside Ana's head. At least, she thought it was her mother, the little girl standing at the seashore with ribbons in her hair.

Ana recognized *El Malecon,* the wharf, a famous landmark in Havana. She'd seen photographs smuggled out of Cuba by relatives, pictures in magazines like *National Geographic.* Recently, there had been a documentary on the island on television. The girl, Isela, had just finished a drink of *guarapo,* the juice made by pressing sugarcane between two rollers. Her mother had always told Ana that she adored the drink, one of the many things she missed here in the States.

Ana could see the girl walking from the juice stand

as the proprietor fed another stick of cane into the presses for the next customer in line. Royal palms swayed with the breeze, making an image so vivid in her head that Ana could swear she smelled the ocean.

Norman spoke like a narrator in a movie, telling her of her mother's great talent. How Ana could be just like her, could access those memories by reliving her mother's life in Cuba, the days spent listening to her grandmother's stories…even Isela's fears when she fled from Cuba as a young woman. These were the memories that were the basis for Isela's talent. What was talent anyway but life experience? How ironic that he might, after all, bring to Ana what she'd always wanted, he told her, give her the thing she'd coveted most. To be her mother—to be Isela Montes.

She saw her mother's life like photographs in the wooden albums Ana's father kept in a cabinet in the den. The cold winter in Spain before coming to California. The years of study and worry in the States, trying to fit into a society that wouldn't accept her, using her angst to write of emotions that she couldn't control. Then meeting Ana's father, a man so completely taken with the very thing Isela despised, her Latin temperament, that he hadn't hesitated to fall in love.

That's when the little girl in the pictures transformed, becoming the woman grown, Ana's mother.

Her eyes filled with characteristic heat, Isela scolded, *"Anita!* You don't want to be me, *mi amor!"*

That vision of her mother became a pail of cold water thrown in her face, as if someone had suddenly hit the pause button on a movie and the director had walked on the screen to explain away the magic. *Pay no attention to the man behind the curtain.* She could still hear Norman's voice, but her focus was now on Isela, feeling her mother's strength in the hard expression she gave her daughter. Ana had that strength inside her, a part of her, just like Isela, buoying her spirit.

All her life, her parents had encouraged Ana to find her own path, to seek *her* life's passion, something unique to Ana. Even in her drugged state, Norman encouraging her to disappear into her mother's memories, the idea of becoming Isela suddenly made no sense at all. It wasn't even a possibility. Soon Ana could no longer hear the drone of Norman's story. Instead, she focused on the echo of her mother's voice encouraging her, Isela's words becoming a catalyst so that Ana could see the room again, though through a continued haze of the drug.

She could see Nick, too, completely focused on her. And she knew, watching him, that her mother was right. Leaving the university, writing her book, Ana hadn't wanted to follow in her mother's footsteps. She was here for herself. To discover her voice after years of trying to silence that need.

But she also understood there was no use running away anymore. There was a part of Isela inside Ana, an emotional legacy she feared enough that Ana had wrapped it up in a corner and hid it away. These past few weeks she'd come face-to-face with that side of herself: the hate she felt for Norman, the passion she felt in Nick's arms, the devotion she needed to give a family of her own. The two Anas coming together inside her, because she needed them both.

In that moment, she knew what she'd wanted all along. To be herself.

Just Ana. Only that.

* * *

It was happening all over again, Nick thought. Just like before, with Valerie. He was screwing up.

But there wasn't anything he could say to change what had already taken place. That asshole had given her the injection, and Ana was slumped in her chair, looking dazed with her eyes half-closed and her breathing too deep. The only sound she made was an occasional moan.

The serum. They had to have used it on Paul. He'd been one of their so-called volunteers. Maybe they'd even discovered he was working for Interpol and figured they'd kill two birds with one stone. It would explain those insane threats to Rachel. His obsession with the girl. He'd figured out what the kid was doing, so they made him one of their guinea pigs. They'd driven him insane. And now they'd do the same to Ana.

Fish droned on about Isela Montes, Ana's mother. How Ana could find Isela inside herself because she carried her mother's memories, telling Ana she should shut out the other voices she might come across and focus only on Isela, search for those memories, those experiences. Isela was there, a part of her.

Genetic memories? Inherited like eye color or intelligence? And Neuro-Sys provided the sophisticated code that enabled them to get this far in their research. They were messing with the neuropathways, using some sort of synthetic compound to access memory?

It didn't seem possible. Memories, if inherited, would have to be part of the DNA, stored there, in a protein of some sort.

Now Fish was talking about some breakthrough Rachel had left on the diskette, something that would make shooting Ana with the serum okay in the guy's mind. But the diskette Nick had read only contained code modeling brain functions. There wasn't any sort of formula or research, nothing that would be a "next step."

Fish thought he had something, something that galvanized him into taking this chance with Ana. But he was talking about science fiction. Phoenix Pharmaceuticals had shit—Nick knew it.

But Fish wasn't listening to anything Nick had to say. The idiot continued his brainwashing, making Ana into something she wasn't, hurting her in a way Nick didn't know he could make right again.

He remembered the time she'd talked about her mother. How much he'd hated the idea that she felt somehow inferior. And now this guy was trying to convince her of just that?

The whole time, struggling with the ropes around his hands and legs, he kept talking to Ana, pleading. As if it could help, telling her he was here for her, no matter what. That he needed her to be just who she was. Ana, a woman who could talk about the beauty of the jungle and make you want to go there. Who could describe books he hadn't even known existed using words that sounded like magic, her eyes lighting up with her special knowledge. She could make him forget Valerie even when he didn't want to, forging a link he'd never wanted to have again.

They'd tied him so tight that his wrists and ankles were jammed back against the chair. The asshole behind him had a gun on him. But Nick kept squirming in the chair, trying to loosen the ropes.

That's when Ana looked at him, as if she could see him and nothing else. In her eyes, he saw that despite all the crap Fish was telling her about her mother, it didn't matter. Ana was still there, looking straight at him.

That look on her face triggered something inside him, making him not care about the gun or the ropes. He didn't even feel pain as he ripped out one hand and then the other from beneath the ropes.

He fell forward and kicked back, pushing the chair into the legs of the guard with the gun, the chair snapping in two with the force of the blow. He untangled his legs and dived at Fish before anyone could stop him.

He knew how to kill a man with his hands. He'd been schooled to react in just this way, part of his training, information he thought he'd buried with Valerie.

By the time he even heard Ana, saw that she was okay, he'd already broken the guy's arm.

"Please, stop." She was shouting at him from the chair. "You're going to kill him."

The minute he hesitated, Fish scrambled away, screaming like a stuck pig at the top of his lungs. Nick jumped to his feet, ready to protect Ana from the expected attack.

Only, what he saw was the guards fighting each other. The one he'd slammed with the chair, the guard with the gun, shot the other man in the knee, then the shoulder so that the wounded guard dropped to the floor, lying there incapacitated.

When Fish reached the door, another shot followed, hitting him in the back of the leg so that he, too, crashed to the floor.

Nick started untying the ropes around Ana's hands, still watching as the guard with the gun—the man he'd hit with the chair—turned the downed guard on his stomach and began tying him up with the man's belt. He glanced at Nick, seeing that he had his attention.

"Help me," he said.

For a second, Nick just stayed there, frozen. Because he couldn't believe what he was seeing. The guard. Nick recognized him.

"Paul?" he asked, disbelieving.

"He didn't inject her with the serum," the guard said, now using his own belt to tie the other man's legs. "I switched the vials. It was sodium pentothal, truth serum. I had to make it look right, her reaction."

He stuffed a rag into the fallen guard's mouth, then looked up to say, "You let him get away."

He was talking about that bastard, Fish. For the first time, Nick noticed the trail of blood leading out the door.

"My God, Paul," he whispered.

He hadn't realized it was him. He'd been too focused on Ana and what Fish was doing to her. Paul looked different. Older. Thinner. But Nick recognized the voice for sure.

"He'll bring help," Paul said, stepping over to them. He took another syringe out of his pocket. He reached for Ana's arm.

"Nick," she said, watching him.

"It's to wake her up," Paul said. "She'll be fine."

It was the strangest thing. Norman had escaped, some guy who looked just like Paul was helping them, and all Nick could do was stare at Ana and hold her.

"Come on, Nick," Paul said, shaking him. "You know the drill."

And he did. He had to focus, get the job done. Think about something other than the fact that Ana was breathing there beside him, that he could hold her again. She needed him to be something different now, the hero, the guy who saved the day.

"Look, we don't have time for this," Paul repeated, this time getting Nick's attention. "We have to go. To help Rachel."

Paul stood and ran to the door. He checked the hall first, said, "Come on," then sprinted ahead, not looking back to see if they followed.

But Ana was already standing. "Is that really him?" she asked, getting her breath.

He nodded. "Paul Hutchings. The crazy guy who kidnapped Rachel." Nick stared at the door, wondering if they should follow even as he pulled her along to the corridor. "God willing, he's not as crazy as I thought."

How is it possible not to change here? Raul has that kind of indelible spirit. But I find myself pliant, changing and absorbing, so insubstantial I barely recognize myself anymore. I smoked the sacred tobacco in two-foot-long cigars balanced on bone forks spiked into the ground. I have a tattoo.

The myth he sang to me hovered on the edge of my consciousness, until I woke one day cured of my illness to decipher its secret. Mystics Incorporated had created a dangerous serum. Something that could kill. And they'd used my research to do it. Raul had come here to stop them, taking credit for what I had done, trying to make himself the target. Trying to save my life.

30

No one could disappoint like family.

Gunnar had learned that lesson with his daughter, Juliet. How he could have such high hopes for this tiny person he'd brought into the world with such care and planning, only to discover that the child couldn't be more ordinary, banal. All that hope turning into something hardly worth his attention.

Magda wanted more children. But with Juliet as the model of what they could produce, why add another failure to his life?

And Rachel. A father could do everything right—put his child in the right schools, make certain she had the right influences—and still, in the end, she would disappoint. She would dress like a slut. She would waste her talent writing poetry. She would run away and betray him.

Gunnar had a theory about such things. Over the years, Rachel had proved him right again and again. The more one did for their children—the more a parent sacrificed and forgave—the less they counted. Those children in the news, the abused ones with the cigarette burns and the broken bones, those children would do anything for their mother or father. Almost as if the crueler you became, the more you mattered.

But it hadn't been in him to treat Rachel with less than kindness and a firm hand. There wasn't anything in the world he wouldn't do for her, no sacrifice that was too great.

He had only asked one thing of her. Loyalty.

"You disappoint me, Rachel," he told her. "Deeply."

"Like I give a shit."

He hit her hard across the mouth. He'd never struck her before. He hadn't known he was this close to losing control.

She came at him like an animal, hitting him, scratching her nails across his face. He grabbed her wrists and pulled her arms behind her back. He pinned her against the wall.

"What is this place? What is Phoenix Pharmaceuticals doing here? What did you do to our father?" she screamed. And when he faltered, loosening his grip, she yanked her hands free. "Tell me where he is!"

He hadn't expected her to ask about Javier. He had been nonexistent in her life. No father, at all. She should realize that he, Gunnar, was all she had—all she'd ever had.

He didn't believe for a moment that Norman had told her the truth. Norman wasn't the type to speak of such things. It was more his style to avoid the ugliness and focus on the glory.

But she knew. He could see it in her eyes.

Her knowledge presented a problem. He could imagine her reaction, and it wouldn't be to cooperate.

"Rachel, you have to understand. Our father was a brilliant man, but he was a dreamer," he said, because it was true. Javier lived for the excitement of the chase, both in his personal and professional life, leaving others to pick up the pieces afterward. She needed to know what Javier had done, forcing Gunnar's hand, that there was no turning back now. "I tried to reason with him. But he didn't listen. He'd convinced himself he was doing the right thing."

"He's dead," she said, dropping into the chair. "He's dead, isn't he? My father is dead."

She appeared suddenly smaller, almost as if the truth were too much for her. Despite himself, he felt pity for her. Javier might have been absent most of her life, but his death would come as a shock just the same.

He knelt beside her. He wanted to help her cope with the emotions he'd shielded her from the past year. "When Norman first proposed your project, we were all ecstatic, beyond ourselves," he told her. "The potential of a functioning brain-simulation program was incredible. But Javier wanted more. He wanted everything, to prove that with Neuro-Sys we could develop a pharmaceutical ready for human trials. He believed in your work that much, Rachel."

They all had—Gunnar no less than Javier or Norman. But Gunnar knew what they were up against. The FDA, feverish competition, and technological breakthroughs that every day turned the world as they knew it upside down.

"He didn't take the necessary precautions," he explained. "He couldn't wait to follow the proper channels, years of testing to achieve FDA approval for the serum we'd developed. He never even considered what his actions might mean to the company if he failed."

"He used the serum on himself?" she said, guessing the truth.

"He thought we were close with our research. Close

enough to start trials, but he wouldn't go through with the experiments unless he was part of it. He wanted to take all the risks."

She was shaking her head. "Why didn't you stop him?"

"Do you think he discussed it with me? That I wouldn't have tried to talk him out of it? But he was that certain of success. Our alpha group." He could see the horror in her face, the realization of what Javier had done. "After the first injection, there was no going back. Do you understand?"

"No, I don't believe you. You're lying again. You always lie. The serum. He couldn't go through all that without help. You had to know, you had to suspect something." She started pounding her fists on his chest until he grabbed her, hugging her against his chest. "You could have stopped him! You could have stopped everything."

"He conducted those experiments without my knowledge or approval," he said, whispering quickly, trying to get the information across before she fell into complete despair. "Yes, he had help, but not from me, I assure you. We have a ready and able staff at his disposal, and trust me when I say that's all Javier needed. Once we lost him, once we started down that path, it was too late to turn back. Too many resources were already at risk."

"No!" But she wasn't struggling anymore. "You killed him." She wasn't pushing him away, either. Instead, she held on to him, crying through the words. "You let my father die."

He closed his eyes, holding her tighter. Didn't she understand that Javier was gone, but not her father? He needed her loyalty now more than ever. "You have me, Rachel. You've always had me. I promised Beatrice. When she died, and I watched Javier turn his back on you because he couldn't look at you—couldn't bear to see Beatrice in your face—I took his place."

She was weeping softly, but he could see he had her attention. She was calmer now, listening. He lifted her face up to his, wiping her tears.

"He was *never* a father to you, Rachel." He kissed her on her cheek, whispering, "For him, it was always about his work. The company, his next discovery. He ignored you from the day you were born. And he did the same thing to your mother. In the end, she had no one to turn to but me."

She frowned. "What are you talking about?"

He didn't hesitate, knowing it was time for the truth. "You know, you look exactly like her." Even with the dyed hair and the tattoos, she couldn't alter her appearance enough to change that. "And while that resemblance may have turned our father away, it only made my love for you grow. You're almost the same age as your mother when we met. Do you understand? I love you…because I loved Beatrice. She meant everything to me."

Her eyes grew wide. "That's…that's crazy." She stood, stumbling back. But he grabbed her arms, making her listen.

"Javier knew that we loved each other—"

"No, no. You were just a kid."

"I was nineteen. Does that shock you?" he asked, surprised. "Javier was twenty years her senior when they married, but it shocks you that she would love me, a man five years younger than she? Listen to me. For all intents and purposes, he abandoned you both. He may be my father, but I was never blind to his faults. He took a brilliant woman who worked for him and once she had his child, he moved on to his next project. But she had me. Both of you always had me."

She pushed him away. "My God, Gunnar. She *killed* herself." There was a harshness in her eyes. An accusation. "If she had you, if she loved you so much, then why did she kill herself?"

He understood that what he'd told her was a shock. But her voice, that tone. She blamed him?

"You have to listen to me." He grabbed her wrist, keeping her there beside him when she would run away. "She was my soul mate. She didn't see that at first, but I knew. I always knew."

But she was shaking her head. "That's why she killed herself, isn't it?" Her voice rose steadily, coming close to hysterical now. "Because it was too much to live with…falling in love with her stepson. Cheating on her husband with his own kid."

She was confusing things. "No. It was nothing like that."

"Did you push her over the edge? You told me you found her! Did you find a note? Did she blame you and that beautiful relationship of yours?" Each word was hurled at him like a knife. "Was killing herself the only way out? The only way she could get away from you, the only way you would leave her alone?"

That she could be so disloyal, to him and her mother.

She couldn't know how it had broken him, Beatrice's death. But it hadn't surprised anyone when she'd taken her life. She had a history, as many brilliant people did.

"Of course, there was a note," he said. "Telling me that she loved me. That she was sorry that she was so weak. That I should take care of you, raise you to be stronger. And that's exactly what I've done, you ungrateful bitch—" shaking her "—because I loved Beatrice to the depth of my soul. I…still…love her."

"Where's my father!" she screamed. "Where's my father!"

He slapped her. "Stop it. You're hysterical."

The shock of the blow caught her off guard so that she stopped screaming, standing silent before him.

"Javier is dead," he said. "He's been dead for almost a year. And he was never your father, not in the real sense of the word."

"No," she said, suddenly very composed. "No, he wasn't."

"You listen to me, Rachel. For once, you'll do as you're told. Now, there's a good girl," he said, seeing that she wasn't fighting him anymore. "I've discussed it with Norman. We have the diskette from the boat, but we need your cooperation."

He took her hand and pulled her to the chair, forcing her to sit. He brought over the tray with the syringe ready.

"There is a very specific protocol for beginning the use of this serum. Not even Norman knows the proper procedure." Gunnar was counting on that, knowing that at this very moment, Norman was injecting Ana with the serum, unknowingly causing her death. Finally he would be rid of that bitch.

"Proper use of the serum involves weeks of preparation," he continued. "If I inject you with this much serum without the ancillary steps, it will overload the brain, resulting in death. Please, Rachel," he said, quietly, "I don't want to use this on you."

Her eyes grew large. "You're going to inject me with the serum?"

He wanted to frighten her. She needed the right incentive, the necessary inspiration. Like those abused children, she needed to listen to him.

"I don't want to hurt you, Rachel. You are all that I have left of Beatrice. Don't force my hand."

At that moment, staring up at him—knowing he had all the power—she had never looked more like Beatrice. Beatrice had always told him that he held her life in his hands. He chose to believe that she referred to his great love for her. He'd never accepted Beatrice's explanation, that their love was cursed, a great sin that would eventually require a great price. But here was Rachel throwing those very words at him. *Was killing herself the only way out?*

Gunnar felt a rage come upon him. Not since he'd found Beatrice's body had he felt such betrayal. Even now, with Rachel docile before him, he could imagine the endless battles ahead. Every step of the way, she would fight him. With each development she offered, he would suspect sabotage.

She was supposed to save him and the company, but if he let her live—allowed her back into the fold, giving her that power over them—she could very well finish what Javier had started and ruin them all. Despite everything he had given Rachel, in the end, she would want only to get away from him. Just like her mother.

He could feel his hand shaking as he held the syringe. He realized Rachel would never return the love he had offered all these years, stepping in to take over Javier's responsibilities. The weight of her disloyalty twisted inside his heart, a pain that he could hardly bear, could hardly breathe through. He felt as if he were losing Beatrice all over again. With Rachel, every day would feel just like this.

End it now. End it here. The syringe still in his hand gave him that power to stop that torment. He was thinking just that when he heard the crash of the door bursting open.

Gunnar frowned as he turned to see Ana race into the room. Behind her came the man from the catamaran, the one who'd come on board to rescue Ana. Both of them froze at the sight of Rachel in the chair and Gunnar holding the syringe.

At first, that picture of them standing there made no sense. It just wasn't possible. He'd given Norman very specific instructions. The procedure should have killed Ana.

Right behind them, one of the clinic guards appeared just as suddenly. He was holding a gun.

"Get them out of here," Gunnar commanded.

The guard didn't move to follow his orders. Instead, the man raised his gun and pointed the weapon at Gunnar.

"Let Rachel go," the guard said.

He recognized the voice, that soft, slow rhythm. He stood, beyond shock.

No. It wasn't possible. He was dead. They'd found the body.

"Frédèric?"

Gunnar could see he'd altered his appearance—the hair lighter, no glasses—but still he recognized him.

"My God," he whispered.

A ghost stood before him. Paul Hutchings, the man they'd turned into Frédèric.

Two years ago, he had come to work at the clinic posing as a brilliant researcher capable of the kind of breakthrough they'd hoped to achieve at Seacliff. Last year they'd discovered he was an agent sent to infiltrate the company. They'd given him the serum then—Gunnar's idea—following the proper protocol so that they might contain his threat but at the same time use him to further their research. Because the very fact that he'd been sent in the first place created a ticking time bomb inside Gunnar, forcing him to put pressure on Rachel and rush ahead to speed up the experiments.

They needed results. Fast. Before others like Hutchings came looking, asking more questions.

When the time came, they'd brought Frédèric here, to the clinic on Marie-Galante. He was possibly one of their best subjects. But he'd died. He'd been burned in that shack.

The body they found, the purported suicide. *Burned beyond recognition.*

"Why, Dr. Hutchings," Gunnar said. "How very clever you are."

Hutchings kept walking toward Gunnar, the gun trained on him.

"How did you do it? The body, I mean?" Gunnar asked, still fascinated. Then, he answered his own question. "Ah, the morgue, of course." Even the locals used the facility for their dead. "Norman did mention the staff here was sub par. I imagine it wouldn't even be that difficult for someone with your training to fool them."

The last time he'd seen Frédèric, he'd been a babbling idiot, just like all the others. But suddenly he stood before Gunnar in complete control of himself.

"The serum," Gunnar asked, entranced by the transformation. There was no way Frédèric could be coherent like this. Unless...

He almost laughed, that delighted with the realization. "You've been working with the serum? You've found something to counteract its effect."

"Enough to keep myself going, yes," Paul answered.

"We've called the police." The other man came forward then. Nick Travis, the corporate spy. Or so he'd led them to believe. But now Gunnar questioned even that.

"Both here and in the States the authorities are on their way," the man continued, standing next to Ana. "Right now, they're probably raiding Seacliff and the Phoenix laboratories. You're made, Gunnar. Just give it up and let her go."

They were all keeping their distance, watching him closely because he still had Rachel. In his hand, he had the syringe with the formula, his only weapon. He realized they were afraid for her. Smiling, he held the syringe to her neck.

"I'll shoot her with it, Ana," he said, addressing the weak link in the group. "There's no antidote. Giving her the serum without proper preparation, it won't precipitate an episode. It will—"

"It will kill me," Rachel said in a low flat voice. "I'll die. Just like everyone else in your life."

Rachel grabbed his hand. Before he could react, she slammed it, syringe and all, into his thigh. She looked right at him as she pushed the plunger, injecting him.

She stood and stepped away as he fell back against

the wall. He slid to the floor, losing the strength in his legs almost immediately. Even as his vision clouded, he couldn't believe what she'd done. "Rachel?"

"It ends now, Gunnar," she told him. "It stops here."

Something wasn't right. Nick could see it. How Paul was staring into space, the gun almost dangling from his hand.

"Paul?"

The minute Nick said his name, Rachel left her brother, running toward Paul. But he warded her off, the gun shaking in his hand.

"Paul?" she said.

"Stop!" He started shivering, staggering back. He turned, pointing the gun at Nick, then swiveling back to point the muzzle at Rachel. "No, don't come near me," he warned, his voice high-pitched, sounding strange.

"Paul, it's me. Rachel." She kept walking toward him slowly. "I'm not scared anymore."

"Be careful," Ana said.

Rachel was stepping closer, her arm outstretched. There was an instant when Paul's eyes met hers. He lowered his hand, and it seemed that everything would be all right.

Until he pointed the gun at himself.

"No!" Rachel screamed.

From behind him, Nick grabbed the gun. They fought over it, rolling to the floor. The gun went off.

Nick felt a sharp pain, as if his entire side were on fire. He could see Ana running, but she was moving in slow motion, almost as if she would never reach him.

Her mouth opened. She screamed.

It was strange, watching her kneeling over him, yelling at him…because he never heard a sound.

Norman Fish typed furiously, following the instructions on the screen, inputting the commands.

He'd inserted Rachel's diskette into the system. He thought he'd just look through the code, maybe find something, anything that might help him out of this mess. He'd tied a bandage around his leg, was even now chewing on a Vicodin. How handy, to be shot in a hospital. But it was difficult to concentrate with the pain.

He needed something, something to give him an out now that everything had turned to shit. But hadn't he known all along that this would not end well? How had Ana put it? He who dedicates himself to the incorrect, he will always face misfortune and just punishment or some such nonsense?

"Come on, Rachel," he said to himself, watching the computer screen. Information was power. And that's what he needed right now, a bargaining chip. Following the instructions she'd sent in her e-mail, he'd plugged in to the main server at Phoenix.

He needed that breakthrough Rachel promised. A discovery to show his colleagues so that they would know how important this research could be, that it was worth the risks he'd taken. Going to prison was one thing—no one could prove he'd known what Gunnar was doing exactly, and he'd be convicted of some white-collar crime at most—but he didn't want to be considered a criminal by the people he respected. And he knew the best defense was a strong offense.

But something strange was happening. He frowned,

staring at the screen. He'd been following the instructions sent by Rachel in her e-mail earlier this week, accessing the main server at Phoenix. It looked promising, but now, the system was changing. It was incredibly odd, how the numbers were taking off, tumbling one over the other, almost as if...

"Oh, God!" He realized then what he'd done. "Oh, Jesus, no!"

She'd hidden a virus in the program. A worm, actually. By accessing the server at Phoenix, he'd inadvertently plugged the virus into the main computer...just as she'd planned for him to do all along.

The backup server—he'd asked her about it just last week when someone at the lab had told him they'd found a problem in the system. Rachel had said she'd take care of it. Which, of course, she would have. Because she'd been planning this demise.

As he typed, trying to stop the virus from destroying everything, he watched in horror as years of work disappeared from the screen. He didn't know how to stop what he'd started. Now, no one would know about the incredible discoveries they'd made.

"Oh my God." He pushed away, panic rising inside him.

Ana was right. At long last, just punishment had found him.

I live in the jungle with the Maçu now, learning from the shaman alongside Raul. I have discovered marvelous things here. That the jungle is timeless, each day flowing into the next. That the morpho butterfly flashes more blue than the most perfect sapphire. And if you swim in the copper-colored waters and lay your hands flat then raise them to the heavens, the water will know your spirit. That even here, in the heart of darkness under trees thick with passionfruit vines, a woman can find love.

Raul and I are one of a handful of men and women who study the canopy in the rain forest in this part of the world. I love to watch him shoot his lines up into the giants, ignoring the vampire insects and venomous snakes in his quest for adventure. He harnesses up to reach the heavens, taking me there fearlessly.

With Raul, I touch the sky.

31

They had taken Nick to the hospital at Marie-Galante where, in a one-bed emergency room, the doctor arrived on a moped wearing Bermuda shorts and announced in broken English that the bullet had shattered Nick's shoulder. He would need surgery. But they weren't equipped to do that kind of repair, so they patched him up and transported him to the main hospital on Pointe-à-Pitre.

The ambulance took Nick and Ana to the ferry. As children ran up and down the aisles of the ship, the attendants lay Nick's gurney across several seats, balancing him there as he groaned in pain. They hung his IV from a potted plant just above his head. When Ana tried to find out if there was any pain medication in the IV, Nick interrupted her feeble attempts at French with a quiet "No." He'd already asked.

The entire ride he was red faced and sweating in pain. On route in the ambulance at Pointe-à-Pitre, the streets still jammed with revelers, a policeman ushered the ambulance through, guiding them in between the krewes in the Mardi Gras parade. Holding Nick's hand, she stared out the grimy windows at a row of youths in skeleton masks wearing black capes, each cracking a bullwhip overhead as they marched behind the ambulance in a funerallike procession.

They reached the hospital just before dark. Following the gurney into Emergency, Ana felt as if she'd walked into a war zone. Patients with open wounds and obvious illness toured the "churgerie," awaiting their turn. She glanced down at Nick's sheets, noticing then they were patched and stained. He didn't have a pillowcase.

When the man on the other side of the curtain began screaming, Nick grabbed her hand and said, "Get me out of here, Kimble."

She called an Air Ambulance service. They allowed her to charge the $25,000 on two credit cards, since she didn't have the credit limit on any one card. The man on the other end of the line said that was quite common.

Now she sat in a Learjet converted into a flying hospital room, exhausted from hours of dealing with doctors and police. Nick was resting peacefully, the paramedic who had come to their rescue checking his vitals. Lying there, with the soft "beep, beep" of the equipment, he reminded her of an Egyptian mummy, entombed in sheets and sleeping on the hospital bed built into the Learjet's tiny interior.

Cramped among the boxes of supplies in the back, Ana peered out at the cold night. The sky was pitch-black, making the stars look so close that she thought she could reach out and touch them through the glass. She was floating, suspended in the night. She'd grown wings.

She pressed her fingers to the window and realized that, for the first time in her life, she could recognize the constellations. Scorpio, Orion. And there, to the left, Acrux.

She smiled, tears of exhaustion in her eyes. She was going home, and there in the sky was the newest constellation she'd come to recognize.

The Southern Cross was rising.

Nick dreamed of Valerie. And, in the dream, she forgave him everything.

He figured it was the drugs, and they had some good ones because he'd never felt this mellow. Like everything would turn out okay. Or maybe it had to do with the fact that he wasn't in pain anymore, that he was finally in a clean room with cute nurses checking on him around the clock, giving him more of those wonderful drugs.

Or maybe it was just Ana.

She hadn't left his side since they'd arrived at the hospital at Newport. It turned out he needed surgery so that they could put a couple of screws in his shoulder. Ana, looking amazingly rested, was ever present. Whenever he opened his eyes, he'd find her perched on the edge of the chair in his hospital room, writing on one of those yellow pads of paper she seemed to always carry around.

She did the professor thing to the hilt, looking attentive as she listened to the doctors, acting as if she understood the medical jargon…as if she and not they were in charge. A born leader, that woman.

At some point, she asked Nick if there was someone she should call. He'd told her, "No." No one, at all. If she called in the troops, his mother and father, his sisters, he'd never get any rest. But most of all, he liked having Ana—only Ana—in charge, taking care of him.

He liked watching how she fixed his sheets and filled

his water cup with ice as soon as it melted. He liked that she plumped his pillows and made certain he got his medications on time, nagging the nurses who looked pretty overworked and acted like she was one major pain in the ass—not that Ana cared. If they didn't snap to, she went out and hunted them down. She brought him magazines from the gift shop.

And she took notes. Lots of them. Hell, she even had stuff printed out from the Internet about the surgery, highlighted for easy reference.

He liked best watching how she drilled the doctor with dumb shit questions such as, "What is your success rate?" and "How often do you do this kind of surgery?" She even interviewed the anesthesiologist. Go figure.

It was nice. Nice to sit back and let her take care of everything as he slipped in and out of consciousness, always knowing that, when he woke up, Ana would be there. She wasn't going anywhere.

She was the first person he saw when he woke up from surgery with three titanium pins drilled into his shoulder.

"You're back" was all she said. And then she smiled.

God, there was nothing in the world like that woman's smile.

He liked having her around so much that he didn't even flinch one day when, out of the blue, he was about to dig into a Salisbury steak—his first solid meal since he'd been shot—and she looked up from the skimpy salad she was picking at, meeting his eyes.

"I always thought I would never want to marry again," she said.

Just tossed it right out there, a slow lob really, making it easy for him with the gentle opener. *How about you, Nick? Ever think about that?*

"Oh, yeah?" He was staring at the steak, already feeling his gut tense up.

"I just wanted to tell you, well, the past few weeks. I don't know how to explain, but you've made me feel…otherwise."

He grinned. The woman was something. "Otherwise?"

"I'm in love with you, Nick."

He put down the fork. "You want to talk about Valerie," he said, knowing where this was heading.

"And you don't. I understand."

"But I've seen how you are with the doctor and nurses, Kimble, how you work them over. You're like a bulldog. You're not leaving me alone until you get the whole story."

"That is absolutely not true, Nick. You do not have to talk to me about your wife."

"See what I mean? There you go again. There's a word for you. I want to get it just right, because I know that sort of thing is your life. Relentless? Nah, that sounds kind of harsh. Tenacious? That's better, don't you think?"

She didn't respond. He knew he hadn't given her much of a chance, painting her into that silent corner.

But the professor was smart. She could always find an out. She just reached for her bag and stood. "I just wanted you to know how I feel. I thought it was…important. I'll be back tomorrow morning."

When she reached the door, he said, "When we first got married, we were working at the NSA." He saw Ana stop, her hand on the knob. "Not like you think, not like the stuff on television. Valerie and I were language experts, looking over foreign newspapers and magazines, searching for hidden messages, codes. Are you going to sit down, Kimble, because it's pretty rude making me talk to your back."

She stood there for the longest time. He thought maybe she might just walk out, that bit about her being relentless pushing her over the edge.

Instead, she turned and walked casually back to the chair as if it were nothing. Putting her bag on the floor, she sat and folded her hands on her lap. He could see that her breathing was short and shallow, but you didn't need intelligence training to read the professor. That face of hers.

"Valerie was really good at what we did," he said, continuing the story as if he'd never stopped.

He hadn't really figured out why he had to talk about Valerie, just blurting it out. He felt as if maybe there was this block wall inside him with Valerie's name painted all over it like graffiti, covering every inch. Maybe he needed to get past that wall. Because if he didn't—if he couldn't—Ana might walk out that door and never look back.

"Me? I got a little bored with the work," he said. "Started trying to see if I couldn't climb my way up the ranks, staying late, making a good impression."

"I assume it didn't take you long." She looked as if she was sitting through a job interview, adding a helpful comment here to make sure he knew she was paying attention. She was pretending to be relaxed, but he'd never seen her more tense.

"Oh, yeah. I was practically running the whole damn team by the time I figured out I had ruined my marriage.

Valerie was going to leave me. There was someone else."

He could see he'd surprised her. Just like when she'd told him about that asshole husband of hers cheating on her. Ana was having the same reaction. Who would ever think he wasn't enough?

"It's complicated." Because his situation wouldn't be anything like the breakup of Ana's marriage. Ana would have given one hundred and ten percent to that damn idiot she'd married, while Nick had given it all to his work.

"Valerie wanted kids, so I thought if I could get the job-security thing out of the way, then we'd get down to the family part. I was looking forward to early retirement, plenty of time on my hands to coach soccer and Little League. Valerie saw things differently."

"That happens a lot, Nick."

"Yeah. Sure. A lot of men are boneheads. The amazing part? I didn't figure it out. I mean, here I was with all this intelligence training and I never saw it coming, never even suspected I'd made my wife so unhappy that some other man could slip into her life, make her think it was time to move on."

Kind of what he thought Ana might be doing when she'd moved to the door just a minute ago. It had given him a jolt, seeing her hand on that door with her shoulders stiff.

Funny thing, he couldn't remember seeing her turn her back on him before. He was sure she'd done it—she'd been in and out of the room a hundred times—he just couldn't remember. But for a second there, just before he started talking about Valerie, he'd thought that image might be burned into his memory. Ana's back as she walked out the door forever.

"Suddenly, I'm this guy who's dedicated to his job twenty-four-seven, you know?" he said, getting past that lump in his throat. "You see, Valerie figured I wasn't going to be around for Little League, much less the happy marriage portion of the program. I begged her to give me another chance. The night she was killed, we were meeting for dinner to talk it over."

She closed her eyes. He hadn't made it easy, just saying it like that. Maybe she'd thought it wouldn't be something so bad. But there it was...worst-case scenario.

"You blame yourself," she said when she could look at him again.

"I was waiting at the restaurant. I had my arguments all lined up. Man, I was willing to do just about anything to get her back—only she didn't show up. Because, she was dead."

He kept wondering how it could still hurt. Three years and it hurt as if he'd lost her yesterday.

"So you see, there wasn't going to be any second chance," he said. "I wouldn't be able to convince her that I could make things right again. We weren't going to have those kids she wanted. There was, in fact, nothing. Nothing I could say, nothing I could do."

"I am...so *sorry*, Nick."

"These things happen."

"But they shouldn't."

He could hear in her voice that she wanted to cry. He hated that he'd put that look on her face, that there was more.

"I don't blame myself the way you're thinking. I wasn't responsible for her death. But Ana," he said, "I was very much responsible for her unhappiness."

He could see he'd left her speechless. The professor wasn't glib. She wasn't going to throw any platitudes.

"So her death," he said, again searching for the right way to tell her, so that she would understand. "My guilt doesn't have to do with my wife being in the wrong place at the wrong time. Not like you think. It goes all the way back. To knowing that Paul would have put her first. Always. That he would have given her kids, come home early, would have loved her better, made her happier. Well, there's just a hell of a lot of baggage there, Professor."

Ana was shaking her head. "You can't know that's true. This happily-ever-after you've imagined for Paul and Valerie. Marriage is never easy."

He looked away, thinking that he did know. Because that's the kind of man Paul had always been.

Setting aside the Salisbury steak, which was cold now anyway, he was trying to tell Ana how he couldn't go to that place inside himself. He couldn't live through all of that again, couldn't care for someone like he had Valerie.

But here was Ana, daring him to do just that. Get back on that wagon? Love again? Which is why he'd told the story. So she could understand just how scared he really was.

But Ana, she could never follow the script.

"Nick, I don't know you that well," she said, this soft, sweet look on her face showing everything she felt for him. "In fact, I hardly know you at all. But I've spent my whole life being careful. And you're the first person who just made me...feel—"

"Ana."

"And I needed to tell you about those feelings. Even

if they aren't reciprocated. I love you, Nick. And that is so freeing to me, to just be able to admit it and believe in it. Not to question myself or try to analyze if it's right or wrong."

"Ana, you are an amazing woman."

"Perhaps. But you may never be able to discover just how amazing...and you don't know how well I understand your fear. But what happened with Valerie. Do you really think that if she'd stayed with Paul she wouldn't have died? That somehow, being with you—choosing you—put her there in the path of that car?"

"Everything we do influences people."

"That's right. So go ahead and isolate yourself." She stood, watching him as if she were memorizing everything about him. "Because now Paul is safe, back with his family. The world has balance again. You took something from him, and now you've given back. Mission accomplished."

"Where are you going?" he asked, afraid of her answer.

"The doctors say you'll make a fine recovery. You don't need me around watching you day and night."

"I might have a different opinion on that."

But she already had her hand on the knob. "I'll be back, Nick. Tomorrow. But there are a couple of things I need to take care of first."

He didn't believe her. There was something in the way she looked at him. She was making his heart go a mile a minute. She was walking out the door and what he feared most at that moment was that she'd never come back.

"Ana," he said, "what are you going to do?"

She thought about it a minute, as if maybe the question was complicated. Something that required careful analysis, the professor thing again.

"I'm going to finish my book," she said. "It needs a good ending, and I have to work very hard to come up with just the right one. Perhaps you could think about that, Nick," she told him, "working for that happy ending."

And just like that, she was gone.

32

Rachel sat in a crazy sterile room. It reminded her of a movie set, or one of those showrooms where they sold furniture. There were a couple of chairs, and a desk with a lamp in the corner, a sofa and coffee table, but no pictures on the walls. Everything looked fake because nobody really lived there.

The guys who brought her called it a safehouse, which she thought was a hoot. She didn't feel particularly safe.

She figured they were in D.C. somewhere, though she wasn't sure. They'd taken her into custody on the island. Paul had told her it was going to be okay, that she should go with the agents they'd sent to pick her up. Ana had already taken Nick to the hospital, so it was just her and Paul and the bad guys to clean up.

They'd used handcuffs and everything. But she wasn't scared. She wasn't sure if she'd ever be scared again. She felt like the room. Sterile, fake. *Nobody living here…*

But then the door opened and she stood, seeing that it was Paul—and there was this rush of emotion. Like an ocean of it. Her throat got all tight, and she thought she might burst into tears, which was crazy because just a second ago she'd felt so empty and dead.

She ran to him and threw herself at him, hugging him, she was that glad to see him. And then she did start crying, hugging him harder even though he kept his hands at his sides.

She didn't know how long they stood there. But at some point, Paul brought his arms up and held her and she fell into that ocean again, sobbing like a baby.

He'd told her that he worked for the government. Some sort of branch of Interpol looking into illegal use of technology. He wasn't a spy or anything, but he knew a lot about the kind of thing she was doing, and he'd had some basic training in intelligence because he'd tested high on some test when he'd first joined the army, so he'd been considered for that kind of stuff. The army had put him through school before he decided he wasn't particularly interested in making the military his career.

He'd been working for a company in Texas when they'd contacted him for a "mission." That's what she thought he'd called it, anyway.

Only, someone at Phoenix figured out what he was doing, so Gunnar made him one of his "volunteers." Once they started him with the serum, he lost it. By the time he escaped, faking his death with one of the bodies from the morgue at the clinic, he was beyond rational thought, focused now on finding Rachel and stopping her—whatever the cost. He'd even fooled the people he was working for, making them think he was okay and on the job so they would leave him alone. But when his family became worried, they sent his friend, the one who'd been trailing her and Ana.

"Are you going to be okay?" she asked, brushing back the tears. "I mean, you work for the government, right? So they can help you now? Find a way to reverse the effects of the serum?"

"They're working on something."

He took her hand and led her back to the couch. He seemed really different now. His face wasn't so sunken with pain. And his eyes, they'd always been clear, almost colorless, but she could see now that they were this really pretty light blue.

He sat her down, then brought over one of the chairs to sit in front of her.

"You look…well, you look really good," she said.

He smiled. She realized she hadn't seen him do that a lot. "They cleaned me up."

"And fed you."

"Yup. That, too."

She remembered how scared he'd always made her. But now, he looked almost kind. "The headaches?"

"Apparently, I wasn't doing so bad with the antidote, though we have a long way to go still."

She was trying to figure out what he meant by "we." Was he talking about the government guys?

She didn't want to make too big a deal about it in her head, didn't want to fool herself into thinking that she could be a part of things still. But when he'd said it—we—he'd been looking at her as if he'd meant just that. Like she could be part of the solution.

"My state of mind made it difficult to take care of myself." He nodded toward the door where he'd entered. "Now I have someone doing that round the clock. He's right outside, waiting."

"That's good."

"They found someone else at the clinic. A girl. She'd been shot, but they patched her up and airlifted her here." He took her hand and squeezed it. "She's going to make it."

"Lynn Stratford," she said, staring at his hand. He seemed almost normal now, sitting there in front of her. "I found her name in our computer system at Phoenix before I left for Guadeloupe." Paul had sent her the name, another one of those notes with the letters clipped out of a magazine. "That's when I started to believe you might be telling the truth, when I found that file."

"That's why I told you about Lynn," he said. "Sometimes, I could actually think clearly. But if I hadn't been under the influence of the serum, I would have done things a lot differently."

She nodded. "I guess I wasn't thinking so clearly, either." She bit her lip, looking up at him. She didn't want to make excuses, but she told him, "I really didn't know what they were doing."

"I realize that now."

She didn't want him to hate her. She was still clutching his hand. "I thought all that Youthful Brain stuff was about keeping people from getting Alzheimer's. Norman said the data I was getting came from the clinic and I just assumed animal trials or some other computer simulation on the other end. I would use the information to write code for Neuro-Sys, make it better, more like what might happen in the brain. Then I would tell the researchers at the clinic how to tweak the serum."

They sat there for a while, neither of them saying anything. She wondered how long she'd have before the guys came back and took her away. But she was glad Paul had come to say goodbye.

"I'm supposed to ask you some things," he said, looking up.

"Oh. Of course." She sat up straighter, letting go of his hand. "This is like one of those debriefings, right? Before I go to jail, I have to tell you everything I know."

"Rachel, you're not going to jail. That's all been taken care of."

He was watching her now with those clear eyes of his. He didn't seem…what was the word? So tortured. The whole time she'd been with him, he'd always been fighting these demons inside his head. But she could see there was something there still. Some fear.

"It's about Gunnar," he said. "We weren't able to save him. Do you understand?"

She sat back. "I killed him."

"No, he's not dead. But he's nonresponsive. The best I can compare his condition to is autism. He's gone, and we may never get him back. But you have to understand, whatever you did, he forced your hand. You acted in self-defense."

She shook her head. "No. I wasn't defending myself."

"From where I was standing—"

"I wasn't defending myself," she said, trying to figure out the right way to tell him. To explain. "I was angry. I *wanted* to hurt him."

Paul pressed his hand to hers again. "In self-defense."

"You know he was obsessed with me. Because I looked like my mother. He was in love with her. They were like having this affair."

There. She'd said it out loud. So that someone else knew.

"I used to hate how much I looked like her, you know? That's why I dyed my hair and wore the contacts.

I wanted to look nothing like her. I mean, here's my father, Javier, avoiding me because I look like my mother. But Gunnar." She shook her head, still not quite believing it. "He took care of me all those years because I reminded him of the woman he loved. That's pretty twisted, huh?" she said, wiping away her tears, refusing to cry anymore.

She'd been thinking about Gunnar a lot since they'd left the island. She was supposed to be this really smart person, but there was so much she hadn't put together. The stuff about the clinic, her father being dead.

"In this really weird way, my brother raised me just like I was his own kid," she said, looking up. "And I basically killed him, like some horrible Greek tragedy."

"He wouldn't have hesitated to inject you, Rachel."

"He wasn't going to give me the serum, Paul." Because he didn't know—he couldn't understand. He'd seen this bad guy who could hurt people so he believed she'd been in some sort of danger. That what she'd done had been necessary somehow. "He was just trying to scare me."

"You can't be certain of that."

But she knew. In her heart, she knew. "He was in love with Beatrice. He was having an affair with her. And I was that last little piece of her." She frowned, thinking about that, knowing the truth. "He couldn't kill me. It would be like losing Beatrice all over again."

"I can see that's what you believe. But in my opinion, you couldn't be more wrong. He wanted to control you, and he failed. You proved yourself a threat. There's no way he could trust you again. And eventually, he'd figure that out, that one day, when he wasn't looking, you'd do something to hurt him again, to bring down his kingdom."

The way he said it, there was no equivocating. He just knew he was telling the truth and that his version of the facts made more sense, and it did, even to her, suddenly putting that weird love of her brother's into a different light, making her wonder.

"I don't know," she said. "Maybe." But even the possibility made her feel as if this big weight were being lifted off her chest.

She shook her head, marveling at how different Paul was now, so calm and sure of himself. Even his voice sounded different. The whole time he'd been in the shack, his voice—every gesture—had seemed tense, edgy. Now he appeared almost placid.

"They're giving you something to sedate you, aren't they?"

He smiled really big this time. "Actually, it's part of the therapy. It helps with the attacks. They're brought on by strong emotion."

She nodded, because that went along with the research she'd been doing. "Why are you smiling?"

"Because before I turned into the insane Frenchman, Frédèric, rogue government agent hunting you down, *this* is who I was. Sedate. Dull." He stared at her, looking completely serious. "I'm a very boring guy, Rachel."

She frowned, but then she got it. That weird sense of humor of his. "I don't believe you could ever be boring."

He seemed to think about that. "Well, we'll just see about that."

Again the idea that it wasn't over yet. That he might be hanging around.

"Okay, maybe you're right. Maybe Gunnar would

have injected me with the serum. But that's not what I believed at the time. I told Gunnar," she whispered; "that I thought Beatrice killed herself to get away from him." Because she wanted Paul to know the whole truth. If they did work together, if he needed her help for the antidote even though he had all these government resources, she wanted him to know exactly who she was.

"I guess," she told him, "I needed to get away, too."

He was silent for a long time, but she knew he understood. He was just searching for the right thing to say to make her feel better when nothing ever could. Because she'd killed her brother, pretty much the only person other than Ana who had loved her, even if that love was horribly wrong.

When she thought about that, it seemed so strange. How she'd been scared of Paul because he was "stalking" her, leaving her these threatening notes. But all along, the bad guy—the man truly obsessed—had been right there beside her. She'd been living under his roof.

"I don't know how I'm going to tell Magda or Jules," she said. "I wonder if they'll hate me for what I did…or if somewhere inside they might feel a little like I do. As if now suddenly they can breathe again." She shook her head. "But that's not right, is it? I'm just projecting my own feelings. He was good to his family. They're going to miss him." Father, husband.

"I'm not a priest," Paul told her. "I can't make any of this right for you. But I will say this, Rachel—and please, forgive me for sounding so cold—Gunnar Maza got exactly what he deserved."

But she didn't want to talk about that, the idea of justice, that she could claim some sort of "right" here. "And my father. I mean, Javier. Do you know how he died?"

"He didn't suffer," he told her. "Gunnar made certain of that, at least."

She could see he wasn't going to say anything more, and she was okay with that. In fact, she didn't want to know. Maybe that was weak or foolish, but she didn't think she could bear the weight of one more piece of this tragedy.

She remembered then something Gunnar used to always say. That she should be strong. He'd been trying to make her into this new Beatrice, a stronger version of the woman he loved, which was probably the closest he'd been to acting like a father. But he hadn't succeeded. She felt fragile and stupid, unable, after all, to cope.

"He was always talking about my legacy," she said, thinking out loud. "That I should make my father proud. I always thought he meant Javier. But I think he was talking about himself. He wasn't my father—not really—but somehow he always acted like I was his creation."

She hated that most of all, how well he'd been able to control her.

"Hey, I know this is tough," he told her. "It's going to take time. And help. Maybe a lot of help. But, Rachel, you will get through this."

And the way he said it, he was almost challenging her. *If I can live through what I have...*

"So here's the deal," he said. "I think you already know that the serum wasn't accessing genetic memories."

She nodded. "Yeah. When I took Lynn's file and read what they were doing with the memories, I started looking stuff up on the Internet about hypnosis and memory. The whole procedure was tainted. Those memories weren't any more real than 'recovered' memories, the kind they stopped using in criminal trials because the process became suspect. There was too much human intervention."

"Exactly. The people they recruited—even me—they searched through their backgrounds and discovered interesting links to the past. The doctor in charge started overreaching, suggesting during hypnosis who they were looking for inside these people's heads. Putting the knowledge there. The serum did the rest, making it all seem real."

"I just hope that you and the woman, Lynn—" she met his gaze "—are going to be okay."

He nodded, looking really sure. She realized that's what she'd come to rely on with Paul. Because he'd been so stubborn, making her realize what was going on, making her face her actions, not play the detached scientist. He'd never given up, finding his way even when the serum had him half out of his mind, because inside he was this really strong man.

She thought of him as *solid.* That was the word that described him best. Which didn't make sense because most of the time she'd known him he'd been just plain crazy.

"Rachel, the government is very interested in Neuro-Sys," he said. "They think it has real potential. Only, all the files at Phoenix have been cleansed by some sort of virus. And someone—I assume it was you—destroyed the backups."

She nodded. "I had access to everything. Right before I left, I made sure there wouldn't be anything available to the company. But the data isn't gone. Fish never really did know that much about computers. I mean, he knew how to use them for research, but the real sophisticated stuff—no way. I gave him a diskette and e-mailed him instructions on how to access the main server at Phoenix once he got the diskette. That's what activated the virus. Only, it really wasn't a virus. The program just moved stuff, sending it in a package through e-mail to me. Like having my own little Swiss bank account, only it's data, not money. I'll show you how to access the files. It's pretty easy, actually. You probably would have figured it out."

He got this thoughtful expression. "I'm not so sure. You're pretty good at what you do."

"I want to be better," she told him. "I want to help with the antidote. I want to fix everything, or what I can, anyway. Maybe find all the victims. Tell their families what happened and how it's my fault. Set up some kind of fund. When I turn twenty-one, I'm supposed to get all this money." She was talking really fast. "I think it should all go to that. All of it—"

"Listen to me. Only three people died, your father and two of his loyal researchers. And they knew the risks."

She closed her eyes. "There were other people at the clinic."

"Yes. At Marie-Galante. Seacliff. But we stopped Gunnar in time and they can be helped." He picked up her hand and this time, he didn't let go until she opened her eyes and looked at him again. "Like me."

She nodded, biting her lip. "I know what you're trying to do. But you can't. I'm not off the hook. I mean, you were right all along. It's my fault. Gunnar couldn't have done any of this stuff without me—"

"Rachel, I know what you're going through is difficult. But you're young, and you have to give yourself a chance."

He looked as if he were going to say something else. She waited, because she wanted him to have the answers. She wanted something to make her feel better. Or maybe she just wanted him to stay a little longer…to be kind for a minute or two more.

"I lost someone once," he told her. After a minute, he continued, "Someone very dear to me. I know it hurts, a pain that can't go away so you wake up each day and remember and wish that maybe you hadn't woken up that day at all."

She thought it was strange how he could put into words exactly how she felt. How she couldn't quite catch her breath. And every morning, she didn't want to get out of bed. She thought maybe he did understand, because he'd put into words the emotions she couldn't describe.

"This past year, what I was doing," he said, "I almost lost myself. I almost killed you. I planned it…I lived for the day I could make it happen, relishing it."

"But that was *my* fault. I did that to you—"

"And Gunnar did the same to you. Maybe he didn't use a drug or hypnosis, but he used you. And someday, you'll make peace with that, the idea that you don't have to wear your guilt like some hair shirt, that you can get beyond those feelings you want to drown in right now. Sometimes, Rachel, we just have to forgive. To let go." And then he told her very quietly, "Let go, Rachel. Just let go."

"You make it sound like it's this simple thing, forgiveness."

"No," he said, shaking his head. "It's the most difficult thing you'll ever do. I had to forgive someone once, and he came and found me, and he saved my life. And I don't want to make that sound like some metaphor for anything, but I think it just might be."

She was watching him, the way he was talking, how eloquent he sounded. It was like meeting him for the first time. "I don't know very much about you, do I?"

He smiled. He had slightly crooked teeth. And dimples. He had dimples. She'd never noticed his dimples.

He held out his hand for her to shake. "Hello. My name is Paul Hutchings, and I'd like you to come work for me."

She stared at his hand, shaking her head because she found herself smiling. He'd always had the funkiest sense of humor.

She took his hand and shook it. "I think I'd like that, Paul. Very much."

"What are you thinking, *mi amor?*"

Ana turned from the window to take the demitasse of espresso her mother handed her. She smiled and answered, "I was thinking about illusions."

"Well, now," her mother said, sitting on the sofa, patting the cushion next to her. "This sounds very interesting."

"Maybe what I mean is delusions." She sat next to her mother, leaning back to rest her head on Isela's shoulder.

Her mother frowned. "I like illusions much better. You tell me of those."

Ana sighed. "This one is about a man, *Mami.*"

"Ah," her mother said knowingly, putting down her coffee cup. "Then we are back to delusions."

Ana snuggled into her mother's arms. Her mother could always make her smile.

"The first time I saw him," she said, thinking back to that night at the airport diner, "I made these assumptions. Because of the way he looked and dressed, how he spoke. He acted…fascinated by my brilliance and that was so intoxicating," she said, remembering.

She wondered if that weren't the draw from the beginning, that singular focus of his. How he could look at her and make her believe there was nowhere else he'd rather be. But she knew somehow those feelings went much deeper, that if the camera lens were turned on her, she would be watching him with the same intensity and desire, as if something inside her had tapped her on the shoulder to say Pay attention—he's the one.

"He called me 'Professor' and poked fun at me, saying I was an intellectual snob. He hung on my every word. And I loved that, thinking that I was smarter, somehow better. After all these years of Norman making me feel as if I weren't enough, I adored for once feeling superior. So I didn't look beyond the obvious. Didn't question inconsistencies."

Her mother put down the coffee cup. "Why do I think I am not going to like this story."

She glanced at her mother. "Because you know it's going to end with a broken heart."

"*¿Qué pasó?*" Speaking now in Spanish. As if such a confession required a change in language.

"I don't know. I mean, I'm not really sure what happened. I think he was just so different than any man I had ever met, and—and I couldn't take my eyes off him, not from that first moment. He showed me the most amazing things, *Mami*. This wonderful burst of light called the green flash, right at sunset, and water that lights up so that you see yourself swimming in stars even though they're still in the sky where God put them."

"Anita," her mother said, turning to look at her daughter. "You sound like a woman in love."

She closed her eyes. "Yes, I do, don't I?"

"This man? He is your illusion?"

She shook her head. "No. Oh, no. He's very real. Very strong. Grounded. Someone who has lived through a great tragedy, so that his spirit shines with the wisdom of surviving that kind of pain." She could feel tears filling her eyes. "He…he's actually quite wonderful."

"Then why are you crying, *mi amor?*"

"Because I think I am the illusion. I lived my life through books all these years because I was too scared of experiencing what was real. I fantasized instead. And the illusion I want now, *Mami,* to live happily ever after with this man." She shook her head. "What if it's just that? Another pretty picture in my head."

"He doesn't love you?"

She hadn't seen Nick for three days. After she'd left the hospital, telling him she'd return, she hadn't found the courage to go back, after all. Suddenly that resistance she had felt from him had a name. Valerie.

"He loves his wife. A woman who died. How can I ever compete with that?" she asked.

"*Ay, mi amor.*" Her mother hugged her. She didn't say another word. She didn't need to.

They spent the rest of the afternoon talking about Ana's book and how excited Isela was about her daughter's "great talent." In Isela's opinion, Ana had finally followed her heart, listening to that voice inside her. The writer's voice. She claimed that Ana had taken a great burden off her mother, who believed Ana had avoided her natural talents because of Isela.

Of course, her mother had a few "suggestions," but she was proud of Ana's book and wanted to show it to her editor. Ana refused, knowing full well that her mother's literary publisher wouldn't be interested in the adventure novel she'd written. But it was comforting, how genuinely proud her mother was of her.

When Ana walked her mother to the door, kissing her goodbye, Isela held on just a little longer.

She whispered in her ear, "Ana. Love is an illusion. You just need to believe."

And then she walked out, letting her daughter contemplate where she might find the faith to do just that.

33

Nick was standing in the shade of a myrtle tree. He liked this spot and came here often. He'd just cleaned the leaves off the marble and set a single rose in a special vase built into the ground. He was standing in front of Valerie's grave, but he was thinking about Ana.

"She said she'd come back," he told Valerie. "Tomorrow, she said. She was very specific. She didn't say 'soon' or 'in a while' or 'when you're feeling up to another visit.' She said tomorrow. But that was a couple of days ago. She didn't come back."

His arm was in a sling. A taxi waited by the curb.

"I kind of expected the professor to keep her word. She's very precise. Businesslike, even. And she's no liar."

He crouched, putting his hand on the stone, his fingers pressing into the cut letters. He remembered asking Ana if she'd done that—touched the inscriptions at Palenque.

That last day at the hospital, he'd wanted Ana to understand why he was holding back. He didn't want Ana to think it was her, not when she was this amazing person. And he knew that ass of an ex-husband had done a number on her.

He'd wanted to make sure she knew it was about him. His problems.

"I guess she figured it out, Val. Stupid me, huh? Clueing her in."

Always trying to think ten steps ahead, examining all the options. But the truth was, he'd had this one chance with Ana, and he'd been too screwed up to take it.

The first place he'd gone after the hospital was to her house. Man, he'd been pissed. She'd left him. Just like that. She'd given up. First she gets him used to her being around—the first person he'd see when he woke up, the last one there when he fell asleep— and then she walks out. Oh sure, he was good and pissed.

He'd never gotten out of the cab when he reached her house. Instead, he'd come here. To see Valerie.

He'd known all along Ana wanted a happy ending. He couldn't blame her now if she didn't want all the baggage he'd brought along dumped in her life. She was probably right to give him some space to work out his issues first. Still he'd been hoping they could work on those together.

And now, he wasn't so sure she'd want him at all.

"What if I screw up again, Val?" he whispered. "And what about you? If you're not the love of my life, if I have someone else? It feels like I'm letting you die all over again. If you're not the first thing I think about in the morning, my last thought before going to bed at night? Who keeps you alive if not me?"

But he knew the answer to his own questions…knew that Paul had been right all along.

Valerie would never want him to die with her.

* * *

Ana opened the door to find Nick, his arm in a sling, waiting for her, a taxi speeding off from the curb, heading down the street.

"Nick, what are you doing here?" she asked, staring at him with this wonder in her eyes.

"What the hell do you think I'm doing, Kimble?" he asked, suddenly angry again. Like she'd flipped this switch inside him and he couldn't contain the emotions any longer. "You gave up on us."

She shook her head. "What are you talking about?"

"So you just have amazing sex with a guy and that's it. You walk away?"

She seemed to think about that. "The sex was…it was good."

He waited. He thought he'd give her a minute.

"It was amazing, Nick," she admitted. "We were perfect. But I never thought I was the one walking away."

Okay. That sounded like as good an opening as he was going to get. Taking her hand, he stepped inside and closed the door. He walked her over to the couch and sat her down.

He didn't sit. He paced.

"I have a list," he told her. "Don't worry, I'm not going to pull out a piece of paper and start reading. It's in my head, this list."

"Okay."

"Number one. I am always going to be afraid. If you're late coming home—if you don't call to give me the heads-up that you're stuck in traffic or the meeting went longer than expected—I'll be thinking that you're gone. That you're dead. And when you walk in the door, all happy to see me, maybe a bottle of wine tucked under your arm for a special dinner, I'll bite your head off. I won't mean to. But I'll do it. I'll do it because I'll be that scared, and once I see you're okay, I'll be pissed."

"I understand," she said.

"Number two. If you think I'm bad now, wait until we have kids. Hell, I would have been irrational even before Valerie died, but now…forget it."

"You want kids?"

"I want kids." And when she was going to say something else, he stopped pacing and held up his hand for silence. "I told you, Kimble. I have a list." She sat back.

"I believe you left off at number three," she told him. You had to hand it to the professor. She wasn't easily intimidated.

"Number three," he said, pacing again. "I get lost in my work. And that's where it all went wrong for Val and me. I don't mean to, but I'll be working on a program or get this idea, and the next thing I know, it's like three in the morning—"

"Home office."

He stopped pacing and he turned to look at her. "That's not a bad idea, Kimble."

"Thank you."

"But I travel. A lot."

"I'll go with you. At least until the kids are in school. You should probably cut back on traveling by then."

He sat next to her on the couch. "I get insomnia sometimes. And I snore like a bear—"

She kissed him, shutting him up. It felt incredible, that kiss. As if they'd never have a problem in the world.

When she finished, she opened her eyes and brushed the hair from his forehead. "I'm not going to let you disappear, Nick. I promise. I'll be there every day, right there beside you. Now, what's number four?"

"I don't know," he said. "You're very distracting, Kimble."

"Do you want to hear my fear, Nick? I only have one. But it's a big one. In all the great literature about lost love, well, Valerie, she's in your heart forever."

"And you think there isn't enough room in there for the both of you?"

She rested her forehead against his. "For love, yes. But not for all the guilt that comes with it."

He didn't even know where to start. But he knew it was important that he get it straight. Not because he wasn't going to get another chance. No way. He was going to keep at the professor. Wear her down until she realized that she needed him just as much as he needed her.

"When you lose someone, you look for ways to keep them alive. I guess I thought that as long as I was alone—when there wasn't anyone else—Valerie was very much alive. Then, when you walked out of the hospital, I felt like I was losing her all over again."

"And how do we fix that?"

He figured that was progress, that all-important word "we." The professor didn't just throw out pronouns as if it was nothing.

"Well, I've been thinking about it. And I came up with a couple of things. Maybe set up some sort of memorial fund. Or get involved with MADD. And I made an appointment to talk to someone. For grief counseling."

She was looking at him as if she could see deep inside to his doubts and his fears. That a part of him thought he was wrong—that he should keep being a martyr, that he deserved just that for letting Valerie die. Afraid that Ana would think he wasn't ready. But he wanted to be, and he thought that should count for something.

"When I was in the hospital," he said quietly, "you were always there, sitting in the chair. If I needed anything, before I even thought about it, there you were, calling the nurse or going down to the gift shop. And then, suddenly, you were gone. Like you didn't think I needed you anymore. So I thought you were right. Moving on." He shook his head. "And I can't. Move on, that is. I just can't go back to things before you. I don't want to work, I can't concentrate. Kimble, I can't *move*. I could only move here. To find you."

She bit her lip, but he could see she wanted him just as much as he did her. And why couldn't that be enough?

"Hey," he said. "What would happen in one of those books you write. The delusional novels?"

She smiled. "*Novela telúricas* are usually quite tragic."

"Then skip it. Skip all the mental anguish of figuring it out. Let's just do it, Ana. Write our own happy ending?"

She smiled that amazing smile of hers. She looked like a kid when she smiled, as if she didn't have a worry in the world, making him believe that she was right. No worries.

"I'd like that, Nick," she said, keeping it simple. "Very much."

34

It didn't take long to bring the villains to justice.
It wasn't even difficult once I pointed the authorities in the right direction. Mystics, Inc. it would
seem hadn't quite dotted its I's or crossed those
all-important T's for the Internal Revenue Service. I understand Nieman Trout and Guzman
Mata had been convicted on several counts of
federal tax evasion.

Even when Guzman and Nieman are free, Mystics will never find me, I've made certain of that,
living in the jungle as I do. Someday, I plan to do
great things again. Find the cure for cancer or
solve the problem of the burnings that continue to
plague the region. But in the meantime, I am content to learn whatever wisdom the jungle might
teach me. I believe I was led here for a purpose
and each trial I survive brings me closer to that
purpose. My struggle is a better one now, to make
things work with Raul and have a happy life together. And perhaps, eventually, one day save the
world from itself.

For you see, the jungle is in my blood now and

*it is not the demon I once feared. It has become
instead my savior.*

Nick put down the manuscript. "It's a hell of a book,
Professor. I mean, you really nailed it."

She smiled, trying to pretend her heart wasn't beating out of her chest. They had been together almost ten
months now. A long time, and no time at all. Nick had
moved in with her, something her father still disap-
proved of. *No one gets married these days?*

Ana picked up the manuscript. She'd stayed up three
nights straight finishing her book, unable to do anything
else, as if she were possessed.

She'd felt a bit like Carpentier's hero. By surviving
the many trials she'd faced back in The Saints, she was
no longer bound by the pounding rhythm of the Galley
Master's mallet—her mother's wonderful talent. She
had come home to set her own pace and discovered that
she loved writing fiction. And now, she'd even found a
publisher.

She'd skated close to the truth in the book. Norman
had received fifteen years, though not for federal tax
evasion. His crimes had been a bit more complex, involving a felonious disregard for life and misuse of
technology. She had hoped the prosecutor could prove
murder, but these days, money could buy an innocent
man's defense.

As for Gunnar, he'd been determined incompetent to
stand trial, incarcerated at a hospital for the mentally
impaired, a victim of his own serum.

"But I was thinking," Nick said. "I mean, if you
don't mind some input here. Don't you think you could
maybe work in a little more action? Juice it up a bit?

And that dumb-shit Nieman, yeah, you nailed him. But the hero. I don't know, Ana. You could have made him maybe…taller? He sounds short, you know? And you could add a few more scenes where he gets to strut his stuff. You have to admit, the guy was kind of a wimp sometimes. You wouldn't want the reader to get the wrong idea."

"Hmm," she said, finding such noncommittal responses best when it came to Nick's input.

"I was thinking." He pulled her on his lap. He'd healed nicely from the surgery, although he claimed his shoulder could predict the weather. "Being in your books," he said, "I mean, it's tricky. Because I was him, right? The Raul guy?"

"You might have inspired a few scenes."

"And if we have a fight or something and you think I'm a jerk for a day, you could write it up? And then it's in print for everybody to read and think about. And, since you're always going to be modeling all your heroes after me—"

"And maybe a villain, or two."

"Well. I don't know. Just sort of makes it all more… public than I'm used to."

She tried to imagine how it would feel to move from the intelligence community to the world of mass-market fiction. "It could be a problem, I admit. From your perspective."

He took in her expression. "And get used to it?"

"Let's just say, it's part of the hazards of being involved with a writer."

"Yeah, okay," he said, taking it in stride, which was how Nick did most things these days. He'd learned a lot about what was important. They both had.

"So," he said, "now that your book is going to get published, what are you going to call it?" He reached over and picked up the cover sheet for the manuscript. "Because, I don't know how to break it to you, Kimble, but what you got here? *A Novel?* Well, that ain't gonna fly."

She smiled, taking the sheet of paper away from him and putting it back on the table. Sitting with Nick, planning a future with him, she remembered that first moment, when she'd let him kiss her despite all the warning bells going off in her head. How, for once in her life, she'd allowed herself the freedom to just get caught up in the heat of the moment. That after years of searching for a soul mate, of living with the idea of love lost, what an easy thing love had become.

"Maybe it's a little like life," she said. "Sometimes you just have to let go," she whispered, kissing him again, "and trust the process."

NEW YORK TIMES BESTSELLING AUTHOR

HEATHER GRAHAM

Toni Fraser and her friends have hit on the ultimate
moneymaking plan. Turn an ancient run-down Scottish
castle into a tourist destination complete with a reenactment
combining fact and fiction, local history, murder and an
imaginary laird named Bruce MacNiall.

So when the castle's actual owner—a tall, dark and formidable
Scot who shares Bruce MacNiall's name—comes charging in,
Toni is stunned...because he seems eerily familiar. And when
the group is drawn into a real-life murder mystery, Toni is
plagued with sinister lifelike dreams in which she sees
through the eyes of a killer....

THE
PRESENCE

"Graham has crafted a fine paranormal romance
with a strong mystery plot and a vibrant setting."
—*Booklist* on *Haunted*

*Available the first week of September 2004,
wherever paperbacks are sold.*

The *New York Times* bestselling author of
16 Lighthouse Road and *311 Pelican Court*
welcomes you back to Cedar Cove,
where life and love is anything but ordinary!

DEBBIE MACOMBER

Dear Reader,

I love living in Cedar Cove, but things just haven't been the same since Max Russell died in our B and B. We still don't have any idea why he came here and—most important of all—who poisoned him!

But we're not providing the only news in town. I heard that Maryellen Sherman is getting married and her mother, Grace, has her pick of interested men—but which one will she choose? And Olivia Griffin is back from her honeymoon, and her mother, Charlotte, has a man in her life, too, but I'm not sure Olivia's too pleased....

There's plenty of other gossip I could tell you. Come by for a cup of tea and one of my blueberry muffins and we'll talk.

44 Cranberry Point

*Available the first week of September 2004,
wherever paperbacks are sold.*

On sale now

girls' night in

21 of today's hottest
female authors
1 fabulous short-story collection
And all for a good cause.

Featuring *New York Times* bestselling authors
Jennifer Weiner (author of *Good in Bed*),
Sophie Kinsella (author of *Confessions of a Shopaholic*),
Meg Cabot (author of *The Princess Diaries*)

Net proceeds to benefit War Child, a network of organizations
dedicated to helping children affected by war.

Also featuring bestselling authors...
Carole Matthews, Sarah Mlynowski, Isabel Wolff, Lynda Curnyn,
Chris Manby, Alisa Valdes-Rodriguez, Jill A. Davis, Megan McCafferty,
Emily Barr, Jessica Adams, Lisa Jewell, Lauren Henderson,
Stella Duffy, Jenny Colgan, Anna Maxted, Adèle Lang,
Marian Keyes and Louise Bagshawe

www.RedDressInk.com   www.WarChildusa.org

Available wherever trade paperbacks are sold.

If you enjoyed what you just read,
then we've got an offer you can't resist!

Take 2 bestselling novels FREE!
Plus get a FREE surprise gift!

Clip this page and mail it to MIRA®

IN U.S.A.
3010 Walden Ave.
P.O. Box 1867
Buffalo, N.Y. 14240-1867

IN CANADA
P.O. Box 609
Fort Erie, Ontario
L2A 5X3

YES! Please send me 2 free MIRA® novels and my free surprise gift. After receiving them, if I don't wish to receive anymore, I can return the shipping statement marked cancel. If I don't cancel, I will receive 4 brand-new novels every month, before they're available in stores! In the U.S.A., bill me at the bargain price of $4.99 plus 25¢ shipping and handling per book and applicable sales tax, if any*. In Canada, bill me at the bargain price of $5.49 plus 25¢ shipping and handling per book and applicable taxes**. That's the complete price and a savings of over 20% off the cover prices—what a great deal! I understand that accepting the 2 free books and gift places me under no obligation ever to buy any books. I can always return a shipment and cancel at any time. Even if I never buy another The Best of the Best™ book, the 2 free books and gift are mine to keep forever.

185 MDN DZ7J
385 MDN DZ7K

Name	(PLEASE PRINT)	
Address	Apt.#	
City	State/Prov.	Zip/Postal Code

Not valid to current The Best of the Best™, Mira®,
suspense and romance subscribers.

Want to try two free books from another series?
Call 1-800-873-8635 or visit www.morefreebooks.com.

* Terms and prices subject to change without notice. Sales tax applicable in N.Y.
** Canadian residents will be charged applicable provincial taxes and GST.
All orders subject to approval. Offer limited to one per household.
® and ™are registered trademarks owned and used by the trademark owner and or its licensee.

BOB04R

©2004 Harlequin Enterprises Limited

OLGA BICOS

66732 SHATTERED ___ $6.50 U.S. ___ $7.99 CAN.

(limited quantities available)

TOTAL AMOUNT $_____
POSTAGE & HANDLING $_____
($1.00 for 1 book, 50¢ for each additional)
APPLICABLE TAXES* $_____
<u>TOTAL PAYABLE</u> $_____
(check or money order—please do not send cash)

To order, complete this form and send it, along with a check or
money order for the total above, payable to MIRA Books, to:
In the U.S.: 3010 Walden Avenue, P.O. Box 9077, Buffalo,
NY 14269-9077; **In Canada:** P.O. Box 636, Fort Erie, Ontario,
L2A 5X3.

Name:_____
Address:_____ City:_____
State/Prov.:_____ Zip/Postal Code:_____
Account Number (if applicable):_____
075 CSAS

*New York residents remit applicable sales taxes.
Canadian residents remit
applicable GST and provincial taxes.

MIRA®